...tarted.

Or... ...houdhury with what
she... ...he structure. Opting
to keep the aperture out of her line of sight as she maneuvered
closer, she rose from her crouch and moved to a point along the
wall where some of the stones had fallen away, providing an
opening through which she could pass. Minding thick vines
and other vegetation, she stepped through the breach, scanning
the ground in front of her before taking each step.

Halfway between the relative safety of the wall and the
structure's opening, Choudhury sensed a hot ache between
her shoulder blades. Freezing in place, she tightened her
hands around the *bat'leth*'s rough leather grips as her muscles
tensed in anticipation.

She was being watched.

Despite all her caution, Choudhury realized her opponent had somehow managed to maneuver behind her and
waited for her to move away from anything that might offer
protection. Gauging her distance from the structure, she
surmised there was no way she could reach it before she fell
victim to attack.

Damn. Damn. Damn!

The curse was all she had time to think before Choudhury sensed movement behind her. Reacting more from
instinct than anything else, she ducked and pivoted to her
left, bringing herself around in time to see the dark form
lunging at her. Fading sunlight glinted off curved metal, and
she brought up her *bat'leth* just as something crashed into
its heavy blade. Choudhury grunted in momentary shock
and felt herself forced backward. Scrambling to her right, she
rotated her weapon for defense as she caught her first clear
look at her newest attacker.

Worf.

STAR TREK®
TYPHON PACT

PATHS OF DISHARMONY

DAYTON WARD

Based upon *Star Trek* and
Star Trek: The Next Generation®
created by Gene Roddenberry

POCKET BOOKS
New York   London   Toronto   Sydney   Andor

For Margaret Clark.
Thanks for everything.

Pocket Books
A Division of Simon & Schuster, Inc.
1230 Avenue of the Americas
New York, NY 10020

This book is a work of fiction. Names, characters, places, and incidents either are products of the author's imagination or are used fictitiously. Any resemblance to actual events or locales or persons, living or dead, is entirely coincidental.

First Pocket Books paperback edition February 2011

POCKET and colophon are registered trademarks of Simon & Schuster, Inc.

For information about special discounts for bulk purchases, please contact Simon & Schuster Special Sales at 1-866-506-1949 or business@simonandschuster.com.

The Simon & Schuster Speakers Bureau can bring authors to your live event. For more information or to book an event, contact the Simon & Schuster Speakers Bureau at 1-866-248-3049 or visit our website at www.simonspeakers.com.

Cover art and design by Alan Dingman; Shar image created by Cliff Nielsen

Manufactured in the United States of America

10 9 8 7 6 5 4 3 2 1

ISBN 978-1-4391-6083-1
ISBN 978-1-4391-9166-8 (ebook)

1

Foul sludge splashed across the ground before Lieutenant Thirishar ch'Thane, and he recoiled in momentary shock as a noxious odor assaulted his nostrils.

"Get away from here!"

Wiping away flecks of the rancid fluid that had hit his face, Shar backed away from the older Andorian who had thrown the filthy water at his feet. The merchant, his blue skin darkened with age, stood stoop-shouldered in the doorway leading into his shop. Shar had seen him tending to the plants outside his storefront on more than one occasion during his walks through this part of the city. In his hands, the shopkeeper wielded a rusted metal bucket, which he now shook before him in Shar's direction.

"Get away from here, you traitor!" the old man repeated, stepping down from the doorway onto the sidewalk lining the row of buildings on this side of the narrow street. He raised one arm and pointed a long, wrinkled finger at Shar. "We don't want you here!"

Shar held up his hands to indicate he presented no threat, still trying to fathom what he might have done—or failed to do—to call forth the aged merchant's ire. He had been warned about isolated instances where other Starfleet personnel—none of them Andorians—had encountered such behavior, but none had been reported here in Lor'Vela. Indeed, he had come to think of this part of the city as his new home, just as many Andorians had in the year since the Borg invasion. The largest population center on Andor to weather the attack relatively intact, the city had served in the months that followed as a rally point for survivors across the neighboring regions, with sprawling refugee camps springing up along the coastline and in the foothills to the north and west. While much of the city lay within and beneath the surrounding mountain range, this section had been constructed aboveground, reminding Shar of his childhood home. The reconstituted, provisional Andorian planetary government now was located here, having summoned lower-ranking officials from cities and provinces around the world to fill the void left by the loss of so many political leaders. Laibok, the former capital city, had fallen to Borg weaponry in the opening moments of the attack, with much of the surrounding region being laid to waste. Had Shar been on Andor when the invasion began, he would have been working there, and certainly would have numbered in the millions of casualties recorded on that day.

And now someone here might want to help correct that oversight. You should go. Now.

"I'm not looking for any trouble," he said, keeping his voice low and doing his best to impart no trace of anger or resentment over what the shopkeeper had done to him. "I'm just—"

The older Andorian cut him off, shaking a fist at him. "I know what you're doing! I've seen you on the newsnets. You and those other traitors, working with the Federation to wipe away our culture. Our very identity!"

Shar rebuked himself for his stupidity. Had he missed a briefing about upswings in anti-Starfleet sentiment within Lor'Vela? So far as he knew, the city had experienced little of the civil unrest that had plagued other areas in recent months, but to expect that not to change at some point was the height of naïveté. This was particularly true in light of the steps Starfleet and the Federation—working in concert with the Andorian government and Homeworld Security—had taken to retain order among the populace as the planet struggled to rebuild from the devastation inflicted by the Borg. Though Lor'Vela had seemed at the outset like a haven of cooperative spirit between Andor and the Federation, current events and the stench of his uniform told Shar that enthusiasm for such an alliance might be waning, at least in some quarters.

Excellent deductive reasoning, Lieutenant.

Opening his mouth in what he knew would be a futile attempt to put the elder at ease, Shar sensed another presence behind him and turned in time to see another Andorian, a *thaan*, approaching him from one of the buildings on the other side of the street. Though he was much younger than the merchant, he appeared to be no less irritated by Shar's presence here.

"You heard him," the new arrival said, stepping closer. "You're not welcome here." Shar recognized him as another merchant—a restaurateur of some sort, if his memory served. Despite his attempts at self-control, Shar felt muscles tensing as the other Andorian came to the boundary of his personal space.

"I understand," Shar said agreeably, though he had no idea what had happened in the five days since his passage through this area of town to so change the way local residents felt about Starfleet personnel in their midst. Taking a step back, he added, "I'm leaving."

A tingle in his left antenna made him duck an instant before a chunk of brick sailed past his face and slammed into the wall to his right. The brick shattered on impact, peppering Shar with debris. Flinching from the rain of shrapnel, he turned in the direction from which the projectile had come to see a young *zhen* standing across the thoroughfare. She glared at him with open contempt, seemingly unrepentant at having nearly injured or killed him. Indeed, her expression seemed to be one of frustration at having failed to do either.

For the first time, Shar allowed an edge to creep into his voice. "I *said* I was *leaving.*" He bit each word, forcing them between gritted teeth as he glowered at the *thaan,* who still stood entirely too close for common courtesy.

"Maybe we shouldn't let you go," the *thaan* replied, glowering at him, and for the first time Shar realized other residents were emerging from doorways and alleys between buildings. A low rumble of disapproval emanated from the people as they began coming closer, drawing a circle around him. Training—to say nothing of mounting trepidation—made Shar scrutinize the threat potential of each new arrival. None appeared to be carrying anything that might be a weapon, but they already had numbers to use against him. A phaser would have gone a long way toward evening the odds, but Shar's weapon was in a locker at the local Starfleet field office.

Tucked away, nice and safe, along with your common sense.

"Let him go," a voice said from somewhere behind him. "Leave him alone. He's not bothering anyone."

"No!" countered someone else. "He doesn't belong here."

"He's no better than the looters from the camps!" shouted a younger *zhen,* whom Shar recognized from the long antennae atop his forehead as a Talish.

"Teach him what happens to trespassers!"

His eyes still locked on the *thaan*'s, Shar regarded his adversary. "If it's a fight you're looking for," he said, hoping his words sounded more convincing to the other Andorian's ears than to his own, "I'm more than happy to provide it."

The *thaan* leered. "You cannot fight us all."

"No," Shar conceded, feeling his pulse beginning to pound in his ears as he resigned himself to the situation, "but I *can* kill *you* first." While he did not want things to deteriorate to that point, it was becoming apparent that he likely would not escape this confrontation unscathed. He would defend himself, and worry about explaining or justifying his actions should he survive the next few minutes.

Always the optimist.

Certain he sensed the *thaan* readying to strike out at him, Shar took another step back, moving into a defensive stance just as his opponent lunged forward. The other Andorian was sloppy, unschooled in unarmed combat, and Shar easily met the clumsy assault. He blocked the *thaan*'s outstretched arm and with a single fluid motion pivoted on his heel, using his opponent's weight and momentum to carry him over his left hip and flip him down onto the sidewalk's cracked pavement. The *thaan* landed hard, grunting from the impact, and Shar followed through by grasping the Andorian's right wrist and twisting the arm until the *thaan* yelped in pain. He tried to break free of the grip, but Shar placed his foot on the restaurateur's throat, holding his arm taut. Seeing other people from the crowd beginning to move forward, he pointed at them with his free hand.

"Stay back!" he shouted. He again twisted his opponent's arm, emphasizing his point as the *thaan* loosed another anguished cry. Shar sensed movement from his left and ducked just as a clenched fist sliced past his face. Releasing his grip on the *thaan*'s arm, Shar dodged right, scrambling for room as he beheld his new attacker, the Talish who earlier had yelled at him. The *shen*'s features were contorted in rage as he lunged forward, swinging again.

Moving to defend against the attack, Shar felt hands on his arms just as someone gripped the collar of his uniform tunic. Another hand clamped around the back of his neck and he was pulled backward, off-balance. He jerked and twisted, his body reacting on instinct to free himself. A face appeared near his right side, and he lashed out, striking the attacker's chin. There was a grunt of pain as the assailant staggered away, then a hand grabbed Shar's wrist, arresting any further movement as he was pushed to the street. As he felt the unyielding stones beneath his back, he looked up to see three Andorians holding him down. One of them was the *thaan* he had first fought, who knelt beside him and thrust a forefinger at his face.

"Traitor," the *thaan* hissed, glaring at Shar.

Shar tried to move, but failed. Continuing to struggle against his assailants, he could only offer a look of defiance as the *thaan* pulled back his hand and formed a fist.

"Release him, and remain where you are!"

The command echoed off the walls of the buildings and cliffs towering overhead, with no easy means to identify its source, followed by short bursts of three electronic tones that commanded instant attention. Only when he heard the low rumble of an engine did Shar know where to look, and he turned to see the familiar form of an aircar, the sort used by the city's police force. It hovered ten meters above the street, its dark, polished hull and sloping, mirrored cockpit windscreen reflecting the rays of the early afternoon sun, and Shar had to squint to shield his eyes from the glare. A row of multi-hued blue lights were affixed to the aircar's roof, and all of them were flashing in rhythmic cadence as the warning tones blared for a second time.

The effect of the police vehicle's arrival was immediate, with most of the protesters and onlookers dispersing. The three Andorians holding him on the ground released him and began moving away. Within seconds, only Shar remained, and he pulled himself to his feet.

"*Disperse*," a voice called through the police car's intercom system. As the command was given, those few onlookers still watching the proceedings retreated. The vehicle moved closer and descended to the street, maneuvering thrusters guiding it to a soft landing atop the worn pavement. Its engine throttled down to a low idle, and its driver and passenger doors lifted open to reveal a pair of Andorians. Their white hair and the fair blue skin of their faces provided stark contrast to the dark uniforms that encased them from the neck down. Even their hands were shrouded by matching black gloves. Shar noted the insignia on their chests and the holstered weapons on their hips as they strode with purpose toward him.

"Take him into custody," the driver said, pointing to the *thaan* who stood with the elderly shopkeeper on the far side of the street. "Disorderly conduct, assault, inciting a public disturbance."

"He didn't do anything wrong!" a female voice shouted from across the street, and Shar looked to see the woman pointing at him. "You saw what he did to him! Why aren't you arresting *him*?"

Raising his voice for the benefit of everyone else still standing on the nearby sidewalks and watching the proceedings, the sentinel spoke in a deliberate, measured cadence. "This incident is over. Leave now, or you'll also be arrested on charges of inciting a public disturbance." He stood watching the remnants of the crowd until he was satisfied that they were heeding his instructions before turning back to Shar. Pausing as he studied Shar's uniform, the sentinel finally asked, "Are you all right, Lieutenant?"

Shar nodded. "Yes, Officer. Thank you."

Indicating the *thaan* with a nod of his head, the police officer said, "I presume you'll want to file a formal complaint against him." His partner was completing the process of taking the *thaan* into custody.

"No," Shar replied, frowning. "I don't think so." He paused, regarding the *thaan* as the other officer escorted him toward the police vehicle. "I believe it was a misunderstanding more than anything else."

"Don't be so sure," the sentinel countered, his expression hardening. "There's a rise in protests against the Starfleet presence in the city."

Trying not to sound bitter, Shar said, "I guess I shouldn't be surprised. There's still so much to do." More than a year after the Borg attack, Andor was still suffering the effects visited not only upon the already beleaguered population but also the planet itself.

The police officer replied, "There also are those who think there's *too much* being done."

Unsure how best to proceed, Shar eyed the sentinel. "I'm not sure what you mean."

"I recognize you from the newsnet feeds," the other Andorian replied. "You are working with that group of scientists and their alien genome project, trying to improve pregnancy and birth rates."

Shar saw no point in denying that easily verifiable fact. "That's right," he said, nodding. While Federation terraforming specialists already had both short- and long-term plans for healing the widespread environmental damage, the effects of the Borg attack had only exacerbated the reproductive difficulties that had affected the Andorian people for centuries. Ever-shrinking periods of fertility coupled with an imbalance between the different sexes made forming a viable bondgroup problematic, and the situation had only worsened with the horrific population losses at the hands of the Borg.

"Indeed," the sentinel pressed, "you are the one who provided the alien genome that was the basis for the research."

Again, Shar nodded. "Ova, actually. From a species called the Yrythny, which we found during an expedition to the Gamma Quadrant." It had been six years since that mission and the discovery of the Yrythny eggs. The genetic key they possessed, and the hope they carried, had driven Shar to return to Andor and offer his findings to his mentor, Dr. sh'Veileth. In short order, the doctor had been able to demonstrate via computer simulations the potential the Yrythny ova held not only to increase the window of Andorian fertility, but also to heighten the potential for multiple births—twins or triplets—something not seen on Andor in more than a century. Shar and sh'Veileth had thought they were bringing wondrous news to their people, but the reactions to the doctor's theories and research had stretched from euphoria to paranoia. For every person who viewed the idea of using the alien DNA to save Andorians from eventual extinction, there seemed to be someone who saw the notion as a means of altering or even supplanting the Andorian species with something altogether different.

The sentinel reached out and placed a hand on Shar's

shoulder. "My name is Tolad th'Zarithsta. Our bondgroup was among the test subjects. My *zh'yi* was able to carry a child to term even though she supposedly had grown too old to do so. Our *shei* recently celebrated her fourth birthday."

It was as though the sentinel's hand had brushed aside an immense weight resting on Shar's shoulders, and he could not help but smile at what he had just heard. "That is wonderful. I'm happy for you."

Though he nodded, th'Zarithsta's expression fell. "We were among the very few fortunate bondgroups, of course."

Shar sighed at the words. Despite the theories Dr. sh'Veileth had put forth, the "Yrythny solution" had not lived up to the promise she had offered to the Andorian people. After the Science Institute gave her permission to start her trials, sh'Veileth began her tests using volunteer bondgroups willing to have their chromosomes augmented with Yrythny DNA. The initial field consisted of twenty bondgroups, expanding within the following year to well over a hundred test subjects. It was soon after this expansion that the first problems began to surface. Unexpected side effects in the forms of failed or troubled pregnancies increased, as did all manner of birth defects among surviving newborns. Even with such problems being recorded, volunteer bondgroups—sometimes as many as a dozen or more in a single day—continued to seek out Dr. sh'Veileth, desperate to avail themselves of the experimental treatment. When the ratio of problem-riddled pregnancies passed fifty percent, the authorization sh'Veileth had been given was retracted, and the trials came to a halt. Despite that action, the effects of the controversial research had left a lasting impact, as Andorians across the planet once again began to consider their potential demise as a species.

"The Science Institute called an end to the program," th'Zarithsta continued, "and probably for good reason, but I'm happy to see that those efforts haven't been completely abandoned. Especially after all that's happened."

"We have new people working on it now," Shar replied. "Much of what Dr. sh'Veileth discovered still has merit, but there are obviously enough incompatibilities between Andorian and Yrythny DNA that more research is required. Professor zh'Thiin is one of our greatest scientific minds. If there's a solution to be found, she'll find it." Marthrossi zh'Thiin had even been a mentor to sh'Veileth, with her own list of impressive accomplishments. In addition to the desire to help her species, zh'Thiin also was driven by a personal agenda to resolve the crisis. Three years previously, she and her own bondgroup had been one of sh'Veileth's test groups, and her pregnancy had ended in miscarriage. It had been zh'Thiin's last opportunity to bear a child, and she now wanted to ensure that the same thing did not happen to other hopeful parents.

Th'Zarithsta seemed to take comfort in Shar's words. "And what of you? You're in Starfleet. Surely there's so much to be done out there." As he spoke, he waved one hand skyward, indicating the vastness of space beyond the planet's atmosphere.

Shrugging, Shar said, "This is my home. I myself was part of a bondgroup, and we volunteered to be one of the test groups for the Yrythny solution. Our *zh'yi* was able to carry a fetus to term, and the child was born without incident." He paused, drawing a deep breath as he relived memories both pleasant and mournful. "I elected to stay here for a while, working with Dr. sh'Veileth, before deciding it was time I returned to Starfleet to resume my duties." He cast his gaze down to the pavement at his feet. "I was en route to what was to be my new posting at Starbase 714 when the Borg came. Though I was traveling alone, my bondgroup decided that they would live with me on the station." He smiled at one recollection that brought him joy in the midst of such tragedy. "We had decided we would attempt to have another child. They were on their way to meet me at Starbase 714 when the transport ship on which they'd booked passage was intercepted by a Borg cube." To this day, Shar remembered with utter clarity the brief, terse subspace communiqué he had received, notifying him of the transport's loss along with all of its passengers. The memories of that day still elicited anguish, which he had tried and failed on numerous occasions to bury in his mind's deepest recesses as he concentrated on his work. "Then I heard about what had happened here; how much damage had been done to the planet, and how much we'd lost." Among the still-uncounted casualties was his own *zhavey*, Charivretha zh'Thane.

"I'm sorry for your loss," th'Zarithsta said, sadness evident in his eyes.

Shar nodded in understanding. "Then I learned that Professor zh'Thiin would be continuing Dr. sh'Veileth's work. I knew I needed to be here, doing whatever I could for our people. I requested permanent assignment to the Starfleet contingent stationed here, acting as a liaison between Starfleet Command and the Science Institute." He shook his head, recalling the minor odyssey he had endured in order to return to Andor. "It took me five weeks to find transportation back here." He had spent much of that intervening time grieving the loss of his *zhavey* and his bond group, and by the time he had returned to Andor, his desire and conviction to help his people in any way possible had overridden every other consideration. There would be no leaving this time, he knew; not until he had helped alter Andor's fortunes in a lasting way.

Feeling a hand on his shoulder once again, Shar looked up to see th'Zarithsta regarding him with an almost paternal air. "If only there were more who felt as you," the police officer said, before turning his attention to those few Andorians who still watched them from the doorways and windows of surrounding buildings. "Perhaps then the troubles our people face might not seem so insurmountable."

"They're not insurmountable," Shar replied, "regardless of what some might think, or want to think, or have been told to think. There is a solution; we simply have not yet found it." As naïvely optimistic as he knew that sounded, he believed that a remedy for the crisis engulfing his home world existed.

He had to believe it, for it might well be the only thing separating Andorian civilization from eventual extinction.

2

Half a dozen clouds of various sizes and shapes were all that blemished the otherwise brilliant blue sky. Jean-Luc Picard wondered with some amusement if they were a deliberate choice of the cadre of meteorological specialists overseeing Earth's perpetually shifting climate conditions, or whether they might have formed of their own volition in utter defiance of the planet's weather-modification network. He preferred the latter possibility, he decided.

Standing on the narrow dirt path that wound its way around the perimeter of the vineyard, Picard turned his gaze toward the evenly spaced rows of trellises stretching for hundreds of meters across the rolling hillside. The slight breeze carried to his nostrils the familiar aroma of organic fertilizers and soil nutrients, the same odor that he remembered permeating his skin and clothes on many a summer day in his youth. Supported by trellises that elevated them to waist height above the ground, the vines were green and lush, and on the closer rows Picard saw bulging grapes clustered among the leaves. His practiced eye noted the grapes' rich color. From the looks of things, this season's harvest would be exemplary.

"Grapes."

A small hand shot outward, one of its short, stubby fingers pointing toward the rows of vines. Adjusting his stance, Picard shifted the small burden resting in the crook of his left arm so it sat higher on his hip, and he felt the toddler's legs wrap more tightly around his waist.

"That's right," he said to his son, René Jacques Robert François Picard, as he looked into the boy's bright, wide eyes that were so much like his own. "Those are grapes, and fine ones, at that." He reached out to brush dirt from René's left knee, noting the abraded skin there from the stumble the child had taken while trying to traverse the uneven ground. "Your mother's going to have something to say about this," he said, gently patting the knee.

"Eat?" René asked, his expression hopeful. At barely one year of age, his vocabulary naturally was limited to a handful of words beyond the usual stream of indecipherable gibberish he delivered with unrestrained enthusiasm. That did not matter to Picard, who often found himself entranced listening to his son's litany of sounds and mangled syllables.

"Perhaps later," Picard replied, unable to suppress a smile. As a boy, Picard and his older brother, Robert, had ruined more than one evening meal by stuffing themselves with grapes from the vineyard, much to their father's consternation. "I think your mother would be upset if I let you spoil your supper." Even as he spoke the words he imagined the expression on the face of his wife, Beverly Crusher, once she learned that he had deviated from the boy's strict dietary regimen. After transitioning to eating solid foods, René had quickly established his likes and dislikes, and Picard mused with no small amount of humor that his son's predilection for grapes as a favorite fruit served only to solidify his place in the family line.

It was René's first visit to Earth following his birth aboard the *Enterprise* more than a year earlier. The baby's delivery, as well as his and Beverly's immediate postnatal care, had been handled by Dr. Tropp, one of the ship's senior medical officers. In true Denobulan fashion, he had fawned over René in the days following the birth as though the infant was one of his own children. Indeed, there seemed to be no shortage of volunteers and stand-in aunts and uncles willing to look after the baby. This allowed Beverly—and Picard himself—to get much-needed rest as they acclimated themselves to juggling parenthood with the demands of their respective shipboard responsibilities. Though he had done his level best to prepare himself mentally and physically for the demands of caring for an infant, no amount of reading or listening to the advice offered by Beverly and other parents had proven sufficient for facing the challenges firsthand.

That goes double for the diapers.

Despite the fatigue and stress that was the reality of parenting a newborn, Picard had not minded such things as the late-night diaper changes and feedings. Indeed, he even had anticipated those activities, taking advantage of the opportunity to bond with the boy. They wasted no time establishing a nightly routine, whereby Picard fed René while softly singing songs from his own childhood. Now such rituals were second nature, as much a part of the captain's daily schedule as reviewing status reports from his first officer and the rest of the *Enterprise*'s department heads.

Was it really so long ago that I felt uncomfortable around children? The question teased him as he regarded René, the boy entertaining himself with the quartet of pips on Picard's uniform collar. For the better part of his adult life and despite spending most of the past two decades in command of those far younger than himself, Picard had never considered himself a father figure. After being appointed captain of his previous vessel, the *U.S.S. Enterprise*-D—the first ship he had commanded that was authorized to carry families—and finding himself in close proximity to children belonging to members of his crew, it had taken him quite some time to warm to their presence. Being viewed as a role model or anything other than the starship's commanding officer was a notion that had required several years to accept.

The idea of raising his own child was one Picard had pondered at infrequent intervals over the course of his life. His first love had always been space and the unparalleled potential it offered for discovery and the furthering of knowledge. Even after marrying Beverly, he at first had resisted the idea of having a child with her, though his reluctance at the time was not born from common uncertainty at the prospect of fatherhood. Instead, it sprang from the fear of what might happen to such offspring in the face of the renewed Borg threat that ultimately had escalated into an invasion ravaging the Federation during the previous year. With Beverly's help, he had seen past his own misgivings and realized that raising a child with her would bring with it joys and celebrations unlike anything else he had experienced. It also might be just one more way he could finally leave behind the doubts, cynicism, tragedies, and loss that had gripped him in the face of unrelenting war and calamity for far too long. While the end of the Borg might mark a new chapter in the history of the Federation, Picard knew that the boy he now cradled in his arms represented the next and perhaps most fulfilling act in his own life.

A life spent aboard a ship among the stars, or with the ground beneath my feet? It was a question he had asked himself more times over the past year than he could count. As he and René wandered the rows of grapevines, it seemed only natural to ponder the query yet again.

It's not as though you'll change your answer. Or, is it?

Turning from the trellis, Picard looked back the way he and René had come, gazing across the vineyard to the modest chateau sitting amid a cluster of tall, overgrown oak trees. The home and the surrounding grounds had belonged to his family for centuries, and generations of Picards had toiled the earth here. Though he had learned the craft and even the art of tending the vineyard under the watchful eyes of his father and Robert, Picard himself never had developed the same passion for the work. Instead, the thoughts and dreams of his youth had carried him far away from the confines of his home planet and toward the stars that shone down upon him each night. His eventual decision to leave the family business and enter Starfleet Academy angered his father, and the two men would remain at odds over the matter until the elder Picard's death.

At another time in his life, the captain would have viewed returning to the Picard family home in Labarre, France, as a burden, an obligation to be completed before returning to the familiar environs of space and the life he had chosen. Robert, having assumed stewardship of the vineyards following their parents' retirement, shared their father's disapproval of Picard's career choices. Indeed, for a time, Robert even had resented his younger brother's apparent dismissal of the family heritage in favor of travel, discovery, and even adventure. Only after Picard's visit to the chateau following the first Borg attack on Earth did the two brothers close the rift between them, putting aside the petty sibling rivalry that had poisoned their relationship since childhood. It was Robert, acting as the unlikeliest of therapists, who helped Picard begin the process of truly coming to terms with what had happened to him during his assimilation by the Borg and his transformation into Locutus.

I thanked you, Robert, but I never really told you what that has always meant to me.

Doing so would never be possible now, as more than a decade had passed since Robert, along with his son, René, had perished in a fire that had nearly destroyed the family home. The house itself had long since been repaired, but Picard still carried the emotional weight of losing his brother and nephew.

"Papa."

The gurgled query, accompanied as it was by the soft stroke of a small hand against his cheek, jolted Picard from his reverie. It was only then that he realized just how far he had walked with his son into the vineyard, as though his legs had of their own volition recalled the correct paths. He was not surprised, given the countless times he had navigated the grounds, at first while playing hide-and-seek with Robert and later working the fields with his father. Every centimeter of the property had long since been committed to memory. Standing between two rows of vine-wrapped trellises, he regarded René and saw the quizzical expression in the boy's eyes. There was no pain or loss there; only the unguarded curiosity that brightened every child's gaze. With his right hand, René was gesturing toward his mouth, his fingers together in a sign Beverly had taught him to communicate that he was hungry. As if in response, Picard felt a mild rumbling in his stomach.

"All right, then," he said, reaching up to stroke the boy's thin auburn hair. "Let's find your mother and Aunt Marie, and see about lunch." Turning back the way he had come, Picard began the long trek toward the house. Ahead of him and beyond the row of trellises to his left side, he caught sight of two heads among the vines; one blond with a liberal smattering of gray, the other a deep red that gleamed in the midday sun. When he reached the next intersection among the rows, he moved over and smiled in greeting at the approach of Beverly Crusher and his sister-in-law, Marie Picard.

"What in the world are you doing all the way out here?" Beverly asked, a chuckle escaping her lips as she drew closer and extended her arms toward René. Unlike Picard, she was dressed in simple, loose-fitting civilian attire, her light-blue silk blouse and matching pants accenting her fair skin.

Picard laughed as René leaned away from him, falling forward into his mother's waiting embrace. "Seemed like a nice day for a stroll." He knew they would soon be back aboard ship, and while the *Enterprise* had always been more his home than any planet, he still remembered his father's belief that a day of fresh air and sunshine was not to be wasted.

"How long can you stay this time?" Marie asked, reaching up to brush away a lock of her hair from where it had fallen across her eyes. "You know you're welcome to stay as long as you like, or at least as long as Starfleet will leave you alone."

"I suspect it won't be that long," Picard replied, unable to keep a small tang of bitterness from lacing the words. "The president of the Federation is usually not in the habit of inviting us back here for holiday."

Eyeing him with a mischievous smile as she noted the soiled, scraped skin on René's knees, Beverly asked, "Are you in trouble again? Did you kidnap another world leader when I wasn't looking?"

"No, but the day's young yet," Picard said, pulling down on the front of his uniform. "Besides, I promised to refrain from such behavior except in the event of presidential approval." His unconventional, unprecedented, and wholly unauthorized "detaining" of George Barrile, planetary governor of Alpha Centauri, had—to put it kindly—ruffled more than a few feathers at Starfleet Command, not that Picard had cared. Barrile, whose home planet had largely been spared the ravages of the Borg invasion, had put forth a great deal of protest at the tens of thousands of refugees who had been relocated to Alpha Centauri from damaged or destroyed planets across the Federation. He even had gone so far as to propose his planet's secession from the Federation. It was not until Picard brought him to Pacifica, a planet that had borne the burden of postwar relief efforts, that the governor saw for the first time the true scope of devastation facing the entire Federation. After that, Barrile even put forth a resolution to the Council that all member worlds reaffirm their commitment to upholding and strengthening the ideals that had first brought them together in the spirit of mutual cooperation and security.

That sudden and very welcome change in attitude had at first not been enough to spare Picard from the wrath of Admiral Leonard James Akaar, the head of Starfleet Command, but he could not argue with the results Picard had brought about. Indeed, Akaar offered him a promotion to admiral and a new assignment overseeing the Federation's post-war rebuilding efforts. Picard, though, managed to convince Akaar that he was of greater service aboard the *Enterprise*, continuing the mission originally given to him by President Bacco.

"Did the orders offer any clue as to what the president wants with you?" Beverly asked, her attention divided between her husband and René, who had begun fiddling with her combadge.

Picard shook his head. "No, but the fact that she ordered us back to Earth rather than sending us somewhere directly tells me this will be different from the assignments we've had to this point."

The *Enterprise* had been ordered to return to Earth with all due haste, the directive from President Nanietta Bacco rescinding or at least temporarily halting Picard's current mission as a sort of freelance asset for Starfleet. For more than a year, the ship and its crew had traveled wherever Picard felt they were most needed and best utilized, responding to all manner of issues and crises of varying size and complexity as the Federation continued to rebuild and restabilize in the aftermath of the Borg invasion. President Bacco had granted Picard broad authority and latitude, his freedom to make rapid judgments and undertake decisive action empowering him to resolve such matters by any means he felt appropriate. Knowing it was a necessary assignment, one for which Picard and the *Enterprise* were well suited, had done little to alleviate his initial disappointment.

Beverly said, "I suppose it's too much to ask that she might send us out to do some exploring."

"Somehow," Picard replied, "I think that might be wishful thinking." After years of war and political turmoil—facing the Dominion, the Romulans, and the Borg, as well as several other comparatively minor threats—the idea of returning to deep-space exploration was one Picard welcomed. Indeed, dispatching starships on such missions seemed important and even vital now, given the Federation's renewed need to find habitable planets with an eye toward colonization and resource replenishment. Millions of Federation citizens remained displaced from homeworlds severely damaged if not outright destroyed by the Borg attack. Supporting so many refugees had long since begun taking its toll on those planets that had agreed to provide aid to survivors, despite Starfleet's best efforts to maintain a constant flow of support personnel, supplies, and other matériel to those in need. Tempers were growing short, morale was falling, and regardless of the progress that continued to be made, despair seemed to be the emotional state of choice.

"I saw the report on your desk last night," Beverly said, pausing to adjust her hold on René. "The one about the latest round of talks with the Tholians. You don't think the president might send us to deal with them, do you?"

Picard frowned, shaking his head. "Sooner or later, someone will have to go, and not just because of the Tholians." Long renowned for its perpetual state of extreme xenophobia, the Tholian Assembly had taken the extraordinary step of aligning itself with a new interstellar consortium now known as the Typhon Pact. The group's forming had placed civilian and Starfleet officials on edge since its emergence in the aftermath of the Borg invasion. Along with the Tholians, the Pact's charter-member states included the Romulan Star Empire, the Gorn Hegemony, the Breen Confederacy, the Tzenkethi Coalition, and the Holy Order of the Kinshaya, each of which at one time or another and to varying degrees had been a figurative thorn in the Federation's side.

"Diplomatic relations with the Tholians have always been strained," Picard said, "and even more so with the other Typhon Pact members, particularly in recent years." Even the alliance between the Federation and the Romulans—cultivated during the Dominion War—had dissolved as that conflict came to an end. Now, tensions once more were on the rise, given the Romulan Empire's status as a driving force within the Typhon Pact.

As for the Pact itself, intelligence analysts were divided on the upstart political conglomerate's potential or even its desire to present itself as a true threat, rather than a simple if inconvenient rival. Still, it had during its short existence already taken steps to undermine the Federation's ongoing recovery efforts. What if the Pact committed an act so bold, so aggressive, that the Federation had no choice but to respond, and what form would such a response take? The notion of facing yet another conflict on any appreciable scale worried Picard. This was not the time to seek out new enemies. Instead, the Federation's focus needed to be on rebuilding what it had lost as well as learning to cope with all that could never be replaced.

"I know that face," said a voice, Marie's. "You're brooding again."

Picard forced a smile as he regarded Marie along with Beverly and René. "I'm sorry. There's just a lot to think about."

"I've been hearing that for years," Beverly countered as she shifted René to a position higher on her hip. "Come on, let's get some lunch. Your son is starting to get cranky."

As though the deities charged with tormenting starship captains were watching over his shoulder, his combadge beeped for attention, its lyrical electronic tones notably out of place in the peaceful vineyard.

"*Enterprise to Captain Picard,*" said the voice of Lieutenant Commander Havers, the ship's beta-shift watch officer, sounding tiny and distant over the communications link.

Tapping his combadge, the captain replied, "Picard here."

"*We have received a message from the presidential office at* the Palais de la Concorde," Havers replied. *"President Bacco is ready to meet with you, sir."*

Offering a knowing smile to Beverly and Marie, Picard nodded. "Thank you, Commander. Notify transporter control at the Palais that I'm standing by at their convenience."

"Aye, Captain," Havers said. *"Enterprise out."*

As the connection was severed, Picard opened his mouth to apologize. "Perhaps we can make plans for dinner?"

Any reply Beverly or Marie might have offered was lost in the whine of the transporter beam, which chose that moment to wash over him.

3

ight reflected off the slashing blade as Lieutenant Jasminder Choudhury lurched to her left, avoiding the strike. She backpedaled, mindful of the uneven terrain as she worked to distance herself from her attacker. The creature kept coming, its oversized battle-ax a blur as it twirled the weapon in its hands. It smiled at her as it moved closer, and Choudhury saw rows of stained, jagged teeth. Her opponent was taller than she and easily outweighed her, by as much as a hundred kilos, if her guess was right. Despite its bulk, an assortment of heavy fur and leather clothing, along with straps and belts crisscrossing its chest, the alien warrior moved with startling speed and grace. Its skin was tight and waxy, and the lack of hair on its head made the creature resemble an animated, muscled skeleton. Dark eyes glared at her, studying her as a hunter might regard its prey before moving in for the kill.

You are one ugly son of a . . .

The rest of the wayward thought vanished as the creature lunged forward, its battle-ax leading the charge. Choudhury halted her retreat and instead stepped into the attack, bringing up the *bat'leth* she wielded and meeting her opponent's blade with her own. Metal clanged against metal and her arms shook from the force of the blow. Howling with rage, the creature pulled back the ax and swung it laterally, aiming for her torso. As she had been taught, Choudhury brought the blade up and around, adjusting her grip as she moved until she held the *bat'leth* vertically to her left side. The tempered blade met the axe with another resounding clash, and this time Choudhury nearly stumbled in the face of her attacker's strength. Once more the alien released an angered cry as it drew back its weapon, readying for another attack.

Oh, no you don't.

Letting instinct and training take over, Choudhury dropped down, sweeping her right leg out ahead of her. She felt her foot catch the creature behind its left knee and sensed it buckle, the alien stumbling at the abrupt loss of balance. It staggered to its left before falling to one knee, removing its left hand from the battle-ax's worn leather grip to steady itself. By then Choudhury was regaining her feet, rotating the *bat'leth* in her hands and stepping forward, angling to strike. Her opponent reacted faster than she had anticipated, already raising its battle-ax in defense. It was going to be close, Choudhury realized as she stepped forward, holding her *bat'leth* over her head as she started to swing.

The *bat'leth* met no resistance until its massive curved blade sank into the creature's skull. There was no blood, no cry of agony. The alien's body simply went limp, its battle-ax falling from its hands to drop to the dirt at their feet. Choudhury just stood there, still gripping her weapon, watching as the creature dissolved in a shower of golden energy.

They're getting tougher each time, she noted as she paused to catch her breath. *Worf, you're going to pay for this.* Choudhury smiled with no small amount of mischief as she pondered just how she might go about exacting vengeance on the Klingon.

Turning from where the latest of the five opponents she had faced had been reclaimed by the holodeck's computer protocols, Choudhury made her way to the crumbling ruins of a low-rise wall from which her most recent adversary had appeared. The structure, obviously the product of a sentient species, was at odds with the trees and other vegetation around her. Choudhury reached up with her free hand to wipe sweat from her forehead, not for the first time wishing she had thought to bring a canteen. She already had unzipped the front of her uniform as well as her gold division shirt in a futile attempt to allow the slight breeze to cool her body. Perspiration ran down her skin beneath her clothes, and Choudhury winced as she noted the sting of a rash in at least one uncomfortable place.

Well and truly, Worf, shall you pay.

She adjusted her grip on the *bat'leth*. When Worf had introduced her to the weapon nearly a year ago, Choudhury had doubted his assurances that she could learn to effectively employ it in close-quarters combat. Designed for the larger, more robust physiology of the typical Klingon warrior, the oversized blade seemed far too heavy and cumbersome for her much slighter frame. Hours of lessons under Worf's expert tutelage had shown her that the *bat'leth*'s size was deceptive, and wielding it was as much art as it was martial skill. Choudhury had actually come to enjoy working with the weapon, welcoming the challenge as Worf increased the level of difficulty he brought to her training.

And today is no damned exception, that's for sure.

Keeping her position behind the wall, Choudhury studied the rectangular structure rising from the jungle floor twenty meters to her right. Partially concealed among the trees, it appeared to be no larger than an oversized cargo container, four or perhaps five meters in height. She surmised it was constructed from the same stones as the wall that now provided her cover. The side of the building closest to her contained an oval-shaped aperture, looking large enough for an average-sized humanoid to enter. Darkness lay behind the portal's threshold, offering no clue as to what might be inside.

It can't be this simple, Choudhury decided. In point of fact, her journey through the jungle to this point had been fraught with all manner of hazards, both natural and otherwise. In addition to the holographic enemies the simulation had sent after her, she also had encountered no less than seven booby traps as she made her way through the thick undergrowth. Not designed to injure, the traps instead were simple sound-concussion grenades of the type used by tactical assault teams as a means of overwhelming an opposing force's attention and reaction time. Deployed as they had been—attached to trees or concealed beneath patches of leaves or other vegetation— they were intended to give away her position should she trip one or more of the devices. Attention to her surroundings and experience with her adversary had taught her what to watch for as she made her way toward her target. Choudhury concluded that these devices were not problems introduced by the holodeck program, but rather by her true opponent, who still lurked somewhere in the jungle.

Now, however, it was the notable lack of such obstacles that worried her. Turning her gaze from the structure, Choudhury focused her attention on the nearby trees and other underbrush. She searched for anything that did not belong, and saw nothing that might be a booby trap or any other sign that the area around the small building had been disturbed. Of course, her adversary knew she would be looking for such clues and would act accordingly.

No sense sitting here, Choudhury mused. Gazing upward, she examined the trees towering over her head, admiring how their branches formed a lush, near-impenetrable canopy. The sounds of indigenous life were all around her, calling out from the jungle's depths. Feeble rays of fading sunlight filtered through the undergrowth, the oncoming dusk casting long shadows that would only serve to provide further concealment as the day gave way to night. *Time to get this party started.*

One last look around the area provided Choudhury with what she decided would be the best approach to the structure. Opting to keep the aperture out of her line of sight as she maneuvered closer, she rose from her crouch and moved to a point along the wall where some of the stones had fallen away, providing an opening through which she could pass. Minding thick vines and other vegetation, she stepped through the breach, scanning the ground in front of her before taking each step.

Halfway between the relative safety of the wall and the structure's opening, Choudhury sensed a hot ache between her shoulder blades. Freezing in place, she tightened her hands around the *bat'leth*'s rough leather grips as her muscles tensed in anticipation.

She was being watched.

Despite all her caution, Choudhury realized her opponent had somehow managed to maneuver behind her and waited for her to move away from anything that might offer protection. Gauging her distance from the structure, she surmised there was no way she could reach it before she fell victim to attack.

Damn. Damn. Damn!

The curse was all she had time to think before Choud-

hury sensed movement behind her. Reacting more from
instinct than anything else, she ducked and pivoted to her
left, bringing herself around in time to see the dark form
lunging at her. Fading sunlight glinted off curved metal, and
she brought up her *bat'leth* just as something crashed into
its heavy blade. Choudhury grunted in momentary shock
and felt herself forced backward. Scrambling to her right, she
rotated her weapon for defense as she caught her first clear
look at her newest attacker.

Worf.

He had removed the heavy ceremonial Klingon baldric
he normally wore over his Starfleet uniform, no doubt with
the intention of moving with greater stealth through the
jungle. Likewise, his combadge was missing, as was the rank
insignia that should have adorned the collar of his maroon
uniform tunic. The only thing to catch the weakening rays
of the sun was his *bat'leth*, which he once again was drawing
over his head in readiness for his next strike. Like her earlier,
holographic adversary, Worf smiled at her, though his expression was not one of taunting. Instead, she sensed the approval
a teacher might show upon realizing the accomplishments of
a prized student.

Recognizing Worf's stance and anticipating the direction from which his next attack would come, Choudhury
pivoted to her right, lashing out with her left leg and kicking him in the stomach. It was not enough to disable the
Klingon, but it did slow him enough for her to bring up her
own *bat'leth* and swing it toward his head. Worf dodged the
strike, sidestepping to his right while keeping his attention
focused on her. Before he could launch another attack of his
own, Choudhury darted at him again, closing the distance.
He was able to bring up his weapon to parry her swing, and

once more the harsh metallic notes of clashing blades echoed through the jungle. With the two *bat'leth*s still pushed together, Choudhury twisted hers in abrupt fashion even as she pulled downward, interlocking the blades. Changing directions and yanking the *bat'leth* up and to her right gave her what she wanted, with Worf's arms crossing over each other to the point that the Klingon was forced to release his grip on his weapon.

"Ha-*hah*!" she cried, unable to contain her enthusiasm.

Worf growled in surprise at being so suddenly disarmed, but Choudhury gave him no quarter as she struck him in the chin with her left elbow. It was not a fatal strike, but it was enough to force him to step back as he raised his arms in what she recognized as a classic *mok'bara* defensive posture. He kept maneuvering backward even as she pressed her attack, swinging and rotating her *bat'leth* in front of his face. There was no fear in Worf's eyes, of course; instead, Choudhury saw the calculation and planning as he gauged her moves, looking for an opening to exploit.

Then his left foot caught on one of the stones loosed from the dilapidated wall, and he stumbled and fell to one knee. He released a particularly colorful—and vile—Klingon oath as he fought to keep his balance and prepare for what he must have expected to be a devastating killing strike from Choudhury. She, however, had other ideas. Taking advantage of his vulnerable position, she kicked out again, this time catching Worf in the chest and sending him tumbling onto his back. Not bothering to wait for his reaction, she dropped her *bat'leth* before turning and sprinting for the structure.

"No!" Worf shouted, and Choudhury heard him scrambling to his feet as he gave chase. She knew he was fast and possessing of great stamina, and more than capable of overtaking her in any prolonged footrace, but could he catch her in just the few dozen meters separating her from the stone edifice? Choudhury already heard his heavy footfalls in the dirt behind her but ignored them, pushing ahead with all her remaining strength. She could not help smiling, sensing the same exhilaration she might once have felt as a child engaged in playground games. Then an excited laugh escaped her lips as she plunged through the aperture and into the structure.

"Yes!"

The edifice's interior lit up in response to her entry, soft illumination cast from sources positioned at each of the room's four corners and revealing the only thing the building contained. It was a pedestal, seemingly formed from the same type of stones used to create the structure itself, and atop which sat a massive expanse of tablet fashioned from a single piece of what to Choudhury appeared to be polished granite. Set into the top of the slab were rows of multicolored jewels, each one placed with utmost precision at equal distances from one another as well as the larger, rounded crystal positioned at the slab's center. Still running at near-full speed as she crossed the ground toward the pedestal, Choudhury reached out and slammed her hand down upon the larger crystal.

"*Contest over,*" said the feminine voice of the *Enterprise*'s main computer. "*Winner: Lieutenant Choudhury.*"

She turned, beaming, as Worf entered the structure. Dirt covered much of his uniform, and some of his long hair had come loose from the thong he used to secure it away from his face. There was no anger in his expression or even bitterness over the computer's cold, matter-of-fact pronouncement. Instead, he stood near the structure's entrance and nodded in unrestrained approval.

"A fine victory," he said, sounding not the least bit out of breath.

Choudhury herself was panting as she leaned against the pedestal for support. "Thanks," she said, nodding. She held up a hand, pointing an accusatory finger at him. "You changed the simulation, didn't you? The goons were more difficult this time around." Pausing, she drew several deep breaths before adding, "Each one seemed to get better as I went along."

Nodding, Worf replied, "I programmed the simulation to evaluate your skills and technique, and to apply lessons learned each time you defeated an opponent. The computer then factored that analysis into its calculations when generating a new adversary to send out against you. However, I also added a threshold that the program could not exceed. You reached that level with your sixth opponent. Had you faced a seventh attacker rather than me, you would have found that the difficulty level had reached its limit."

"I honestly wasn't paying *that much* attention, Worf," Choudhury replied, shaking her head before releasing a tired chuckle. Her breathing had almost returned to normal, and the immediate aches and discomfort she had felt in her muscles from the prolonged exertion were already beginning to fade. Of course, she knew the real pain would come tomorrow. *Nothing a hot bath and a nice bottle of wine won't cure.*

Stepping closer, Worf appraised her with an expression of stark admiration. "Your progress with the *bat'leth*, as well as your *mok'bara* training, has been exemplary, Jasminder. I am proud to have been your teacher." He paused after the last word, his features warming as he regarded her.

"That's not all you're proud to be, is it?" Choudhury asked, allowing a hint of suggestion to lace the question.

Worf shook his head. "Not at all." The faintest of smiles tugged at the corners of his mouth, but he remained where he stood, his hands at his sides. Despite his stoic demeanor, Choudhury saw what lurked just beneath the surface of the Klingon's practiced façade. In addition to making for one hell of an efficient team as members of the *Enterprise*'s senior staff, the past year had also served to strengthen the personal bond they now shared. What had begun as her simply needing the emotional and physical support of someone she trusted had evolved into something far surpassing any relationship she previously had enjoyed. Worf, who at first had expressed some anxiety over the intimacy they had shared insofar as it clashed with the traditions of his people, had finally come to terms with such concerns. He and Choudhury had allowed things to progress at a natural pace, each mindful of the other's feelings, to the point that the time they shared, along with everything else, simply felt, as ship's counselor Hegol Den described it to her during one of their frequent discussions on the topic, "right."

Choudhury moved to stand close enough that she could place her hand on Worf's broad chest. "You know what else you are?"

"No," Worf answered, playing the game.

Choudhury bobbed her eyebrows as she looked up at him, her hand reaching for his uniform's front closure. "The loser. Now pay up."

The bath and the wine could wait.

4

"Almost there. Just a little bit more. Easy now. Yeah, that's it."

Standing just to the port side of the *Enterprise*'s main deflector-dish assembly, Commander Geordi La Forge leaned back so he could look up through the faceplate of his environmental suit's helmet. The chief engineer held his right hand out and away from his body, his fingers unconsciously moving as though he were wielding the controls of the Starfleet workbee hovering just overhead. In his left hand he held a tricorder, and his attention was divided between the device and the maintenance craft as it maneuvered ever closer to the ship. He watched as the workbee spun on its axis, the clusters of tractor-beam emitters also shifting as they grasped the deflector's replacement particle emitter.

As the workbee stopped its rotation, the voice of its pilot, Lieutenant Var joresh Dahk, sounded in La Forge's ears, breaking up the monotonous tones of his own breathing as it echoed inside the helmet. "How's that?"

La Forge held up his free hand with his thumb extended so that the Tellarite pilot could see him through the workbee's cockpit canopy. "Looks good. Keep it coming like that." Taking his attention away from the small maintenance craft, he directed his gaze toward the other side of the deflector array and the suited figure standing there. The engineer's view was partially obscured by the thick black cable connecting the emitter to the deflector housing, and for a moment he watched as the line—which actually was a shielded conduit housing power relays as well as wiring for connecting the emitter to the *Enterprise* computer's optical data network— went taut once again, pulling in the slack created as the work-bee pushed forward. "How are we looking, Taurik?"

Positioned beyond the base of the deflector dish and also holding a tricorder, Lieutenant Commander Taurik replied, "The umbilical cabling is retracting normally, Commander. All connections are active and appear to be operating within expected parameters."

"That's what I like to hear," La Forge said, nodding in approval. Though the installation of the new emitter was a routine task performed by one of the crews assigned to the Farber Station maintenance facility positioned in geo-synchronous orbit above Australia, he had exercised his chief engineer's prerogative in order to oversee the installation himself. Getting his hands on one of the upgraded particle emitters and installing it had been on his list of goals for general ship improvements for months. According to the specifications he had read in a Starfleet technical journal devoted to the latest advances and enhancements for *Sovereign*-class vessels, the upgraded unit would offer a broader range of configurations as well as allow greater power to be channeled to it from the ship's warp engines. Many of the improvements to the emitter's design had come from lessons learned in harsh fashion during various engagements with the Borg, and relayed to Starfleet Command via reports submitted by chief engineers aboard starships throughout the quadrant. Considering how many times La Forge had been called upon to rig the deflector to channel power in some unorthodox manner for one reason or another—and almost always while trying to resolve an emergency situation or deal with a threat to the *Enterprise*—if a new model of the unit was available, then he wanted it.

La Forge's wants and desires aside, the *Enterprise*'s mission tempo had been such that coordinating time at a starbase or other facility along with obtaining one of the new emitters and having it transported to that location had proven difficult. He had almost given up on the idea until the ship's next scheduled biennial maintenance cycle. It was fortunate happenstance that a scheduling window at Farber Station coincided with the starship's unplanned visit to Earth. No sooner had La Forge heard about the abrupt change of orders than he dispatched a subspace communiqué to the facility's commanding officer, requesting the new particle emitter be made available for installation upon the *Enterprise*'s arrival.

Stepping back as the bottom of the particle emitter dropped closer to the socket where it would rest within the deflector assembly's housing, La Forge motioned with his free hand toward the workbee. "Almost there."

"Commander," Dahk said over the comm frequency, *"the sensors and associated instrumentation installed into this craft are operating within acceptable parameters."* When he spoke La Forge noted the less-than-subtle hint of irritation in the Tellarite's voice.

The chief engineer looked up to the workbee and offered what he hoped was a disarming smile. "Not trying to tell you how to do your job, Lieutenant. I'm just a bit of a mother hen where my ship's concerned. Call it an old habit."

Rather than offer an intelligible reply, Dahk merely

grunted, continuing to maneuver the workbee closer. A few seconds later, La Forge watched the emitter settle into the socket. He felt a series of small reverberations emanating from the hull plates and into the soles of his boots as, one after another, each of the twelve locking clamps closed around the assembly's base, securing the component into its proper place.

"That's it," he said, nodding. "Nice work, Dahk."

By way of reply, the lieutenant maneuvered the workbee up and away from the deflector array before tilting the craft so he had an unobstructed view of La Forge standing on the hull. Inside the cockpit, Dahk raised his right hand to his temple, offering an informal salute.

"Happy to be of service, Commander," the Tellarite replied, its gruff voice still offering a tinge of annoyance at La Forge's hands-on supervision of the installation. *"Is there anything else you require?"*

La Forge shook his head. "I think we can take it from here, Lieutenant. Thanks for your help."

"Very well, Commander," Dahk replied. *"Safe journey to your ship and crew."*

As the workbee backed farther away from the ship, the chief engineer turned to his pair of assistants. "Okay. Taurik, Veldon, engage magnetic constrictors," he ordered. Turning from the array, he made his way with slow, deliberate steps across the hull to one of the three independent magnetic interlock control consoles positioned along the outer rim of the dish housing the deflector. A computer display screen was waiting for him there, with the message "MAGLOCK SYSTEMS OFF-LINE." It took only a handful of commands keyed into the console's manual interface to change the status to "MAGLOCK ONE ENGAGED."

Across the deflector dish from him, Taurik was bent over one of the other consoles. "Maglock Two engaged, Commander."

"Maglock Three engaged, as well, sir," said Lieutenant Veldon, one of the junior specialists assigned to the *Enterprise*'s engineering team. Even with the distance separating them, La Forge could see the hint of vapor clouding the inside of the Benzite's helmet. Her environmental suit had been configured to provide her with an atmospheric mixture approximating conditions on her home planet.

"I'd say that's it for the hard part," La Forge said.

Reaching for her own tricorder as she bent back over her console, Veldon replied, "Initiating diagnostic program now to confirm all the connections are secure."

"We might need to make a few settling-in adjustments," La Forge said. Even though the components designed for *Sovereign*-class starships—and, indeed, many of the systems incorporated into the different models of Starfleet vessels— were intended to be interchangeable to facilitate efficient installation and repair, it had been the chief engineer's experience that not everything always proceeded according to that well-intentioned master plan.

Reaching for his suit's communications controls, he keyed a new frequency. "La Forge to Commander Worf." At last report, the first officer was off duty and had informed the engineer of his intention to undertake one of his preferred calisthenics drill simulations—complete with *bat'leth*s at the ready—on the holodeck with Lieutenant Choudhury. For a moment, La Forge wondered if Worf, perhaps engaged in simulated combat against a holographically created enemy, would even answer the call.

As it happened, there was a noticeable delay before the Klingon's deep voice rang in La Forge's helmet. *"Worf here."*

"I know you're off duty, Commander," the engineer said, "but you asked to be updated when the particle emitter was installed. We've got it in place, and we're running through the final adjustments and diagnostic checks now. I figure another hour once we get back inside and run the last few installation protocols from engineering, and we'll be set."

"Thank you for the report, Commander," Worf replied. There was a slight pause, during which La Forge sensed the first officer was waiting for him to say something, before he added, *"Is there anything else?"*

Unable to resist the opening, the chief engineer said, "If you've got time, I was just checking to see if you might want to come out here and review the installation for yourself."

The grunt of mild irritation, low as it was, still managed to get conveyed through the open comm channel. *"That will not be necessary, Mr. La Forge,"* Worf said after a moment. *"I have full confidence in your ability to oversee the task to its proper completion."*

La Forge smiled even though the Klingon could not see it. Worf's dislike of any activity that might require him to venture outside the confines of the ship into the zero-gravity environs of open space was legendary aboard the *Enterprise*. "Well, okay," he said, allowing a bit more of his gentle ribbing into his voice. "If you say so."

"He says so!" answered the higher-pitched and noticeably irritated voice of Jasminder Choudhury, catching La Forge only slightly by surprise. *"Worf out!"* The last word was punctuated by a snap of static as the connection was severed.

The laugh La Forge released was short and full of mischief. "Uh-oh. I guess *she* meant it when he said he was off duty. Looks like I'm in trouble."

Taurik's arching right eyebrow was visible through the Vulcan's helmet faceplate. "I presume that you mean your call interrupted Commander Worf and Lieutenant Choudhury's . . . extracurricular activities?"

"I don't know if I'd put it quite that way," La Forge countered. "Or *any* way, for that matter." While the relationship between Worf and Choudhury was no secret, the two officers still had endeavored to maintain discretion, if for no other reason than they valued their privacy. "Probably better for all of us if we didn't bring this up the next time we see either of them."

Not that it will stop Choudhury from trying to dissect me with that bat'leth *of hers.*

5

In Picard's experience, the interval separating a high-ranking official's "being ready" to do something and that activity actually occurring varied, often to absurd degrees. Though arranged with the noblest of intentions, the schedules that defined such a person's agenda on any given day often were crowded to the point of bursting, with overworked assistants struggling to find some previously undiscovered slice of time into which a new appointment or matter requiring their superior's attention could be fit.

Such appeared to be the case with President Bacco, at least today.

So far as Picard had been able to determine, during just the few short minutes it had taken for the Palais de la Concorde's Starfleet transporter control center to authorize his being beamed from Labarre to Paris, the president obviously had been confronted by at least one such interruption. Though he wore no chronometer on his wrist and there were no such timekeeping devices in the foyer outside Bacco's office, he was certain that he had been waiting here for nearly half an hour.

Maybe I should have walked.

Picard sobered as he considered what might have seen fit

to disrupt the president's already-hectic day. An emergency on one of the numerous planets still struggling with reconstruction a year after the Borg invasion? Some bit of posturing by one of the adversarial interstellar powers? Something else entirely? At the very least, Picard took comfort in knowing that it could not be the Borg presenting some kind of renewed danger. If indeed they did pose a risk, he was certain he would be aware of it.

It took him an extra moment to realize that he had been sitting in the president's reception area, his eyes closed as he . . . what? Listened for some sign of life from what had been the Collective?

They're gone, he reminded himself. *Dead, and gone to dust. Leave them there.*

"Captain Picard?"

Opening his eyes with a start, Picard looked up to see Sivak, President Bacco's personal assistant, standing just a few steps away from him. He was dressed in a dark, formal two-piece ensemble that featured script embroidered in his native language over the left breast. Though Picard possessed a rudimentary understanding of certain Vulcan dialects, the symbols on Sivak's attire were lost on him. How had he failed to register the aide's arrival in the foyer? "Yes," Picard said, rising to his feet and straightening his uniform jacket. "My apologies, Mr. Sivak. I was lost in thought for a moment."

Sivak, standing with his hands clasped behind his back, offered an understanding nod. "President Bacco is ready to see you now, and apologizes for the delay."

Nodding, Picard cleared his throat. "Of course. By all means, lead the way." As he followed Sivak across the foyer, a pair of ornate doors—each emblazoned with the presidential seal—parted at the Vulcan's approach. Beyond the portal lay the lavishly appointed suite that served as President Bacco's office.

The first thing Picard noticed was the large panoramic window that served as the room's rear wall. With the curtains drawn aside and allowing the rays of the early afternoon sun to warm the office, Picard was greeted by a brilliant, cloudless blue sky framing the Paris skyline.

"Madam President," Sivak said, observing the customary protocols for visitors to the president's office, "Captain Picard." He waited until Picard had entered the room before stepping back into the foyer and allowing the doors to close behind him.

Rising from behind her desk, President Nanietta Bacco smiled in warm greeting. "Captain, thank you for coming, and I'm sorry to have kept you waiting." She shook her head. "There never seem to be enough hours in the day anymore."

"I can certainly sympathize with that, Madam President," Picard said as he took Bacco's proffered hand in his own. Even before crossing the office to greet her, he had taken stock of the room's other occupants. "Admiral," he said, nodding toward Leonard James Akaar, Starfleet's commander-in-chief, who stood to the left of Bacco's desk.

The towering Capellan, the locks of his long white hair lying across the shoulder boards of his uniform tunic, smiled in greeting. "Always good to see you, Jean-Luc."

Picard replied, "The pleasure is mine, sir."

"I believe you know my chief of staff, Esperanza Piñiero," the president said, indicating the human woman who had risen from one of the chairs positioned before Bacco's desk. Piñiero stepped forward and she and Picard shook hands.

"Good to see you again, Captain." Picard noted the firmness of her grip. In her mid to late fifties, as he recalled, her dark hair featured no small amount of gray, doubtless owing to the high-pressure nature of her job. There were deep lines in her forehead and around her mouth, and bags under her eyes. If Picard had not known better, he would have sworn Piñiero had not slept in the months since he had last seen her.

Turning to the fourth member of her assemblage, Bacco said, "And this is Professor Marthrossi zh'Thiin." The professor was an Andorian female, possessing stark-white hair and soft, indigo features. To Picard's eye, she appeared to be nearing middle age, at least by the standards of her species.

He bowed his head in formal greeting. "An honor to meet you, Professor." Her name seemed familiar, though Picard could not place it.

"The honor is mine," the Andorian replied, her antennae shifting atop her head to point in his direction. "Your reputation precedes you, Captain Picard."

"She's the reason I've gathered you all here today," Bacco said, before directing the group to the pair of couches and a matched quartet of parlor chairs situated in the far corner of her office. The president indicated for everyone to find a seat as she took her place in one of the chairs situated so that she had an unobstructed view of her guests. Looking to Picard, Bacco asked, "Captain, what do you know of the current situation on Andor?"

Picard settled himself in one of the other chairs so that he was comfortable and facing Bacco. "It sustained massive damage during the Borg attacks, Madam President. Hundreds of thousands of lives lost, to say nothing of the extensive destruction of its infrastructure, along with contaminated water and food supplies and any number of problems arising from ongoing medical and reconstruction issues."

"The same on worlds spanning Federation space," Bacco

said, "though in Andor's case, the damage inflicted by the Borg has only served to exacerbate existing troubles already plaguing the Andorian people."

"You're talking about the issues pertaining to procreation," Picard replied. The problem had slowly yet inexorably been escalating for more than two centuries, and already had caused the near-extinction of the Aenar, an Andorian subspecies. Turning to Professor zh'Thiin, who was seated to the president's left, he said, "Now I remember where I've heard your name. You're heading up the science team on Andor, working on ways to solve the crisis."

The professor nodded. "That is correct, Captain. The project originally was overseen by a former colleague of mine, Dr. sh'Veileth, but she was killed during the Borg attack."

Trying to recall what he knew of the research, Picard said, "I've read reports of civil unrest on Andor, in reaction to some controversial theories and solutions being proposed."

"That's a very polite description for what happened," Akaar replied from where he stood just behind President Bacco and over her right shoulder.

"Dr. sh'Veileth's hypothesis for dealing with my people's reproductive crisis was greeted with all manner of volatile opinions," zh'Thiin added. "There were those who reacted with unrestrained joy at the prospect of saving our people from extinction. Many more were skeptical, of course, and there also was a very vocal contingent who were convinced that Dr. sh'Veileth's ideas would do no less than wipe out the very essence of the Andorian people in order to replace it with something new; something *alien*."

Picard remembered more of what he had read. "You mean her idea of possibly needing only two Andorian sexes, rather than four, to complete the reproductive process?"

Zh'Thiin nodded in approval at the captain's astuteness. "Precisely. As you likely are well aware, the four-gamete fertilization paradigm would seem to be unique, or at least extremely rare, so far as our present knowledge of xenobiology would seem to indicate. Dr. sh'Veileth simply applied what she had learned from the Yrythny ova and extrapolated a course of action to benefit my people. There are those who believe that taking such action to ensure our survival engenders too great a cost to our cultural identity."

"I can imagine," Picard said. He held no doubts that Dr. sh'Veileth had been acting with the best interests of her people as her first priority, likely rationalizing that any arguments to culture, history, or even faith could be saved for another day, after resolving the immediate crisis. "However, there were problems with the proposed Yrythny solution."

Her expression darkening as her antennae curled downward, zh'Thiin replied, "Yes, there were. Several of the *zhen* within the test groups where the ova were applied have experienced unanticipated side effects. There were a number of miscarriages, as well as instances where the child died in the womb before being carried to term." She paused, and Picard was sure he caught a flash of pain and sorrow crossing her features before her passive demeanor returned.

Clearing her throat, she added, "Other children who survived to birth now suffer from a variety of genetic deficiencies. We are still trying to learn what has caused this, but the obvious theory is that something in the Yrythny ova that has escaped our detection to this point must be at the root of the problem. Until this anomaly can be isolated, further testing has been halted, but our research into other alternatives continues."

Shaking his head, Picard allowed a small sigh to escape

his lips. "It astounds me that even with the combined medical and scientific knowledge of the entire Federation, something like this can still be without resolution."

"It certainly isn't for lack of trying, Captain," Bacco said, shifting in her seat. "In addition to carrying on Dr. sh'Veileth's research, Professor zh'Thiin and her team have been looking under every rock they can find in search of anything which might offer a clue to solving this problem. I even convinced the Federation Council to authorize her group to access whatever data we have on genetic engineering, even of the sort we banned centuries ago."

This caught Picard by surprise. "I can't imagine that not causing a public outcry."

Bacco nodded. "Which is why that order and that aspect of Professor zh'Thiin's research remain highly classified."

"Several planets scattered throughout Federation and surrounding territories are known to engage in various types of eugenics research," Akaar added. "There have already been a few covert overtures made to the governments of those worlds. As for our own research, we've even cracked open the vaults and pulled out the work of notable figures like Arik Soong. More than two hundred years ago, he attempted to reconstruct some of the advances in genetic engineering made during the late twentieth century. Perhaps the Chrysalis Project sounds familiar to you?"

"Indeed it does," Picard said, making no effort to hide his surprise. "The Chrysalis Project was what brought about the Eugenics Wars. It gave birth to misguided souls like Stavos Keniclius and tyrants such as Khan Noonien Singh." Looking to Bacco, he asked, "Madam President, are we sure this is a precedent we want to be following?"

Bacco held up a hand as she shook her head. "Don't

worry, Captain. It's not our aim to throw open the doors and declare open season on eugenics, not that there's really a whole lot of information to go on, anyway. You know that records from that period of Earth history are, to put it kindly, fragmented. Still, if there's something, even a shred of information locked in whatever's left of that data, that might point Professor zh'Thiin and her people in a new direction, then it's an avenue we can't ignore."

"Agreed," Picard replied. To zh'Thiin, he said, "And Professor, it was not my intention to imply otherwise."

Zh'Thiin smiled. "Worry not, Captain. I understand it is your responsibility to point out potential dangers and undesired consequences of any actions your superiors might contemplate. I would expect no less from a man of such conscience and principle as you are known to be."

Somewhat embarrassed by the unexpected compliment, Picard said nothing for a moment. As an explorer—a man dedicated to the pursuit of knowledge in order to better not only himself but the people he represented and even swore an oath to defend—examining all possibilities without allowing emotion to enter into the equation came as second nature to him. However, reality had shown Picard that unfettered access to knowledge rarely was accompanied by the wisdom to properly employ it. Indeed, he often had been called upon to resolve issues stemming from such disparity, with those undertakings rarely being simple or pleasant.

It was this thought that caused Picard to turn once more to Bacco. "Madam President, I realize this is a sensitive and ongoing issue, but what do you require of me and the *Enterprise*?"

"Well, as you've probably already figured out," Bacco replied, "even with the additional information at their disposal, Professor zh'Thiin and her people are still seeking answers."

"That is true," zh'Thiin added. "Despite several leads that hold great promise to assist my people, much of the information we've gathered or studied remains inconclusive with respect to our unique problem. Meanwhile, there is growing discontent among the Andorian populace, given how the effects of the crisis we face have only been worsened by the lingering effects of the Borg attack."

"More civil unrest?" Picard asked.

Akaar said, "In some areas, particularly those cities that are home to Federation embassies and Starfleet installations. There's a growing anti-Federation movement on the ground there, Jean-Luc. People feel like they've been abandoned, that solutions aren't being found fast enough, and that the Andorians are being left to eventual extinction. So far, it's just a few isolated incidents, but our people on-site feel that it will only get worse before it gets better."

Leaning forward in his chair, Picard frowned. "Given what we've all had to deal with over the last year, it's easy to let emotion take over in the face of adversity, to try and find someone else to blame." He had seen that sort of reaction on multiple occasions in recent months. "But you're not suggesting we reduce the Federation or Starfleet footprint on Andor?"

"On the contrary," Bacco said, rising from her chair and indicating with a gesture for everyone else to remain seated. "Instead, we're going to hold a conference in the new capital city." She made her way to her desk, where an etched crystal carafe of water sat on a silver tray. As she poured some of the water into one of the matching glasses, she continued, "Andor's new presider, Iravothra sh'Thalis, has requested it be held there, and she's invited prominent scientists from across the Federation as well as a few nonaligned worlds where eugenics research has been conducted. If anything, we want to show that we're as committed as ever to helping Andor fight this crisis. By hosting the conference there, and bringing some of the Federation's prominent scientific minds to participate, we hope to put a public face to the effort being expended to solve this problem."

Now, Picard understood his role. Looking to Akaar, he asked, "You want the *Enterprise* to transport a delegation to Andor?"

The admiral nodded. "Not only that, but your crew can also augment the existing Starfleet security detachment without being too obvious about it. The *Enterprise* has been our ship on point for a year, moving from planet to planet and spearheading the resolution of problem after problem as we continue our rebuilding efforts. Having it in orbit while the conference is in session will, hopefully, go a long way toward discouraging anyone from getting any bright ideas about disrupting the proceedings."

Picard could agree with the subtle tactic. While Starbase 7, the base nearest to Andor, could provide ships and personnel to reinforce the Starfleet contingent already on the ground, none of those vessels carried the same high profile as the *Enterprise*. Likewise, the resources Picard commanded would likely be more than enough to handle any issues that might arise. Still, it was not his habit to take such things for granted. "Are we expecting that sort of trouble?"

"I have seen several instances of unrest, Captain," zh'Thiin said. "So far, they have been small, yet still organized. We suspect that a few activist groups may be working in concert to organize a larger, more formal protest during the conference."

Akaar added, "Though our Starfleet units on Andor haven't yet picked up anything that might imply active resistance or attacks being planned, you know how things can go from bad to worse if and when tempers start flaring."

"It's worth noting that there also are many among my people who understand and appreciate the Federation's efforts on our behalf," zh'Thiin said. "Groups representing this viewpoint have been working to make their voices heard as well. I expect they also will be present when the conference convenes."

"Our Starfleet assets are already working with Andorian counterparts to prepare for the security issues we know this will bring," Bacco said, still holding her water glass. "And, as always, you've got my authority to take whatever action you deem appropriate. I'm obviously hoping things won't get that far, but if I've learned anything during my time in politics, it's to be ready for anything and everything."

Offering a small, knowing smile as he contemplated what had been asked of him, Picard nodded. "As it happens, my choice of career has provided me with that very same life lesson."

6

The doors to her quarters parting to allow her entry, Lieutenant T'Ryssa Chen stepped through the portal, tossing her tricorder in a broad arc to land atop her bed on the other side of the room. Once the doors closed behind her, she released a sigh of contentment as she allowed the tranquility of her private space to wash over her.

Be it ever so humble.

The trouble with being a contact specialist, Chen had learned quite some time ago, was that when there was no one or no thing to contact, such talents were not required, largely leaving the possessor of such expertise with nothing to do. In the first weeks after her permanent assignment to the *Enterprise*, Chen had taken to assisting Commander La Forge and his engineering staff with whatever assignments might require an extra set of hands. Her atypical childhood and wealth of experience in a number of areas had given her a diverse set of skills that proved handy when it came to the rather lengthy list of tasks and chores required to keep a starship operating at peak efficiency.

"I really should just make the permanent transfer to engineering and get it over with," she said to no one as she reached for the closure on the front of her uniform. Unlike a lot of days, today Chen had managed to avoid coming into contact with lubricants or other fluids and grime from plumbing the depths of the ship in search of problems to fix. That did not stop her from wanting to take a shower, however, in order to get on with the evening's activities. Though tonight was not her regularly scheduled dinner with Taurik, the Vulcan's recent promotion to lieutenant commander required a proper observance, which Chen had insisted upon despite Taurik's objections. Ignoring the engineer's appeals to the illogic of wasting time on such frivolities, Chen had compromised with respect to how the milestone should be celebrated: a simple meal in one of the ship's recreation halls, followed by the poker tournament scheduled to begin at 2100 hours. She had learned to play during her childhood, and was surprised to learn that Taurik also enjoyed the game, though the Vulcan had admitted to not playing for quite some time.

Yeah, I've heard that one before, she mused, smiling at the notion of Taurik deliberately understating his competence for the game as a means of luring her to play. Though he did not often display it, Chen knew from experience that the Vulcan possessed a sly sense of humor. When she had asked early on during their friendship if he ever had any fun, his cryptic response had been, "At regular intervals." It had taken her a moment to grasp the reply's multilayered meaning, after which she had laughed in unvarnished appreciation of his dry, deadpan wit. In the year or so in which they had spent as colleagues as well as friends, Chen had come to appreciate the many facets of Taurik's personality, including those he did not easily share.

Stepping out of the uniform that now lay in a crumpled heap at her feet, Chen opened the front of her gold tunic as she moved toward the trio of sloping windows set into the bulkhead above her bed. Nothing but stars greeted her, unlike the past few days when her view had been obstructed by the support structure of Farber Station. That was at least one small comfort as the *Enterprise* warped away from Earth toward its next assignment, as she had grown accustomed long ago to falling asleep while being treated to an unfettered view of the stars.

It's the simple things.

She had removed the rest of her clothing and was on her way to the lavatory and the luxurious shower awaiting her when the door chime sounded. Chen frowned, having no idea who might be calling on her. If there had been a situation or task requiring her attention in engineering, Commander La Forge or a member of his staff would simply have raised her via the comm system. For a brief, playful moment, Chen considered just standing naked in the doorway for her unexpected visitor, but just as quickly discarded the notion. With her luck, it would be Commander Worf or, worse yet, Captain Picard himself.

"That'd look good on my performance evaluation," she muttered as she retrieved a silk robe from her closet and donned it, securing its belt at her waist before announcing for the benefit of the ship's computer. "Come in."

The doors slid open, the brightness of the corridor lighting sharply contrasting with the dimmer illumination Chen preferred inside her quarters. Dr. Crusher stood in the doorway, wearing as was her habit a Starfleet blue medical smock over her standard uniform. In her hands she carried a narrow burnished-copper box with ornate patterns engraved into its sides.

"Lieutenant Chen?" the doctor asked, offering a warm

smile. "I hope I'm not disturbing you. I was told you'd just come off duty."

Chen shook her head. "Not at all, Doctor." She gestured toward her. "Please, come in. You caught me on the way to the shower." In deference to her visitor, she called out, "Computer, increase lighting thirty percent."

"I promise I won't keep you long," Crusher replied, stepping into the room as the internal illumination increased. "I was hoping I might impose upon you for a favor."

A favor? This was interesting, Chen decided. "What can I do for you?" she asked, indicating for Crusher to have a seat in one of the two straight-backed chairs positioned at the small table near the center of her room.

Moving to the table, Crusher set down the box. Its polished exterior reflected the lights, the engraving eliciting a multitude of colors that played off the table's glass top. "I've been told you're rather inventive when it comes to fixing things," the doctor said, dropping into one of the chairs.

Chen adjusted her robe as she took the seat across from Crusher. "I like to tinker, if that's what you mean," she replied, shrugging. "Hazards of an atypical childhood, I suppose. What's in the box?" She watched as the doctor's hand lay atop the box for a moment, her fingers caressing its surface.

"I suppose you could call it an heirloom," Crusher said after a moment. "It's a very special memento belonging to the captain. It was damaged when his ready room was destroyed during that Hirogen attack last year. He lost a lot of keepsakes, but this one was spared, at least partially."

Nodding as she recalled the events of that day, Chen reached with her left hand to massage her right arm. It had been badly burned during the Hirogen assault on the *Enterprise* and the *U.S.S. Aventine* following the two Starfleet

ships' venture to the Delta Quadrant. In a bid to fight a holding action against Borg ships via the network of subspace
tunnels to the Alpha Quadrant during their final invasion,
the two starships had found themselves targeted by a pack of
ten Hirogen ships. The predatory alien race, knowing nothing of the Borg's campaign, had seen the vessels merely as
another prime hunting opportunity, and launched a devastating assault on both ships.

Those were the days.

Crusher reached to undo the closure on the box's front
and raised its lid, revealing its contents to Chen. Inside,
nestled within a foam pad that Chen could tell had dried
and cracked as though exposed to extreme heat, lay a slender
metallic rod. Sporting its own series of elaborate engravings,
it also featured several holes along its length. It took her only
a moment to recognize the object, at least in general terms.

"It's a flute?"

Nodding, Crusher replied, "A very special flute, the only
one of its kind. It was . . . a gift to the captain some years ago,
following a rather unusual first-contact mission." She paused,
and Chen noted the look of recollection on the doctor's face.
"It means a great deal to him."

"I'm surprised it even survived at all," Chen said.

"He normally kept it in our quarters," Crusher replied.
"He often played it as a means of relaxing. During the Borg
crisis, when he was spending so much time in his ready room,
he played it once in a while as he tried to work out various
problems and decisions he was facing. It was only fortunate
happenstance that the box was closed when the fire broke out
in his ready room. That was enough to protect it from being
destroyed, but the heat still managed to damage it to the
point where he can no longer play it."

Chen had seen the damage inflicted upon Captain Picard's private sanctum, and remembered the various artifacts and keepsakes it had contained, reminders of a long, fruitful life as well as a distinguished Starfleet career. She recalled how visibly shaken the captain had been upon viewing the charred remains of the ready room, and the sorrow he had exhibited upon learning how many of those prized possessions he had lost. Though Chen herself valued very few such mementos, those she did retain were irreplaceable, and she could only imagine the grief she might experience if faced with their loss. Still, she knew that such items were only inanimate objects, far less valuable than one's life or the love of a cherished family member or trusted companion. She also was certain that Captain Picard felt the same way. So, what was it about the flute, this object, that carried within it so much emotional resonance for him?

That must be one hell of a story.

"You'd like me to have a go at fixing it?" Chen asked.

Crusher smiled. "If you're willing."

Reaching toward the box, Chen used utmost care to lift the flute from the foam pad in which it was ensconced. It had been cleaned with care, she surmised, and a light blue tassel encircled it near the mouthpiece. "It looks to be in pretty good shape, overall," she said.

"He polished it and the box to remove the soot, and replaced the tassel," Crusher said, "According to the captain, it has an internal mechanism that helped to provide its distinctive sound. Though the outer casing survived the fire, that piece was damaged. I don't know why he's never asked anyone to even take a look at it, much less try to repair it." She shrugged. "Maybe he's worried it'll be damaged even further."

Though she possessed very little in the way of knowledge

with respect to musical instruments, Chen nevertheless found herself intrigued by the challenge of repairing the flute. Eyeing Crusher, she said, "It's been more than a year. Why now?"

Crusher shrugged. "I'd pretty much forgotten about it until I found it in the back of a drawer in our quarters the other day. He hasn't displayed it since it was damaged. I guess he just doesn't want to be reminded of what he lost." After a moment, she added, "Of course, he might also be simply hiding it from René. He's at that stage where everything needs to be opened and thrown onto the floor."

"I was doing that just this morning," Chen countered, unable to resist the small joke as she returned the flute to the box and closed its lid before patting it with her hand. "I'd be happy to take a crack at it, Doctor, though I'm surprised you came to me."

"He trusts you, Lieutenant," Crusher replied. "Therefore, so do I. He's talked often about how impressed he is with you, despite your . . . shall we say . . . unorthodox methods?"

"That's me," Chen said. "Lieutenant Unorthodox."

Leaning closer, the doctor said, "Anyway, I thought this might make a nice present—from René—so I obviously want it to be a surprise."

"Oh," Chen said, feigning worry. "So, no pressure or anything like that."

Smiling, Crusher added, "Well, I need somebody I know can keep a secret from the captain. You seem rather good at that."

"I'd like to think of it as having an exceptionally good poker face," Chen replied. "Which reminds me, I'm going to be late for dinner and cards."

Crusher nodded, rising from her chair. "Of course. Thank you, T'Ryssa. I owe you one."

"Remember that the next time I need a doctor's note for missing calisthenics class," Chen said as the doctor made her way to the door and exited the room. Once Crusher was gone, the lieutenant turned and gazed once more upon the box, pondering its contents. For Crusher to bring the prized instrument to her implied a trust beyond simple confidence in her ability to carry out her assigned duties. Though Chen long ago had grown comfortable aboard the *Enterprise* and believed that she was indeed a valued member of the starship's crew and perhaps even its "family," this sense of inclusion she now felt seemed altogether different.

So, I should probably try to avoid screwing this up.

7

It was on days like this that Presider Iravothra sh'Thalis wished her office window opened.

With her arms folded across her chest and one of several reports she was supposed to be studying held in her right hand, sh'Thalis stood before the curved transparasteel barrier that served as the window at the front of her tastefully appointed private chamber and gazed at the lush green lawn eight stories below. The immense courtyard was attended with utmost care, thanks to the efforts of a twenty-person crew devoted to the maintenance of the Parliament Andoria's exterior areas. Today, the sky was a vibrant blue and the sun was out, bathing the courtyard in its warm rays. According to the forecast she had seen during an early-morning newsnet broadcast, it was a glorious day to be outdoors. With such weather, it was almost too easy to forget that other areas of her world lay in permanent ruin.

"Presider," a voice said from behind her, "are you all right?"

Sh'Thalis turned to see her assistant, Loqnara ch'Birane, standing in the doorway leading from her office. The young Talish wore a beige robe that offset his deep blue skin and complemented his long, stark-white hair, which was pulled back from his face and secured at the base of his neck, further emphasizing the long antennae atop his forehead. In his hand he carried the ubiquitous data reader that seemed to be an extension of his body.

Shaking her head, sh'Thalis replied, "I was just wondering about the possibility of venturing into the city. I know I called for a party Enclave today, but it's simply too wondrous a day to be trapped inside, and the change of pace would do us well, don't you think?" The notion of spending the afternoon ensconced in the underground cavern that had been designated as the new Enclave chamber on a day like today galled her. "Why not take to the fresh-air spaces of New Therin Park?" She had not yet had the chance to visit the public recreation area, located at the center of the city's teeming downtown business and government district, since its rechristening after the relocation of the parliament to Lor'Vela. The park had been renamed not only in honor of Shantherin th'Clane, a Starfleet officer who had distinguished himself with great bravery more than a century earlier, but also the original Therin Park—likewise named for him—which along with its home city of Laibok had been destroyed during the Borg attack.

"It would indeed be a nice deviation from our normal schedule," ch'Birane conceded, "but you can expect protest from some of the more traditional party members. Beyond that, I'm certain I can already hear Commander th'Hadik lodging a preemptive formal protest as we speak."

Unable to stifle the chuckle that escaped her lips, sh'Thalis smiled at her aide's observation. So far as her personal safety was concerned, Commander Jaedreq th'Hadik, the leader of her protective detail, was as zealous as he was thorough. To his credit, the commander was aware of his propensity for erring on the side of caution and withstood sh'Thalis's humorous barbs at his expense with great aplomb. On the other hand, his reputation and professionalism also were among the primary reasons she had requested him for her staff shortly after taking office.

"You're probably right," she said. "Still, it was a pleasing thought." Stepping away from the window, she moved to the other side of the room where her expansive, curved desk was situated so as to afford her a view of the cityscape beyond the complex's perimeter wall. Most offices she visited were furnished so that windows like hers were at the occupant's back, but sh'Thalis could not see the logic behind such a choice. What was the point of a window, particularly if it framed a picturesque view of a city as alive and full of energy as Lor'Vela, if one could not easily look out it? Taking a seat in the high-backed gray chair positioned behind her desk, she asked, "What can I do for you, Loqnara?"

Pressing a control on his reader, ch'Birane ejected a small data-storage card from the device and stepped closer to sh'Thalis's desk, offering the card to the presider. "We've received word from President Bacco. The *Enterprise* is on its way, bringing with it Professor zh'Thiin, along with several experts from Starfleet Medical and prominent Federation civilian agencies."

"Excellent," sh'Thalis replied, nodding in approval at the report. "And what of the other conference attendees?"

Without consulting his reader, ch'Birane answered, "A few have already arrived, and they've been situated with appropriate accommodations. The mansion has plenty of space to house all the invited guests, and I'm told that book-ings are up in lodgings throughout the city. People from all over the world are traveling here to attend, Presider."

"I hope that's a good thing," sh'Thalis said, her eyes moving to look down at one of the several reports provided by Commander th'Hadik. "According to the assessments I've been getting, security is worried about protest groups trying to stage events designed to draw the attention of the newsnets."

"It's not just th'Hadik and his people, Presider," the young Talish countered. "Captain ch'Zandi has similar concerns."

Nodding, sh'Thalis said, "Yes, I know. I've read his reports as well." As commander of the Homeworld Security brigade located on the outskirts of Lor'Vela, Captain Eyatra ch'Zandi oversaw any threats to the city deemed too large to be faced by local law enforcement. Most of the time, the brigade's role was the same as for other military units stationed around the world, charged primarily with the defense of Andor itself when faced with global threats. During the Borg invasion, nearly half of the Andorian military's ships were destroyed, and a sizable percentage of those that survived had suffered significant damage.

"We're getting a lot of questions from the newsnets about Homeworld Security's presence at the conference," ch'Birane said, studying his data padd. "There's concern that they're taking on a role that should belong to the police."

Sighing, sh'Thalis replied, "These are special circumstances. The nature of the conference and the controversy it's stirred demand we take extra precautions. We have to keep people safe; not just the attendees, but private citizens who will be in the city once the event gets under way. As for the concerns of the news media, they're coming from people who are deliberately trying to generate controversy, and I've no time for such nonsense." With respect to operations on Andorian soil, Homeworld Security's involvement was minimal, as mandated by law, and relegated to assistance and relief efforts in the event of natural emergencies such as fire or extreme weather, and only then after being called to active service on order of the presider. It also was within sh'Thalis's authority to summon military assets for other reasons, up to and including any threat to public safety regardless if it was believed to be within the scope of local police agencies. In the aftermath of the Borg attack, Homeworld Security units had been assisting government and civilian organizations around the world with reconstruction as well as security efforts, and in many people's eyes the line between the military and the police had blurred to the point that any distinction was insignificant. It was not a view sh'Thalis took lightly, and she had taken steps to ensure that the roles of both groups were defined with no ambiguity whatsoever.

"They're pressing our staff for answers, Presider," ch'Birane warned.

Sh'Thalis waved away the statement. "If they want to have this fight, they can do it on their time, not mine."

"There are those who consider your time to be their time," ch'Birane said, his expression and tone neutral.

Shrugging, sh'Thalis said, "They're right, to a point." Moving aside a stack of reports she had already read, she added, "But the people who elected me did so with the understanding that I'd know where to direct my energy. Given the choice between real or manufactured issues, I'll go with the former." During her short tenure, she had managed to avoid getting dragged into petty squabbles that seemed to fill the days and nights of her political opponents, choosing instead to focus on the genuine matters of governance, of which there were many. "If they want to replace me, they're more than welcome to do so."

"Continue to talk like that," ch'Birane said, his antennae bending in her direction, "and even your opposition will vote for you in the next election."

"Well, we can't have that, now can we?" Sh'Thalis paused, shaking her head. "There are days when I feel as though I've been at this job my entire life." Little more than a year ago, she had been a magistrate in the former presider's administration, overseeing the Natural Resources Conservation and Protection Committee. Along with those of several other low-ranking departments, her offices were here in Lor'Vela, rather than the capital city of Laikan. As such, only she and various other subordinate members of the former presider's staff survived the Borg attack. Being the official among the survivors with the most seniority, sh'Thalis was elevated to the position of presider, promoted through tragedy and fate to be the new head of Parliament Andoria in its adopted home.

She consulted the schedule displayed upon the computer terminal set into the center of her desk, angled so that she could read it without having to lean over it. "Are the plans for the reception dinner still going forward?"

Ch'Birane nodded. "Yes, Presider. Commander th'Hadik is working with the staff to ensure all security provisions are met, and in a matter as unobtrusive as possible for our guests. Given that Starfleet will also be represented, the commander is advocating several additional measures be put into place."

"I trust th'Hadik's judgment," sh'Thalis replied. "Speaking of which, I understand that the *Enterprise* captain, Picard, is something of an aficionado when it comes to Earth wines as well as a few made on other planets. Please have something selected for presentation as—"

The rest of her sentence was cut off by the piercing shriek

of an alarm siren. Sh'Thalis flinched at the unexpected sound, rising from her chair at the same time ch'Birane moved toward her. No sooner did he place himself between her and the door to her office than the door slid open, revealing a pair of agents from her security detail, th'Perene and ch'Mahlaht. Both agents entered the room with weapons drawn, ch'Mahlaht standing in the doorway and keeping his attention focused on the corridor beyond as th'Perene stepped into the room.

"We're sorry for the interruption, Presider," th'Perene said, his voice tense as he called out over the sound of the klaxon, "but we have an intrusion alarm."

"What?" sh'Thalis asked. "Where?"

Ignoring her query, the agent turned and gestured to ch'Mahlaht, who then stepped into the office, allowing the door to close. He reached for the control pad set into the wall and entered a string of commands. The colored panel on the keypad changed from blue to orange, indicating that the door was now locked and impossible to open from the outside. The sound of metal against metal caught sh'Thalis's attention, and she turned to the window in time to see heavy protective shutters lowering over the transparasteel pane, blocking her view of the courtyard and the surrounding city. In response to the loss of natural light, the illumination in her office increased automatically.

Th'Perene reached to his belt and retrieved a communications device, lifting the unit to his mouth. "This is th'Perene. The presider is secure."

"Acknowledged," replied a voice through the device's speaker, one sh'Thalis recognized as belonging to Commander th'Hadik. *"Other teams have taken up position outside the presider's office. Our initial report counts two intruders on*

the grounds, and we're still securing the rest of the compound. Stand by and await further instructions."

"Understood," th'Perene replied before severing the connection and returning the communications unit to his belt. Turning to face sh'Thalis, he said, "I apologize for the disruption, Presider."

Drawing a deep breath, sh'Thalis nodded before turning to ch'Birane, whose expression had turned to one of worry. She reached out, placing a reassuring hand on his shoulder. "It will be fine, Loqnara, though I suppose this means we're not going outside today."

Shar stepped from the lift, emerging into the sunlight. Raising his face skyward, he smiled as he breathed the fresh air. The temperature was mild, and he felt a slight breeze. Only a few small clouds accented the otherwise clear blue sky. He had hoped being outside would soothe him, but any fleeting relief he might have felt dissolved as he turned his attention to the object he now held, and which had been waiting for him upon his arrival earlier this morning.

The locket seemed to weigh heavily in his hand, all the more so for what it contained. It was a *shapla,* a traditional Andorian betrothal symbol, which he found upon opening to contain a lock of dark hair, its color and texture making it obvious that it could not have come from any Andorian. It had been intertwined with a similar segment of thicker, stark-white hair. Any lingering doubt as to the symbol's meaning was erased by the small paper note he had found tucked inside the locket, with a single word written by his own hand: *Someday.*

How long had it been since he had last seen Prynn Tenmei? He pondered the question as he walked the path that ran parallel to the perimeter wall encircling the parliamentary compound's courtyard. His last contact with Prynn had been just prior to her departing Andor and after his decision to remain with his bondgroup and undertake the *shelthreth* mating ritual. It had been Shar's original intention to return to Deep Space 9 following the birth of the bondgroup's child, but circumstances saw to it that he stayed, continuing to assist Dr. sh'Veileth with her research when it became apparent that the Yrythny ova protocol was not the solution to Andor's ongoing reproductive crisis. Despite that desire to contribute to work that might save his people, Shar still thought of Prynn often.

Why did you not contact her?

The question burned in Shar's mind, harassing him for an answer he did not possess. Though his bondgroup had dissolved for a time following the birth of their first child, Thiarelata ch'Vazdi, a decision eventually was reached to make a second attempt at procreation. Shar had at first resisted the notion, electing instead to return to Starfleet, but his bondmates made the choice to join him at his new posting on Starbase 714.

Then the Borg came, and took away Thia, Anichent, and Dizhei, along with the child they had created together.

Finding a bench woven from strands of thick, fibrous vines that had been placed before one of the gardens situated around the courtyard, Shar sat and listened to the tranquil sounds of the small waterfall that fed the garden's reflecting pool from an underground spring. It served only as a momentary distraction before his attention once more was drawn to the box in his hand. Though the months immediately following the Borg invasion had been unforgiving as he returned to Andor and devoted his energies to helping with relief efforts, why had he not contacted Prynn? He had not even sent her a message to inform her of his decision to remain with his bondgroup. Was he frightened at the prospect of seeing her again? For that, Shar had no answer. Of course, Prynn had seen fit not to contact him, either, but he knew that was for different reasons. Their parting had been very upsetting for her, and at the time, Shar was certain that any renewed communication would serve only to deepen any feelings of sadness that had gripped her.

Now, however, things were different. A year had passed, and while Shar still grieved the loss of his bondgroup and their child, other feelings were beginning to make themselves known. Loneliness, desire, yearning.

For Prynn. Any concerns that she might not feel the same way seemed to dissolve in the face of the *shapla* in his hand. When might they finally meet again? Shar smiled at the memory of the small note he had placed inside the locket. *Someday.*

The serenity of the courtyard was shattered by the shrill tones of what Shar recognized as an intrusion alarm. Muscles tensing, Shar rose from the bench, looking for the source of the alert. At the far end of the compound, he was able to see several figures, all wearing the dark uniforms of Homeworld Security, running down various paths and around the courtyard's trees and gardens. Had someone attempted to breach one of the compound's security gates?

Something scraped against the stone wall to his left, and Shar turned in time to see a figure dropping from the top of the wall and down behind a row of tall hedges near the garden's outer edge.

"Hey!" he yelled, his eyes widening in shock as an Andorian emerged from the hedges. Dressed in some kind of woven, dark-brown single-piece garment, the intruder halted at the sight of Shar. They both froze, standing on the stone-tiled path running parallel to the wall as their eyes locked, each trying to read the intent of the other.

Reaching up to slap his combadge, Shar was able to call out, "Ch'Thane to security! Intruder alert! Quadrant three," before the Andorian drew a knife from a pocket along his right thigh and charged forward.

"Lieutenant ch'Thane!" a voice erupted from his communicator. *"What's your status? Lieutenant?"* Shar ignored the question, concentrating instead on his opponent. Light reflected off the curved blade in the intruder's hand, and Shar backpedaled, giving himself room to prepare for the attack as the other Andorian closed the distance. Shar could tell by the way his opponent wielded the weapon that he had no real experience with knife fighting, but that did not mean he could not still inflict injury if given the chance.

So, don't give him that chance.

With a warbling cry Shar assumed was meant to startle him, the Andorian raised his knife hand as he lunged forward. Shar set his feet, waiting for the exact moment when his opponent would be the most vulnerable. When the Andorian was close enough, Shar stepped into the attack, his hand rising to block the intruder's blade arm on the downward swing. Drilling his right fist into the Andorian's torso and just beneath his raised arm, Shar heard the satisfying grunt of shock and pain. He pressed his attack, not giving the intruder any opportunity to recover or react. Grasping the assailant's knife arm, Shar twisted it down and away before driving it up and behind the other Andorian's back. He bent the wrist until his opponent cried and loosened his grip on the knife. The blade fell to the ground and Shar kicked it

away before tightening his hold on the Andorian. He drove
him down to the ground, jamming his knee into the small of
the Andorian's back and resting on him with his full weight.
Only then did he realize that his opponent had to outweigh
him by a minimum of two dozen kilos.

*I guess those close-quarters combat classes weren't a waste of
time, after all.*

"Lieutenant ch'Thane!" shouted the voice from his combadge. He was about to say something when a shadow fell
across the tiles of the walkway in front of him. Jerking his
head to the left, he saw another Andorian running at him.
Shar started pulling himself to his feet, releasing his prisoner
and trying to get his hands up and ready for any kind of
defense, but by then it was too late.

The Andorian hit him at full speed, tackling him while
he was still rising to his feet. Shar shouted in pain as their
bodies collided just before he slammed against the ground, his
head striking one of the large tiles forming the walkway. Stars
exploded in his vision and he lashed out blindly, hands connecting with his new attacker's head. Twisting, pushing, and
pulling with all his remaining strength, he wormed his way out
from beneath the other Andorian, continuing to strike at him
with both hands. Then something hit him in the side of his
head and he felt his body go limp as he collapsed to the grass.

Get up! Get up!

His mind screamed the words and he struggled to push
himself to his hands and knees, but his limbs would not
cooperate. Tiny daggers jabbed at his skull. Through blurred
vision he saw both Andorians scrambling to their feet, and
Shar was gripped by fear and helplessness. With a growl of
frustration he forced himself to one knee, unwilling to face his
attackers while floundering in the grass like a wounded animal.

Then a high-pitched whine pierced the air, making him wince as twin beams of angry red energy passed over his head to strike his opponents. For an instant, both Andorians were enveloped by undulating crimson cloaks before they staggered and fell unmoving to the ground. Shar stared at them for a handful of seconds, waiting for them to rise to their feet or for their bodies to twitch.

Satisfied that they were staying where they were, Shar promptly followed suit, sinking back to the grass. Above him, the sky twirled and stretched, dancing in his pain-racked vision. His stomach lurched and he felt bile rise in his throat.

From somewhere behind him, he heard the sounds of running footsteps, and a moment later a head, big and blue as it whirled before his eyes, peered down at him.

"Lieutenant ch'Thane?" a voice asked, distant and hollow. "Remain still." The new arrival pulled away from him, shouting something Shar could not understand.

Another Andorian appeared in his vision, kneeling near his left side, and Shar heard a mild electronic warbling next to his ear.

"Lieutenant," a new voice said, "can you hear me? I am Specialist ch'Gelosine. You were stunned by the blow to your head, but you've suffered no serious damage. I'm going to give you something to help with the pain."

Shar heard a hiss of compressed air, accompanied by a pressure on the left side of his neck, and a moment later the pain in his head began to diminish. The world stopped spinning before him, and the sensation of nausea began to pass.

"How do you feel?" someone asked, and Shar turned his head to see Commander th'Hadik kneeling beside him. The security leader's expression was one of concern.

Coughing as the medic on his left side helped him to a

sitting position, Shar replied, "Like somebody landed on me with a shuttlecraft." He winced as residual pain stabbed at his temples, and when he reached for his head his fingers touched something wet.

"It's not serious," ch'Gelosine said, reaching toward him, and Shar noted the familiar smell of antiseptic solution as the medic dabbed at the side of his head with a treatment wipe from his field aid kit. "He had a metal band sewn into his glove. The cut's not that deep. It will only take a moment to treat with a dermal regenerator."

"Can you tell me what happened?" th'Hadik asked.

Shaking his head, Shar replied, "I don't know. I was taking a break from my work and came outside to get some fresh air." He waved to where the two intruders now were standing, their hands locked into security cuffs as members of the commander's detail looked through the various items found in their possession. "I guess they jumped over the wall? Are there more of them?"

"No," the commander said. "At least, we haven't found any more. We're still searching the mansion and the rest of the compound."

Shar pulled himself to his feet, an action he regretted as a fresh wave of nausea washed over him. Ch'Gelosine reached out to steady him, and Shar nodded in appreciation. "What do you think they were doing?" he asked.

"We don't know yet," th'Hadick replied. "They weren't carrying anything more than a knife, so far as weapons are concerned. No explosives or firearms, and no identification or anything else of use, for that matter." He paused as though contemplating a notion he did not like, and then said, "They couldn't possibly think they could just climb over the wall and get across the courtyard to something or someone of value. Either they're idiots, or perhaps they were deliberately testing our responses to an intrusion alarm."

With the conference just days away, were potential enemies already probing the compound for weaknesses? What else might they be planning? "You don't believe they were idiots, do you?" Shar asked.

Th'Hadik released a long, slow sigh, looking over his shoulder at the prisoners, who were still being questioned by members of the commander's security team. When he turned back to Shar, the expression on his face was one of resignation.

"What I believe is that this is just the beginning."

8

She was tired, she was hungry, and the idea of a shower and bed was beginning to take a firm hold on her, but Beverly Crusher ignored it. There was still too much to do.

Sitting with René at the dining table in their quarters, Beverly divided her attention between her son in his high-chair to her left, and the computer interface resting on the table itself. Seeing all the padds and reports scattered atop the table as she watched René eat his supper, Beverly was struck by a sudden sense of déjà vu. How long had it been since she had last found herself in this position, setting aside her work as she fed young Wesley? Thirty years?

Thirty-four, my dear doctor.

Not for the first time, Beverly smiled at how even the simplest of interactions with René spurred a memory of doing something similar with her firstborn son. Likewise, it never failed to make her wonder where Wesley might be at that moment. Having become a Traveler—one of a race of beings possessing the ability to move about time and space at will—his visits had become increasingly infrequent over the years as his abilities evolved. He had returned in order to attend his mother's wedding to Jean-Luc Picard, and he also had arrived shortly after the birth of his new baby brother. Beverly trea-

sured those as well as Wesley's other visits, irregular and brief
though they were. Though she understood on an intellectual
level what he had become and the path he had chosen, and
that he had grown into not simply a fine man but also so
much more, Wesley was still her son; her baby. On those rare
occasions when he came home to her, she was able to put aside
at least some of the sorrow she sometimes felt at not having
him in her life.

"You're not going to leave me, are you?" she asked, reaching out to caress René's cheek. "And if you do, would you
promise me that you'll do something a bit more normal with
your life? Something that lets you come home more often
than once every couple of years?" In response to her questions, the child gurgled something unintelligible as he smiled
around a mouthful of mushed carrots.

Good enough for now. Sighing, she reached for the glass
of water she had all but forgotten amid the mess littering the
dining table. As she brought the glass to her lips, she heard
the distinctive pneumatic hiss of the doors parting behind her
and turned as Jean-Luc entered their quarters. Upon seeing
her, his face warmed into a smile.

"I'm sorry I'm late," he said as he crossed the room toward
her. "After spending most of the day with some of our guests,
I was getting caught up on the message traffic from Starfleet
Command. Have you eaten?"

Beverly nodded. "I had to feed René, anyway." Indicating
the work spread across the table before her with a wave, she
added, "And I wanted to get back to this, but I'll probably
wait until we put him down for the night."

After bending to kiss her, Jean-Luc stepped over to René,
kissing him on the top of his head before reaching out to

caress the boy's thin, dark hair. "Thankfully, the delegation we're transporting is proving to be very easy to handle, at least in comparison to some of the other times we've been assigned this sort of duty. I have to say, I almost miss some of the theatrics."

"That's what happens when the politicians stay home," Beverly said.

"Indeed," Picard replied, releasing a sigh. "As for the other, you know, there was a time when I could review that material in far less time. Am I slowing down with old age, or is there just that much more to read?"

"Yes," Beverly teased, smiling as she watched him move to the replicator. When he ordered the unit to provide a tossed-greens salad with a raspberry vinaigrette dressing, she could not help the small chuckle that escaped her lips. "I see you're following the diet card I wrote up for you."

The replicator delivered his salad, which Jean-Luc retrieved before turning back to the table. "As if I had any choice."

"Well, you *were* a bit overweight at your last physical," she said, her tone teasing as Jean-Luc settled into the seat on the other side of René. For his part the child had forsaken the remainder of his own meal and was now watching his father with rapt attention.

He regarded her across the table, his eyes narrowing. "You said yourself that I'm in fine condition for a man of my age."

"True enough," Beverly replied, "but it's in my best interest to keep you in top form." She bobbed her eyebrows in suggestive fashion before taking another sip of water from her glass. "And don't think I won't check the programming for the replicator in your ready room."

"I've already asked Commander La Forge to place it under voice print lockout," Jean-Luc said, playing the game. "Captain's prerogative."

Beverly shrugged. "Maybe, but Geordi wants me to introduce him to my new medical intern, Dr. Harstad, so he owes me a favor or two." Tamala Harstad was a recent addition to the *Enterprise* crew, replacing Dr. th'Shelas, who, like a handful of other Andorian crew members, had resigned his Starfleet commission and returned to his homeworld to assist with rebuilding efforts. At last report, th'Shelas was working in a small hospital in one of the isolated southern regions that had survived the Borg attack yet sustained massive damage and thousands of casualties.

"It's always something, isn't it?" Jean-Luc asked as he picked up his fork and stabbed at the green leaves on his plate. He had barely put the first bite in his mouth when René indicated that he was done with his supper by extending both arms toward his father.

"Well," Beverly replied, "it doesn't hurt that she seems interested in him, too."

As he reached for the boy and brought him to his lap, Jean-Luc said, "So, we're adding matchmaker to your list of talents, are we?" When she chose to offer as her only response a knowing smile, he changed the subject, nodding to the computer interface. "I take it you're reviewing Professor zh'Thiin's research?"

"Just getting started," Beverly replied, shaking her head. "Genetic resequencing has never been a strong suit of mine." Rolling her eyes, she added, "Maybe you remember that mess with Barclay?" Reviewing zh'Thiin's logs had only served to remind her of the unfortunate series of events that had transpired after her attempt to treat Lieutenant Reginald Barclay for the Urodelan flu he had contracted. Her chosen remedy was to use the synthetic version of a form of white blood cell—thymus lymphocytes, or "T cells" as they were colloquially known—to help him fight his infection. An unknown anomaly affecting the lieutenant's genetic structure resulted in an unanticipated mutation of the T cells, activating a latent gene that, when working in concert with the Urodelan flu already in his body, triggered a bizarre transformation in Barclay, causing him to "de-evolve." The mutation, spurred by the flu virus, also became airborne, eventually contaminating everyone on the ship, save for Jean-Luc and their dear, departed friend, Data. Off the ship at the time of the outbreak, they had returned to find the degenerating crew, and Data was the one who had fashioned a cure to reverse the regression process.

Pausing with a forkful of salad poised before his lips, Jean-Luc replied, "Will tried to eat my fish, as I recall."

"Well, understanding what happened then is nothing compared to trying to make sense of Professor zh'Thiin's work." Beverly gestured toward the terminal. "Reading this makes me feel like a first-year student all over again."

Jean-Luc placed his fork down on his plate, freeing his hand to situate René in a better position in his lap. "Come, now. You've done your share of work in this area, thanks in no small part to several encounters we've had with previously unknown species and diseases, to say nothing of the role you played in helping to complete Dr. Galen's research. I wouldn't think twice about pitting your hard-won experiences in the field against any academic's theories and dissertations." When René reached for the salad, his father pushed back his chair, widening the gap between his plate and his son's determined grasp.

"The Barclay incident wasn't your fault," he continued. "I read the report and paper you submitted to Starfleet Medical. His condition was unique, offering no means of anticipating the effects of your treatment. Still, I'd think that experience would have proven to be a valuable learning opportunity with respect to genetic mutation or manipulation."

"Maybe," Beverly replied, reaching up to massage the back of her neck, and unable to resist smiling in appreciation at her husband's steadfast support. In the hope of aiding her current research, Beverly had even revisited some of the notes recorded by Jean-Luc's late mentor, Federation archeologist Richard Galen. It was Galen who had discovered fragments of four-billion-year-old genetic code contained within the DNA of dozens of humanoid species throughout the quadrant, and his research eventually had revealed this commonality to be a deliberate machination, left by an ancient and now-extinct humanoid civilization. After exploring the stars and finding no other beings like themselves, these humanoids had seeded this genetic code into primeval, evolving forms of life on numerous worlds, providing a common link to uncounted races throughout the galaxy.

"I have to tell you, Jean-Luc," she continued, "the work zh'Thiin's done is nothing short of remarkable. I'm just beginning to scratch the surface, but some of the theories she's postulating about gene therapy and resequencing are mind-boggling. Some of it looks as though she was inspired by the research Dr. Galen performed, but in many respects, zh'Thiin has charted her own course."

Jean-Luc frowned. "How do you mean?"

Reaching to turn the computer terminal so he could see it, Beverly said, "According to her notes, she's been working to develop an artificial strand of DNA code that can be resequenced within living DNA—in this case, Andorian—to repair the defective genes. This isn't like other gene therapy, where existing DNA is resequenced to repair birth defects, Jean-Luc. We're talking about introducing something entirely new into the equation, which is the part of zh'Thiin's research that's causing the controversy on Andor. But, if the computer simulations she's run are any indication, this could be the best chance of helping the Andorians to solve this crisis, once and for all."

"And she's developed this artificial DNA on her own?" Jean-Luc asked.

Beverly nodded. "According to her notes, which are extensive. Her work on this aspect of her research goes back almost a year, but you can see hints of it going back farther than that. She was working on this problem even before joining the project in an official capacity, making her the best choice to continue in Dr. sh'Veileth's stead. It's really quite something."

His meal forgotten as he divided his attention between René and the computer display, Jean-Luc turned to regard Beverly. "If only the Andorian people were as receptive to the professor's ideas as you seem to be."

"Not all Andorians are against zh'Thiin," Beverly countered, reaching once more for her water glass. "The best estimates say that opinions are divided pretty evenly on the subject. It wasn't always that way, but the Borg attack changed a lot of minds. There are many segments of Andorian society who now believe that if drastic action isn't taken, the species is doomed within just a few generations."

"Is there any truth to that?" Jean-Luc asked, leaning over to lower René to the floor. Now free, the boy walked on unsteady legs away from the table, searching for one of the toys he had left near the sofa in the suite's main room.

Beverly shook her head. "No hard proof, but the data we have is so uncertain that one could draw that conclusion and not really be seen as a paranoid reactionary." Shrugging, she added, "I suppose that's enough to explain the sharp division in opinions."

"Well," Jean-Luc said, rising from his chair and taking his plate back to the replicator, "hopefully, this conference can raise the level of debate on the issue."

Eyeing her husband as he turned from the replicator and walked to where René had busied himself playing, Beverly said, "The debate's your problem. I've got my hands full just understanding how this will work." For a time, she watched in silence as her husband and son interacted, with Jean-Luc having taken a seat on the floor next to René as the boy proffered a toy his father had made for him—a replica of a *Constitution*-class starship placed inside a transparent, unbreakable bottle.

"Do you have to go back up?" she asked, after a moment.

Resting on the floor with his back against the couch, Jean-Luc nodded as he pulled René into his lap and accepted the toy. "Yes, but it can wait until he goes to bed. Admiral DeSoto forwarded me several reports on Tholian, Breen, and Tzenkethi ship movements. He's worried that the Typhon Pact might be trying to get away with something in some of the outlying systems while our attentions are elsewhere."

"What do you think?" Beverly asked.

"So far," Jean-Luc replied, "every move the Typhon Pact has made, regardless of the ultimate goal, has been carried out with deliberation and patience. Whatever they're doing, it's for a reason."

Beverly nodded in agreement. For the past year and for the most part, the Typhon Pact had seemed content to carry on with their affairs in private, though a handful of incidents had flown in the face of such proceedings. The theft of top-secret information and plans pertaining to Starfleet slipstream propulsion technology had been traced back to the Breen and no doubt sanctioned by the Pact. Incidents of interstellar merchant shipping running afoul of pirates believed to be working as contract agents with ties to Pact members were on the rise. The Romulan Empire was believed to be spearheading efforts to bring the Typhon Pact's goals into focus, for purposes as yet unknown.

Just what we need, she thought as she reached up to rub her temples, *Romulans with goals.*

Noting his wife's apparent distress, Jean-Luc asked, "I take it you're working late again tonight?"

"I think so, yes," Beverly replied, stifling a sudden urge to yawn as she regarded the work arrayed before her. There was still so much to read, and she had taken copious notes on what she had already reviewed. The idea of waiting until the baby was put down for the night before resuming her work brought back yet another memory: caring for young Wesley at the same time she was completing her final year at Starfleet Medical Academy. There had been a lot of long days and nights then, too, many of them made all the more difficult and oftentimes exasperating due to her late husband, Jack, being gone on assignment aboard the *Stargazer*.

The more things change, she mused.

It did not matter how tired she was or how frustrating her work might be, Beverly decided. All of that was easy to forget in the face of the joy she now felt, to say nothing of the ever-strengthening bond between her and Jean-Luc. If anything, it fueled her desire to see this through; to contribute to Professor zh'Thiin's efforts in any way possible. If those labors were successful, then anyone on Andor who sought such happiness, to say nothing of zh'Thiin herself, would be able to enjoy the feelings Beverly now was experiencing.

That had to be worth at least a few more sleepless nights.

9

"What *are* you doing?"

Looking up from her desk, Chen turned to see her friend Lieutenant Dina Elfiki standing in the open doorway leading from her quarters. "How did you get in here?" she asked.

Elfiki regarded her with an almost Vulcan-like expression, her right eyebrow arching as she smirked. "You just told me to come in."

"I did?" Chen asked. Then, blinking several times, she shook her head. "Whatever." Swiveling her chair back to face her desk, she looked down at the mess she had created.

"What is all that?" Elfiki asked as she strode across the room. "Wait, don't tell me. You broke one of Commander La Forge's diagnostic scanners again, didn't you?"

Reaching across the desk for her tricorder, Chen replied, "I wish it were that simple. This is something I'm working on for Dr. Crusher." Arrayed before her atop a rubber work mat were the components of the flute. After running a thorough scan of the instrument and capturing a complete schematic of its construction, she had disassembled it with painstaking care, recording each step of the process with her tricorder so that she could reverse the procedure when the time came.

"It's a flute?" Elfiki asked, frowning as she looked over Chen's shoulder and read the tricorder's display.

Chen nodded. "A very special, one-of-a-kind flute. Irreplaceable, I'm told." One evening after her duty shift, she had accessed the mission logs from Picard's tenure as captain of the *Enterprise*-D, reading the report filed after the ship's encounter with the automated probe launched by the long-extinct population of the planet Kataan. Chen had read with rapt fascination the accounts of the bridge officers on duty when the probe incapacitated Captain Picard for a period of twenty-five minutes, but it was the captain's own recounting of what he had experienced during that brief span that had prevented Chen from sleeping that night. The report, written with a level of passion and detail unrivaled even by Picard's usual meticulous attention to such matters, had compelled Chen to keep reading without regard for the lateness of the hour. During the time Dr. Crusher and the rest of the bridge crew thought Picard to be in a coma, he instead was in communion with the probe, which transmitted into his mind the life experiences of a Kataan native, Kamin. From Picard's point of view, he lived for decades as Kamin, raising a family and watching as Kataan suffered the effects of an extended drought that ultimately doomed the planet. After the connection was severed, an inspection of the probe revealed that it contained—among other mementos—the flute Kamin had played throughout his life; the same flute that now lay disassembled on Chen's desk.

Reading and rereading the report, she could not see how Picard's experiences at the hands of the probe, which had imbued him with the history and culture of a civilization dead and gone for more than a millennium, had not affected him on some fundamental level. There was the flute, of course, which, according to Dr. Crusher, was among the captain's most prized possessions. Even damaged as it had been from the destruction to his ready room, Picard had kept it, cleaned it, replaced the decorative tassel, and held on to it despite being denied the pleasure and comfort he derived from playing the instrument.

"*Enterprise* to Lieutenant Chen."

It took an extra moment to remember that she was not alone, and Chen blinked away her reverie and turned to look at Elfiki, who now was regarding her with amused skepticism. "What?" she asked, shaking off the last bit of distracted remembrance.

"Wow," Elfiki said, "you really beamed out there for a minute, didn't you? Widest possible dispersion and everything." Indicating the dismantled flute, she asked, "How long have you been working on that thing, anyway?"

Chen shrugged. "A couple of days. Dr. Crusher gave it to me the night we left Earth."

Shaking her head, Elfiki frowned. "Can't you just replicate what you need? Better yet, why not just replicate a whole new one?"

"It's not that simple," Chen said, "and that's not the point, anyway." If such a solution truly were viable, she believed that Picard would have done so himself by now. That he had not spoke volumes about the sentimental value of this object. Chen knew from her tricorder scans as well as her own visual inspection of the instrument that she would have to replace at least some of its internal components, but she planned to do so without relying on a replicator to speed up the process. Instead, she had decided to fashion any necessary replacement parts herself, with her own two hands. So far, she had found the exercise of disassembling and studying the flute to be a surprising form of relaxation. It was a creative challenge that she welcomed, and she had no intention of shortchanging her own satisfaction at completing the task given to her.

"You really respect him, don't you?" Elfiki asked. "Captain Picard."

Looking up from the tricorder in her hand, Chen turned to her friend. "Yeah, I do. You know what's weird? I can count on one hand, with fingers left over, how many people I respect that way. I knew how tough he could be before I came aboard, how rigid and proper and all that, and I figured I'd shoot myself in the foot within the first day, but that didn't happen." She smiled. "Sure, we bumped heads a few times, but that's to be expected when we're talking about me, right? He probably could have thrown me off the ship if he'd wanted to a dozen times over, but instead I've had more opportunities to contribute something here than at any other time since I joined Starfleet. I don't get it."

Elfiki shrugged. "Maybe he just sees through that rebellious façade you like to put on, and found whatever it is inside you that makes you a decent Starfleet officer. I just wish he'd tell the rest of us, because I've tried scanning with full sensors and haven't been able to find it."

That made Chen laugh. Deactivating her tricorder, she set the device on the desk next to the work mat before turning back to her friend. "Okay, enough of that. What's up?"

"We were going to play racquetball tonight, remember?" Elfiki asked, crossing her arms. "Konya and Faur have been making noise about challenging us to a rematch, and I'm in the mood to wipe the court with them again. If we're going to beat them even worse than we did last time, we should probably get in some practice before we officially throw down the gauntlet."

Chen could not help laughing at the aggressive edge her friend was now exhibiting. When she had met Dina Elfiki upon first reporting for duty aboard the *Enterprise* a year earlier, the young science officer had always seemed content to spend her off-duty hours holed up in her quarters. Her favorite pastime appeared to be reading, often while accompanied by music from her rather large and diverse collection featuring selections spanning most of the Federation's member worlds. During the ensuing months, Chen and Elfiki had become friends, with Chen learning that in addition to possessing a razor-sharp wit and a penchant for practical jokes, Elfiki harbored a competitive edge almost as deep-seated as her own. She only needed someone of like mind to bring her out of her shell after the normal period of adjustment to a new duty assignment.

Busted out of her shell, is more like it.

"What are they saying now?" Chen asked.

Elfiki replied, "That our win in the tournament was a fluke. They're calling us out, Trys. You know we can't just let that pass."

From chess to poker to racquetball, the science officer was a formidable competitor, employing a level of tenacity and even stubbornness that had become the stuff of much good-natured, respectful ribbing aboard ship. Chen and Elfiki had won an informal tournament last month, defeating the heavily favored team of Lieutenants Rennan Konya and Joanna Faur. The match had been broadcast live for the benefit of anyone who might want to watch it, and according to what Chen had heard, the betting was fast and furious. Only a handful of brave souls came out winners, but their reward reportedly was substantial after casting their allegiance—and their credits—with the underdogs.

"So, they're talking a big game, are they?" Chen asked, unable to suppress a mischievous grin. "Fine, here's what you do. Tell them we accept their challenge, but the losers have to run naked through the officers' mess during dinner." She bobbed her eyebrows. "Let's see how brave they are after that."

The smile faded from Elfiki's face, though only a bit. "Whoa, there. I don't know about that. What if we lose?"

"We're not going to lose," Chen countered, her grin widening. "Besides, it's been a while since I've seen Rennan naked."

Elfiki eyed her with suspicion. "Everything okay between you two?"

Realizing how what she had just said might be misinterpreted, Chen waved away her friend's concerns. "Oh, no. Nothing like that. We were never really that much of a thing, despite . . . well . . . you know."

"You mean the security lock on your door all those nights?" Elfiki asked.

"It wasn't anything more than that," Chen insisted, rising from her chair. "We both knew that going in." Crossing her quarters to the replicator set into the far wall, she ordered the computer to provide her with a glass of chilled water. As the glass materialized, she said, "You know he's been seeing Dr. Hegol, right? He had a pretty tough time of it after the Borg."

Nodding, Elfiki said, "He's mentioned it a few times, but we've never really talked about it."

"He says he's doing a lot better," Chen said before taking a sip of her water, "but there's definitely something different about him the past couple of months. He's always been serious about his work, but lately that's the only thing he seems to care about. I've gone looking for him, you know, after hours, and more often than not I've found him in the holodeck running some kind of security training simulation, and I don't mean the normal range of drills, either. I'm talking about full-blown tactical exercises, crisis and threat situations, combat. You'd think he was making a move to ground forces or something."

"You know what he told us," Elfiki said, her expression one of concern. "He admitted he was feeling something like survivor's guilt. It's what he talked to Dr. Hegol about."

Chen nodded as she sipped her water. She and Rennan Konya had shared an on-again, off-again casual romantic relationship for quite some time now, though Chen would certainly classify it lately as more of the "off-again" variety. During one of the times they had been together, several months earlier, Konya had admitted his troubled feelings to her, and the discussions he had undertaken with Dr. Hegol Den, the *Enterprise*'s senior counselor. Konya had expressed his feelings of inadequacy, blame, and dishonor at having survived the Borg war while many of the men and women he had ordered into battle had died in action. Dr. Hegol, according to Konya, had been understanding yet straightforward when telling the security officer that he had to find a way to examine the scorn and condemnation he had heaped upon himself.

Apparently, Rennan Konya's prescription for dealing with the guilt he carried was to immerse himself in his work. If he was not on duty, then he was undertaking some form of training class or conducting a simulation or other exercise drill on one of the holodecks. His physical-training regimen was much talked about among the ship's junior officers. Along with the usual scheduled workouts in which he participated with his security teams, he often was seen in the fitness center exercising alone. Though he remained pleasant and approachable, Chen and others had sensed an air about him that communicated his desire not to engage in small talk or other social interactions whenever he was focused on a particular task, which seemed to be all the time. His duties and any means he might employ to improve himself in those areas seemed to have become his primary focus, to the near exclusion of everything else.

Including me, at least a lot of the time.

As though reading her thoughts, Elfiki said, "Are you sure you two are okay?"

Chen made a dismissive wave with her free hand before drinking the last of the water in her glass. "Yeah, of course. He's just working things out. You know how it is."

"God," Elfiki said, rolling her eyes. "I could write a book about the men I've known who've had to go off and work things out. I'm pretty sure I'm the thing they're working out, though." Then, her eyes narrowed. "You're not seeing some-body *else,* are you?"

The way she stated the question made Chen regard her with suspicion. "What's that supposed to mean?"

"Oh, come on!" Elfiki said, moving across the room to sit on Chen's bed. "Are you going to tell me there's nothing going on with you and Taurik?"

Chen's eyes nearly bugged out of their sockets. "Wait. What? No! What are you talking about?" Were rumors cir-culating about her and Taurik? If so, how had she not heard about them before now?

Smiling, Elfiki said, "Relax. I'm just teasing you. Still, he's not such a bad guy. You could do a lot worse."

"You make that sound like some sort of challenge," Chen quipped. "Have we met? I'm the queen of doing a lot worse." Her track record with dating was, in a word, disastrous. What she had shared with Konya easily was the best relationship she had ever experienced, and even that was more physical than emotional. Or, was it?

Shut up, she chided herself.

Elfiki laughed. "Well, you two *do* have some things in common."

"What?" Chen asked. "That we're both from Vulcan? You do realize that if it wasn't for the ears, nobody would ever know I had *any* Vulcan heritage. If Surak himself were alive today and met me, he'd probably renounce logic and all that other stuff just long enough to drop-kick me out an airlock."

"Maybe," Elfiki said, "but I doubt Taurik would do that. You know that you'll have to make the first move with him, right? He's pretty shy, according to the gossip I've heard."

"As you've so cleverly pointed out," Chen replied, "he's a Vulcan. We're all shy."

"Even you?" Elfiki asked.

"I'm the exception that proves the rule." The friendship Chen shared with Lieutenant Commander Taurik was one she could not explain, having begun as it had under less-than-ideal circumstances as each confessed to the other underlying grief they both had been feeling due to the loss of family members during the Borg invasion. While they shared occasional meals or other social activities, Chen had never seen the relationship advancing to the next level, and she was fairly certain Taurik felt the same way. "Anyway, we're just friends."

"Whatever you say," Elfiki said, offering another impish smile. Clapping her hands together, she pointed to the chronometer on Chen's desk. "Okay, forget that. We're wasting time. You up for racquetball or not?"

Frowning, Chen asked, "Does it have to be tonight?"

"It does if you don't want to run naked through the officers' mess," Elfiki countered.

"And I don't." Returning the empty water glass to the replicator, Chen gave in to the inevitable. "Okay, fine. Let me get my stuff." She was turning to head for her closet when her door chime sounded. "Come in," she called over her shoulder.

The doors parted to reveal a lone figure standing at the threshold. His hands clasped behind his back, Lieutenant Commander Taurik regarded Chen with his usual stoic expression. "Good evening, Lieutenant." His eyes caught sight of Elfiki, still sitting on the bed, and he added, "I'm sorry. I hope I'm not intruding."

"Oh, not at *all*, sir," Elfiki said, rising to her feet. Though Elfiki's expression remained passive, Chen heard the inflection in her words and shot a death glare in her direction.

"Is there something I can do for you, Commander?" Chen asked, immediately regretting her choice of words and silently hoping that Elfiki would not react to any possible double entendres lurking within her question.

Taurik, in the finest Vulcan fashion, appeared unfazed by any of the silent communication passing between the two women. "This isn't an official visit, Lieutenant." He paused, his eyes shifting for the briefest of moments to Elfiki before returning to Chen. "I was wondering if you had any plans for the evening. However, I see that is the case."

"Well," Chen said, glancing to Elfiki, "we were—"

"I was just leaving, sir," Elfiki said, cutting her off. "I've got an experiment running up in my lab, and I need to get back to it, if you'll excuse me." As she made her way toward the door, she turned to look at Chen. "Remember what I said about that first move."

I'm going to kill you, Chen thought, schooling her features to reveal nothing. Elfiki masked her grin before turning back to face Taurik, who stepped aside in order for her to leave the room.

"Good evening, Commander," she said as she passed him.

Taurik nodded. "Good evening, Lieutenant." Waiting until she had gone, he turned his attention back to Chen. "Well, I suppose that my original question remains valid. I have just ended my duty shift and have not yet eaten today. If you have nothing scheduled for this evening, I was wondering if you might like to have dinner with me."

In all the time she had known him, Taurik had never once come to her quarters for such a purpose. It was a welcome gesture, so far as Chen was concerned. "I haven't eaten yet, either, so that sounds like a fine idea."

Nodding, Taurik said, "Excellent." Stepping aside once more as she approached the doorway, he added, "Perhaps we can discuss this first move Lieutenant Elfiki mentioned."

That was almost enough to make Chen trip over her own feet. "What?" she blurted, and then just as quickly covered that with, "I'm sorry. I meant . . . that is . . . excuse me?"

Taurik tilted his head and his right eyebrow arched as he regarded her. "I assumed that you and Lieutenant Elfiki were discussing chess. As you know, it's a favored recreational activity of mine, but I don't recall you ever mentioning an interest in the game. If I'm in error, then I would welcome a discussion on the topic, and perhaps even a game after we finish our meal, if you have no conflicting appointments."

I could get used to this, Chen mused. "I've been known to play a game or two. You're on."

As they made their way down the corridor to the nearest turbolift, Chen could almost hear Dina Elfiki snickering in triumph.

10

The doors to the *Enterprise*'s main crew lounge parted, releasing the festive atmosphere of the Happy Bottom Riding Club into the corridor as Dr. Hegol Den approached. He smiled as he entered the room, pleased to see most of the club's tables and bar stools occupied by off-duty personnel as well as a few civilians. Still more people congregated in groups of varying sizes, carrying on all manner of conversations. With no small amount of amusement, Hegol wondered if the notable absence of any delegates or science specialists making the trip from Earth might well be contributing to the overall positive vibe enveloping the lounge.

Now, now, he reminded himself. *No need to be that way.*

Through the years he had spent as a counselor, Hegol had come to understand that one of the fastest ways to gauge the morale of a starship's crew was to observe them when they were off duty. Taking that one step farther, he had cultivated the habit of visiting recreational areas such as the Riding Club, ostensibly for the purposes of unwinding in the company of his shipmates while enjoying a drink or two. When doing so, he made a point to downplay his role as ship's counselor, often couching his true purpose by accepting an offer to join a group at the bar or to play poker, chess, or some other game that might be under way at one of the tables.

Making his way deeper into the lounge, the doctor scanned the faces of its patrons, looking for one in particular, and it took only a moment to find the person he sought. She sat alone at one of the lounge's smaller tables in the room's far corner, her attention focused on a padd she held in her left hand while her right rested around a glass sitting on the table. Like most of the lounge's other occupants, the young Andorian officer was still in uniform, even though Hegol knew that her duty shift had ended nearly three hours earlier. A plate with what appeared to be the remnants of a forgotten meal rested near her left arm. As he drew closer, he noted that the image displayed on her padd was that of a blue-white planet, with no accompanying text.

"Ensign?" he asked as he drew close enough for her to hear him.

Looking up from the padd, Ensign Ereshtarri sh'Anbi regarded him for a moment before recognizing that she had just been addressed by a superior officer. Her expression changed to one of surprise and uncertainty, and she moved to rise from her seat.

"Lieutenant," the young Andorian began.

Hegol gestured for her to remain seated. "We're off duty, Ensign," he said, offering his best disarming smile. "I was just coming off shift, myself, and thought I'd stop in for a drink." He paused to glance around the room as though taking in the crowd and the notable lack of empty seats before saying, "Would it be all right if I joined you?"

"Certainly," sh'Anbi replied, indicating the seat across from her. Hegol settled into the proffered chair, nodding toward the lounge's bartender, Jordan, as he did so. As sh'Anbi deactivated her padd and set it aside, he noted that she appeared to be struggling to suppress uncomfortable or perhaps even unwelcome thoughts. He expected as much, given that he had spent the better part of the past two days talking with the other sixteen Andorian members of the *Enterprise* crew. Each of them had expressed some form of misgiving or apprehension about returning to the world of their birth, but so far Ensign sh'Anbi had declined his offers to meet with him in his office. Hegol suspected what might be at the heart of the young officer's reluctance to talk with him, but he wanted to hear it from her. More importantly, he felt sh'Anbi needed to hear it herself.

Movement from the corner of his eye caught his attention, and Hegol turned to see Jordan stepping up to their table, carrying a single squat glass half-filled with a green beverage. The bartender placed the glass on the table in front of Hegol.

"I managed to nab a case just before we left Earth," Jordan said, smiling in conspiratorial fashion. "My normal supplier didn't have any, but I was able to find some through my network of emergency providers. Consider yourself lucky." Leaning closer, he lowered his voice. "Only you and the captain even know it's here, so keep that classified."

Hoisting the glass and offering it up in salute to the bartender, Hegol said, "A secret I'll take to my grave. I'm in your debt, good sir." He took the first drink, savoring the beverage's rich, potent flavor.

"What is that?" sh'Anbi asked as Jordan turned and walked off to see to patrons at another table.

"Aldebaran whiskey," Hegol replied. "I acquired a taste for it years ago, and since then nothing's come close. Maybe it's because it's not made with synthehol." He had never learned to like the artificial alcohol substitute, likely the result of many years spent drinking the real thing while still a young man living on Bajor. By the time he joined Starfleet and was introduced to a beverage made with synthehol standing in for actual whiskey, his palate was beyond convincing.

"So," he said after taking a second drink and setting the glass back down on the table, "what brings you here?"

Sh'Anbi indicated the plate to her left. "Dinner. I didn't feel like eating in my quarters or the mess hall." Shrugging, she added, "I guess I just wanted a change of scenery."

"Fair enough," Hegol said. After a moment spent spinning his glass in slow, clockwise motions across the tabletop, he said, "Ensign, if you don't mind my saying so, you look to be a young lady with a lot on her mind."

Looking up from her own drink, sh'Anbi regarded him with suspicion. "Doctor, with all due respect, is this supposed to be some kind of counseling session?"

"Nothing so formal, Ereshtarri," Hegol replied, keeping his tone level. "May I call you that?" When the Andorian nodded, he added, "Then please call me Den."

Sh'Anbi nodded, and Hegol could see the lingering doubt in her eyes. "All right," she said, "so, what can I do for you, Den?"

"You can tell me how you're feeling tonight," Hegol replied.

Frowning, the ensign shook her head. "How am I feeling? I don't understand the question."

"In the interest of total honesty," Hegol said, "I'll tell you that I'm here on behalf of Lieutenant Choudhury, who's expressed some concerns for your well-being. She seems to think that you're a bit distracted so far as our current assignment is concerned."

Now sh'Anbi's expression turned to worry. "Lieutenant Choudhury said that?"

Lifting a hand in a gentle, calming gesture, Hegol said, "It's not what you think, Ereshtarri. The lieutenant is merely worried that something's bothering you, and that you're keeping it to yourself. This was not motivated by anything punitive on her part, I assure you. Given that we're going to Andor, it's reasonable to expect that the Andorian members of our crew, particularly those who lost loved ones during the war, might have reservations and troubled feelings." He knew from reading her personnel file that sh'Anbi's family had been living in the former capital city, Laibok, when the Borg struck, and numbered among the millions of Andorians lost on that tragic day. Sh'Anbi herself, stationed aboard the *U.S.S. Khwarizimi* during the Borg assault, had later requested a transfer after that vessel was assigned to retrieve debris from destroyed Borg ships as part of a larger research effort being conducted by Starfleet Security. According to the information in her file, sh'Anbi had cited personal objections to the project, owing to the grief she still felt after the loss of her family, which was not an uncommon reason behind numerous requests for transfer or resignation from Starfleet in the aftermath of the war. Her request had resulted in her posting to the *Enterprise,* where, according to Lieutenant Choudhury, she had been nothing less than a model officer with great potential.

Sh'Anbi sat in silence for a moment, her hand playing at tilting her glass from right to left and back again, watching as the liquid it contained sloshed from side to side in a slow, rhythmic motion. When she looked at him again, Hegol saw the pain in her eyes.

"This is the first time I've been back," she said.

Nodding in understanding, Hegol asked, "Since the attack?"

"That's right." She shrugged, frowning as she cast her gaze back toward her glass. "There didn't seem to be any reason to do so before. Everyone I knew—my family, my friends, everyone—was lost when Laibok was destroyed. I was offered leave on several occasions, but I always declined." Shaking her head, she released a slow, small sigh. "And now we're going back."

"And you feel guilty for not returning sooner?" Hegol asked.

Sh'Anbi looked up, her eyes wide. "Yes. Maybe I should have gone home, to attend the memorial services, or something. I thought about going, but every time I changed my mind. What was I going to do there? There was no one waiting for me. I couldn't even go to salvage anything from my . . ." Hegol said nothing as tears formed in the corners of sh'Anbi's eyes, which she wiped away. Then, in a stronger voice, she said, "There was nothing there for me, so I decided I might as well focus my efforts where I was needed."

Leaning forward in his seat so that he could rest his forearms on the table, the counselor said, "What you're experiencing isn't unusual, Ereshtarri. You're harboring what you consider to be guilt because you survived, when so many of the people you love did not. For what it's worth, I've spoken with several people who feel exactly as you do." It was a common sentiment among the patients Hegol had treated in the year following the invasion, all of them looking for answers to the grief overwhelming them. "Captain Picard and Lieutenant Choudhury are going to need you once we get to Andor. The *Enterprise*'s security teams will be heavily involved with overseeing protection for the conference. Chances are you'll be assigned to a detail on the surface. Is that something you feel you're capable of doing?"

"Of course," sh'Anbi snapped, and she regarded him with open indignation. Then, as though realizing how harsh her response had sounded, she added, "I'm sorry, Doctor."

"Den," Hegol said, smiling.

Nodding as a small grin formed on her lips, the ensign replied, "Den. I'm sorry, Den. Yes, I'm capable of handling this assignment. I suppose I've simply been letting myself think too much about going home."

"There's nothing wrong with what you're feeling," Hegol said. "It's only natural. What's wrong is if you let those feelings paralyze you, or make you start to second-guess decisions you've made or—more importantly—decisions or actions you might undertake. One way to prevent that from happening is to talk to someone when you think such feelings are becoming too much to deal with. You don't have to do it alone, Ereshtarri."

After a moment, during which she focused her attention once more on her glass, sh'Anbi said, "This is the first time I've spoken with a counselor. Since the war, that is. You're not what I expected."

"I should take that as a compliment?" Hegol asked, reaching for his own drink.

Sh'Anbi laughed. "Yes, that's a compliment. By the way, my friends call me Tarri."

"Okay, then, Tarri." Satisfied that his young charge seemed at ease—for the moment, at least—Hegol said, "Now, do you mind if I eat dinner?" He gestured toward a table near the center of the room where several officers were playing poker. "I don't want my stomach grumbling when I get in on the card game."

Sh'Anbi shook her head. "Be my guest." She nodded toward the game in progress. "So, you like to play?"

Offering an expression of mock innocence, Hegol shrugged. "Yes, but I'm not very good."

"Ah," the ensign replied with a wistful smile, reaching up to scratch her chin before making a show of examining her fingernails. "What a coincidence. Neither am I."

"Commander La Forge?"

Sitting alone at a table near the window ports at the front of the main crew lounge, his attention all but buried within his padd's rapid-fire scroll of information, it took La Forge a moment to realize that he had heard someone calling his name for the second time. Looking up from the padd, he saw Tamala Harstad, the newest member of Dr. Crusher's medical team, standing behind the unoccupied chair across from him and greeting him with a smile.

"I'm sorry, Lieutenant," he said, starting to rise from his seat. "Can I help you?" Even as he spoke, he searched his memory, trying to remember if he had ever seen Harstad in the lounge before this evening, and coming up with nothing.

But she's here now. That, of course, begged a series of new questions for which La Forge had no answers. Not for the first time he was struck by just how attractive the doctor was, her fair skin and thin features seemingly all but overwhelmed by the dark, straight lines of her Starfleet uniform. Her black hair was cut in a short, feminine style that left her neck exposed, reminding La Forge of his late friend and former *Enterprise*-D security chief, Natasha Yar. Indeed, Harstad's high cheekbones and piercing eyes also were reminiscent of Tasha's.

Nodding toward his padd, Harstad asked, "I'm not disturbing you, am I?"

"No, not at all," the chief engineer replied, gesturing toward his glass, which still held most of his beverage. "I just came off duty and decided to have a drink while I figured out what I wanted for dinner. I also needed to catch up on some of the technical journals I keep meaning to read." He indicated the chair on the opposite side of the table. "Would you like to sit down?" As he spoke, he hoped his words did not sound as uneasy to her as they did to his own ears.

"Thank you," Harstad said. As they both took seats, the lounge's bartender, Jordan, came to the table and took her drink order—a vodka martini. Once Jordan departed, Harstad smiled again, leaning closer so that she could be heard over the sounds of music and other conversations filling the lounge. "Is it always like this in here?"

La Forge shook his head. "Only for the first few hours after each duty shift. I only get up here once every couple of days myself."

"I've heard you like to tinker around down in engineering," Harstad said.

"There's always something to do," La Forge replied. "The days are never boring, that's for sure. What about you? From what I've heard, you don't have anything against hard work. Is it true you did a year of residency at a hospital on Vulcan?"

Nodding, Harstad said, "All true."

"Is it common for human doctors to do something like that?" La Forge asked. "I mean, that early in their careers? I'd think residency would be hard enough without adding that kind of pressure to the mix."

"It was a challenge," Harstad replied, "but I enjoyed myself, for the most part. My roommate at Starfleet Academy was a Vulcan, and she also was going to medical school after we graduated. She convinced me it would be a rewarding experience working on Vulcan, and she was right. I admit I thought it would be all logic and that famous Vulcan stoicism all the time, but there's just so much to see and do there. I may even decide to move there when I retire."

"We had a Vulcan doctor for a while," La Forge said. Then, remembering, he added, "I mean, back on the *Enterprise*-D. Dr. Selar was her name."

"The name's familiar," Harstad replied, "but I can't say I've ever met her."

La Forge set his drink back down on the table. "She was CMO on the *Excalibur* for several years." He paused, realizing that nearly two years had passed since he had read the official Starfleet report listing Selar as having died while on assignment in Sector 221-G. Clearing his throat, he returned his attention to Harstad as he reached for his glass. "So, Dr. Crusher tells me you're doing research into the newest generation of ocular implants, and that you might want to talk to me."

Her smile fading and her expression turning to one of mild confusion, Harstad asked, "I beg your pardon?"

"I guess because I've had both a VISOR and implants," La Forge said, "I might make a good candidate for an upgrade."

Harstad's frown deepened. "It's true I've been doing some research into the field, and that I'm writing a dissertation on it, but I didn't mention anything to Dr. Crusher with respect to talking to you about it."

Well, La Forge thought, fighting to school his own facial features, *this just got awkward.* Taking another sip of his drink to stall for time, he finally said, "Oh?"

Harstad said, "She did tell me that you were wanting to talk to me about questions you had pertaining to your own implants."

What is she talking about? "I'm sorry," La Forge said, "but I . . ."

"No, no," the doctor replied. "I'm the one who should be sorry. It's just that I have a cousin who was injured in a shuttle crash and lost sight in both eyes. He was given ocular replacements, and I became interested in the subject while checking up on him. It's a fascinating field of study, and the potential for continued advancement is limitless. Of course, I don't need to tell you any of this."

The conversation paused as Jordan returned, this time bearing a tray atop which sat Harstad's martini. Setting the glass on the table in front of her, the bartender smiled and offered a small bow before turning and heading off toward another table. In the time it took for all of that to happen, La Forge realized what was going on here between him and Harstad.

"I—" he said, stopping to consider his next words. "That is, I think there's been some kind of misunderstanding here." As he spoke, he was unable to suppress a small, nervous smile.

To his relief, Harstad returned the smile. "I think Dr. Crusher might be up to something."

Not sure of his footing, La Forge decided that honesty had to be the best approach. "Well, for what it's worth, and in the interests of full disclosure, I did ask her about you when you came aboard. I just didn't expect her to do anything like this."

"Like what?" the doctor asked. "You mean, set us up?"

Several seconds passed with both of them looking at each other, before they both laughed. La Forge liked the sound of her laugh.

"Look," he said after another moment spent composing himself, "I'll be the first to admit that I'm not very good at this kind of thing, and I understand how the abruptness of all this might make you feel, and that's the last thing I'd want."

Taking a sip of her own drink, Harstad nodded in approval at the martini before returning her attention to him. "Well, I'm not very good at this sort of thing, either, but so far we both seem to be doing okay. I guess this is also the part where I admit I asked Dr. Crusher about you, too."

"Really?" The question was out before he could stop it, and La Forge loathed the way it sounded as he spoke it aloud. *Do I really sound that pathetic?*

If Harstad thought that, she was kind enough not to mention it. Instead, she said, "Guilty as charged. Anyway, we're here now, and you said you were thinking about getting some dinner. If you don't have any other plans, neither do I. Want some company?"

The evening, La Forge decided, was most definitely looking up.

11

Picard awoke.

In the near darkness of his and Beverly's shared quarters, he opened his eyes and took stock of the curved ceiling above his head. Something had roused him from sleep. Then René whined again and Picard sighed in understanding. He glanced to his left and saw Beverly lying on her side, her back to him, unmoving beneath the light comforter and silk sheet. She had not stirred, itself an unusual phenomenon. Normally, she was the first to awaken in response to any sounds uttered by their son in the middle of the night. It was a testament to how hard she must have been working these past few days for her to not already be out of the bed and heading across the family suite to the crib where their son slept.

Duty calls.

Moving so as not to disturb his wife's slumber, Picard folded aside the bedclothes and rose from the bed, padding barefoot across the carpet. He did not bother with anything more than the soft glow of the indirect lights mounted beneath the row of slanted windows to his left. The illumination was sufficient for him to navigate his quarters without running into furniture or any errant toy René might have left as a booby trap for his unwitting parents.

Even before he reached the crib, Picard saw the boy's small head peering over the side, tiny hands gripping the railing as René regarded his father with wide, puffy eyes. Drawing closer, Picard could tell that his son had been crying, though he had managed to avoid employing the ear-splitting, teeth-rattling wail that on more than one occasion had shattered the silence in the middle of the night. Such instances were infrequent these days, far removed from the nightly ritual they all had endured during the first weeks after his birth. Instead, René was looking up at him, his breathing coming in short, rapid gasps that Picard recognized as the prelude to full-blown crying.

"What's the matter?" Picard asked, his voice low and soothing as he reached for René and took him into his arms. The boy immediately found purchase atop Picard's chest, his head nuzzling into the spot beneath the captain's chin as his small arms reached as far as they could around his father's shoulders. With his left forearm supporting the baby beneath his bottom, Picard turned from the crib and made his way toward the windows. "Did you have a bad dream?"

René's response was to press himself even closer against Picard's chest, uttering a quiet, indecipherable gurgle, though Picard heard the boy's breathing already slowing and becoming more regular. His small body, tense at first, had begun to relax, almost going limp.

"That's a good boy," Picard whispered into his son's ear. "Back to sleep."

Standing at the window, he took in the view of the warp effect surrounding the *Enterprise* as the ship made its way through subspace toward Andor. He had darkened the windows prior to retiring, subduing the light cast by the streaking stars, but that did not diminish their brilliance, at least to him. After all the years he had spent in space, the stars still called to him as they had when he was a boy, looking up at them from that tree in the Picard family vineyard.

"You don't know what you're missing," he said, reaching up with his right hand to stroke René's hair. His son had drifted to sleep, his arms having fallen to his sides and his breathing now soft and slow. Not quite ready to return the child to his crib, Picard instead turned from the windows and made his way to the small room that had been configured as an office, set off to the side of the main area that dominated the family quarters. There, he glanced at the chronometer set into the base of his desktop workstation, noting that at least on this occasion, René had waited until less than an hour remained before Picard himself needed to awaken for the coming duty day.

"Well," he whispered, exiting the office on his way back to the crib, "that was certainly considerate of you." With slow, gentle movements, he was able to return René to his bed without rousing him, and the boy promptly rolled over and commenced a light snoring as Picard covered him with a blanket. Whatever had troubled the child earlier, there appeared to be no remnant of it to disturb his sleep any further.

I wish I could be so fortunate, Picard mused, smiling as he shook his head. Now resigned to the reality that he was awake for the day, he saw no reason to waste this quiet time before the computer called on Beverly in something less than an hour. After all, there would be no shortage of status reports and other briefing papers waiting for him, despite the best efforts of Commander Worf and his own yeoman to insulate him from the worst of the lot.

A quick check of his message log showed incoming communiqués from the Office of the Federation President, though the attached message header indicated that the request was not of a high priority. Picard read it anyway, nodding in approval at the personal message President Bacco had dispatched to him offering her thanks for his taking on this assignment. Such gestures rarely moved him, but given that the president was not at all obligated to thank him for carrying out her lawful orders, he found the note to be uncommonly heartfelt.

Perhaps you're simply getting soft in your old age.

The next message in the queue was from Admiral Robert DeSoto at Starfleet Headquarters. It also did not have a priority flag attachment, and there was no video component, simply a text entry indicating the admiral's desire to speak at Picard's earliest opportunity. The captain frowned, knowing his old friend was not given to melodramatic displays. Indeed, Robert DeSoto was a man of minimalist tendencies, at least when it came to official matters, never using ten words to convey an idea or instruction when five would do. Picard even had joked with him that his inclination toward brevity likely would get him into trouble once he began navigating the upper echelons of the Starfleet hierarchy and all of the political dodging and weaving that entailed. Most of the inhabitants of that rarified air liked to talk, often to excess, much to Picard's chagrin.

After donning exercise attire—hoping as he did so that he actually would be able to avail himself of the ship's fitness center before commencing with the day's official schedule, and ordering a cup of hot Earl Grey tea from the office's small replicator—Picard returned to his desk. "Computer," he prompted, "what is the current time at Starfleet Headquarters on Earth?"

"The current time at Starfleet Headquarters is fourteen fifty-

three hours," replied the warm, feminine voice of the *Enterprise*'s main computer.

Nodding at the report as he sipped his tea, Picard said, "Computer, open a channel to Admiral Robert DeSoto at Starfleet Command."

"Acknowledged," the computer answered, after which there was a delay as the request was channeled through the communications system and the message transmitted via subspace to Earth. Picard busied himself during those moments by reviewing the latest personnel and ship's status report as submitted by Worf just prior to the end of his duty shift the previous evening. A similar report had also been filed by the beta-shift watch officer, and another glance at the desktop chronometer informed him that—if his guess was right—the report from the gamma-shift watch officer should be coming anytime now.

The bland, predictable nature of the reports was broken a moment later by a tone from Picard's workstation, followed by the voice of the computer: *"Communications link established."* On the computer's display screen, the seal of the United Federation of Planets on its black background faded, replaced by the grizzled, aged visage of Admiral DeSoto. His hair, now completely white, had receded to the point that nearly the entire top of his head was visible. Was it possible that his friend looked even older than he did the last time they had spoken, mere weeks earlier?

"Good afternoon, Admiral," Picard said by way of greeting.

On the screen, DeSoto shook his head, the corners of his mouth turning upward in a wry grin. *"Jean-Luc, we've been friends since we were fresh-faced cadets at the Academy. How many times do I have to tell you to please call me Robert?"*

Picard shrugged. "Old habits die hard, I suppose."

Glancing away to something off-screen that Picard could not see, the admiral said, *"The computer's telling me it's oh five thirty hours, shipboard time. What's got you up so early?"*

"René," Picard replied. "He had a dream or something. Beverly's still sound asleep, but I thought that since I was up, I might as well get started."

DeSoto laughed. *"Welcome to parenthood, Jean-Luc. You'll be happy to know that you can start sleeping in again once he leaves for college, or Starfleet Academy, or whatever it is he eventually decides to do. Until then? Well, it's just like the old days when we were know-nothing ensigns on the* Antares. *Grab those catnaps when and where you can."*

"Duly noted," Picard said, smiling at the memories his friend had recalled. He and DeSoto had been friends or shipmates from the earliest days of their careers. Their paths through the ranks had diverged in radical fashion, following Picard's assignment to the *Stargazer* and his subsequent rapid promotion to captain following the tragic events that resulted in the death of the ship's commanding officer and the incapacitation of its second-in-command. Still, DeSoto had distinguished himself on numerous occasions over the years, particularly during early engagements with the Cardassians as well as the Jem'Hadar at the height of the Dominion War. A skilled diplomat despite Picard's good-natured teasing to the contrary, DeSoto had helped negotiate treaties with the Romulans, Cardassians, and the Breen, and his temperament and ability to see the "big picture" was well suited to his current role as Starfleet's director of postwar rebuilding efforts.

"You sent a message, asking me to contact you at my earliest opportunity," Picard said, reaching for his tea. "Now's as early a time as any, I suppose."

DeSoto nodded. *"It wasn't urgent, but I appreciate the call-*

back just the same. I thought you might like to know that Admiral Hasslein has decided to retire."

"Eric Hasslein?" Picard asked, the hand holding his teacup freezing at the midpoint between the saucer and his mouth. "Really?" He shook his head in disbelief. "He's been the director of Starfleet's exploration and colonization division for . . . how long has it been?"

"Longer than either one of us wants to admit," DeSoto replied. *"There's already talk about who his replacement might be. Admiral Akaar hasn't said as much, but I get the feeling he's thinking about hitting you up for the job."*

Sighing, Picard placed the teacup back on its saucer. "Robert, we've been over this. I'm more useful out here than I'd ever be sitting behind some desk." Pausing, he shrugged. "Though, I have to admit, that particular desk has more appeal to it than some of the others I've been offered." Then, realizing what he had just said, he smiled again. "No offense meant to you, old friend."

"I know," DeSoto replied, waving away any notion of having been troubled by the remarks. *"And for what it's worth, I think you're right. Even Akaar seems to know what your answer will be when he asks you. Whatever you said to him the last time he asked must've made an impression. That said, Starfleet's going to need someone making sure our priorities are where they need to be with respect to renewing our exploration efforts. We're getting back on our feet in that department, but you and I both know we've got a long way to go."* Pausing, he leaned closer to the screen and lowered his voice, as though worried someone might overhear the conversation. *"That division needs someone who's not a politician, but who can at least speak the language when it's time to fight for resource allocation and prioritization. The people who can pull that off, and who also have a genuine,*

vested interest in exploration, make for a very short list, Jean-Luc, and your name's at the top."

Picard said nothing at first, choosing instead to sip his tea and consider his friend's words. This was a topic that had not gone away as he originally had hoped, and even had increased in frequency over the past year. The strain and stresses of guiding Starfleet and the Federation through the post-invasion rebuilding efforts were proving too great for a large number of people occupying the higher levels of authority within both hierarchies. Good people, men and women with whom Picard had served or was at least acquainted, were tendering their resignations, opting to spend their twilight years with their families. For many, it was the only way to address the lingering feelings, doubts, and even depression they harbored after surviving the Borg attack.

The result was that a lot of vital positions within the Starfleet command structure were being left unattended, and officers were being reassigned or promoted to fill those vacancies. The domino effect of that action was increasing, if the promotion bulletins Picard read as part of his daily Starfleet status-briefing package were any indication. With that in mind, he had on numerous occasions asked himself how much longer he might forestall the inevitable. Might the time to accept a promotion be now, or coming soon? If so, would it not be prudent to accept an assignment that at least kept him in touch with those functions of Starfleet that had drawn him to the service in the first place?

"There's something else," DeSoto said, after a moment. *"More scuttlebutt, about you."*

"I am rather popular, it seems," Picard replied, placing his now-empty teacup on his desk.

DeSoto chuckled. *"More than you realize. The diplomatic*

*corps has had their eye on you for a while now, too. They've even
made their case to President Bacco herself, inquiring about your
possible availability and interest in becoming a new Federation
ambassador."*

That caught Picard by surprise, and he made no effort to
hide that from the admiral. "An ambassador? Me?"

"Face it, Jean-Luc," DeSoto said. *"You've got the skills and
the track record to pull it off. Hell, your diplomatic record is better than some of the people who do it for a living. If nothing else,
this past year has only made your case that much stronger."* He
offered a warm smile, and the two men regarded each other
as the friends they had been for all of their adult lives. *"Take
it from me, old friend: Sooner or later, they're going to have no
choice but to bump you up the ladder. At least make sure that
when they do it, you can still make some kind of difference when
the dust settles. Otherwise, you might as well retire; maybe go
pick grapes from that family vineyard of yours."*

For the admiral's benefit, Picard nodded. "There's a lot
to consider, Robert, but I can't say I'm not interested in the
notion."

"Well, consider this," DeSoto replied. *"The life of an ambassador is a hell of a lot less dangerous than that of a starship
captain. Plus, don't forget that you've got other people to think
about, as well."* He pointed to the screen. *"Do you want that
son of yours growing up running the halls of that ship, or on a
planet with real grass and dirt beneath his feet? Besides, how
much longer can the three of you share quarters before somebody
has to move out? Are you planning to turn one of the cargo bays
into an apartment?"*

Picard actually smiled at that. Sharing living space first
with Beverly and then René had necessitated definite changes
in the captain's quarters. The rooms Picard had occupied

aboard the starship for years were adequate even for two people, but adding a child was something else altogether. While the *Enterprise*-E did not feature the same lavish interior-space allocations as its *Galaxy*-class predecessor, the design still allowed for some modular reconfiguration of different interior spaces. This had already occurred in the case of several members of the ship's complement who also had their families aboard. The result was a home that might not measure up to a luxury apartment on Earth or some other world, but was still a far cry from the single berth and locker Picard had enjoyed as a young Starfleet officer.

"It's an interesting offer, Robert, but this isn't something I can concern myself with right now. We still have much to do before we reach Andor, and then my full attention will be there at least until after the conference concludes. Once that's done and I've received orders for my next assignment, I'll give this the attention it deserves. I promise."

Once more offering a knowing smile, DeSoto nodded. *"I know you will. For what it's worth, even though I know I'm doing some good here, there are days I wish I was still out there. Felt like that just this morning, in case you were wondering. You take care of yourself, Jean-Luc, and I'll talk to you soon."*

"You do the same, Robert. Picard out." The computer automatically severed the link, and DeSoto's face disappeared, now replaced once again with the UFP seal and the message "COMMUNICATION ENDED," along with the current time.

Sitting alone in his office, the rest of the family quarters now silent, Picard was able to hear the soft sounds of René snoring in his crib. Only a few minutes remained until the computer roused Beverly. How better to spend these few precious moments of solitude than in careful contemplation of the future? Not simply his own, but also that of his family?

He found himself revisiting thoughts he already had pondered on several occasions since René's birth. Was life aboard a starship really in the boy's best interest? It was one thing when his son was still an infant, but what about just a few years from now, as his intellect developed and he began wanting to explore the world around him? Was it fair to limit that world to the decks of the *Enterprise*? Even with all the ship's expansive facilities and wondrous technology at his fingertips, Picard knew it was no substitute for living on a planet, with fresh air and sunshine. Though it might not be an issue at present, Picard knew this was a question he one day would have to revisit.

But not today.

12

"*So, as you can see, Professor, everything is in order, and both patients are progressing as expected. As you might imagine, they both are very excited.*"

Marthrossi zh'Thiin smiled into her computer station's visual pickup as she beheld the image of her assistants, Dr. Eluqunil sh'Laenatha and Lieutenant Thirishar ch'Thane, transmitted via subspace communications relay from Andor. "I wasn't expecting news to the contrary, Doctor, but it's nonetheless gratifying to hear it."

Despite being away from Andor, zh'Thiin had kept apprised of the current status for each of the twenty-three bondgroups that had volunteered to be test subjects for her gamete gene-therapy protocol. After all the time she spent devising the new regimen to reach a point where she was ready for testing on living hosts, she had no intention of being uninformed simply because she was off world. The first two of the *zhen* who had volunteered for the trials now were nearing the end of their pregnancies, and the latest reports from sh'Laenatha, who was serving on zh'Thiin's staff as its resident obstetrician, all were favorable with respect to the patients' conditions. The prognosis was for both *zhen* to conclude their pregnancies with the birth of healthy babies.

"I trust you conveyed my best regards and that I look forward to seeing them upon my return?" zh'Thiin asked.

On the terminal's display, sh'Laenatha nodded. *"Indeed I did. They are most anxious to share their anticipation with you. I'm told there are celebrations being planned to herald the birth of both children, for which you are to be the guest of honor."*

"That is," ch'Thane added, *"if you don't mind sharing the spotlight with the new arrivals."*

Laughing at that, zh'Thiin nodded. "Please tell them that it would be my great privilege, Lieutenant. Barring unforeseen circumstances, I expect to be back on Andor before our patients' next examination. I look forward to seeing them again."

Sh'Laenatha said, *"I for one look forward to you announcing the success of this new protocol to the people of Andor at the upcoming conference. After everything our people have endured over the past several generations, I cannot imagine this news will be greeted with anything but the most heartfelt support, at least by the majority of the populace."*

"If only that were true, my friend," zh'Thiin replied. Given how her predecessor's work and theories were treated by some segments of Andorian society—a negative reaction even before the flaws in the Yrythny DNA approach were discovered—zh'Thiin expected that resistance to her own ideas and the tests she already had conducted would be even greater than that shown to the late sh'Veileth. "Still, we can certainly hope for the best." Directing her attention to ch'Thane, she said, "Lieutenant, before I forget, please instruct my computer to transmit any incoming correspondence to the *Enterprise*." With the starship still more than a day's travel from Andor, she figured culling her burgeoning backlog of subspace communiqués and other message traffic would go a long way toward passing the time.

The young Andorian Starfleet officer replied, *"I have already done so, Professor."*

As if on cue, zh'Thiin's desktop terminal emitted a pointed telltale tone, alerting her to incoming messages. "Your ability to anticipate my needs never ceases to amaze me, Lieutenant."

"Indeed," sh'Laenatha added. *"I have given serious consideration to requesting his transfer to my own team."*

"There will be no kidnapping of my staff members," zh'Thiin said, smiling.

Looking uncomfortable at being the sudden focus of the light banter, ch'Thane asked, *"Is there anything else I can do for you, Professor?"*

Zh'Thiin shook her head. "Find a way to transport me from one planet to another without having to travel by starship?"

"Engineering's not my specialty," the lieutenant said, *"but I will look into it. Good day, Professor. Ch'Thane out."*

Leaning back in her desk chair as the image of her colleagues dissolved, zh'Thiin reached for the cup of tea sitting near her right hand. She had done her best to program the replicator in her guest quarters so that the device would produce her preferred herbal blend, but after several attempts the computer's approximation of her personal recipe still left much to be desired.

One more day, she reminded herself, *and you'll be able to enjoy proper tea.*

"Computer," she said, turning her attention back to the desktop terminal, "retrieve private correspondence."

"Working," replied the *Enterprise*'s main computer. Another series of melodic tones sprang from the interface before a scroll of text filled the terminal's screen. Zh'Thiin studied the list of senders' names, along with the date-time

stamps on each of the entries. In her absence from Andor and despite continuous efforts to remain up to date with the constant flow of correspondence to and from her office, a backlog of unanswered messages was beginning to accumulate. The professor sighed in resignation, knowing she would have to devote at least one entire evening upon her return home toward clearing out her message queue.

One entry on the list caught her gaze, and she reviewed the sender's name a second time to be certain she had correctly read it. According to the entry's header text, the communiqué was an audio-visual message, as was all of the correspondence sent to her by this individual. Reaching across the desk, she used the terminal's manual interface to open the message. The data list vanished, replaced by the image of a Gallamite. She normally experienced no overt reactions when encountering even some of the most acute variations in appearance to be found among the myriad species populating the known galaxy. Still, zh'Thiin nevertheless felt uncomfortable whenever she beheld a member of this specific race. To her, at least, there was just something unsettling about being able to look upon the oversized brain—seemingly floating within a thick, lucent fluid—that was visible through the upper portion of a Gallamite's enlarged, transparent skull.

Or, zh'Thiin reminded herself, she simply could be having an adverse reaction to this particular Gallamite.

"Greetings, Professor zh'Thiin," said the prerecorded voice of Eronaq Sintay, who stared out from the display with wide eyes and a broad grin consisting of two rows of gleaming, perfectly spaced teeth. *"It is my pleasure to pass along the best regards of our mutual benefactors."*

Benefactors. The word all but burned in zh'Thiin's mind as she beheld the Gallamite's recorded visage. *I'm trying to save a civilization, all while this parasite acts as a gatekeeper and earns money from my work.* She knew that, in truth, Eronaq Sintay gained no monetary value from her endeavors. He was, in the parlance of those who cared about such distinctions, an "information broker," acting as an agent whose primary task was to pass data between two or more parties. This usually was done while observing and safeguarding the anonymity of at least one participant in whatever transaction the agent was managing. In this case, he was protecting the identity of her mysterious sponsors, who had seen fit to convey through this bizarre means information that had proven to be of such aid to her research that its value could not—in her opinion, at least—be measured in any material sense.

"Our mutual friends," Sintay continued, *"have reviewed the information you've sent, and are quite pleased with the progress you've made. It seems their faith in your expertise and abilities was not misplaced, and they wish to express their utmost delight that your test trials appear to be advancing as you projected. We can only hope that the Andorian people will come to appreciate what you seem to have accomplished."*

Zh'Thiin felt a twinge of anxiety at the mention of the "information" she had sent for review at the request of her unnamed supporters. She had provided data and materials relating to her volunteer test subjects, including detailed notes about each *zhen* currently implanted with gametes enhanced in accordance with her experimental gene-resequencing protocol. There was no arguing that she had violated any number of regulations and laws surrounding patient privacy and the release of confidential medical information, but doing so was just one of the many conditions and parameters to which she had agreed in order to receive the assistance her benefactors had so far imparted. While she had been able to convince herself that what she had done and continued to do was justified if it aided in her quest to help her people, she was not a fool. If her actions ever came to light, there would be those among the Andorian populace who would take great exception to the sacred trust she had breached.

But perhaps their children and grandchildren will live to one day debate the merits of what I've done.

On the computer monitor, Sintay continued, *"As to your request for additional information regarding genetic manipulation, my clients have expressed a reluctance to provide that at this time. I was told to pass on reassurance that you currently possess all that's required for you to continue your work."*

As grateful as she was to hear such affirmation, zh'Thiin yearned to know more about the enigmatic party or parties responsible for what she had so far accomplished. It was they who had contacted her, using Eronaq Sintay as a conduit, informing her of their knowledge of her research and, incredibly, an interest in rendering assistance. At first zh'Thiin had balked at the notion, engrossed as she was in the voluminous research notes and data files compiled by Dr. sh'Veileth in the years before her death.

That was until Sintay transmitted a mere sample of the information his client wished to impart. From the first moment she reviewed the data given to her, zh'Thiin knew she had to see where this mystifying liaison might lead.

"Given the controversial nature of your research," Sintay said, *"and regardless of its potential benefits, our friends wish to avoid being the focus of attention, at least for the time being."* From the outset, maintaining secrecy as to the source of the data was one of the conditions for her having access to the information being offered by the Gallamite's client. So far she had honored her part of that arrangement, keeping the truth behind her

research hidden even from Dr. sh'Laenatha and Lieutenant ch'Thane. So far as anyone knew, zh'Thiin herself was the sole architect of the contentious theories she had put forth.

To her surprise, Sintay said, *"Besides, while they provided the catalyst for your research, they have no desire to claim credit for the very real and necessary work you performed in order to bring about a viable gene-manipulation procedure."*

"Catalyst," zh'Thiin said to no one, given that she was alone in her quarters. "That is an understatement of almost criminal proportions." As intriguing as the data sample given to her by Sintay had been, it was not until she received a larger, more comprehensive information packet—itself encrypted in such a way that she had to wait for a subsequent message from her most peculiar caller to arrive containing the decryption key—that she realized the scope of assistance her apparent supporters proposed to offer. Though she was one of the foremost genetic scientists in the Federation, she had been unprepared for the knowledge now in her grasp.

Most of the information given to her revolved around gene sequences of a complexity that dwarfed the deoxyribonucleic acid found in most known life-forms. The sample strands of DNA provided with the information packet, according to her benefactors, represented a cross section of more than a dozen forms of plant and animal life developed in a laboratory setting. There was no mistaking the common bond shared by the samples, with each specific DNA strand possessing a varying number of chemical base pairs relating to the life-form in question. Each strand also carried within it chemical pairs that, in zh'Thiin's opinion, appeared to act as a form of barricade between the first set of pairs and the remainder of the staggering amount of genetic information contained within the respective sample.

As for that information, in addition to what zh'Thiin could identify, the DNA strands contained molecules unlike anything on record, and defied classification despite the professor's best efforts.

Zh'Thiin was certain that all of it obviously was artificially engineered, but by whom, and for what purpose? So far as she knew, no species in the charted galaxy possessed the ability to create genetic code of such complexity. She had reminded herself on more than one occasion that anyone harboring such knowledge might very well be keeping it themselves, given the Federation's long-standing views on the practice of selective or "enhanced" genetic engineering. It was that attitude that had prompted Sintay to instruct her not to consult Federation or Starfleet medical and science databases in search of more information on this phenomenon. The genetic code, she was told, was far too valuable to allow the entire galaxy free access to it.

It's easy to hold such values when your very survival is not part of the equation.

Setting aside her initial concerns surrounding her unidentified advocate, she had spent months studying the convoluted genetic code and learning about its adaptive qualities. Armed with that hard-won knowledge and using the perplexing artificial DNA as a guide, zh'Thiin developed a resequencing protocol that would allow her to apply her own version of the engineered genetic modifiers to fertilized gametes taken from an Andorian bondgroup's *shen*, and prior to implantation in the uterus of the *zhen*. The resulting zygotes, if all proceeded according to her theory and expectations, would gestate and be carried to term as with any problem-free pregnancy. Would it work? So far, that seemed to be the case, but the final questions remained unanswered, at least until zh'Thiin's first two test subjects delivered in just over three months' time the babies they currently nurtured.

The recorded image of Sintay was smiling now, an expression that annoyed zh'Thiin. *"There is still much work to be done, for which you require no more immediate assistance from our friend. For now, you are instructed to proceed as you have to this point. If it becomes necessary to offer additional guidance, rest assured that it will be provided. Until then, my client and I wish you continued success with your work. Good day, Professor."* The UFP seal appeared on her monitor, advising her that the transmission had ended. In what had long ago become a habit, zh'Thiin reached for the terminal and pressed the control to delete the message and all archived copies from the *Enterprise*'s main computer.

Additional guidance. Zh'Thiin considered the phrase and decided that, under the circumstances, it was an interesting choice of words. In addition to the insights her research had provided toward possibly saving the Andorian people from extinction, she had become convinced that the delightfully complex strands of synthetic genetic code given to her for study were not complete. Could there really be even more to the already-remarkable DNA, beyond the overwhelming amount of knowledge zh'Thiin was sure remained to be gleaned from the samples currently in her care? If so, why keep that information from her?

As always seemed to happen every time she was contacted by the infuriatingly unflappable Sintay, zh'Thiin was left with a lingering frustration that in time would fall beneath the onslaught of a wholly different emotion: determination.

Sooner or later, she vowed, she would learn the truth. All of it.

For now, zh'Thiin decided, and as Eronaq Sintay himself had said, there remained much work to do.

13

Sitting in his customary place at the head of the conference table in the *Enterprise*'s observation lounge, Picard crossed his legs and hoped the stain gracing his right pants leg—split pea soup, courtesy of René—which he hadn't seen while feeding his son lunch, was not noticeable. Even if anyone among the party assembled in the lounge observed the unsightly blemish, Picard was certain that none of them, with the possible exception of T'Ryssa Chen, would say anything.

"Thank you for coming, Professor zh'Thiin," Picard said, nodding to where the Andorian sat in the chair nearest to him along the table's left side. "I know that you and Dr. Crusher have been immersed in your research since leaving Earth, but I hope you can appreciate our desire to obtain as much first-hand knowledge and experience as possible regarding Andor's current political and social climate."

Zh'Thiin replied, "Of course, Captain. I'm eager to assist in any way possible. It's the least I can do after all the help you and your wife have provided me since I came aboard your ship, and for the tasks you will soon undertake on behalf of all of Andor. Dr. Crusher has already provided some ideas that might well simplify the process and make it more easily available on a mass scale."

Hoping that the professor's sentiment was one shared by many Andorians—and knowing that likely was not the case—Picard merely offered a formal nod in acknowledgment of zh'Thiin's kind words before turning to where Commander Worf sat to his right. "Number One, what's our ETA at Andor?"

"Five hours, thirty-seven minutes at our present speed, Captain," the Klingon answered without hesitation, and while using no padd to confirm what he had just said. Picard suppressed a small smile, knowing that Worf took great pride in presenting information without benefit of notes or anything else that might be interpreted as a crutch.

"We have already been contacted by Andor's orbital operations command," added Lieutenant Choudhury, from where she sat next to Worf. "They're awaiting our arrival and have made available a docking berth at their primary space station in the event we wish to make use of recreational and other facilities for our off-duty personnel."

Picard nodded. "Please extend my thanks and gratitude to the operations commander. Given the multiple demands I expect to be placed on our people once the conference is in session, I'd rather the *Enterprise* not be docked anywhere." Leaning back in his chair, he clasped his hands and rested them in his lap. Much to his irritation, the soup stain registered in his peripheral vision, but he ignored it. "Which brings us to the next topic on the agenda. What can we expect to encounter before and during the conference?"

Sitting across from Choudhury and to zh'Thiin's left, Lieutenant Chen cleared her throat and sat straighter in her chair, and Picard noted how her gaze shifted ever so briefly to Professor zh'Thiin before returning to him. "As you know, sir, Andor has experienced a resurgence in anti-Federation sentiment in recent years. While there is a wide spectrum of political ideologies, the two major parties, the Progressives and the Visionists, tend to dominate much of the dialogue. Then there are activist groups, such as the one calling itself the 'True Heirs of Andor,' which have been quite aggressive in spreading their message of hewing to traditional Andorian values. While some work to foster mutual cooperation and banding together, particularly during these trying times, the T.H.A. and groups like it are holding to the notion that Andorians are second-class citizens, subsuming their needs to the greater good of the Federation."

"In their defense, Lieutenant," zh'Thiin said, her voice low and even, "all such groups do not operate with a single agenda, nor do many of them even agree with one another. That said, it is worth noting that some of these factions do have legitimate criticisms. Federation efforts on Andor's behalf with respect to our procreation crisis can be interpreted by such groups as . . . less than enthusiastic."

"And I would take issue with that viewpoint, Professor," Picard said, measuring his own words so as to keep the tone of the discussion civil. "The very real truth is that the unique nature of Andorian biology has been its own worst obstacle. You above anyone know that some of the brightest minds, from your people to the Federation science community, have wrestled with this issue for decades."

Zh'Thiin nodded. "My apologies, Captain. I did not mean to infer a genuine lack of effort or commitment on the Federation's part."

"I apologize to you, as well, Professor," Chen added. "It wasn't my intention to generalize or diminish any genuine grievances Andorians of any affiliation might have."

The professor reached out to pat the lieutenant's hand,

a very human gesture that Picard found surprising, coming from the Andorian. "Worry not, Lieutenant," she said. "There are more than enough issues to address, without us inventing things about which to disagree. Think no more of it, and I hope you will excuse my interruption."

Looking to Picard, who nodded for her to continue, Chen said, "Based on our reports, the True Heirs of Andor, while among the largest and most vocal of such groups on Andor, stand in unity with the Visionist party and have never really taken any radical steps so far as trying to spread their message. While some splinter groups have committed acts of vandalism or hijacked computer network hubs and broadcast media outlets to distribute propaganda, the T.H.A. has taken steps to remain in the background. There's some speculation that they're doing this on purpose, while at the same time funding the smaller, more extremist groups."

"Not exactly an original strategy," Worf said.

Chen nodded. "And actually not a bad idea. Have the hard-line activists do all the crazy stunts and get all the attention, both from the media as well as any law enforcement agencies investigating their activities, while you sit back and look fairly reasonable by comparison. The former Andorian presider, who aligned with the Visionist party, was a supporter of the T.H.A., as were several members of his administration, though they were outnumbered by members who identified themselves with the Progressive party."

"Of course, most of the Andorian government was wiped out during the Borg attack," zh'Thiin said. "As for Presider sh'Thalis, she is actually not affiliated with either of the two major parties. She describes herself as an independent or—as she likes to say—a social Progressive and a fiscal Visionist, supporting issues valued by either party as well as some of the smaller groups. Still, if forced to classify her, most pundits usually opt to describe Presider sh'Thalis as a Progressive."

"A rather arbitrary designation, it seems," Picard said. The notion of labeling groups of people in order to define the parameters of discussion and problem solving had always seemed to him little more than a fool's errand. Ideas, so long as they were constructive and based in facts and reality rather than hysterics and the propagation of ignorance and fear, were worth exploring regardless of their presenters' ideology. Unfortunately, the history of many worlds, including his own, was rife with examples of a less evolved approach to political discourse. Such tactics often came to the forefront during times of adversity, employed by opportunists and charlatans of every stripe, and demanded even greater vigilance to ensure such divisive and ultimately harmful concepts and actions did not acquire any lasting traction among a troubled populace.

"It's worth noting that this issue has supporters and detractors across both major parties," zh'Thiin said. "Still, many Visionists now serve within the new government, and several of those have used their position to make clear their stance on many of the issues currently plaguing my people. The controversy surrounding the use of the Yrythny ova as a means of stimulating windows of fertility within bondgroups seeking to procreate was at the forefront of the Visionists' agenda even prior to the Borg invasion. It's now a prime focus for the new government, as Presider sh'Thalis has come out in favor of continued and even expanded research for alternatives to the Yrythny solution, which despite its faults still offered much promise toward helping my people. She's hoping this conference will raise awareness of such alternatives, not only to the people of Andor but also across the Federation."

Picard nodded. "A noble effort, to be sure." Shifting in his seat, he looked to Worf and Choudhury. "We can be certain the conference will attract a diverse range of viewpoints. Prudence demands we be prepared for every eventuality."

"Already on it, Captain," Choudhury replied. "As you know, I've been in contact with the commanders of the Homeworld Security brigade as well as the Starfleet detachment stationed in the capital city. *Enterprise* security personnel will augment their people once the conference starts, as well as provide additional logistical support from the ship. That's naturally going to ruffle some feathers among the more hard-line anti-Federation groups, but we're stressing that it's Homeworld Security who's running the show on the ground."

"Besides the formal protests we can expect to see," Picard said, "is there any indication that one or more of these activist groups might be trying to carry off some other sort of display? Perhaps even something violent?" It was a question that gnawed at the captain in the evenings while reading Choudhury's continuous stream of updated security assessments as she worked to finalize preparations for her department.

"A few such groups are worth keeping under observation," Worf replied. "In particular is a group calling itself the *Treishya*. They describe themselves as an offshoot of the Visionist party, dedicated to bringing attention to the issues the elected politicians are afraid to address. They are specifically committed to denouncing the role of any 'outsiders' who would—as their propaganda states—pollute Andorian blood with alien genetic engineering or other artificial means of resolving the reproductive crisis."

Zh'Thiin said, "I've heard of the *Treishya*. The name

is derived from ancient Andorii religious texts, and means 'Children of the Light.' They're radicals, believing that if our people are to survive these trials, then they will do so by their own hands or die as a race, rather than accept the assistance of non-Andorians."

Chen nodded. "That's them. They're small yet vocal, but the reports we're getting from Homeworld Security and our people on the ground suggest that the *Treishya*'s extreme viewpoints are starting to gain acceptance in some quarters."

"It's not out of the question that they might be planning to take advantage of the attention the conference will receive," Choudhury added. "With that in mind, anyone connected with the conference or on the attendance list is being screened for possible connection to the *Treishya*."

Frowning, Picard asked, "Has this group made any statements or announcements indicating they might attempt to use the conference as a platform to make some kind of statement?"

"Nothing overt, sir," Choudhury replied. "Though the security detail assigned to parliament has reported a handful of incidents with suspected *Treishya* members attempting to enter the grounds. So far they've been classified as little more than nuisances, but we're not ruling out the possibility of them stepping up their efforts as we continue our preparations."

"Very well," Picard said. "It's obvious that these groups have grievances against the Andorian government, and that dissatisfaction will likely extend toward the increased Starfleet presence once the conference is under way. However, given the sensitive nature of this situation and the proliferation of anti-Federation sentiment, it's important that our presence on Andor not be perceived as an attempt to quash dissenting views or opinions."

"The safety of the conference attendees is our primary focus, Captain," Worf said. "I do not believe Lieutenant Choudhury's efforts to this point have been motivated by any other concern."

Picard nodded. "I don't mean to imply otherwise, but make no mistake: Our every action while on Andor will be scrutinized and—in some cases—conflated or distorted in order to further an agenda at odds with what the conference is trying to accomplish. We must avoid fueling such dissent, but so long as protesters observe the laws regarding peaceful assembly, we must not do anything that might be perceived as an infringement on their civil liberties as defined under Andorian law."

"And if these protest groups step beyond the law?" zh'Thiin asked.

"Then we take the appropriate, measured actions, Professor," Picard replied, "in order to keep the peace and ensure that the conference proceeds with minimal disruption." Turning once again to Choudhury, he said, "I understand that you're walking a fine line, Lieutenant, but it's the price we pay for maintaining the ideals we hold dear. Be vigilant, certainly, but do not allow these preparations to devolve into a witch hunt. No doubt the Homeworld Security brigade commanders have some knowledge and experience in this area, so do continue to consult with them. They'll know how best to deal with their people."

"According to the reports we've received so far," Chen said, "they've already begun gathering information on conference attendees and possible affiliations with the *Treishya*."

Picard said, "That's their prerogative, Lieutenant, but *we* are not in the business of investigating or harassing citizens on the basis of their legally protected associations. Besides, you'll have enough to worry about once the conference is under way. Until then, I thank you all for your work to this point. Dismissed." As Professor zh'Thiin and his officers rose from their seats to return to their duties, Picard remembered a point he had forgotten to address at the meeting. "Lieutenant Choudhury."

Walking behind Worf as he headed toward the bridge, the security chief turned back to face Picard. "Yes, Captain?" As she did so, Lieutenant Chen moved to stand near the bulkhead.

"I've read your report about involving Commander La Forge and members of his engineering staff to augment security procedures at the conference venue. Given what we just discussed, are you confident you can employ these measures in a way that does not attract undue attention?"

Choudhury replied, "Yes, sir, I think we can." The lieutenant's recommendations had included the use of transporter inhibitors as well as portable force-field generators—similar to systems already in place at the Federation embassy there as well as those deployed around the Parliament Andoria complex—in the event it became necessary to isolate or even protect conference attendees from some form of attack. At first, Picard had considered rejecting the suggestions as being too heavy-handed. After reading the more recent security briefings and now knowing what he did about the tumultuous situation on Andor and what they likely would encounter in the capital city once the conference got under way, he had been forced to reconsider his initial reaction.

Nodding in approval, Picard said, "Very well, Lieutenant.

Make it so." He watched as Choudhury turned and exited the room, returning to the bridge and leaving him alone in the conference lounge with Lieutenant Chen. When she said nothing after a moment, he eyed her with a questioning look. "Was there something else, Lieutenant?"

Her expression betraying nothing, Chen asked, "Sir, did you know you have a green stain on your pants?"

14

Ensign Maureen Granados made a dramatic show of studying the cluttered cargo bay. "You know what we're missing here? More crates."

Geordi La Forge could not help the smile that escaped his lips in response to the junior engineer's remark. Glancing around the cargo bay, he was impressed by the amount of matériel that had been assembled in such a short time. Each of the containers arrayed around the chamber was packed with tools, components, and other supplies to be utilized by him as well as the teams he would soon dispatch to the planet's surface. There, they would assist Andorian technicians and other specialists in a variety of tasks for which Captain Picard had pledged the resources of the *Enterprise* and its crew.

"We do have a way of over-preparing, don't we?" La Forge said, chuckling as he consulted the inventory report displayed on his padd. Keying the device, he reviewed the listings of equipment being readied for transport to different locations around the planet.

"Given the effort we will be expending," said Lieutenant Commander Taurik from where he stood on the far side of an antigravity pallet holding several smaller crates, "and the importance of returning these facilities to full operational capability, such preparation is a logical course of action." Also holding a padd, the Vulcan engineer continued his inspection of the crates and the equipment they contained.

La Forge nodded. "My thoughts exactly." Each of the locations to which he would be sending people for their first assignments—a power plant, a water-reclamation facility, a hospital, and a new command-and-control center for Home-world Security—had required extensive repairs, having suffered major damage during the Borg attack. Though Andorian engineers had completed most of the heavy renovations—or, in the case of the water-reclamation plant, a complete reconstruction—there still remained a long list of adjustments, fine-tuning, and other "settling in" modifications in order to bring the facilities online. Once operational, the plant would service the water-usage needs of more than three million residents of nearly twenty small villages and other prefectures along the Ka'Thela continent's southern perimeter.

Not bad for a day's work, mused the chief engineer, *if we can get it all done.*

Stepping back from the container she was inspecting, Granados reached up to run her free hand through her dark-red hair. Though she wore her hair in a bun, an occasional rebellious lock still managed to work its way free of whatever knot or accessory she employed, to drop across her eyes. "Well, with the stuff we have here, we could build a starship drydock, or three, down there." She paused, her expression sobering. "Come to think of it, that might not be such a bad idea."

When she said nothing else, La Forge realized that the young woman's off-the-cuff remark now was conjuring memories of friends and loved ones lost during the Borg invasion. Granados had told him one evening over a drink in the crew lounge that her fiancé had been a security officer serving aboard the *Potemkin* when that ship was destroyed during the Borg's devastating attack on the now-dead planet Deneva. Her story was similar to uncounted others among the *Enterprise* crew. Like Maureen Granados, those who had endured the war were forced—almost from the moment tragedy struck them—to put aside their anguish in order to continue performing their duties under the most extreme of pressures and stress. Now those burdens were gone, replaced by all-new difficulties, and required those same survivors to weave in and around their continuing responsibilities the grief, mourning, and whatever other periods of reflection they might need. This was not the first time La Forge had seen one of his people, or some other member of the *Enterprise* crew, take a brief respite from their duties in order to engage in a moment of "emotional self-maintenance," as Dr. Hegol had once called it. The ship's counselor had explained this to the senior staff, encouraging them not to be overly concerned about the behavior—so long as it did not interfere with a critical task, of course.

Seeing Granados's attention appearing to wander away for the briefest of intervals, La Forge said nothing as the young engineer snapped back to the here and now, drew a breath, and composed herself before turning back to face him. Their eyes locked, and La Forge said nothing, opting instead to offer a simple, slight nod of understanding. Granados's expression changed, and her mouth formed a silent reply. *Thank you.*

Then, as though to reassure the chief engineer that she remained on point so far as her assignments were concerned, she said aloud, "According to my inventory, the shipments for the power plant are ready to go. We can transport them down anytime you're ready, Commander."

"Outstanding," La Forge said, refocusing his own attention to the matters at hand. "Looks like we're almost ready with the shipment for the power plant. Taurik, what about the hospital and the brigade's command center?"

Looking up from his padd, the Vulcan replied, "We are requisitioning some final components for the brigade consignment, which, by my estimate, should arrive here in sixteen point three minutes. The containers assigned to the hospital are also nearly complete, though we are waiting for some items that are due to be delivered by Dr. Crusher's medical staff."

"They're here," another voice said from behind La Forge, one the engineer recognized with no small amount of pleasant surprise. He turned to see Tamala Harstad walking toward him, an oversized medical bag slung from each shoulder while she cradled a third such parcel in her arms. The doctor smiled as their eyes met, an infectious smile of which La Forge had grown particularly fond during the past days.

"Dr. Harstad," he said, hoping as he spoke the words that his attempt at professional decorum sounded less hollow to Granados's and Taurik's ears than they did to his own. He stepped toward her, moving to assist with the bags she carried. "You could have had a couple of orderlies bring these down."

Harstad shrugged as she allowed La Forge to take the bag she carried in her hands. "Dr. Crusher wanted a final verification before we sent anything down to the hospital, and I was on my way to lunch, anyway, so here I am."

"Given that sickbay is on deck seven and the officer's mess is on deck two," Taurik said, his right eyebrow lifting as he regarded the doctor, "it would seem impractical for you to travel here to deck eleven on your way to consume your midday meal."

"Commander Taurik, *sir*?" said Granados, her tone such that La Forge turned to see her doing her best to suppress a smile as she held out her padd to the Vulcan. "If you could verify the inventory on this consignment, I'll see that it's ready for transport to the surface." As Taurik took the device from her, she glanced toward La Forge and made a show of rolling her eyes in melodramatic fashion.

Also seeing this, Harstad laughed. "News travels fast, I guess."

"On the *Enterprise*?" La Forge asked. "At warp ten." He reached for the strap suspending the bag from her left shoulder, then turned and led the way to one of the cargo containers holding equipment for the hospital.

"And about that," Harstad said, her voice taking on a quieter tone, the kind La Forge had heard more than once over the years.

Steeling himself for what he was sure was coming, he turned to look over his shoulder, keeping his expression neutral. "Yeah?"

Harstad stepped closer, as though concerned that her words might carry across the open cargo bay, and reached out to lay a hand on his arm. "I just wanted to say I really did enjoy last night."

"You already told me that," La Forge said, smiling in spite of himself. "This morning, remember? On your way out the door?"

Her expression changing to one of regret, Harstad squeezed his arm. "I know, and I'm really sorry about that." She waved toward the container. "It's just that I knew today was going to be hectic, getting ready for all of this, and I needed an early start." Then her smile widened. "Besides, I honestly hadn't planned on what happened last night." She punctuated the last word by bobbing her eyebrows at him.

That made La Forge laugh. "Well, you've got me there. To be honest, I was a bit surprised by it, too."

"But not disappointed, right?" Harstad asked.

La Forge shook his head. "Not for a nanosecond." The previous evening had begun in similar fashion to their first encounter, unwinding over dinner and drinks in the crew lounge. It was a relaxing way to end what for the chief engineer had been a double shift spent making preparations for his staff's tasks on Andor. The key difference on this second "date" was that the conversation had come far easier on this occasion, which in turn served to set the stage for what had come afterward.

"I'm sure that'll make its way through the ship's rumor mill at top speed, too," Harstad said, smiling again.

Holding up a hand as though swearing an oath, La Forge replied, "Not from me."

She patted him once more on the arm before taking away her hand. "So, there are still a few gentlemen left wandering the galaxy, after all? Lucky me." Reaching for the strap over her right shoulder, she lifted the bag from her arm and placed it in the lone remaining space within the cargo container.

"When are you beaming down?" La Forge asked. He knew that Harstad, like Dr. Tropp and other members of the ship's medical staff, would be transporting to the hospital in shifts to assist with the installation and calibration of new patient-care equipment provided by Andorian manufacturers as well as items and components delivered by the *Enterprise*.

"Not until tomorrow," Harstad replied. Brushing some of her hair away from her face, she eyed him with a playful expression. "You?"

Nodding back over his shoulder, he said, "I'm taking the first team down later this afternoon, to get a look at the power plant before we go to work. The Andorian engineers already on-site are pretty good at what they do, so I'm hoping this is more formality than actual heavy labor on our parts." The initial reports from the facility were promising, but La Forge, a creature of habit particularly when it came to his work, wanted a firsthand inspection to satisfy his own curiosity.

"Well," Harstad said, "if you make it back in time for dinner, call me. I might be in sickbay tending to some last-minute stuff, so the break will be nice."

La Forge shrugged. "What if I'm too late for dinner?"

"Call me anyway," Harstad said, poking him in the chest before turning and heading for the cargo bay's exit, leaving the chief engineer standing alone, watching her leave and making no effort to hide the satisfied grin he now sported.

The grin faded as he turned around and saw Ensign Granados studying her padd with an uncommon intensity, and Commander Taurik studying him with a passive, unreadable expression.

"What?" La Forge asked.

Without looking up from her padd, Granados replied, "Nothing, sir. Not a thing."

"And what about you?" the engineer asked Taurik.

The Vulcan said, "I have no additional comments or observations, sir."

Shaking his head, La Forge stepped back to the pallet where he had been working and retrieved his padd. "Let's get back to work."

Only when he was sure neither of his junior officers was looking at him did he allow the grin to return.

15

The familiar tingling on his skin faded as the transporter beam released him, and Picard found himself standing in a well-tended atrium. Multicolored stone tiles formed a circular mosaic beneath his feet, around which was arrayed a variety of flora and fauna. The atrium in which he, Lieutenant Chen, and Ensign sh'Anbi had materialized was open on three sides, overlooking a lush, manicured lawn, and in the distance Picard could see a tall, imposing stone wall.

"Nice," Chen remarked.

Picard nodded. "Indeed." A path constructed from similar stones led a few meters from the atrium to a covered walkway running alongside the exterior wall of the mansion that now served as the seat of power in the city of Lor'Vela for the Parliament Andoria. The surrounding compound housed an array of stone walking paths winding around and among ponds, gardens, rock formations, and waterfalls. To Picard's practiced eye, every last flower petal and blade of grass seemed the product of meticulous, even loving care. "As I recall, this building once housed elements of the regional government, but they graciously offered the complex to the parliament when it was decided this city would serve as the new capital for the central planetary government."

"There's a lot of space here," said sh'Anbi, the security officer assigned to accompany Picard. She indicated the expansive courtyard with a wave. "If this is where the conference is being held—even wtih most of the facility underground—security will definitely prove challenging."

"I would imagine so, Ensign," Picard replied, "which is why Commander Worf and Lieutenant Choudhury have spent the past several hours since our arrival meeting with their Andorian counterparts." The Enterprise had barely settled into orbit when his first officer and head of security transported down to the capital city, ostensibly to discuss final security preparations with the local Homeworld Security units as well as the Starfleet contingent based in Lor'Vela. Of course, Commander Worf also had used the opportunity to conduct his own sweep of the Parliament Andoria complex, including the mansion housing the offices of the presider as well as the subterranean auditorium and meeting rooms where the conference was to be held. Only after being satisfied with the security of the compound had he allowed Picard to transport to the surface. With respect to the safety of his captain, Worf had proven as intractable as Will Riker ever had been, a trait he obviously had taken to heart after years serving alongside the Enterprise's former first officer.

Noticing a change in sh'Anbi's expression as she continued to study the courtyard, Picard asked, "Ensign? Is there something wrong?"

"I . . . I mean, no, sir," the young Andorian replied, shaking her head. "My apologies, Captain. I was just thinking about . . . something else."

It took Picard a moment to make the connection, but then he remembered what he had read in sh'Anbi's personnel file when the ensign had first joined the Enterprise crew several months earlier. He also recalled a report filed by Dr. Hegol just a few days ago with respect to the young officer's fitness for duty.

"Ensign," Picard said, "if you're uncomfortable being here . . ."

Again, sh'Anbi shook her head. "No, sir, I'm fine. I was just distracted for a moment by how beautiful everything here looks, compared to . . . other areas of the planet." Though she said nothing else, Picard knew she was envisioning her home city, now little more than craters and ash a year after the Borg attack. Like many worlds across the Federation, jagged, scorched canyons, kilometers long where cities once had stood, mutilated Andor's once-beautiful landscape. Millions of tons of ash, dirt, and soot had been thrown into the atmosphere, heightening the danger of global cooling as well as the rising risk of respiratory illness, particularly in children and the elderly. Brilliant scientific and engineering minds such as those assigned to Starfleet's Corps of Engineers had hit on the notion of modifying planetary weather-modification satellites and networks to act as rudimentary, field-expedient atmosphere scrubbers, assisting with the monumental task of cleaning toxic pollutants from the air. The ploy was not nearly so all-encompassing as a true terraforming operation, but neither was it as time- and resource-intensive. Still, it would take years before all of the atmospheric impurities were removed from the air.

No doubt sh'Anbi had viewed reports from the Federation News Service, broadcasting footage of the destroyed cities not only on Andor but on worlds throughout the quadrant. Perhaps such images were forever burned into her memory, and she was cursed to carry them with her all the days of her life. Picard could sympathize, given how his own mind still harbored the memories of the battle at Wolf 359, and the ships whose destruction he had witnessed while imprisoned by the Borg Collective as their unwilling spokesperson, Locutus.

Enough, he chided himself. *The Borg are gone. Forever.*

"Ensign," he said, keeping his voice soft, "do you feel incapable of carrying out your duties due to personal matters?" It had been Dr. Hegol's idea to include as many Andorian *Enterprise* crew members as possible into the various details and away teams scheduled to transport to the surface in support of the conference. The counselor's reasoning was that it would send a silent yet still strong message to the conference attendees that Starfleet and the Federation stood alongside the Andorian people. At the time it had seemed like a reasonable request on Hegol's part, though Picard had considered the idea that there might be an Andorian crew member still shaken by what had happened to their homeworld—particularly upon firsthand viewing of the devastation. What he had not anticipated was a reaction like sh'Anbi's, who now confronted an area of the planet that had been spared annihilation while regions where her family had lived were not so fortunate.

Drawing a deep breath, sh'Anbi said, "I'm fine, Captain. With your permission, I'd like to remain on this detail."

Picard offered her a small, paternal smile before laying his hand on her shoulder. "Very well, Ensign. Thank you."

Footsteps echoed off the stone tiles behind him, and Picard turned to see a group of Andorians emerging from a doorway several dozen meters down the walkway running parallel to the mansion. The small party's most prominent member was a female Andorian dressed in a flowing multi-colored robe that clothed her from neck to feet. Behind her followed two other Andorians, whom Picard guessed to be aides or assistants, and the entire party was flanked by a quartet of male Andorians dressed in black leather uniforms that he recognized as those worn by soldiers of Andor's Homeworld Security contingent.

"Captain Picard," said the female Andorian as the group came closer. Smiling, she reached out to take his hand in both of hers. "I'm Presider Iravothra sh'Thalis. Welcome to Andor. Your reputation precedes you, and it is an honor to have you here."

"The honor is mine, Presider," Picard replied with the practiced ease of an experienced diplomat. "The importance of this conference cannot be understated, and it's a privilege for me to be a part of it." Turning to indicate Chen with his free hand, he added, "May I introduce Lieutenant T'Ryssa Chen, the *Enterprise*'s contact specialist, and Ensign Ereshtarri sh'Anbi, a member of the ship's security detail."

Turning to regard Chen, sh'Thalis asked, "And what does a contact specialist do in a situation such as this, Lieutenant?"

"Anything the captain tells me to do, Presider," Chen replied, her expression remaining neutral even when Picard flashed a mild rebuking glance in her direction.

The response was enough to garner a small laugh from sh'Thalis, who next turned to regard Ensign sh'Anbi. "You honor us with your service to the Federation, Ensign."

"Thank you, Presider," sh'Anbi replied, offering a formal bow of her head.

Returning her attention to Picard, sh'Thalis asked, "Do you have many Andorians among your crew, Captain?"

"Seventeen at present, Presider," Picard replied. "We had fourteen others, two of whom requested assignment to the Starfleet contingent stationed here on Andor. The others elected to resign their commissions and return as civilians to aid in recovery and reconstruction efforts." It had been a similar story with several members of the crew, but most especially from those whose homeworlds had survived the Borg invasion while still suffering varying degrees of damage.

Nodding, sh'Thalis said, "We must each follow wherever our conscience chooses to lead, and a path of service in any capacity is not to be questioned."

"Indeed," Picard replied. "Particularly now, I'd think. On that subject, I must say that it's quite remarkable what you've been able to accomplish so far as reestablishing the parliament. My understanding is that ninety percent of government officials were lost in Laibok." As he spoke the words, he glanced to Ensign sh'Anbi, whose expression revealed nothing.

"We have very detailed plans of succession to thank for our ability to reorganize so quickly," sh'Thalis said. "Though such plans still do not always allow for some of the more interesting choices to be made during a reconstruction effort like the one we've faced. Before the Borg came, I was the leader of a low-level committee, which kept mostly to itself. I oversaw efforts to protect natural resources and government-owned land such as parks, wildlife and nature preserves, as well as historical and culturally significant sites around the world." Shaking her head, she released a small laugh. "That I was elevated to the office of presider should tell you all you need to know about just how deeply the Andorian central government was affected."

"You could have resigned," Picard said, "or simply refused the appointment, and yet you chose to serve. A daunting task, to be sure."

Again, sh'Thalis smiled. "To be sure." Gesturing for Picard to walk alongside her, the presider stepped toward the stone path leading away from the mansion and into the courtyard. As the party moved, her security detail once again took up their protective formation, keeping sh'Thalis and the rest of the group between them. "I wanted to personally thank you for the assistance you've offered for some of our reconstruction efforts. I imagine your crew's technical expertise will be an invaluable asset in the coming days."

"Think nothing of it, Presider." Among the tasks to which Picard had committed *Enterprise* resources and personnel were the repairs to several facilities scattered around the planet. Commander La Forge and his teams of engineers would soon be dispatched to assist with various tasks at those locations, to include getting a power generation plant back online and providing energy for a network of small villages and other provinces located in an isolated region several hundred kilometers south of Lor'Vela.

"Your help is greatly appreciated," sh'Thalis said. "As for other daunting tasks, that brings us to the subject of the forthcoming conference. I'm told that you have several concerns regarding security and the safety of the attendees."

"Yes, Presider," Picard replied, falling in step with her as they moved farther into the courtyard. "Given the reports we've received regarding certain activist groups and their opposition to the work of people like Professor zh'Thiin, I'm sure you can see why I might be wary."

"Understandable," sh'Thalis said, reaching out to pat Picard on the arm. "My security people have been collecting information on these groups for quite some time now, and they were a point of interest for my predecessor, as well." Shaking her head, she released an audible breath. "Considering all that's happened to our world, you would think those of us who survived could strive to put aside such petty differences and instead turn that effort toward salvaging what remains of our civilization. How anyone can believe that Professor zh'Thiin and those like her are working to destroy our race is, to be honest, beyond me."

"In times of crisis," Picard said, "people often embrace whatever previously provided them comfort. Your world and its people have been through a terrible ordeal, which has also served to heighten a problem you were already facing. That some people might react in fear to the propositions being offered even as they struggle to rebuild what they've lost is not unusual."

The path they traversed came to an end at a line of foliage that acted as a natural barrier between the courtyard's perimeter and the mansion. Stone gave way to grass, and out here the afternoon sun warmed Picard's skin as a slight breeze worked to cool him. Looking up, he saw the blue sky laced with only a few clouds; perfect weather.

I hope that's a good omen.

Movement from the corner of his eye caught his attention, and he turned to see Worf and Choudhury walking toward him at a brisk pace along the stone path leading from one of the courtyard's picturesque gardens. "I don't know if you've yet met my first officer, Presider."

"Not yet, no," sh'Thalis replied, and Picard introduced Worf and Choudhury.

"Mr. Worf, do you have a report for me?" Picard asked.

Drawing himself up to his full, impressive height, the first officer replied, "Yes, Captain. We have just concluded our initial meetings with the Homeworld Security brigade commander as well as the officer in charge of the local Starfleet detachment. As expected, the preparations already under way for the conference are proceeding on schedule and with no significant trouble."

Choudhury added, "We're currently in the process of integrating *Enterprise* security personnel into the overall plan developed by the brigade commander. I don't expect to run into any problems, sir."

From behind sh'Thalis, one of her aides, a younger male carrying an electronic device that Picard took to be the equivalent to a padd, said, "Presider, I've just been informed that the preparations for your midday meal have been completed."

"Excellent," sh'Thalis replied. Turning to Picard, she said, "I do hope you and your officers can join us, Captain. After all, there is much to discuss, both official and otherwise."

His interest piqued, Picard asked, "Otherwise, Presider?"

"As I told you, my prior post involved the management of Andor's numerous historical locations. Among those are several archeological sites, including one or two only recently discovered. Overseeing such culturally significant finds is a personal treat for me, as archeology was a subject for which I held great affection earlier in my life, before politics took over everything. Still, I was able to travel to some of those sites as part of my official duties, but now even that small pleasure has been curtailed in the face of my current responsibilities. I'm told you are something of an archeologist yourself."

Shaking his head, Picard replied, "I'm strictly an amateur, Presider, despite the best efforts of one of my professors at Starfleet Academy. There was a time when I did consider pursuing a career in that field, and it's a subject I revisit as I'm able."

"Then you should avail yourself of just such an opportunity while you're here, Captain," sh'Thalis said. "We have a new discovery, something completely unknown to us until recently, that I think you'll find to be nothing short of fascinating."

"Assuming time and my duties permit such a venture," Picard said, "I'm certainly open to the idea." The notion of doing some actual exploring intrigued him, and would without doubt provide a welcome change from the responsibilities he had shouldered these past several months. What was it that Andorian archeologists had found? Since the presider had deigned not to reveal specifics to him at this point, Picard figured she must be trying to preserve something of a surprise for him when and if he found time to visit the site. With any luck, the opportunity would present itself sooner rather than later, but for now, there were other matters requiring his attention.

Diplomat before explorer, Jean-Luc.

16

Looking around Professor Marthrossi zh'Thiin's well-appointed office, Beverly Crusher found herself feeling more than a bit envious. The private chamber was lined with shelves fashioned from a dark, stained wood and set into the room's curved walls. Each of the shelves was filled almost to overflowing with books, their shapes and the text printed on their spines or covers telling Beverly that the professor's collection featured works from planets throughout the Federation, as well as a few nonaligned and even adversarial worlds. Most of the books were medical volumes of one sort or another, spanning more subjects and specializations than Beverly could remember seeing even at the museum wing of the Starfleet Medical library on Earth.

Scattered among the books were mementos from zh'Thiin's long career, as well as what Beverly guessed to be cherished keepsakes from family or friends. The office's far wall contained what appeared to be an old-fashioned wood-burning fireplace. Opposite the fireplace and behind zh'Thiin, a large oval-shaped window overlooked a small pond. The pond itself was part of the courtyard that encircled the building serving as a base of operations for the Starfleet contingent assigned to the new Andorian capital city of Lor'Vela. Off to one side of the fireplace was a small kitchen unit complete with replicator but also featuring a simple stove with two burners, atop one of which sat an oversized stone urn. A faint, sweet odor permeated the room, and Beverly realized the professor was brewing some kind of tea on the stove.

"Maybe I need to reconsider private practice," Beverly said.

Looking up from where she sat behind a curved desk that to Beverly appeared to be carved from polished marble, zh'Thiin smiled. "Not exactly something you'd find aboard a starship, I'm sure."

"You can say that again," Beverly replied. Despite her best efforts to transform her office in the *Enterprise* sickbay into something warm and inviting, it still was little more than a room aboard a spaceship. That much was unfortunate, considering the hours she often spent there, completing required reports, conducting research or personal consultations with patients, or simply hiding away for a few minutes to catch a bit of rest during the course of a long duty shift. Even her husband's ready room, she long ago had conceded, was more appealing than her own office, and zh'Thiin's private refuge made both of those spaces pale in comparison. Here, there was no omnipresent hum of warp engines reverberating through the bulkheads and the deck plates. There would be no Red Alert sirens, and with them the possibility of a hostile alien vessel or other threat destroying her office and the rest of the ship surrounding it.

I could certainly learn to live without that sort of thing.

"Are you scheduled to see any more patients today?" Beverly asked.

"No," zh'Thiin replied, standing and making her way around the desk. She crossed the office to where the urn still sat atop the small stove, steam rising from its narrow top opening. "The two *zhen* we saw earlier were the only patients on the day's schedule." As the professor had explained, she might have deferred seeing even those two, given that the *Enterprise* had just arrived at Andor. However, her trip to Earth had disrupted her normal schedule, and zh'Thiin had not wanted to wait any longer than absolutely necessary to see how the patients were doing with their respective pregnancies, both of which were quite advanced. "Once I'm finished here, I was planning to go home. I'd offer to host you and Captain Picard for dinner, but I know that you likely would rather return to the *Enterprise* and your son."

Beverly smiled at that. "Is it that obvious?" Since René's birth more than a year ago, there had been only a handful of occasions where she had been away from him for more than a day. During her duty shifts aboard ship, René, along with a half dozen children of comparable age, was looked after in a nursery established by Dr. Tropp just a few doors down from sickbay on deck seven. A civilian spouse of one crew member, both of whom were the parents of a child a few months older than René, had accepted the daunting task of supervising the toddlers. Even though Beverly worked in such close proximity to her son and made frequent visits to see him during her duty shift, it was not the same as the time she and Jean-Luc spent with him after the workday was completed.

Reaching to a shelf above the stove, zh'Thiin retrieved a pair of stone mugs that looked to be a match for the urn. "Several of my friends and colleagues are parents themselves, so I'm familiar with the body language, expressions, and other unspoken signs of a mother or father who misses their child." She paused, and Beverly saw the professor's expression change as her antennae drooped. "I had hoped to experience such feelings of my own one day."

"I'm sorry," Beverly said. Zh'Thiin had told her of her own failed pregnancies, along with the pain of realizing she would never know the joys of nurturing her own child. Rather than dwell on that loss, the professor instead had devoted her intellect and efforts toward finding a way to ensure other parents did not have to experience the sorrow she would forever carry with her.

"It's quite all right, Doctor," zh'Thiin said, busying herself for the next moments with pouring tea into the pair of cups. Returning the urn to the stove, she took the cups and offered one to Beverly, who accepted it with thanks.

Bringing the cup to her nose, Beverly inhaled the tea's aroma. "What is it?"

"My own private blend," the professor replied. "I grow the plants in a small garden in my home, using seeds I've acquired from different worlds during my travels. It took some time to find the proper mixture and determine which combinations weren't toxic, to me and my friends as well as the occasional non-Andorian visitor." As though anticipating such a reaction based on any number of past conversations on this topic, she turned to look at Beverly and offered a reassuring smile. "It's perfectly safe for humans, but I won't feel slighted should you choose to inspect your cup with a tricorder."

Chuckling at that, Beverly shook her head. "No need for that." She brought the cup to her lips and took a sip. As sweet as the tea had smelled while brewing, it was not nearly so saccharine to the taste as she had expected. It was, she decided in a single word, exquisite.

Zh'Thiin was directing her to the chair situated on the

right-hand side of the professor's low, curved desk when a soft chime echoed in the room. "Enter," zh'Thiin called out, and the door to her office slid aside to reveal a young Andorian male dressed in a Starfleet uniform. The tunic he wore beneath his black and gray jacket was the blue of the Sciences Division, and the rank pips on his collar identified him as a lieutenant. Beverly was sure he was not a member of the *Enterprise* crew, but he still looked familiar.

"Good afternoon, Professor," the Andorian said, before turning and offering a formal nod to Beverly. "Dr. Crusher, welcome to Andor."

Smiling in reply, Beverly said, "Thank you." Then, recognition finally rescued her. "Of course. You're Lieutenant ch'Thane, from Deep Space Nine."

"That's correct, Doctor," the Andorian replied, "though it has been a few years."

"Indeed it has," Beverly said. Already familiar with the work and research of Professor zh'Thiin's predecessor, the late Dr. sh'Veileth, she had reacquainted herself with the doctor's research materials during the *Enterprise*'s voyage to Andor. Shar, acting in his role as sh'Veileth's assistant, also had compiled volumes of supporting documentation for the research the doctor was conducting, and which zh'Thiin was now continuing. "I think it's wonderful that Starfleet has allowed you to stay on here and continue the research efforts."

"He's been an invaluable assistant to me," zh'Thiin said. "He has a true gift for research, which I have been only too happy to exploit."

Shar cast his eyes downward for a moment before replying, "I felt it was the correct thing to do, given that the Yrythny ova have not proven to be the solution to the troubles plaguing our people."

"Perhaps not," zh'Thiin countered, "but that's what is so wonderful about science. It allows us to revisit ideas and theories and examine them with fresh eyes once new information is added to the mix. Dr. sh'Veileth's work is extraordinary, and despite the setbacks we've experienced, there's still so much to build on."

"We are fortunate to have Professor zh'Thiin on this project," Shar told Beverly. "Her insights have been invaluable. She has gleaned more from Dr. sh'Veileth's research than anyone, and has been able to put those ideas into practice with what so far has been remarkable success." Stepping toward the professor's desk, Shar offered to zh'Thiin a Starfleet-issue padd. "On that matter, I have completed the reports on the patients you saw today. They are ready for transmittal to the Science Institute once you've given your approval."

"Excellent," zh'Thiin said as she took the padd. "I'm sure the Institute is as anxious to see these as I am to provide them."

Beverly had observed the patient examinations conducted by zh'Thiin and Dr. Eluqunil sh'Laenatha, her handpicked obstetrician, earlier in the day. Both *zhen,* who each had suffered a miscarriage a few years earlier, had with their respective bondgroups volunteered to be test subjects for the professor's experiments with the new gene-therapy protocol she had developed. She was pleased to see firsthand the *zhen*'s progress during this, the final months of their respective pregnancies. If zh'Thiin's calculations were correct, the births would occur within days of each other; and both babies were perfectly healthy according to every test and scan conducted by the professor.

"Would it be all right if I received a copy of those reports?" Beverly asked, reaching for the cup of tea she nearly had forgotten atop zh'Thiin's desk. "I almost feel like I know them, at this point." She already had read the professor's notes and case files for both test subjects, and had been updated by zh'Thiin during the journey to Andor from Earth.

Looking up from the padd, the professor nodded. "Of course. Both bondgroups have already authorized the release of this information to you at my request. I'll see to it that a copy is dispatched to you aboard the *Enterprise* when I send it to the Science Institute."

Beverly took another sip of her tea, relishing the taste. "I wouldn't mind if you included the recipe for this tea with that." She set the cup down on the desk again before leaning back in her chair. "How much involvement has the Institute had in your work?"

"Almost none," zh'Thiin replied. "We keep them informed about our progress, and in turn we enjoy a great deal of latitude, though I don't always sense great enthusiasm or support for what we're doing. If anything, I believe they're deliberately keeping a distance between the Institute and our group, mostly because of the political controversy our work has caused, all while trying to avoid the appearance of actually doing that."

"I can certainly see that," Beverly said, "given the mixed public reaction." She had seen reports about protests carried out in the time since Dr. sh'Veileth originally proposed using the Yrythny ova to modify Andorian genes to treat or even cure the issues surrounding conception and pregnancy. The media coverage given to Dr. sh'Veileth's and now Professor zh'Thiin's work was being filtered based on political, scientific, and even religious bias to such a degree that both supporting and dissenting viewpoints of any real merit were being drowned out by extremism on both sides. That much had even been a topic of conversation with both *zhen* during their individual examinations with zh'Thiin. "Speaking of that, what about your patients? Someone has to know why they're coming here."

"They do indeed, Doctor," Shar replied. "We've had to enact security measures to ensure the professor's patients are safe. Their identities are kept secret, and they are brought here from their homes via transporter so as not to attract the attention of protesters outside the compound."

"Not that it matters," zh'Thiin added. "They always seem to know when I'm seeing patients, even if they don't know who those patients might be."

Frowning, Beverly asked, "So they're outside right now?"

"Oh my, yes," zh'Thiin replied. Turning in her seat, she gestured toward the window behind her. "Not many, at least compared to the crowds that gather to protest the parliament and Presider sh'Thalis out by the main gates, but they make up for their lack of numbers with passion."

Beverly rose from her seat and looked through the window, gazing out across the hundred meters or so of courtyard grass, trees, and shrubbery to the perimeter wall surrounding the Parliament Andoria complex. She saw three Andorians, each wearing the uniform of a parliament security officer and spaced at regular intervals along the barrier, watching a small group of Andorians milling about on the public street beyond the wall. They appeared only to be standing and watching; Beverly saw no placards or other signage, nor were any of the onlookers shouting or otherwise trying to attract attention. If it was a protest, it was one of the more peaceful such endeavors the doctor had ever seen.

"They seem harmless enough," she said.

Zh'Thiin nodded. "They usually are, but there have been

occasions where security has had to react to one disturbance or another."

"How long have they been carrying on like this?"

It was Shar who replied. "This group has maintained a regular vigil for the past two months. I don't always see the same people, so they must be organized to operate in shifts. Their numbers fluctuate, though never by more than five or six members. They don't identify themselves as representing the True Heirs or the *Treishya,* but a few of them have expressed support for those groups' causes."

"So," Beverly said, crossing her arms to ward off a sudden chill as she watched the assemblage, "what do you think they're doing?"

Professor zh'Thiin shrugged. "If I was forced to offer a theory? I'd say they were waiting for something to happen."

17

I offended someone in a past life. That's the only explanation.

"This is main engineering," Lieutenant Choudhury said, leading the Andorian diplomatic delegation through the massive shielded double doors and into the expansive workspace that formed the heart of the *Enterprise.* The multi-leveled compartment was awash with activity, with personnel manning workstations or moving from one task to another. "Every onboard system is monitored from here. With the use of configurable as well as direct interfaces to the main computer and its host of subsystems, the chief engineer and his staff have total control over every facet of the ship's operation, maneuverability, and defense."

As she spoke, Choudhury noted the presence of security personnel standing watch at various positions around the room. Though not a normal occurrence, she had suggested the extra precautions for engineering as well as other sensitive areas when Captain Picard informed her of Presider sh'Thalis's desire to tour the ship along with members of her diplomatic cadre. The captain had agreed to Choudhury's request and left the details to her, though he had added the caveat that the enhanced security measures should not feel so conspicuous as to make the visitors feel unwelcome. With that in mind, Choudhury had worked with her team leaders to set up a rotating detail of security teams to those areas of the ship to be included in the tours, opting for enhanced surveillance of the groups while moving from point to point. So far, the plan she had put into place seemed to be working, with the security officers proving to be a visible yet mostly unobtrusive presence.

What it had not done was alleviate Choudhury's boredom.

The tours themselves were largely uneventful. Presider sh'Thalis had been among the first group to come aboard, and had asked all manner of thoughtful questions designed to spark engaging conversations. The topics had ranged from ship operations—with only occasional detours whenever the conversation drifted too close to what Choudhury considered to be sensitive information—to the role of Starfleet in the "new reality" in which the Federation now found itself. Rather than dispense with the notion that Starfleet was needed for anything other than assisting in the reconstruction of worlds devastated by the Borg assault, sh'Thalis had inquired as to Choudhury's interest in returning to the *Enterprise*'s primary mission of exploration. So far as the presider was concerned, that was what the Federation needed in order to begin looking forward again. Rebuilding was important, of course, but so too was seeing to the future. To her own surprise, Choudhury had come away from the tour asking herself the same questions, and thanking sh'Thalis for the stimulating conversation.

It was now two days later, and all Choudhury wanted was to do something—anything—that did not require her to answer the same basic, mundane questions over and over again.

"It's so clean. I would have expected it to be more utilitarian," remarked one of the delegates, a mid-level attaché in Presider sh'Thalis's administration, as Choudhury remembered from the information she had been given about each visitor in this latest group. This was her fifth such tour in the past two days, and names and details were starting to blur together.

"It's important to remember that the computer oversees most of the mundane tasks," Choudhury replied, forcing a smile. "It employs some of the most sophisticated software ever designed, to the point that the ship theoretically could operate itself indefinitely in the event the crew becomes incapacitated for any reason. There are limits to that, of course, such as the service or replacement of physical components. For that, there are passageways and crawl spaces throughout the ship that provide for easy access to the various systems. This section is primarily for monitoring those systems, which includes modulating their performance or rerouting power to those areas that need it the most, such as when the ship sustains damage."

Indicating the cadre of engineers who had volunteered to conduct individual tours of the engineering spaces, Choudhury said to her entourage, "Commander La Forge is not available at the moment, as he's working with Captain Picard on some of the technical aspects for the conference, but he has placed several members of his staff at our disposal. They're happy to guide you through this section, and please feel free to ask them anything you wish."

As the group dispersed, with each of the delegates meeting a member of the engineering crew and allowing themselves to be led to different areas of the chamber, Choudhury realized after a moment that she was not alone. Sensing the presence behind her, she turned to see one of the Andorians regarding her. "May I help you, sir?"

"Starship computer technology has always been quite impressive," the Andorian replied. When Choudhury regarded him with a confused expression, he bowed slightly. "My apologies, Lieutenant. I was once a Starfleet computer systems specialist. Threlas ch'Lhren, formerly of the *U.S.S. Trinculo*, though I suppose you likely already know that."

"Indeed I do, sir," Choudhury replied, smiling to remove any edge from her remark. She and her team had reviewed information on each delegate or other visitor scheduled to board the *Enterprise*, flagging for additional scrutiny those with possible ties to the known activist groups on Andor. Though ch'Lhren's name had not been connected to any such groups, his prior Starfleet service record had caught Choudhury's attention. Grateful for the distraction from inane conversations about cleanliness, she said, "You were a commander, serving aboard the *Trinculo* during the Dominion War as well as the Borg invasion."

Ch'Lhren nodded. "Correct, though it's important to stress that my role during those conflicts was nothing memorable. Despite holding an A6 computer-expert classification, I was often regarded as . . . what is the human expression? A background player?"

"Not to me," Choudhury said. Placing her hand on ch'Lhren's arm, she guided him away from the row of workstations where two *Enterprise* engineers were working and where another was answering questions from one of the Andorian guests. "Computers account for far too much of a starship's operation to dismiss them, much less the people responsible for their care and feeding."

Releasing a small laugh, ch'Lhren said, "An interesting observation, and one I wish others shared. Not that it matters. That part of my life is behind me. Now I serve Presider sh'Thalis and the people of Andor." He paused, casting his gaze downward. "It seemed the appropriate thing to do after all that's happened."

"I can certainly understand that sentiment," Choudhury said, her tone somber. "Several friends of mine, both here aboard the *Enterprise* as well as on other ships and planets, feel the same way. One of my closest friends from the Academy just resigned her commission last month. Her planet was spared from the attacks, but she joined a group of missionaries who've volunteered to assist in reconstruction efforts on Pacifica and a few other worlds." Then there was her former shipmate, Miranda Kadohata, who had requested a transfer from the *Enterprise* in order to take an extended assignment on Pacifica. It was a notion Choudhury also had considered. Though she could of course offer no help to her homeworld of Deneva, the once-vibrant planet now reduced to little more than a scorched, lifeless rock, there still were survivors in need of assistance. Denevan refugees had settled on several planets, including Andor, though until now Choudhury could not bring herself to visit any of the encampments that still were filled with displaced survivors. Despite herself, she had been able to run a thorough check of the camps' population rolls, confirming that no members of her family were living anywhere on the planet.

"And yet," ch'Lhren said after a moment, "you remained in Starfleet."

Choudhury nodded. "At the time, it seemed the most sensible course of action—for me, anyway. I really didn't have any other place to go, and staying in Starfleet felt like the way I could be most useful." For a time, she also knew that remaining aboard the *Enterprise* offered one of the best ways to locate her family, whose final fate remained unknown to her a year after the Borg invasion. As the months passed and any lingering hope of finding her loved ones faded, the *Enterprise*—its crew and its familiar, comfortable environs—had come to be her home; the only home left to her.

"There are many Andorians who feel the Federation failed us during the Borg attacks," ch'Lhren said. "I imagine there are those from other worlds who feel the same way. With Andor, there is hope our planet and our people will one day regain at least some of what we have lost, but others are much less fortunate."

There was a moment of awkward silence, which was filled by the constant, omnipresent hum of the warp core at the center of the room. Despite her best efforts, Choudhury could not force away the images of Deneva's devastated surface. She saw herself standing with Worf on the scarred, desiccated soil once occupied by her family home along with the entire province of Mallarashtra where she had lived as a child. So many warm, happy memories had, along with the town itself, been reduced to ash and scattered upon the winds.

"Starfleet and the Federation did everything it could," she said, the words little more than a whisper. "You know what the Borg were like, what they were capable of. We were outmatched. If not for the Caeliar, we all would have been wiped out." As she spoke, Choudhury reminded herself to maintain her bearings, not to allow her emotions to get the best of her while in the company of the visiting dignitaries.

Frowning, ch'Lhren replied, "I do not disagree with what you are saying, Lieutenant, but consider the point of view of someone living on one of the worlds affected by the disaster. There are those among my people who feel that the Federation gave up on certain planets because it believed they were beyond saving. I would think you of all people would at least be sympathetic to such views."

"Six starships were lost defending my planet," Choudhury countered, now requiring effort to keep her poise. "Twice that many were lost here, along with half as many Klingon vessels. I'm not sure how someone could view that as giving up on Andor."

Ch'Lhren said, "Chaos breeds all manner of perspectives."

Does this guy want me to kick him in the throat?

"I'm sorry, sir," she said, but only after she was certain the words would come out with utmost control and offer no hint to the emotions roiling within her. "I need to check in with my deputy security chief prior to the first of our teams beaming down to the surface."

His expression one of worry, ch'Lhren said, "If I have given offense, please allow me to apologize."

Choudhury shook her head, scrambling to cover her awkward attempt to extricate herself from the troubling conversation. "No, sir. It's nothing like that. I simply lost track of time, and I need to check in. If you'll excuse me, I should only be a few moments."

If ch'Lhren sensed the real reasons for her wanting—or needing—to depart, he chose not to say anything. Instead, he replied, "Of course, Lieutenant. There is much here to hold my interest until you return, but I doubt the discussion will be as engaging."

Offering a demure nod, Choudhury said, "Thank you, sir," before turning and heading for the exit. She forced herself to walk at a casual pace toward the door, all while her mind was screaming at her to run like hell.

Threlas ch'Lhren entered his office, locking the door behind him after it finished cycling closed. The office was a small, windowless affair, lacking the lavish appointments and furnishings that were characteristic of the office space utilized by Presider sh'Thalis, her senior advisory staff, and the magistrates overseeing the various committees. Like the offices of his peers—secondary and tertiary department supervisors—ch'Lhren's office occupied space on the complex's first subterranean level. The only indicator of the passage of time was the small chronometer on the wall above the door. It was not uncommon for him to enter the office before dawn and work until well after dusk, during which time he rarely ventured outside to bask in the sun or even to take in a breath of fresh air.

The arrangement suited ch'Lhren, offering him the privacy he needed from time to time, such as now.

Moving to the small desk that was covered with reports, data-storage cards, and other bureaucratic nonsense about which ch'Lhren could not care less, he settled himself atop the backless chair he preferred to use while working and entered the combination to unlock the desk before reaching to open a drawer to his left. Inside the drawer was a box composed of duranium, the same material used in the construction of starship hulls. Set into the box's top was another combination keypad as well as a biometric lock. After entering the proper combination, ch'Lhren bent over the box, positioning his right eye over the retina scanner. It took an extra moment for the scanner to recognize him and disengage the lock.

Inside the box was a portable computer interface, a commercial model popular both in the government and private sectors. Accompanying the interface was a communications adapter, of a type most definitely not available to the public, the government, or even the military. While his workspace contained its own dedicated computer interface, his use of that device as well as his access to the complex's information sharing network and any communications he logged beyond the confines of the Parliament Andoria would be recorded. That was something ch'Lhren could ill afford at the moment.

It took only a moment for him to set up the interface and connect the communications adapter. Once the unit powered up and completed its self-diagnostic, he activated several software routines designed to mask his presence within the larger data network. The software responded in short order, informing him that his activities were not being monitored by the central computer or any of the security protocols currently active in the network.

That was the easy task, he mused. For someone of ch'Lhren's skill and experience, accessing the complex's computer core and accompanying network—and doing so undetected—was a simple process. All it required was for him to know how the security measures worked, where the vulnerabilities were, and how to navigate through those gaps in the protection schemes without triggering any of the numerous alerts programmed into the system's oversight software. He had discovered the complex network's astounding number of weaknesses within the first weeks of assuming his position within the administration. That his role involved overseeing information security for the entire network was a point of no small amusement, not only for him but also his friends and compatriots. The same skills that ch'Lhren had employed to receive this assignment had aided him on numerous occasions, allowing him to perform all manner of data-manipulation tasks, such as altering his own personnel file to remove any mention of his interest in organizations such as the True Heirs of Andor as well as the group to which he now professed allegiance, the *Treishya*.

Adjusting himself to a more comfortable position on the chair, ch'Lhren entered a series of commands to the computer. "Now we see if our efforts were worth it," he said to no one. Talking to himself was a habit he had acquired as a youth, and later reinforced as a cadet at Starfleet Academy; a means of helping him retain the vast amounts of information he was required to absorb in short periods of time.

The wait for the connection he had initiated from his computer to be completed seemed interminable, a sensation made only worse by his repeated looking to the chronometer above his office door. When the computer emitted a tone indicating success, ch'Lhren smiled in satisfaction as he read the status message on the interface's display, rendered in Andorii text: ACCESS ACQUIRED.

Excellent. Another string of commands resulted in the native Andorian glyphs and other graphics to be replaced with a Starfleet standard primary-interface menu bearing a logotype that read LCARS—Library Computer Access and Retrieval System—along with the platform on which the software was operating: *U.S.S. ENTERPRISE, NCC-1701-E. MAIN ENABLED*. Checking his session status once again, ch'Lhren was pleased to see that his own security software was unable to find any sign that his presence in the starship's computer network had been detected.

It had worked.

Upon first hearing the idea as presented to him by his friend, Lynto sh'Vasath, ch'Lhren had been prepared to dis-

miss the engineer and her outlandish notions without any
further thought. Then he had witnessed sh'Vasath's practical
demonstration of the device she had designed specifically for
the covert infiltration of secure computer networks. Her first
test had been on the systems belonging to the regional government offices in Lor'Vela, the transmissions between her
computer and the device she had planted embedded within
the normal flow of communications traffic throughout the
network. The test had been an unmitigated success, after
which sh'Vasath followed with another such experiment, this
time on the Parliament Andoria network. As before, access
had been obtained with almost no difficulty.

Lynto, your deviousness is unmatched.

Reaching into the box in his drawer, ch'Lhren retrieved
a small octagonal device and held it on the palm of his hand,
studying it appreciatively. Not even so big as one of the smaller
coins still used by merchants in the town square, there was
nothing to identify it or its purpose. The transceiver had been
scratch-built using components obtained from a variety of
sources, and designed with a single task in mind. With the
knowledge that a transceiver in constant operation within a
secure computer network would inevitably be detected, this
model was intended to receive a one-time burst packet of
instructions from a designated contact node, after which it
would load software components into the targeted computer
network. Once that operation was complete, the transceiver
would go dormant.

A twin to the transceiver in ch'Lhren's hand currently
resided beneath a workstation in the *Enterprise*'s engineering section. Having already completed its primary task of
accessing the ship's main computer system, the device had
required only a short interval to finish loading its compressed

software packets into the data directories of a low-priority subsystem, one unlikely to be the target of routine security checks. In this case, ch'Lhren had chosen the files and subroutines belonging to the system's clothing replication processes. Once activated, the software kernels ch'Lhren had deposited would begin a covert infiltration of other systems, slowly inserting new subroutines and other protocols that he could trigger when the time was appropriate. As for the transceiver, its final act prior to deactivating itself would be to wipe its memory, leaving behind no clues as to its origin or purpose. By the time the device was detected by whatever security measures succeeded in finding it, the damage would have been done.

Planting the device was easier than he had anticipated. After two days of conducting their tours, the crew in the engineering spaces had grown complacent with the frequent visitors. Ch'Lhren had observed as much simply from watching them interact with his own tour group. The only true obstacle had been the *Enterprise*'s security chief, Lieutenant Choudhury. Still, the series of questions he had asked her, playing upon the loss of her family at Deneva and designed to unsettle her to the point where she might leave the engineering section, had proved more than effective. It was then a simple matter for ch'Lhren to spend several moments following other members of the crew about the chamber as they answered questions posed to them by the delegates. While inspecting one of the status-and-control workstations, he had surreptitiously placed the transceiver on the underside of the console. Shielded so as not to interfere with any other interface, the device was all but undetectable, short of employing a tricorder with the intention of seeking out such things.

Child's play.

On his interface, the display informed him that the transfer of software components into the *Enterprise* systems was complete. For now, they would continue to work autonomously, lying in wait until they were needed.

When would that be?

Soon, ch'Lhren hoped, and not soon enough.

18

"You'll want to watch your step up here. Sometimes ice can give way due to the constant foot traffic. A slip here would be rather unfortunate."

Picard could not help but smile as he followed Reniel zh'Yemre, his Andorian guide, up the narrow path leading from the plateau that had been designated as a landing site for shuttle transports. It also was where Picard and the security detachment accompanying him had beamed down from the *Enterprise,* forsaking the starship's comfortable environs for the unforgiving climate of this ice-covered mountain range. According to the sensor report he had been given prior to leaving the ship, the captain knew that they were only a short distance from Andor's northern pole.

"That's a long way down," said Lieutenant Rennan Konya from where he followed the trail behind Picard, raising his voice to be heard over the wind.

A single glance to his left was enough for the captain to confirm that both zh'Yemre and Konya were employing the art of understatement to wonderful effect. Less than ten meters from the edge of the winding path, the ground fell away, and from his vantage point Picard could see that nothing but air beckoned to him. In the distance, the ghostly, gray-white silhouettes of distant mountains formed a back-drop for the clouds, which he noted were below his eye level.

Leaning into the wind that drove down from the mountains, he felt a blast of cold air reach the exposed skin of his face and neck. He adjusted the hood of his Starfleet-issue parka, securing a protective flap across his throat. The wind was kicking up the fresh snow that had fallen earlier in the day, necessitating those working at this site to wear goggles. Some of the snow stuck to his parka as well as the matching padded trousers and boots he wore. Flexing his fingers inside his insulated gloves, Picard kept his eyes on the ground in front of him, tracing zh'Yemre's footprints in the thin layer of snow.

"I'm pretty sure this is as cold as I've been in my entire life," said Lieutenant Rachel McClowan, one of the *Enterprise*'s archeology and anthropology officers, who had asked to accompany Picard on this excursion. She was walking behind Picard and to his right, carrying an equipment satchel over her left shoulder and all but entombed within her parka. "And that includes the month I spent on Delta Vega."

"This is actually quite mild for this time of the season," replied Ensign Ereshtarri sh'Anbi, who had taken up position next to McClowan on the captain's right side. Though the young Andorian wore protective clothing like the rest of the away team, she of course showed no signs of being affected by the cold.

Glancing over her shoulder, zh'Yemre added, "You should come back after the solstice. The sunsets are something truly beautiful." Then she smiled. "Of course, that's also the rainy season. You'd probably want to avoid the floods."

"I'm sure I would," McClowan said.

Glancing ahead of zh'Yemre, Picard saw that the trail

curved to the right as it crested a small rise, and even with rock formations obstructing some of his view, he still noted some of the artificial structures comprising the encampment that had been established here. Not quite obscured by the wind was the low hum of what he guessed to be a power generator. They passed a pair of large boulders, and the path widened into a broad, reasonably flat expanse of snow-covered terrain, upon which sat a dozen temporary structures of varying sizes and shapes. The buildings reminded Picard of the Starfleet emergency shelters—uncounted thousands of them—that had been deployed on world after world across the Federation in the aftermath of the Borg invasion. Entire cities had been built using such shelters, with far too many survivors still calling them home as they struggled to rebuild something of what they had lost during the war.

One day, Picard reminded himself. *One day.*

Despite his best efforts to heed Beverly's advice about allowing himself to relax, if only for a short time, the captain nevertheless had been unable to completely divorce himself from his numerous responsibilities. The day had begun with a review of the latest intelligence briefings dispatched to him from Starfleet Command. Concern about the movements of Breen, Tholian, and Tzenkethi vessels in and around the fringes of Federation space continued to stir up concern among Starfleet's senior tactical minds. Attempts to engage Typhon Pact diplomatic representatives had met with resistance despite the ongoing presence on Earth of the one-time Tholian ambassador to the Federation, who now acted as an envoy not only for her own people but also for the Pact's other charter members. According to the most recent communiqué Picard had received from Admiral DeSoto, the situation was growing more tense by the day.

Picard's next act was to visit two of the refugee camps situated outside Lor'Vela. The Andorian government had undertaken commendable effort to make the camps' inhabitants as comfortable as possible, and their continuing initiatives to relocate refugees to permanent accommodations within the new capital city or at other sites around the planet had garnered notice from the state leaders of worlds across the Federation. Despite the progress that had been made, and though the conditions at the camps were far better than similar facilities on other planets still besieged by thousands of survivors, Picard knew that there remained much work to do. His schedule during the past few days had been dominated by meetings, the topics revolving around the current need for personnel and resources to continue the rebuilding efforts, as well as briefings and updates with respect to the conference's ongoing preparations. With all that out of the way, Beverly had advocated a brief rest period, suggesting he take up Presider sh'Thalis's offer to visit this archeological site over which so much fuss had been made.

Following zh'Yemre, they made their way to the center of the compound, around which the buildings were organized in a roughly circular pattern. Picard now saw that several of the buildings actually were constructed from multiple modular components fitted together, no doubt in order to expand the amount of usable interior space. He noted that each structure featured a ground-level entrance that faced inward, toward the "courtyard." On the wall near each door was text printed in native Andorii script, which Picard could not read. As though sensing his minor plight, Ensign sh'Anbi stepped up to stand beside him.

"It looks as though half the buildings are living quarters," she said, "with the other half devoted to equipment and supply storage, an infirmary, a dining facility, and a lab for examining artifacts retrieved from the site."

Hearing the conversation, zh'Yemre turned to face them. "Professor ch'Galoniq has an office in the lab building. It doubles as the command post here at the site." She gestured to indicate the camp. "As you can see, we keep things simple here, endeavoring to limit our footprint to the absolute minimum so as not to disturb the environment too greatly. At some point, we'll have to move the camp to another location, as this area likely will be excavated."

"The find is that big?" McClowan asked, her tone betraying her barely harnessed curiosity. "I'm sorry, it's just that reports we were given about this site were pretty vague."

Zh'Yemre nodded. "And with good reason, I assure you. Until we're ready to share what we've found, we'd prefer not to have too many people making their way up here and disturbing the site. It won't be long before we're ready to share it with everyone." She smiled as she waved again, this time to indicate the surrounding terrain. "If what we've already found is any indication, it's larger than anything we've ever seen." She then smiled. "Of course, if I tell you any more, Professor ch'Galoniq will get upset. When he gets upset, he threatens to throw people off the mountain, and it's already been me three times this trip." Turning, she started walking toward one of the smaller buildings. "His office is this way, Captain."

It took only a moment to reach the structure, and they stepped through the entrance into a small vestibule, which Picard recognized as a sort of airlock, though in this case it was designed to ease the transition from the frigid outdoors to the warmer environs within the building. With the five of them inside and the exterior door shut, zh'Yemre keyed the control to open the inner door, and Picard caught the wave of warm air washing over him. Reaching up, he pushed back his hood and removed his goggles before undoing the parka's fasteners and opening the garment, relishing the change in temperature.

"Very cozy," he commented, allowing himself a small, wry grin.

The room in which he found himself was designed for functionality, with rows of storage nooks along the walls to his left and right. Various items of cold-weather clothing hung on hooks and racks mounted wherever something else did not block wall space. Zh'Yemre indicated nooks to Picard's right. "You can store your gear there for now. The shelter's interior climate is very comfortable."

As Picard and his team were shrugging out of their parkas, the door at the room's far end slid aside, revealing an older Andorian. Though his body was lean, his face seemed to Picard a bit puffy around the mouth and eyes. His white hair, long and unkempt, hung freely past his shoulders. When he smiled, his entire face seemed to be pushed aside by a mouthful of large, gleaming white teeth.

"Captain Picard?" the Andorian asked, stepping forward. "I'm Professor Nisra ch'Galoniq, leader of this expedition. I was informed by Presider sh'Thalis's office to expect you. It's an honor to have you here. Welcome!"

"It's a pleasure to be here, Professor," Picard replied, before introducing the rest of his away team. "I'm told by the presider that you have something rather remarkable to share with us."

As impossible as it might have seemed to the captain, ch'Galoniq's smile grew even wider as he nodded with no small amount of enthusiasm. "Indeed. We've had our share of visitors from various universities and museums around the world." He paused, casting a gaze downward. "Those that survived, of course." Then, as though shaking off the momentary melancholy, he said, "It's created quite a stir among the science community, though we've managed so far to keep it to ourselves and off the newsnets. I imagine we'll have all the attention we can handle once we make our discoveries public."

Stepping forward after storing her cold-weather gear in one of the unused nooks, McClowan adjusted the strap of her utility satchel. "Professor, are you saying this is a classified operation?"

"No, no," ch'Galoniq replied, shaking his head. "Nothing like that. It's just that considering the size of the find, and that we still don't know how big it actually is, we're working to determine the true scope of the site so that we can protect it from the curious." He paused again, adding in a lower voice, "Well intentioned or otherwise."

Picard asked, "You're concerned about profiteers?"

"Exactly," the professor answered, "and not just those native to our planet. I'm well aware of the black markets that have sprung up along the various trade routes through Federation space as well as the nonaligned worlds. Opportunists of every stripe are taking advantage of our current plight. It's shameful."

Picard nodded. According to one of his intelligence briefings, the Typhon Pact was even believed to be behind some of the activities, as well. "People deal with adversity in different ways," he said. "To go from living without want or need to standing in line to receive the very basic necessities for simple survival cannot help but be traumatic."

Still, having read more than a few reports detailing problems such as that hinted at by ch'Galoniq, Picard could sympathize with the professor. Plundering and looting had been a concern, particularly in the days and weeks immediately following the war, as governments at every level on those worlds spared from destruction welcomed hordes of survivors into their embrace, doing what they could to ease the pain and suffering of those who had endured so much. Martial law had been commonplace early on and still was in effect on some planets, and there had been uncounted reports of thefts from private homes and businesses as well as burial places, religious institutions, and even hospitals. No one was immune from such crimes, and though Picard felt that much of this activity was the result of people simply doing what they thought was necessary to survive, he knew that others were motivated by far less honorable agendas. It had taken authorities more than a bit of time to adjust to what should have been a predictable outgrowth of the chaos into which a normally peaceful, ordered society had been thrown.

"I know," ch'Galoniq said, "just as I know that with all the problems we're facing, an archeology field trip seems like a waste of time and resources. But, Presider sh'Thalis not only authorized the expedition, she encouraged us to come here once the initial find was made." He offered another, more reserved smile. "After everything we've been through, it was a welcome change to return to my work." Indicating the door through which he had entered the room, he said, "If you'll follow me to our communications center, I'd like to show you what's had our attention these past months."

With zh'Yemre volunteering to show Konya and sh'Anbi where they could find something warm to drink, Picard and McClowan followed ch'Galoniq out of the locker room, their boots echoing on the metal flooring. Like the chamber, the passageway and the rooms lining it were utilitarian in appearance, with much floor space devoted to crates and other containers of supplies and equipment. Andorians occupied several of the rooms, all of which looked to be laboratories or work spaces of one kind or another.

"You can probably guess that space is at a premium," ch'Galoniq said as they proceeded down the cramped hallway, which was so narrow that they were forced to walk single file. "We thought about erecting a few more buildings, adding more space for berthing and labs, but we decided we could hold out until it was time to move."

"Zh'Yemre mentioned something about that," Picard said. "You believe the area beneath the encampment might be part of the find?"

Ch'Galoniq nodded without looking back over his shoulder. "It appears so. Our preliminary examinations of the areas adjacent to the primary site are very promising."

The corridor turned ninety degrees to the right, terminating abruptly at a closed door. Examining it and the surrounding bulkheads, Picard was able to see that this was a part of the building where two modular components had been connected. Interlocking pins joined to sections of wall were held in place with clamps of a sort he might find in an engineer's emergency conduit-repair kit. For a brief moment and with mild amusement, he wondered what Geordi La Forge—himself a master of improvisation—might think of the skill and ingenuity employed by the expedition's members as they constructed their base camp.

Reaching for the door's locking lever, ch'Galoniq pulled it up before pushing the door inward. "Hello," he called out as he stepped through the portal, with Picard and McClowan following him. "Joshi, I brought guests."

The room beyond the door was stuffed to the point of overflowing with computer equipment, storage containers, and a variety of items Picard could not identify. There barely was enough space for someone to navigate between the five workstations arrayed around the room. Seated at a workstation along the far wall, which itself was positioned before a viewscreen set into the wall in front of him, was another Andorian. Somewhat portly in appearance, he swiveled his chair to face the new arrivals. "What are you talking about, Nisra?"

Ch'Galoniq gestured to Picard and McClowan. "Captain, Lieutenant, allow me to introduce you to Trejoshi th'Sivelrak, one of Andor's leading archeologists. Joshi, this is Captain Picard and Lieutenant McClowan from the *Enterprise*. The lieutenant specializes in archeology, and Captain Picard is something of an aficionado in his own right."

As though grateful to be in the presence of kindred spirits, th'Sivelrak smiled and rose from his chair. "Ah, yes. Now I remember. Nisra mentioned something about a visit from the commander of the Starfleet ship. Welcome, Captain, and to you, Lieutenant."

"Thank you," Picard said, offering an informal nod. "We're delighted to be here."

Chuckling, th'Sivelrak said, "Delighted? I suppose that's an appropriate enough description. As for myself, I have been and continue to be awestruck. It's a wonderful feeling." He punctuated his remarks with another laugh, one loud enough to make the metal walls vibrate.

Picard stepped farther into the room. "Well, my interest has been rather piqued since Presider sh'Thalis invited me up here."

"Yes, yes," ch'Galoniq said. "I think we've kept you in

suspense long enough." Turning, he stepped across the room toward the viewscreen. "Tell me, Captain, what do you know of the Aenar?"

Frowning, Picard glanced to McClowan before replying, "They were a subspecies among your people, very limited in number as I recall."

"Limited is an understatement, sir," McClowan said. "They were believed extinct until the early twenty-second century, when a settlement of just a few thousand was found living in a subterranean complex in the Northern Wastes. They used telepathy to communicate, and they were blind, supposedly as a result of countless generations spent living underground."

Picard nodded. "The Romulans captured a number of Aenar, forcing them to utilize their abilities to remotely pilot unmanned vessels during the Earth-Romulan War."

"That's correct, Captain," ch'Galoniq said. "One of the darker periods in our history, to be sure. So far as we know, the last known remaining Aenar died more than a century ago, and their underground complex was destroyed during the Borg attack, but they leave behind a wondrous legacy we're only now truly beginning to uncover." Turning to the workstation next to th'Sivelrak, he bent over the computer interface there and tapped a series of commands across the rows of controls lining the blue-tinted console. Above him, the viewscreen activated, coalescing into an image of what Picard recognized as a massive dig site. A crater had been excavated through ice, dirt, and rock; and contrasting against the dark, rough edges of the chasm walls were the straight lines, sweeping curves, and sharp angles of artificial structures. Crystal gleamed beneath the rays of sunlight, and while there were obvious signs of damage, Picard's initial assessment was that the condition of the find was remarkably good.

"What is this?" he asked, his voice barely a whisper.

"A city," th'Sivelrak replied. "An Aenar city, buried beneath dozens of meters of ice. There are no records of it. Until a year ago, no one knew about it. A scouting party studying the ruins of L'Uvan, a city north of here that was destroyed by the Borg, found signs of something beneath the ice while passing over this area on its way back to Lor'Vela. Their transport's onboard sensors detected the presence of manufactured metals and structures, and the initial data they collected showed a handful of crystal spires jutting from the ground. So far as we have been able to determine, the Borg weaponry appeared to have caused a series of earthquakes throughout this region, loosening ice and creating a new network of gaps and valleys." He nodded to the viewscreen. "This was beneath one of those valleys."

"This is extraordinary," Picard said, stepping so close to the viewscreen that he imagined he could see the individual pixels working in concert to render the images.

Standing next to him, McClowan asked, "You've dated these structures?"

Ch'Galoniq replied, "Indeed we have, Lieutenant. This area of the find is approximately five thousand years old. Much of what we've found is composed of a type of crystalline composite that was common to known Aenar construction techniques, but on a scale far more massive than anything we've ever encountered, even in previous excavations we've determined to be of Aenar origin. The scientific and historical value of this find is incalculable." After a moment, he asked, "So, I take it you might be interested in examining the site firsthand?"

"Is that a trick question?" McClowan asked.

Unable to resist smiling, Picard turned from the view-screen. "Are all Andorians so gifted with respect to under-statement?" There was no stopping the feelings now stirring within him. The idea of spending any amount of time down there, walking among the ancient structures and whatever artifacts might be there after lying untouched and unseen for millennia, was already galvanizing him in a way he had not felt for years. Only his wedding day and the birth of his son had filled him with greater passion. "Would it be too forward of me to ask when we might leave?"

"I think we can arrange something in short order, Captain," ch'Galoniq said, making no effort to suppress the pride he felt at what he and his team had accomplished here. "We've been wanting to share this with anyone other than ourselves for a while now."

McClowan said, "I have to say, I find this interesting on another level. From what I remember reading about the Aenar, they also were faced with a choice between preserv-ing their species or compromising what many viewed as their cultural identity and integrity. They chose the latter, and we all know how that appears to have turned out."

"And now we have the chance to learn from what they've left behind," Picard replied. "How tragic it would be, after being presented with such an opportunity, for the Andorians to follow the same path."

19

From where he stood on the restricted walkway that snaked just beneath the curved ceiling of the massive subterranean auditorium, Worf surveyed the floor of the cavern with a critical eye. Several members of the *Enterprise*'s security contingent, as well as soldiers from the local Homeworld Security brigade and officers of the city police agencies, intermingled on the Enclave chamber's main floor, conferring in small groups or working on the installation of various equipment. He scrutinized the scene in slow, methodical fashion, searching for flaws, weaknesses, or points of vulnerability that might be exploited. There were several, Worf decided, though none that could not be secured.

"I hate places like this," said Lieutenant Bryan Regnis, who stood to Worf's right on the catwalk. "I stopped counting doors when I ran out of fingers."

Leaning against the railing to the left of the *Enterprise*'s first officer, Lieutenant Choudhury replied, "We'll secure most of them. Just like access to the antechamber on the surface, entering the main hall will be controlled."

Worf nodded, eyeing the cavern's layout. There were numerous entrances, fifteen to be exact, set into the chamber's limestone walls along its ground level, though they did not concern him quite so much as the three levels' worth of private viewing balconies each carved from the rock and positioned along three of the four walls. Each possessed an unfettered view of the raised stage at the front of the hall. Put another way, each balcony offered a direct line of sight to any potential target on the dais.

As though reading his mind, Choudhury said, "Given the number of attendees, sealing off the balconies isn't really an option."

"We could deploy force-field emitters," Regnis said, gesturing toward one set of balconies. "The people sitting in those seats will still have clear views of the stage."

Shifting her position so she could rest her elbows on the catwalk's railing, Choudhury replied, "Want to take bets on how well *that'll* go over? We're talking about government and scientific leaders from all around the world, as well as their counterparts from almost two dozen different planets. You can be sure they'll already be irritated when they see how we're controlling access to and from the chamber. You can count on at least some of them throwing a fit when they find out they have to sit behind a force field just to watch the show."

Regnis shrugged. "But aren't the steps we'd be taking for their safety, too?"

"If you're going to start injecting logic into this discussion," Choudhury said, "I'm chucking you right off this catwalk."

After listening to the banter between the security officers, Worf said, "Mr. Regnis, Lieutenant Choudhury's observations are valid, but you raise a legitimate concern. The balconies present a potential security risk, and yet simple numbers tell us we'll need those seats in order to accommodate all of the conference attendees. Captain Picard's instructions were that our measures must be visible, and yet understated. With respect to the balconies, do you have a suggestion?"

The lieutenant took another moment to study the venue, and Worf noted that he appeared to do so just as he might survey unfamiliar terrain while searching for targets or other threats. Possessing expert ratings with every model of phaser currently used by Starfleet—along with weapons favored by several Federation allies and adversaries—Regnis owned most of the sharp-shooting records at Security School and all of those tracked by the *Enterprise*'s security detachment. Even Captain Picard, himself an accomplished marksman, had tested the lieutenant in an informal match on the ship's firing range. Like all previous challengers, the captain lost that bet, and Regnis had enjoyed a bottle of Chateau Picard, vintage 2347, later that same evening.

After a moment, Regnis pointed toward the balconies. "We deploy the emitters to cover the balconies, but leave them inactive unless a situation calls for us to use them. They can all be controlled from our command post," he said, referring to the base of operations Choudhury had established in a meeting room above the grand hall leading into the Enclave chamber. "We could designate the balconies as VIP seating only—people who were specifically invited and vetted, heads of state and so on—and leave the main floor for the general-public attendees."

Worf turned to Choudhury. "Lieutenant?"

The security chief nodded. "Sounds like a plan. As for force fields, we can also set up a grid that would throw a blanket over the entire building above- and belowground. Obviously we'd only pull that switch if things got totally out of hand, but I think it's a nice card to play should something happen and we want to keep people in or out."

"I'd suggest keeping that card close to the vest, Lieutenant," Regnis said. "In fact, I'd restrict knowledge of force field or other emergency containment measures only to those who absolutely need it to carry out their duties."

"You don't trust our Andorian hosts?" Choudhury asked.

Regnis shrugged. "Not all of them. I mean, we haven't vetted everyone, including everyone from the local Homeland Security brigade or even on the police force."

Worf said, "According to the security briefings we've received, groups like the True Heirs of Andor and the *Treishya* have boasted having members, supporters, and informants within the different levels of government as well as law enforcement and the military." Even for those individuals who passed the stringent screening procedures and background checks being performed on conference attendees, there still was no way to be certain that none of them had ties to one of the groups.

"They already know about the transporter inhibitors," Choudhury said. "There's no way to hide those, or any force-field emitters we deploy inside the building."

Regnis shrugged. "I don't think we can get around that. The best we can do is demonstrate that they—along with the other measures we're putting into place—are intended for emergency use, rather than making the attendees feel like they're entering a prison."

"I agree," Worf replied, nodding in approval. Choudhury and her team had spent two days examining the grounds, and she had devised a comprehensive security plan. A series of transporter inhibitors had already been positioned around the Enclave chamber, as well as in or near key spots within the subterranean structure's three other levels. More of the devices had also been arranged on the lawn surrounding the chamber's exterior and the rest of the parliament compound, and security teams would be stationed at points along the courtyard's perimeter wall.

Choudhury said, "We'll control everything from the command post. We've still got a couple of days before the conference starts. Plenty of time to run a series of drills to test everything."

"Excellent," Worf replied. Indicating for the other officers to follow him, he turned from the railing and strode toward the elevator. "Be sure to coordinate the drills with the brigade commander and the leader of the presider's protection detail." The first officer knew that all three organizations, despite working together to provide security for the event, also had their own distinct procedures for handling such matters, to say nothing of the differences in training and even experience level. Worf wanted to see how those differences came into play once they were set into motion at the same time in response to an emergency or other atypical incident.

"I'm hungry," Choudhury said as the trio entered the elevator, "and I was told by a lieutenant with the Homeworld Security brigade that there's a nice little restaurant just outside the compound. They offer dishes from around the planet, as well as several other Federation worlds." When Worf glanced at her, she added, "I forgot to ask about any Klingon selections on the menu."

"Will they serve Starfleet types?" Regnis asked. "I've heard some of the local merchants are refusing service to anyone in a uniform."

The elevator had begun to descend when a tremor ran through the entire car. All around him, Worf felt the walls rattle, and there was no mistaking the reverberations in the floor plating beneath his feet.

"What the hell was that?" Choudhury asked.

Frowning, Regnis replied, "Power spike?"

Worf reached up to tap his combadge. "Worf to command post. Report."

"Command post. Cruzen here," said the voice of Lieutenant Kirsten Cruzen, another member of Choudhury's security detail. *"We've got a situation on the main level, sir. Some sort of explosive just detonated. We have teams on the way."*

"Location of the explosion?" Worf asked.

"The atrium, sir," Cruzen replied, *"just north of the elevator lobby near the main entrance to the auditorium."*

Regnis said, "Isn't that pretty close to where we're . . ."

The elevator doors parted, and there was time for Worf to detect movement in the passageway beyond before Choudhury's shout of warning echoed inside the car.

"Down!"

Harsh blue energy sliced the air inside the elevator as Worf threw himself against the wall to his right, the beam close enough that he felt his exposed skin tingle. To his left, he saw that Choudhury had shoved Regnis against the opposite wall, with both officers avoiding injury.

"Did you see him?" Regnis asked, pushing past Choudhury and lunging out of the car, phaser already in hand. "He was wearing a police uniform!"

"Lieutenant!" Worf called out, following after Regnis. There was a thin haze of smoke in the corridor, and the first officer noted the telltale odors of scorched metal and burned wood. Members of the *Enterprise* security team as well as Andorians in Homeworld Security and police uniforms were in the curved, high-ceilinged hallway, running in different directions. Ahead of him, Regnis was heading for one of the transparasteel doors leading outside, and Worf caught sight of an Andorian wearing a police officer's uniform and running across the open courtyard.

"Secure the grounds!" Worf shouted over his shoulder toward Choudhury before running for the door. He reached it in seconds, using his left elbow to force it open and out of his way. His other hand had already retrieved his phaser from the holster on his hip. Barely ten meters ahead of him, Regnis had stopped, extending his arm and aiming his phaser. Worf watched as the lieutenant's arm moved to his right, tracking the running Andorian before firing. The weapon spat a pulsing beam of orange energy that crossed the space in the blink of an eye, striking the Andorian in his back and sending him stumbling to the grass.

The *Enterprise* officers ran to where the Andorian lay unconscious on the ground. Worf, a few steps ahead of Regnis, bent over the prone interloper and rolled him onto his back. A quick inspection told the first officer that the Andorian's police uniform appeared to be in order, including the identification card suspended on a lanyard around his neck. Worf reached for the lanyard and pulled, feeling it snap in his fingers. Handing the card to Regnis, he said, "Verify his identity."

"Aye, sir," the lieutenant replied, reaching to his right hip for his tricorder. Looking past him, Worf saw Choudhury and other members of the *Enterprise* security team heading in their direction.

It took only a moment for Regnis to scan the card before he looked up at Worf. "This card's a fake, Commander. A good fake, but not good enough. Neither the name nor his face matches anything we have in our database for any personnel assigned to conference security."

Worf nodded, not at all pleased with the report, as Choudhury and her team approached.

"Are you okay?" she asked.

"Yeah," Regnis replied before shaking his head. "As well as can be expected, I guess."

Indicating the fallen Andorian with her phaser, Choudhury asked, "Who is he?"

"We have no idea," Worf answered, "except that he is an apparent imposter."

"Even if he's a plant," Choudhury said, "that doesn't explain the uniform or how he got on the grounds, to say nothing of the bomb he planted. He had to have help."

After instructing the security officers standing over the Andorian to take him into custody and transport him to the holding area the Homeworld Security team had established, Worf turned back to Choudhury. "What about the bomb? What did you find?"

Shrugging, the lieutenant said, "Not much, really. It wasn't a very large device, and didn't do that much damage. We scanned for residue and were able to find trace amounts of two substances at the point of detonation. By the looks of things, the device was constructed from some form of pretty crude binary explosive, combining two otherwise harmless compounds that are in fact designed to work together in this manner. That's probably how he got it in here in the first place, waiting until he was inside to create the actual explosive."

"It is a common tactic," Worf said, "often used by covert operatives. Klingon intelligence agents have been known to use a compound called *qo'legh*, which is made by blending three inert ingredients." Though he found the use of such weapons to be without honor, Worf had been forced to grudgingly admit that they had their uses. "What was the target?"

Choudhury shook her head. "That's the weird part. The

device was detonated inside a waste-disposal bin. The charge wasn't big enough to cause any real damage, so I can't figure out what he was trying to do."

"He was probing," Regnis said. "Testing our defenses. The Andorian security details have had some problems with this. Remember the report of what happened at the Parliament Andoria complex?"

"You believe he was testing to see if he could get a bomb past security?" Worf asked. "To what end? Now that we know how the bomb was made, we can scan for those substances."

Shaking her head, Choudhury said, "I don't think that's it."

"What do you mean?" Regnis asked. "You think it was just a prank to see what we'd do?" He nodded toward the Andorian. "Seems like a pretty stupid thing to volunteer for, don't you think?"

"Not if he's a member of the T.H.A or the *Treishya*," Choudhury countered, before nodding in the direction of the perimeter and the city that lay beyond it. "Lots of buildings with windows facing this direction. You willing to bet that none of them are watching the grounds and collecting intel on us right now?"

Worf frowned. "That would be a sensible tactic."

"Absolutely," Choudhury said. "I'll bet every credit in my account that this wasn't about a bomb. This was about our response."

"Even if that's true," Regnis replied, "anybody watching us has to know we'll adjust our procedures to account for this kind of thing."

Nodding, Choudhury said, "Yeah, but you're forgetting something." She pointed to the Andorian who was now in the custody of three members of her team. They were leading the alleged imposter to the holding area, where he would wait to be questioned by her or Worf. "Somebody had to let that guy in here. Maybe it's one person, loyal to the True Heirs or whatever, but what if there are more?"

Worf holstered his phaser, feeling his jaw set in determination and his anger beginning to rise as he thought of the blunt betrayal to which they had just been exposed.

"We will simply have to be ready."

20

"You do realize that sitting in such an awkward position for extended periods of time has a detrimental effect on the spinal column."

Looking up from the computer terminal occupying one corner of the crowded desk in her cramped office, Beverly Crusher smiled at the sight of Dr. Tropp standing in her doorway. "I didn't hear you come in," she said, straightening her posture and reclining into her high-backed chair.

"A benefit of being light on one's feet," the Denobulan physician replied as he stepped into the room. "It proves useful when keeping up with the clandestine activities of my offspring. When you're the father of eight of your own children and parent twenty-six more, you exploit every advantage you can find."

"And I thought just one at a time was hard," Beverly said, gesturing toward the guest chair in front of her desk. "How do you do it?"

Settling into the seat, Tropp replied, "I stopped sleeping fifty-six years ago, a practice I never abandoned after my youngest child left home."

"That has a familiar ring to it," Beverly said, reaching for the cup of tea she had summoned from the replicator. Taking a sip, she frowned at how cold the beverage had grown. How long ago had she requested it? "Professor zh'Thiin didn't warn me that this blend sours so quickly once it starts to cool." Rising from her seat, she asked, "Would you like something?"

Tropp shook his head. "No, thank you. I was on my way to eat when I saw you working in your office. You've spent a lot of time here in recent days. That's rather unusual for you."

"Don't worry," Beverly said as she stepped to the replicator set into the bulkhead to the right of her desk. "I don't plan on making it a habit." She preferred to spend the bulk of her duty shifts in the sickbay's patient-treatment or laboratory areas, even if there were no pressing matters requiring her attention. More often than not, she worked from one of the computer stations in the main sickbay, allowing her ease of interaction with patients as well as members of her staff. "It's just that I've been so caught up in Professor zh'Thiin's research." Instructing the replicator to provide a fresh cup of tea, she waited as her original cup and saucer dematerialized and was replaced by a new set, the cup filled with the steaming beverage. She retrieved the tea and brought the cup to her nose, relishing the aroma of the exotic blend. Sighing in contentment, she returned to her desk. "Jean-Luc can have his Earl Grey."

Tropp sat silent for a moment, waiting for her to take her first sip of the tea before saying, "I've only had time to give Professor zh'Thiin's material a cursory review, but some of her theories and conclusions seem rather extraordinary."

Nodding, Beverly set the cup down on its saucer. "I'd say that, given the circumstances, extraordinary is exactly what's required."

"I agree," Tropp said. "I've also been keeping apprised of the political situation on Andor. It's unfortunate that more people don't appear to share your view of the professor's work."

"There's not much we can do about that," Beverly said, leaning back in her chair and gesturing toward her computer terminal. "On the other hand, there doesn't seem to be much I can do with this, either."

Frowning, Tropp asked, "What do you mean?"

"I mean that I'm finally convinced I'm out of my league when it comes to this material," the CMO said. "I've spent the past five days reading through her early research notes—which, by the way, took me most of those five days just to understand. The theory she presented for altering the genetic code in an Andorian gamete is straightforward enough. It's really not all that different from the types of DNA resequencing we use now to correct simple genetic disorders, at least so far as she presents it. However, the unique nature of Andorian physiology, particularly their reproductive systems, does present a host of potential problems we likely wouldn't encounter in other species. Her research even acknowledges many of those issues with respect to any new resequencing protocols."

Tropp said, "You seem reasonably well-informed on the topic. What do you feel you're not understanding?"

Shifting her position so she could lean forward, Beverly rested her left arm atop her desk and reached for the computer terminal, swiveling it on its base so the Denobulan could see its display. "It's where she charts her new protocols that I get lost." She tapped the terminal's manual interface, calling up a computer-generated representation of a dense, multicolored double helix. As the image resolved, it began a slow counter-clockwise rotation, with the computer supplying pointers and blocks of informative text drawn from the medical database. "This is one of the simulations zh'Thiin created to test her theories on inserting new recombinant DNA sequences into a sample of Andorian genetic code." She paused the graphic's rotation, and then pointed to seven different strands spaced at irregular intervals within the helix, each of which highlighted in bright blue in response to her touch. "These are the new sequences, created from a hybrid of Andorian DNA as well as wholly new code intended to fill the gaps left by genetic deficiencies contained within an original gamete after fertilization. All of this is chronicled in great detail in her notes. The problem is that when I look through the rest of her notes, there's a small yet very noticeable gap between the previous set of test sequences and the one she finally developed for use on volunteer patients on Andor."

Leaning forward in order to afford himself a better look at the display, Tropp's eyes narrowed as he regarded the information before him. "I am not a geneticist, but it seems to me as though the gap between the two generations of recombinant DNA is such that establishing a bridge shouldn't prove that difficult."

"That's what I thought, too," Beverly said, tapping her desktop with a fingernail. "I ran some simulations of my own, but the computer wasn't able to fill in the missing link between zh'Thiin's latest recombinant DNA sequencing and what her notes say is its predecessor."

"Inspiration born of desperation?" Tropp smiled, the corners of his mouth stretching so that his speckled cheeks rose almost to touch his temples. "Some accidental by-product of an otherwise failed experiment she was conducting? Stranger things have happened in the course of history, particularly in the fields of science and medicine."

Beverly shrugged. "Maybe, but wouldn't you think she'd want to document that? I mean, we're talking about pulling an entire civilization back from the brink of extinction, if what she's developed ends up working." She gestured again to her computer. "Based on the reports I've read detailing the progress of her test subjects, the babies developed from gametes modified with her new resequencing protocols are going to come to term with no detectable defects. The mortality rate of fetuses enhanced with previous versions of test recombinant DNA sequences she developed was only marginally better than those created using genetic code derived from the Yrythny ova. Such a leap forward is incredible."

"Are you suggesting that Professor zh'Thiin is employing an untested medical procedure?" Tropp asked, his expression turning to one of concern.

Frowning, Beverly replied, "I don't think it's that simple. I have no doubt that she has the well-being of her patients as her top priority, and there's no denying the effort she's expended postulating, documenting, and testing her theories, both before and after she arrived at this specific sequencing protocol. There's just this one gap that troubles me. Considering the detail she's paid to her research notes, it seems very odd to be lacking in this one particular area."

"It could be a simple case of overprotectiveness," Tropp said. "The current political climate on Andor isn't anywhere near being completely supportive of her work or even that of her predecessor. Perhaps she's worried about further angering a populace that's already polarized by what many see as a dilution of the Andorian species. Widespread protests might persuade the government or even the Science Institute to order her to stop what she's doing."

Beverly nodded. "I'd considered that, myself. A lot of what alienated people to Dr. sh'Veileth's early theories was her focus on only requiring two sexes in order to complete the reproductive cycle, which presumably would replace the current four-gender paradigm. Professor zh'Thiin's method should be getting far more support, because it's compatible with existing Andorian physiology." She shrugged. "Still, it's possible zh'Thiin is worried that she's somehow strayed too far from the notions of simple genetic resequencing and instead embraced methodologies too reminiscent of what eventually spawned the Eugenics Wars on Earth, or even what happened to the Klingons two hundred years ago."

"Of course," Tropp said, unable to suppress a wry grin, "what happened to the Klingons was an outgrowth of human experiments in augmenting human genetics. Considering what it endured, it's no wonder the Klingon Empire took so long to warm to humanity."

"Fair point," Beverly conceded, smiling.

Pointing to the computer screen, Tropp said, "As for whether she might be harboring concern about her work running afoul of Federation edicts with respect to eugenics, it's worth noting that she was given access to all available information on the subject, including any surviving records from the project that spawned the Eugenics Wars as well as later research conducted by Arik Soong and even the work he did that eventually was used by the Klingons. Though she was given strict parameters in which to work, she also enjoyed unprecedented freedom in this arena."

"But was that enough?" Beverly asked. "I mean, what if she exhausted all of that information while searching for a viable Andorian regimen, and found nothing? What would be her next step?"

Tropp shrugged. "I suppose she might seek out other parties with experience in advanced genetic manipulation. My people, for example. It's common knowledge that Denobulans employed genetic engineering for several generations to treat many diseases and other disorders, while managing to avoid most of the societal and political problems experienced by other cultures." After a moment, he added, "So long as she violates no actual laws or regulations, seeking out such counsel is hardly illegal, or even unethical, unless she somehow neglects to credit any assistance provided to her by other parties when publishing her findings for formal review." He paused, his features clouded in suspicion. "Is there some reason you've not approached Professor zh'Thiin with your concerns?"

"Because I just don't have enough information," Beverly replied as she reached up to rub the bridge of her nose, "and I don't want to come off as though I'm accusing her of wrongdoing. Right now, we're only talking about a puzzle that's missing a piece, no matter how large or important that piece might be. I need more data, and then I'll figure out what to do next."

"And what if the information you seek gives you even greater cause for worry?" Tropp asked, his tone gentle yet pointed, as it always was whenever he adopted the demeanor of the accomplished parent and mentor that he was.

Beverly sighed, having no immediate answer for that.

21

His attention divided between the tricorder in his hand and the massive control console dominating the forward wall of the operations center, La Forge watched as the station's array of status gauges and indicators slowed from their initial chaotic frenzy and settled into patterns and readings more in line with what he wanted to see. The console's fifteen computer monitors, positioned on the wall at or above eye level, displayed various combinations of graphics and Andorii text, most of which he could not decipher. To assist him with the translation, he had attached a portable computer interface to the workstation, which now relayed to him in Federation Standard summarized versions of the information on the computer screens.

"From what I can see," he said after a moment, "everything's working just fine now."

"Indeed it is," replied Kilamji ch'Perine, the power plant's main operations manager. The burly Andorian was standing next to him at the control console, his gaze directed at the various indicators. "You and your people are most impressive, Commander La Forge."

Smiling as he closed his tricorder and returned the device to the holster on his right hip, La Forge said, "Your team did the hard part. We just pitched in a bit to help with the settling-in adjustments." There had been more to it than that, of course, but he saw no need to nitpick over such details, particularly in light of the work the Andorian team of engineers had accomplished despite the obstacles before them.

Beyond the walls of the operations center, La Forge could hear the constant, steady hum of enormous storage cells, twenty-six of them, as they worked to draw current channeled to them from the expansive field of solar-energy collectors surrounding the main facility. His ocular implants picked up residual heat on the walls, cast off by the massive cells as they harnessed the energy they were provided. Once the proper commands were issued from the operations center, the cells would begin redistributing that amassed energy along transmission lines to more than three dozen small villages and other provinces located within a five-hundred-kilometer radius of this facility. For the first time in more than a year, those population centers would no longer need to rely upon portable generators and whatever meager supplies of energy could be redirected from other power plants in the western region of the Ka'Thela continent that had survived the Borg attack.

"Given what you had to work with," La Forge said, "this place is really something." He pointed to the control console and the technical schematic of the facility. The image depicted the field of solar collectors, arrayed in an expanding circle with the plant itself at its center. "I've seen schematics for something like it a few times, but never the real thing. It's impressive, Kilamji." Another engineering feat involved the decision behind the facility's location. Constructed atop a massive artificial foundation, the entire structure was elevated fifteen meters above the surrounding terrain. As such, it was protected from the dangerous floods caused by the unpredictable torrential rainfall to which this region was subjected during warmer seasons.

Ch'Perine nodded, though La Forge sensed the Andorian was uncomfortable with the praise. "I did not devise the idea. That credit belongs to one of our younger engineers, Vayith zh'Belegav. It took her some time to convince those of us who—according to her—were more than a bit closed-minded when we began researching how to rebuild this facility. We had intended to simply repair the existing infrastructure and return to producing energy via the *noprila*-fired plants, but Vayith insisted that this new method could provide more power without the need to reestablish the mining and transporting of the raw *noprila* materials here for processing."

"Yeah," La Forge said, remembering what he had read about the *noprila* mineral, similar in many respects to the coal used for energy production on Earth for centuries. "Not the cleanest stuff to be working with, I imagine."

"Indeed," ch'Perine replied, smiling. "Vayith also went to great lengths to argue that the elimination of waste products created by the *noprila* would, over time, be beneficial to the environment. There was no arguing that point, and it was enough for the government to grant us the funds and resources needed to rebuild the plant to collect and distribute solar energy." Nodding toward the technical schematic, he added, "According to the specifications, once this plant is running at full capacity, it will be able to generate and distribute more than double its prior output."

"Well," La Forge said, tapping the console with the palm of his right hand, "the specs were right. You and your team can be proud of the work you've done here. The big question now is what do you plan to do with all the excess energy you'll be generating?"

By way of reply, ch'Perine leaned over the console and tapped a series of commands into one of its manual-input interface stations, with keys and other controls laid out in a circular pattern. When he finished, he pressed the larger key at the station's center, and in response to his commands one of the screens changed its image to depict a map of what La Forge recognized as the Ka'Thela continent. Along the map's southern boundary, several areas had been indicated by pulsing blue dots, which the engineer knew represented those villages that soon would be drawing energy transmitted from the plant. Another series of dots, these a faded, static green, also appeared on the map, farther inland than the locations currently serviced by this facility.

"Work is continuing on other plants that normally provide power to these regions I've highlighted," ch'Perine said, pointing to the map. "Several of those plants were completely destroyed during the invasion, to the point that rebuilding them is considered a waste of time and resources. Those plants that survived intact or, like this one, only suffered repairable damage are being converted to the new solar model. Once we resolve the remaining issues with this facility, the lessons we learn here will be used to finalize work on the other plants." Turning from the console, the Andorian looked once more to La Forge. "The power-conversion modules you installed were the key. So, you see, Commander, your team's efforts will have a lasting impact on the work we're trying to do here."

Nodding in satisfaction, La Forge said, "And that, sir, is all the thanks I need." In point of fact, the team of Andorian engineers—dozens of dedicated individuals supported by a crew of more than two hundred construction workers and technicians representing myriad fields of expertise—had spent the better part of a year repairing the facility as well as designing and building the enhancements needed to facilitate the transition to producing solar energy. Simply constructing the farm of collectors had taken months, and that was with the assistance of Starfleet replicators used to create the components necessary to build the mammoth energy-collection units and their accompanying storage cells.

La Forge's team of *Enterprise* engineers had been brought in to help resolve issues that had sprung up during the final phase of the project—being the upgrade of the transmission lines sending energy from the collectors to the plant and then redistributing that power outward to the receiving population centers. What had seemed like a straightforward idea during the design stage had become more complex when it became apparent that the equipment used to govern the flow of power into and out of the complex was inadequate for the task of regulating the new, greater demands now placed upon it. The existing equipment had overloaded on each occasion it was tested, necessitating the deactivation of the entire collection process until the issue could be resolved. After an inspection of the facility by teams from the *Enterprise,* Ensign Granados had suggested the installation of dynamic mode conversion modules—specifically of the type used aboard Starfleet vessels when there was a need to interface with the often-incompatible power systems of another ship—to help with upgrading the power flow. According to her, it was a trick she had learned from her grandfather while working to install a "wind farm" energy-collection system on her family's ranch on Ophiucus III. While perhaps not the most glamorous means of solving the problem, the tactic had worked here, as well, and the flow of energy into and out of the facility was now well within operational specifications, with none of the spikes and ebbs experienced prior to the *Enterprise*'s arrival.

Further, the converters were easily replicated, requiring no special or hard-to-obtain materials.

Sometimes, La Forge mused, *the simplest solutions are the best ones.*

Turning back to the master control console, he said, "Well, I think we're done here." He reached for the portable computer interface he had brought with him and ended its link session with the console and—by extension—the facility's own network. He was in the process of disconnecting the unit for return to its carrying case when the console emitted a melodic sequence of tones, followed by a voice.

"Operations, this is Security Station One. We have a situation here."

Ch'Perine reached for a row of controls near the center of the workstation and pressed a large yellow key. "Operations. This is Supervisor ch'Perine. Report."

The voice being filtered through the communications circuit replied, *"Three ground vehicles have just arrived, Supervisor. They parked fifty meters from the main entrance, and their passengers have begun gathering just outside the security perimeter. So far, we count twenty-four individuals."*

Before ch'Perine could respond, another voice—this one female—said, *"Operations, this is Security Station Three. We have the same thing here. Approximately twenty persons have just arrived in four small ground vehicles. They're shouting at us, but we can't understand what they are saying."* Within moments, three more security stations reported in, offering similar accounts of groups massing near their respective entrances to the facility.

"There are five main gates, right?" La Forge asked.

Ch'Perine nodded. "That is correct. The gates and the protective perimeter are designed to inflict a mild stun to anyone who comes into contact with them from the outside. They will be rendered unconscious for several moments; long enough for one of our security teams to take them into custody." As he spoke, he entered new commands to the stations overseeing one of the entrances.

Pointing to one of the screens, La Forge asked, "Are there any other ways into the plant?"

"Yes," ch'Perine said. "We have a network of service tunnels underneath the grounds, but all entrances from the surface have been secured, and are equipped with their own intrusion countermeasures." He leaned once more over the console, tapping the computer interface and calling up a new set of technical diagrams. On one of the screens, La Forge recognized a map of the facility, and ch'Perine pointed to it. "According to this, all entrances to the plant are secure."

As they watched, the map dissolved into a maelstrom of static before the image faded altogether, leaving behind a dark screen.

"I don't like the looks of that," La Forge said. "Can your security measures be overridden?"

"Only by someone with access to our computer network," ch'Perine replied, "but it's encrypted and requires specific authorization and decryption keys."

La Forge nodded toward the console. "Somebody's got it. Can you lock out any other point of access to the system from here?"

"Yes," ch'Perine said. "I can do that now."

As the Andorian worked, an alarm sounded in the operations center, followed by a male voice speaking in a droll, monotonous cadence. *"Attention. Unauthorized computer system access, high clearance memory. Intrusion countermeasures activated. Terminate control mode. Activate matrix storage."*

"What is that?" La Forge asked.

His hands playing over different sections of the console, ch'Perine replied, "The system has activated an emergency core dump to secondary off-site storage. That's standard procedure in the event of a system breach, prior to a complete shutdown and the transfer of all system-control protocols to the backup operations center." He stopped as the image on another monitor changed. "Commander, look."

La Forge felt his stomach lurch as he watched status indicators on the main control board shift from blue to harsh crimson. Energy levels were beginning to rise, and warning gauges were flashing alert messages.

"It's an overload in progress," ch'Perine said. "Someone has severed the power-distribution network and deactivated the balancing and regulator protocols. The temperature inside the storage cells is rising. If this is allowed to continue, the result will be catastrophic." He pointed to another status monitor. "We have less than three minutes now. Once it reaches critical levels, the process can't be reversed."

Stepping closer to the console, La Forge studied the banks of controls, indicators, and monitors. "Can't we stop it?"

"Not in the time available," ch'Perine replied, before releasing a hiss of frustration between gritted teeth. "The emergency discharge circuits are off-line. They've been locked out! I do not understand how that's even possible. Someone on the outside should *not* be able to access our system, let alone do *this*."

La Forge grunted. "My bet is that they had help from someone on the inside." He was about to suggest possible courses of action when his combadge beeped.

"Granados to Commander La Forge!"

"La Forge here," the engineer replied, hearing the anxious tone in the ensign's voice.

Static crackled through the communications frequency before Granados said, *"Sir, are you seeing this overload? We're reading it on the control monitors here."*

As if to accentuate the point, the computer system chose that moment to announce, *"Attention. System overload in progress. Evacuate the facility immediately. This is not a drill."*

"We know!" La Forge shouted. "Granados, where are you now? Is the rest of the team with you?"

Granados replied, *"Affirmative sir. We're in the secondary control room on level two. All hands accounted for."*

"Okay, sit tight, I'm calling for evac," the engineer said before tapping his communicator again. "La Forge to *Enterprise!* Lock on to everyone in this facility and prepare to beam them out of here on my command."

"Commander," replied another voice, this one belonging to Worf, *"coordinates have been relayed to transporter control. What is your situation?"*

Moving around ch'Perine to examine another bank of status indicators, La Forge replied, "Somebody's accessed the power plant's main computer system and started an overload. We've got about two minutes before the whole place goes up. Get somebody on tracking the source of the breach!" To ch'Perine, he said, "Kilamji, we need to go. *Now!*"

From his combadge, Worf's voice said, *"Coordinates plotted, Commander. We are ready to transport on your order. According to our scans, detonation will occur in approximately one hundred seconds."*

The Andorian uttered a cry of rage before slamming both fists on the console. "There's nothing I can do!"

"Then we're out of here," La Forge said. *"Enterprise,* beam us up!" He was aware of the column of energy coalescing around him and the tingle washing over his body, which was over almost as soon as it began. Then the operations center was gone, replaced by one of the *Enterprise* transporter rooms. Behind the transporter console, Lieutenant Attico stared back at him with wide eyes and a nervous expression.

"Check with the other transporter rooms," La Forge said as he stepped down from the pad. "Is everyone out of there?"

Looking down at one of the console's displays, Attico nodded. "Yes, Commander. Our people are accounted for, and the rest of the Andorian factory workers are coming up now."

"La Forge to bridge," the engineer said, his voice command automatically activating the ship's internal communications system. "Worf, are you monitoring the power plant?"

"Affirmative," the first officer replied. *"The overload is continuing to build. Estimated time to detonation is . . . standing by."*

Stand by? What the hell is he talking about? "Worf," La Forge said, confused. "What's going on?"

Several seconds passed before the Klingon replied, *"Commander, the overload has been aborted. According to our scans, the power plant's energy levels are lowering, with the excess being discharged through emergency circuits."*

"That's impossible!" ch'Perine snapped, and La Forge turned to see him stepping off the transporter pad. "Those systems were locked out!"

"He's right, Worf," La Forge said. "Those circuits were deactivated by whoever accessed the system and started the overload."

The first officer said, *"We have no explanation. From what we can tell . . ."* There was another pause before Worf added, *"Commander, we're receiving a message from someone claiming to speak for the* Treishya. *The source of the signal is being masked."*

"What?" La Forge could hardly believe what he was hearing. "Worf, what are they saying?"

"*Stand by,*" Worf replied. "*We're routing the transmission to you.*"

A tone sounded over the link before a new voice said, "*We are the* Treishya, *the guardians of Andor, assuming that sacred trust on behalf of a government unwilling to do all that is necessary to protect our people and their identity. For too long we have allowed ourselves to be led by those weaker than us, who do not share the same values we hold dear, and who choose of their own volition to insert themselves into matters which are not their concern and which they can never understand. Outworlders, our message to you is simple: We do not want you here. Leave us, and do not return. If you choose to stay, then you do so as uninvited and unwelcome intruders.*"

"Are they serious?" La Forge asked, staring in disbelief at ch'Perine.

"*We did not ask for your assistance,*" the voice continued, "*and we will survive without it. Further, the* Treishya *calls on the children of this world to impede the efforts of any outworlder to further defile our planet, through any passive or active means at their disposal.*"

After a moment, Worf's voice returned. "*That's the entire message. We're attempting to trace the source of it, as well as the power plant's computer-system breach, but we aren't having much success. I am contacting Captain Picard, along with all* Enterprise *and Starfleet personnel, to be on the alert.*"

"The captain's down there?" La Forge asked.

There was yet another pause before Worf replied, and when he did, the engineer heard the tension in his friend's voice.

"*Yes.*"

22

Columns of ice, hundreds of meters in diameter and spaced as far apart, rose from the depths of the cavern to tower high overhead. His eyes tracing the ascent of the mammoth pillars, Picard studied how they expanded as they melded with the curved ceiling far above him, wondering if the vast chamber was a natural formation or the result of deliberate action at some unknown point in Andor's mysterious, unrecorded history.

"This is simply incredible," he said, his voice but a whisper that still seemed to echo off the surrounding ice. Standing on a ledge carved out of the wall leading down from the cavern's entrance, Picard enjoyed an unobstructed view of the portion of the underground city that had so far been excavated. He had been anticipating this moment since seeing those first images on Professor ch'Galoniq's monitor back at the base camp, but even the quality and beauty of those pictures paled in comparison to standing here, beholding the subterranean Aenar city with his own eyes.

Standing next to him, Lieutenant McClowan replied, "Forgive me for going with the obvious turn of phrase, sir, but what you see here is quite literally the tip of the iceberg."

"The lieutenant is right," said ch'Galoniq, standing to

Picard's left. "According to the sensor data we've collected, more than ninety percent of the city is still buried. We've tunneled into different areas of the cavern, and everything we've found so far is perfectly preserved within the ice."

Picard nodded in amazement as he beheld the sight before him. By his estimate, the cavern's concave ceiling was perhaps a hundred meters above the floor. Rising out of that floor and encircling each of the more than two dozen columns scattered throughout the chamber were structures created via artificial means. "I've seen images of the Aenar city discovered in the Northern Wastes in the early twenty-second century, and there are obvious similarities in design." To his practiced eye, however, the city before him lacked much of the artistic flair that had characterized the wondrous subterranean metropolis believed to have been home to the last surviving members of the Aenar race.

"We're currently operating under the theory that the Aenar had not always been blind," ch'Galoniq said, "but rather their apparent genetic disposition toward blindness occurred as a consequence of generations spent living underground." He gestured toward the city. "How might someone who could not see create something of such beauty? By our best estimates, this find predates that city by almost one thousand years. Definitely preindustrial by any standard measure, but as you can see, that did not appear to be a hindrance. Most of what we've found suggests the builders here were working with more conventional materials, rather than the composites that comprised much of the structures to the north." He pointed to one of the closer columns and the massive edifice encircling much of it. "Foundations and other support structures are embedded deep into the spires, anchoring the surrounding construction, which actually accounts for perhaps forty percent of the building's total habitable space. The rest is carved into the column itself."

Picard tried to envision the interior of the artificial construct, drawing on what he knew of ancient as well as modern Andorian architectural techniques. "It's a fascinating parallel to Vulcan engineering," he said, "substituting ice for rock to achieve similar results."

Chuckling, ch'Galoniq offered a wide, tooth-filled smile. "And considering the rather tumultuous history my people share with Vulcans, you can just imagine how such comparisons might trouble some of the more disagreeable members of Andorian society."

"Indeed," Picard replied, nodding in understanding and unable to suppress a small grin. Vulcan and Andor, Earth's long-standing interstellar allies, had spent centuries embroiled in bitter conflict. With Earth's help, they had set aside their differences in order to join humanity as part of the original Coalition, which had ultimately evolved into the United Federation of Planets. Still, Picard held no illusions that segments of each society still retained some form of animosity toward the other.

"It looks almost as if it could be inhabited," McClowan said, shaking her head in wonder.

Ch'Galoniq replied, "The quality of preservation is astounding, even for this region. Other finds we've made this far north usually have suffered damage from cave-ins, seismic or volcanic events, and so on. This site, however, appears to have been spared those sorts of misfortunes, which is ironic, of course. If not for the Borg attack, it might have been years before we discovered this on our own. I suppose on that count, we actually owe the Borg a debt of gratitude."

A number of responses flashed in Picard's mind, but the

captain chose against offering any of them aloud. Instead, he asked, "Have you been able to find any indications as to what might've happened here? Where the population might have gone?"

The professor shook his head. "Nothing as yet. There's still much of the city to explore, so perhaps there are clues yet to be found. We've dispatched messages and other information to the Science Institute, requesting research into the historical archives, but so far we have received no reply." He shook his head, casting his gaze to the snow and ice at his feet. "There is much that remains unknown about the Aenar, even after all this time, and so much we likely will *never* know."

"And yet," Picard said, "still so much to learn. I envy you, Professor. Not only is this a remarkable find, but it's also a window into a period of your world's history that's remained closed for far too long. Rather than dwell on what you likely won't find, I wish you the best of luck with the discoveries you surely will make here."

Smiling, ch'Galoniq nodded. "Thank you, Captain. Sometimes, it's easy to forget the rewards my work can bring me, if I would only allow it."

Interesting choice of words, Picard mused. He had spent a significant portion of the past year pondering his current duties and wondering if he might be better suited either to take some other assignment or simply retire altogether. From his talks with Beverly, either at the start or conclusion of what more often than not had been very long days, he knew that he likely had failed to take away the proper level of appreciation for what he and his crew had accomplished as worlds across the Federation continued their rebuilding efforts. Though he might desire to spend his time and efforts on other pursuits, he knew that for the time being, he was where he needed to

be. There remained much to do, but there also was much to
be proud of, and with Professor ch'Galoniq's innocent comment, Picard realized he should probably remind himself of
such things from time to time.

"I don't suppose I could convince you to extend your stay,
Captain?" the professor asked him. "Though the odds of dis-
covering anything of note today are remote at best, one never
knows what tomorrow might bring."

Picard shook his head, forming a response, when his
communicator badge chirped.

"*Enterprise to Captain Picard,*" said the voice of Commander Worf, and there was no mistaking the tension lacing
even those few words from the first officer.

Frowning, the captain reached up to tap the badge where
it was affixed to a patch on his Starfleet-issue parka. "Picard
here. Go ahead, Number One."

"*Captain, there has been an incident with one of our away
teams,*" Worf replied. "*Commander La Forge and his engineering detail were attacked while working at a power-generation
facility. Members of the* Treishya *have claimed responsibility for
the action, during which they at least threatened to destroy the
facility. We were forced to evacuate the team and all planet personnel to the ship.*"

Startled by this news, Picard asked, "Was anyone hurt?"

"*No, sir. The facility appears to have been the primary target, though mostly as a means of forcing an evacuation. However, they broadcast a message stating their intentions to interfere
with the activities of any non-Andorian civilians or Starfleet
personnel. I have already issued orders for all* Enterprise *personnel to return to the ship, and I—*" An audible snapping sound
belched from the combadge.

"Mr. Worf?" Picard called out before tapping the combadge once more. "Picard to *Enterprise*." When no one answered, the captain repeated the attempt and achieved the same result. Turning to ch'Galoniq, he asked, "Professor, are you employing any equipment that might interfere with communications?"

The Andorian shook his head. "None of our equipment should have any effect like that."

A feeling of unease beginning to grip him, Picard turned toward the passageway leading back to the surface. "Something's not right here," he said. "Let's go."

They were nearly to the tunnel opening, the bright blue sky of late afternoon beaming through the aperture and reflecting off the ice, when Picard heard the distinctive sounds of energy weapons exchanging fire: Starfleet phasers and Andorian disruptors. Gesturing for the trio to halt their advance, the captain reached into a pocket of his parka and extracted his own phaser, verifying that it was set to stun. A glance over his shoulder told him that McClowan was mimicking his movements.

"What's going on?" ch'Galoniq asked, his light blue complexion paling in worry. "We're under attack?"

Picard nodded, splitting his attention between the Andorian and the weapons fire being exchanged somewhere outside the tunnel. "It would seem so, Professor." He considered what Worf had managed to tell him before their communication was interrupted. "If the information my first officer received is correct, the *Treishya* is launching an active campaign against any non-Andorians."

"That's outrageous!" ch'Galoniq said, all but spitting out the words. "They have no right to interfere with your peaceful efforts to help us, particularly if we've *asked* for your assistance!"

Standing behind him, McClowan replied, "The *Treishya* see it differently, Professor."

For his part, Picard was irritated with himself. After the earlier disruption experienced by Worf, Lieutenant Choudhury, and her security team at the conference site, should something like this escalation have been foreseen? Perhaps, he granted, but that concession was of little help at the moment.

The sound of someone shouting carried down the passageway just before a shadow moved across the mouth of the tunnel. Picard turned toward it, extending his arm and aiming his phaser just as a figure stepped into view less than ten meters away. He recognized the white hair and antennae of an Andorian at the same time as he registered the disruptor rifle the new arrival brandished. The intruder saw him, too, and started bringing up the muzzle of his weapon as soon as his eyes locked with Picard's.

The captain fired first.

Hot orange energy belched from his phaser, striking the Andorian in the chest and sending him tumbling to the ground outside the tunnel. There was an instantaneous reaction from somewhere outside, and Picard heard several voices shouting out in alarm. "Let's go," he said, gesturing with his free hand to turn and head back down the passage.

"Where are we going?" asked ch'Galoniq, his tone one of protest though he allowed McClowan to guide him by the arm.

Holding his position as McClowan and the burly Andorian began jogging back the way they had come, Picard replied, "Whoever it is, they know we're in here. We need cover." Another shadow darkened the tunnel opening, and Picard saw another Andorian, dressed like the first intruder in a dark brown leather shirt and leggings. He also wielded a disruptor rifle, which he fired down the passage without truly aiming. Picard threw himself against the wall to his left as blue energy struck the ceiling. Chunks of ice tumbled to the floor and the captain raised his free arm to protect his head as he returned fire. This Andorian had better reflexes than his compatriot and avoided being hit, ducking out of view.

Picard spared a quick glance over his shoulder to see McClowan and ch'Galoniq had cleared the tunnel. Turning his attention back to the tunnel opening, muscles tensing in anticipation, he dropped to one knee, crouching close to the floor. He was ready when the Andorian emerged from cover on the opposite side of the aperture, doing his best to catch the captain off guard. From this distance, Picard was able to adjust his aim and fire before his opponent could target him, and when he fired this time the phaser burst caught the Andorian in the left shoulder, spinning him up and away from the tunnel entrance.

Not waiting for anyone else to follow, Picard scrambled to his feet and sprinted back down the tunnel. He sensed someone at his back as he emerged into the larger chamber and dove to his right, out of the line of fire—just before another disruptor burst sliced the air where he had been. Phaser fire from his left echoed in the cave, and Picard rolled onto his side in time to see McClowan kneeling against the opposite wall, aiming her weapon up the tunnel. Behind her, ch'Galoniq plugged his ears with his fingers as the lieutenant fired twice more in rapid succession before looking across to Picard.

"There're at least three of them up at the entrance," she said, then ducked back against the wall as a storm of disruptor energy howled down the passage. "I think they're pretty mad at us, sir. Why hasn't the *Enterprise* tried to beam us up yet?"

Checking the power setting on his phaser, Picard replied, "Whoever cut off our communications must be using some kind of jamming field to prevent the ship's sensors from locking onto us." This, of course, begged the question: If this was the *Treishya,* how were they being supported? Who was providing the logistical assistance? Someone in the Andorian government or military? It was a sobering thought, Picard decided.

Another disruptor blast chewed into the tunnel wall near Picard's head, spraying him with icy shrapnel. One large chunk of debris caught him in the shoulder, and though his parka absorbed much of the impact it was still enough to knock the captain off balance. His knee gave way from beneath him and he dropped to the ground in a disjointed heap. It was not until he tried to roll back onto his feet that he realized he had lost his grip on his phaser, the weapon skipping across the ice, well out of reach.

"Captain!" McClowan shouted, rising from her crouch as though preparing to move toward him.

Picard waved her off. "Stay there. Protect the professor!" The echoes of weapons fire and heavy footsteps clamoring down the tunnel were growing louder with every heartbeat, and he turned to look for his phaser just as McClowan fired again. There was no way to reach the weapon before their attackers were on them, he realized. At the same instant he heard another disruptor burst echoing in the passageway, followed by a grunt of pain and surprise from McClowan. Turning, Picard saw the lieutenant reaching for her leg, stumbling away from the wall and falling to the ground. He had no time even to shout her name before the first Andorian emerged from the tunnel, the muzzle of his disruptor rifle aimed at McClowan.

"No!"

The cry of rage that spat from Picard's lips was enough to startle the Andorian and he flinched, halting his determined stride as he turned toward the sound of the voice. By then Picard was on him, running into him at full speed and sending them both crashing into the nearby wall. The captain followed his attack with an elbow to the Andorian's face, feeling something shift or break beneath the force of the strike. His opponent loosened his grip on his disruptor and Picard grabbed at it with one hand, but the Andorian's strength was formidable. He required almost no effort to leverage Picard off balance, his other arm rising above his head as though readying to deliver a killing blow.

Then the familiar and quite welcome whine of a Starfleet phaser erupted from the tunnel behind the Andorian, and his body jerked. His expression went slack as he collapsed to the ground, nearly dragging Picard with him. The captain managed to disentangle himself from the now-unconscious Andorian and let his attacker fall to the ice, just as he heard more footsteps in the tunnel.

"Captain?" asked Ensign Ereshtarri sh'Anbi as she stepped into view, wearing a Starfleet parka and holding her own phaser so that its muzzle pointed skyward. "Are you all right?"

Picard released a pent-up sigh of relief before lowering his weapon and gesturing to where McClowan still lay unconscious. "The lieutenant needs medical assistance." Hearing new footfalls in the tunnel, he turned to see Lieutenant Choudhury and a security team, all wearing parkas, emerge into the chamber. "Good to see you, Lieutenant," he offered, reaching over to rub the elbow he had used against the Andorian.

I really am getting entirely too old for this sort of nonsense.

Nodding in greeting, Choudhury said, "Glad you're okay,

sir." She gestured to one of her security people and directed him to see to McClowan and ch'Galoniq before returning her attention to Picard. "Sorry for the delay in getting to you, Captain. Our sensors were blocked by some kind of localized jamming device. Lieutenant Konya's tracking it down now and should have it disabled in no time."

"Excellent," Picard said, turning as sh'Anbi moved toward him, holding out the phaser he had dropped during the firefight. "What happened up there?"

Choudhury returned her phaser to a pocket of her parka before replying, "About a dozen infiltrators stormed the base camp. Their weapons were set to stun, thankfully, so there were no casualties. Once my team and I got down here, it didn't take long for us to secure the site. From what we can tell, they hiked up the same trail you took to get here." She paused, regarding Picard with a raised eyebrow that would have made any Vulcan proud. "Speaking of that, sir, you *do* know the transporters are working? When our sensors aren't being jammed, that is? You don't really *have* to go traipsing up and down these mountains."

"Indeed, Lieutenant," the captain replied, grinning. "Duly noted for future reference."

The security chief pointed to the unconscious Andorian behind Picard. "Counting him, we have all twelve in custody. I'm guessing Homeworld Security will want to talk to them."

"I'd imagine so," Picard replied. "Though I'll want you involved with any interrogations."

"Aye, sir," Choudhury said, "and there's something you should know. We were able to capture one of the Andorians topside without disabling him. The only thing he said was that more attacks like this would be coming."

Picard sighed in quiet acceptance. *Of course they would.*

23

Worf hated doing nothing.

On an intellectual level, he was aware that he wasn't actually doing nothing. As first officer, he knew it was his responsibility to direct the actions of others, often waiting for subordinates to bring him information upon which he could base decisions. After his lengthy service to Starfleet, he thought he might eventually have found a way to suppress his innate desire to be doing something, *anything*, other than sitting in the captain's chair at the center of the *Enterprise* bridge, presenting the outward appearance of calm and control. He always had admired the air of authority and unyielding demeanor affected by those who had commanded him— Benjamin Sisko, Martok, and, of course, Jean-Luc Picard— all while struggling to emulate it. Even his years spent as a diplomat, a profession that by definition required the ability to present the façade of utter patience and bearing, had only softened his distaste for such inactivity. For a younger officer, such periods could always be filled with some task or, barring that, some form of drill or other training that formed a large portion of a security detachment's schedule aboard a starship. Now, however, as second in command with the captain off the ship, Worf's focus was here, on the bridge, waiting.

"Ensign Balidemaj," he snapped. When the young officer turned from the tactical station, her eyes wide with uncertainty, Worf realized the summons had come off with greater severity than he had intended. Pausing, he composed himself and made a point to lower his voice and soften its tone. "Ensign, do have anything new to report?"

Abigail Balidemaj shook her head. "No, sir. All our attempts to track the source of the transmissions have failed. Whoever they are, they definitely know what they're doing."

In truth, Worf had anticipated that exact response from the ensign, who would not have waited to be asked before providing any worthwhile updates to his progress. Balidemaj and every other member of the *Enterprise*'s crew were aware of their duties and carried them out with unparalleled efficiency. Worf, like Captain Picard, had never expected anything less in that regard.

Therefore, Commander, the Klingon chided himself, *be at ease.*

Sitting idle was difficult enough when nothing of apparent consequence was happening. Doing so while others performed any number of tasks vital to the security not only of the ship but also the forthcoming conference was all but impossible. Beneath the veneer he forced himself to affect in the presence of the bridge crew, Worf seethed. His captain and chief engineer as well as several other valued members of the *Enterprise*'s crew had been in harm's way while he remained safe aboard the ship. That the incidents had occurred on the surface of one of the Federation's founding member worlds only served to further gall him. Worf would rather channel that energy into something useful, instead of sitting here and taking out his mounting irritation on the officers around him.

Even the prospect of utilizing his churning emotions to conduct interrogations of those attackers currently held in custody by Andorian Homeworld Security was unavailable to him. That duty fell to Jasminder Choudhury, and though he harbored no doubts that the ship's security chief could handle that task with aplomb, it did not dilute his desire to yell at someone deserving of his wrath. Resigning himself to the situation, Worf made a mental note to increase the level of difficulty for his evening calisthenics regimen. If he could not face a real enemy across a table, then he would settle for a holographic adversary on a computer-generated battlefield, and vent his frustrations upon it.

"Commander Worf," Balidemaj called out from her station, "I'm picking up another broadcast being transmitted across the planetary network. It's visual this time, but I think it's them again, sir."

Rising from the captain's chair, the first officer nodded. "Play back from the beginning, on-screen."

A moment later, the image on the bridge's main viewscreen shifted from a view of Andor from high orbit to that of a figure shrouded in darkness. The silhouette—obviously Andorian, judging by the presence of antennae atop his or her head—was a flat black form rendered against a light blue background, and it took Worf a moment to realize that the backdrop featured symbols he recognized as Andorian in origin, accompanied by groupings of Andorii text. For a moment, Worf wondered if the image was being computer generated.

"See if you can enhance the image," he said, not taking his eyes from the screen. "I want to see his face."

"Greetings, people of Andor," the figure said, with a voice that sounded as though it was being processed through some

kind of audio-filtering software, obviously intended to disguise the speaker's gender. *"I speak to you again on behalf of the* Treishya, *your protectors during this time of great uncertainty. Many of you have doubtless heard of our attempts to convince outworlders to take their leave of this planet. Likewise, I harbor no illusions that our government will report these incidents as nothing less than violent attacks against innocent victims. If you believe as I do, that our duly-elected leaders are little more than puppets controlled by their Federation masters, then discount anything they might choose to say."*

"Wow," said Lieutenant Elfiki from where she sat at one of the science stations against the bridge's port bulkhead. "Talk about stretching facts to fit a point of view."

"As I speak to you," the shadowy figure continued, *"your government, with the able assistance of the Starfleet vessel currently orbiting our world, is marshaling every available resource to track me and my followers. Were they to find me, should I believe that I will be afforded due process under the law? Or, is it a wiser course to presume that I will be treated as a terrorist; a threat to the security of the Andorian people?"*

"You appear to be nothing more than a coward to me," Worf said, his voice low and menacing as he folded his arms across his chest. Glancing to Balidemaj, he asked, "Ensign, can you track the transmission?"

The young Indian woman shook her head. "I'm trying, sir, but the signal's being bounced around different hubs throughout the entire worldwide data network. There's no easy way to sort it out."

As though able to hear their conversation, the figure on-screen said, *"To the Starfleet ship in orbit above us: Don't bother trying to trace the source of this broadcast. Your time and efforts would be better spent recalling your people from the surface. We urge you to do so in peace, for we have no desire to harm anyone, but do not question or underestimate our resolve. We will no longer tolerate outsiders wishing to interfere in our affairs.*" For the first time, the silhouette moved, an arm rising into the picture to aim a closed fist and pointed finger at the visual pickup. "*Too much of our cultural identity and purity has already been tainted or lost by such intrusion, despite grand Federation protestations about observing and respecting the sovereignty of its individual member worlds. I have devoted my entire life to the defense of this planet and its people against all manner of threats, and I stand ready to do so again, even if that threat comes from those who once dared to call themselves our ally.*"

"What about filtering the image?" Worf asked.

At the science station, Elfiki replied, "No good, sir. Whatever processor they're using to render the video portion of the broadcast, it's designed to thwart any attempts at deconstruction for identification purposes. Whoever these people are, they have some pretty sophisticated toys at their disposal."

On the screen, the figure said, "*We do not believe our demands are unreasonable. On the contrary, we simply ask that Starfleet and—by extension—our own government uphold what is believed to be one of the fundamental principles upon which the Federation was founded, that being a civilization's right to self-determination.*" The speaker paused, and when he or she continued, it was with a lower, almost conversational tone. "*Of course, the Federation in recent times has allied itself with parties who do not value such tenets. Indeed, the ship in orbit is currently commanded by a Klingon. He represents a people whose history is rife with conquest rather than cooperation, let alone a belief in individual liberties and societal free will, at least so far as it extends to anyone they deem weaker than themselves. The very notion that such a people would honor that which we hold dear is laughable, and yet the* Enterprise's *esteemed captain sees fit to leave one of Starfleet's most powerful vessels in the hands of a soldier from a race of invaders, all while he parades the most powerful member of our government before us like a pet on a leash."*

"How can anyone be so stupid as to believe any of this?" asked Lieutenant Joanna Faur from where she sat at the conn station.

"Don't discount the power of passionate rhetoric," Elfiki said, shaking her head in wonderment. "And don't think there aren't people down there who aren't eating up every word of this."

Faur looked over her shoulder at the science officer. "Anyone who's spent five minutes in a children's history class should be able to see what this guy's trying to do."

"At ease," Worf said, keeping his voice low. "I'm not nearly as concerned about his nonsensical blathering as I am about his apparent knowledge of the captain's movements, to say nothing of being aware of who's been left in command while he's off the ship." Though he was forced to admit that the speaker's comments about the Klingon people caught him by surprise, he gave the remarks no credence. He was well aware of the legacy of the Klingon Empire as forged from centuries' worth of battle, and required no history lesson from someone who possessed not even the courage to show his face.

"It is time for you to act, citizens of Andor!" When the figure moved again, this time it was to lean closer until his filtered, opaque visage all but filled the screen. The voice was louder now, the words laced with churning rage. *"Do you wish to have your future decided by outworlders, or would you rather face the destiny you choose for yourself? Yes, the Federation may well offer us life, but what kind of life can it be, if what they offer*

changes us from that which we've been since the dawn of our civilization? And what will be the price for this gift they so magnanimously see fit to bestow upon us? Are you prepared to bear that cost? If so, then you doom our people to eventual extinction as surely as the crises our people now face, except that in the case of the former, you do so at the expense of everything our ancestors forged from the very depths of the world beneath your feet. If not, then stand ready, for the day of reckoning is fast approaching."

The figure promptly vanished from the viewscreen without anything resembling a formal conclusion to his remarks, replaced by the image of Andor slowly turning beneath the *Enterprise*. After several moments spent in silence broken only by the cadenced litany of tones and indicators from the bridge's various workstations, Elfiki was the first to speak.

"So, do you think anybody saw that?"

There was a chorus of mild chuckles, which Worf tolerated as he returned to the command chair. "Apprise the captain of this latest message," he said, gripping the arms of the chair while reminding himself not to rip them from their mountings. "Continue efforts to track the transmission to its source, and to ascertain the identity of the speaker. Ensign Balidemaj, monitor the planetary newsfeeds for reactions to the message, and forward any relevant information to Lieutenant Choudhury as well as the security liaison at the Parliamentary Andoria complex."

With orders issued and his people turning to their respective tasks, Worf was left alone at the center of it, as he had been all along.

Waiting.

24

"That's it," Admiral James Akaar muttered to no one, as he was alone in his office. "I'm hungry, I'm tired, and I quit."

Rising from his chair, Akaar surveyed the landscape of padds, reports, and other administrative debris littering his desk. All of it contained matters of great import, at least to someone else. To him, they represented the chain and weights that had hung from his neck for what seemed an eternity. It was necessary work, of course, overseeing every aspect of Starfleet and the ships, stations, starbases, and personnel that ultimately answered to him. Despite a cadre of admirals and their respective staffs to which authority could be delegated—and beneath them, ship and station commanders and their staffs who in turn were empowered to act independently with broad discretionary powers—when it came to any of the thousands of decisions that could be made by those individuals during a single day, the responsibility for all of that eventually fell to him as the Starfleet commander. Knowing his staff would apprise him of anything requiring his attention, he did not trouble himself with the routine, even boring reports passed to him via the chain of command. Instead, he preferred to trust in those officers who had been granted the rank and commensurate responsibility to take the correct actions for the appropriate reasons. As for the truly vital issues demanding his immediate consideration, Akaar already had commented or acted on them as appropriate, and now felt confident that whatever remained could wait until morning.

Of course, by then, he reminded himself, *the pile will have quadrupled.* His staff was nothing if not efficient in that regard, seeing to it that the admiral was provided with such reports and other data in a timely manner. *Curse their competent souls.* Looking through the bay window that formed his office's rear wall, Akaar surveyed the cityscape before him, highlighted by the thin band of orange on the horizon that signaled the end of another day. San Francisco was coming alive as night fell, lights from buildings as well as the Golden Gate Bridge painting the city in a vibrant array of colors and energy. The scene called to Akaar, imploring him to shrug off the mundane duties of his office and instead plunge into the vibrant atmosphere of his adopted home planet. He decided he would walk home this evening, and if he happened to come across one or two establishments catering to those who sought the pleasures to be found in fine beverages of the spirited persuasion, then so much the better.

He made it halfway to the door when it slid open to reveal his aide, Lieutenant Commander Jennifer Neeman, standing at the threshold. A slim human female with brown hair, high cheekbones, and a small yet prominent nose that gave her face an almost regal air, she held a padd in her hand, her expression one of apology as she nodded to him in greeting. "Good evening, Admiral."

"Commander Neeman," Akaar replied, his tone communicating that what he was about to say was intended in jest, "your talent for anticipating my desire to vacate these premises, to say nothing of your ability to initiate a timely disruption of my escape plan, is uncanny."

"I'm sorry, sir," Neeman said, playing along with their all-too-familiar game. "Were you on your way out?"

Akaar chuckled. "Don't you ever have the desire to flee this prison, Commander?" he asked, indicating his office's drab gray walls with one hand. "To leave behind the shackles of duty and responsibility, and instead enjoy life the way it's meant to be lived?"

Nodding, his aide replied, "Every day, Admiral, but then I remember that I work for you."

This time, Akaar's laugh echoed off the walls of his office. "I hear that a lot." Turning from the door, he gestured for Neeman to follow him back to his desk. "What can I do for you, Commander?" he asked as he returned to his high-backed black leather chair.

Her expression and demeanor returning to something more formal, Neeman took a seat in one of the two chairs situated before the desk. "We've received an unusual report from our information security division. It seems that a request was submitted to the Starfleet central data banks, and when it yielded a negative result, search-query protocols were directed to the archive facility at Aldrin City."

"What's so unusual about that?" Akaar asked, frowning.

Neeman replied, "It's what happened after that, sir. According to the facility's commanding officer, Captain Randolph, the search arguments included with the request apparently contained key words and phrases that, when used in a particular context, triggered an alert in the archive center's main computer banks. According to the report we received, the computer canceled the request, flagged the search terms, and initiated what the computer people at Aldrin City are calling a 'containment protocol,' which includes pro-grammed instructions to notify the Starfleet Commander of its activation."

Having next to no idea what his aide had just said, Akaar leaned forward in his chair and rested his muscled forearms atop his desk. "I certainly hope *you* understand at least some of that."

"From what I can tell," Neeman said, "a century-old com-puter program has been triggered, alerting us that someone has attempted to access information so restricted that it's not even catalogued in the data banks of any Starfleet computer facility, at least not officially. According to the containment protocol, the information can only be released by authority of the Starfleet Commander and the Federation President."

While it was not an unusual request, Akaar conceded, it still was an irregular occurrence. The computers and data-storage facilities that played home to the vast store-houses of information Starfleet had amassed in its more than two centuries of existence contained their share of closely guarded secrets. More than a few of those secrets, while not maintained even at one of Starfleet's centralized data-management locations, could still be found at the secure archival repository located in Aldrin City on Earth's moon. Access to that facility was limited primarily to the select crew of personnel tasked with managing and protecting its contents. Special requests to obtain information stored there normally required the approval of a flag officer, after which such inquiries still fell under the authority of the Chief of Starfleet Operations.

"So," Akaar said, "what was being requested?"

Neeman shook her head. "I don't know, sir. The contain-ment protocol called for the immediate isolation of any relevant data files or other information related to the query. It's been quarantined until it can be reviewed, by both you and President Bacco."

Akaar decided this was the point at which things were beginning to make less sense. Frowning, he reached up to rub the bridge of his nose. "Who requested this information?"

Consulting the padd in her hand, Neeman replied, "Commander Beverly Crusher, chief medical officer—"

"Picard's wife?" Akaar asked, interrupting his aide. He had just spent the last hour reviewing Jean-Luc Picard's latest reports about the situation on Andor and the escalating incidents of civil unrest, including attacks on Starfleet and *Enterprise* personnel.

"That's right, Admiral," Neeman replied. "On the *Enterprise.*"

Scowling, Akaar said, "I'm aware of her current posting, Commander." This bit of information did nothing to alleviate his increasingly foul mood at having his evening's agenda delayed or—worse—possibly scuttled. While he certainly wished nothing but happiness to Picard and Beverly Crusher, the admiral had never warmed to the idea of married officers serving together on the same starship. For a time, Akaar had suspected Crusher had been behind Picard's outlandish kidnapping of Governor George Barrile last year. He was certain that she had spurred her husband to show Alpha Centauri's planetary leader the scope of the suffering and relief efforts under way on Pacifica and—by extension—worlds across the Federation. Even though Picard had vociferously denied that allegation, taking full responsibility for his actions, the admiral still had wondered just how much influence the *Enterprise*'s chief medical officer might have over the decisions made by the starship's captain. Akaar eventually had relented, realizing that Picard's noteworthy career was defined by the orders and regulations he had flouted as much as it was by the standards and principles he had sworn and acted to uphold. Likewise, he knew that Beverly Crusher was an officer of similar character, and that Jean-Luc Picard of all people would never allow anyone of lesser moral fiber to serve as a member of his crew, let alone stand beside him as his wife.

"What was the nature of the records search she was performing?" he asked.

Now it was Commander Neeman's turn to frown. "That's the part I don't get, sir. On the face of it, Dr. Crusher's request seems rather benign. It deals primarily with genetic research. Specifically, she was looking for any information relating to complex, artificially created DNA structures and genome engineering. With the *Enterprise* at Andor and Dr. Crusher assisting Professor zh'Thiin, it at least sounds like information she'd be looking at as part of the ongoing research effort." Pausing once more to look down again at her padd, she added, "There's some medical or scientific formulae here, which I assume are related to words I actually *do* understand, but I'm not making sense of any of it."

"But the Archives' computer obviously knows what it is," Akaar replied, shaking his head. "And that's what triggered a lockdown? That's ridiculous. Does Dr. Crusher know what's happened?"

Neeman replied, "No, sir. According to Archives, her request resulted in the transmittal of some data to her, but obviously not whatever's been quarantined. That seems to also be a part of this containment protocol."

That seemed logical, Akaar mused, at least from an operational security point of view. "This can't be the first time something like this has happened. Surely someone has made a similar kind of innocent request from Archives and been denied. Is there a record of this kind of reaction happening before?"

"Already ahead of you on that one, sir," Neeman replied. "Obviously, search queries are inspected and some are flagged for security reasons, and requests similar to the one made by Dr. Crusher have been approved without incident. Something about this is different, and I'm guessing it has to do with the science gibberish she included as part of her search criteria."

Indicating the computer terminal on his desk with a wave of his hand, Akaar asked, "So, how do I access these mysterious data files that I need to either approve or deny Dr. Crusher's ability to review?"

"You can't, Admiral," Neeman replied, shifting in her seat as though she suddenly felt uncomfortable. "The files in question aren't even stored in any of the Starfleet Archives' data banks. According to Captain Randolph, they're sealed in a series of three archival containers, where they've been for more than a century."

Akaar knew that off-line storage was but one of several effective means of preventing easy access to classified materials, even considering the formidable security protocols engineered into the complex software that was the heart of Starfleet information technology. "That's a common enough practice," he said.

Holding up her hand, Neeman replied, "There's more, sir. Captain Randolph says that unlike normal archival procedures, these containers possess no instructions for when their contents are to be released and made available for public access. So far as the data banks are concerned, these files are never to be opened, and even that gets better. She also says that the inventory codes as listed in the Archives' main computer don't match the codes on the containers themselves. In all three cases, two sets of numbers—the first and last pairs—were transposed."

"If the codes don't match," Akaar said, "then how did the computer know where to find the files and issue a quarantine order?"

Neeman shook her head. "According to Captain Randolph, the containment protocol knew about the error. She doesn't understand how that's even possible and is speculating that it's not an error at all, but instead a deliberate mislabeling, perhaps to keep someone from stumbling across them during a routine archives search."

Releasing a sigh of exasperation, Akaar leaned back in his chair. "You're telling me all of this is because someone tried to access a set of computer records from more than a hundred years ago, which somebody apparently stuck in a box with the wrong label? *On purpose?* What could possibly be so important that it requires this level of secrecy?"

"I have no idea, Admiral," Neeman replied, shaking her head. "But you're about to find out. The archival containers are on a Starfleet shuttle on its way from the moon right now. It'll be here within the hour."

Akaar rose from his chair, stepping around his desk so he could pace the carpet in the center of his office. As he began the slow circuit toward the front wall, he interlocked his fingers above his head and lifted his elbows toward the ceiling, stretching the muscles in his back and welcoming the respite from sitting. He had anticipated a nice walk in the mild evening air to reenergize himself after spending far too long trapped behind his desk, but it now was looking as though his habitual circuit back and forth across his office floor was all the exercise he would get this evening.

"Has the president been informed of this?" he asked as he reached the front wall and turned, retracing his steps across the carpet toward Neeman.

The commander shook her head. "Given that it's only coming up on four in the morning in Paris, I held off on sending any messages to her aide."

"There's no sense waking her at this hour," Akaar said, "not until we've had a chance to see what this is all about. Still, make sure to get me on her morning schedule." He sighed, resigning himself to the evening's forthcoming activities as he made his way back toward the window at the rear of his office. "I imagine I'll be doing a lot of reading before tomorrow, so kindly inform the steward to keep the coffee hot."

"I don't suppose I'm allowed to help review whatever it is that's coming?" Neeman asked.

Akaar replied, "You probably don't possess the necessary security clearance. For all I know, *I* don't have the proper clearance, considering I have absolutely no idea what this is about."

Stopping before the picturesque view of San Francisco before him, the admiral considered the beautiful cityscape, wondering about the sealed files currently on their way to him. What did they contain, and of what value might they be after being locked away for more than a century?

"Maybe we're all better off with nobody knowing what's in those containers," Neeman said from behind him.

Though he did not turn from the window, Akaar shifted his gaze until he could see his aide's reflection in the transparasteel. "Perhaps you're right," he replied, though he admitted to himself that he now was motivated to uncover this odd little mystery as much by his own curiosity as by his official responsibilities. "Somebody wanted that information hidden away, perhaps forever. I just hope that when we crack the seals on those files, we're not opening Pandora's box."

25

Standing before the large windows at the rear of Presider sh'Thalis's office, Picard watched the crowd that had gathered before the main entrance to the Parliament Andoria complex. A police barricade cordoned off an area leading up to the gate itself, should a ground vehicle require access. Picard counted at least a dozen police officers on the street before the main gate, with others in vehicles scattered among the crowd.

"That's a lot of people," said T'Ryssa Chen, from where she stood next to the captain.

Picard nodded. "Quite." Even from this distance, it was easy to see that the gatherers had separated into two distinct groups, with members from each party holding signs displaying a broad spectrum of slogans, questions, and demands. Most of the signage was written in different Andorii dialects, though a few also had been printed in Federation Standard or decent approximations. As with the assemblage itself, the signs depicted variations on two basic themes: support and disdain for a continued Federation—and Starfleet—presence on Andor.

"At least they're remaining peaceful," said Presider sh'Thalis from behind her desk, her chair turned so that she could look out into the courtyard and the throng of citizens milling on the streets.

Standing on the other side of the wide desk, her hands clasped behind her back, Lieutenant Choudhury said, "I don't expect that will last for very long, Presider. From what we've learned so far, everything that's happened to this point is just prelude."

Sh'Thalis swiveled her chair until she faced the *Enterprise*'s security chief. "I've reviewed the reports submitted by Captain ch'Zandi and Commander th'Hadik, Lieutenant. They spared no detail."

"Then you must know that we cannot allow the conference to continue," Picard said as he turned from the window and stepped around the presider's desk to stand next to Choudhury. "It's almost certain the *Treishya* will attempt to disrupt the proceedings, either by direct assault or simply by inciting civil unrest in the streets outside the compound. Of course, the latter might also prove to be an effective distraction to pull security personnel from their assigned stations while an actual attack is launched against a vulnerable location."

Choudhury said, "That's what I'd do."

"Given that many members of the *Treishya* are believed to be military veterans," sh'Thalis said, "such a scenario wouldn't seem at all far-fetched. However, Captain ch'Zandi's report from questioning some of the prisoners stated that the *Treishya* is not interested in harming anyone. Their actions to this point would seem at odds with that stance."

Picard replied, "It's a public disinformation campaign, Presider, designed to incite sympathy for them and animosity toward any non-Andorians. The tactics used against my people haven't just been aggressive. It's only fortunate happenstance that no one was seriously injured, or worse. If this situation continues to escalate, there may come a point where casualties are unavoidable."

"Or even desirable," Chen said. When Picard glared at her, she added, "What I mean, sir, is that sooner or later, if we don't do what they want, they're going to use greater force. I know I'm not one to throw this term around lightly, but it's the only logical evolution of their tactics. They don't have any problem threatening property, and even though the weapons we confiscated from them were all set to stun, it stands to reason that, eventually, they'll consider a few people injured or even killed as worth whatever goal they're after."

Resting her hand atop her desk's polished surface, sh'Thalis caressed the smooth, obsidian finish with her fingertips. After a moment, she said, "The reports we've received about the *Treishya* all make a point to emphasize how well-organized they seem to be. That much is implied by the news-net broadcast we all saw."

Picard had reviewed the original message, along with three follow-up dispatches, upon his return to the *Enterprise* following his own encounter with *Treishya* operatives. Like the original message, the subsequent communiqués were characterized by a recurring theme: anger at the presence of outsiders determined to interfere with matters they knew nothing about, undermining the cultural heritage of the Andorian people. The messages had provided fodder for much propaganda now being broadcast around the planet. It was enough for Picard to order all Starfleet personnel on Andor to remain at Starfleet or Federation locations around the planet. Advisories also were sent to non-Andorian civilians, many of whom had heeded those warnings and transported to those same secure facilities.

In the case of each *Treishya* transmission, there had

been no visual component save for an unidentifiable silhouette of what appeared to be an Andorian. The voice on the audio broadcasts had so far defied the *Enterprise* computers' attempts to determine the speaker's gender, or even to declare with any certainty whether the voice was genuine or completely fabricated by computer software. What the broadcasts *had* contained was the unmistakable air of confidence, even arrogance, as though the speaker perceived himself to be in total control of the current situation, calling for the expulsion of all non-Andorians from the planet. This, at least to Picard, begged an obvious question: What did the originator of the message know that was not being shared with those to whom he issued ultimatums?

"That broadcast highlights another issue," he said, pointing toward the window. "There are those among the populace who *will* answer the call if summoned to take action at the *Treishya*'s behest."

Sh'Thalis nodded. "Just as there are those who will rally to support *us,* but even that presents a problem. We can't very well have a civil war breaking out before our very eyes even while we work to save our species." Sighing, she added, "If only I could convey that to these protesters. How can they not see what we risk by turning away ideas and assistance from whoever might offer it? I simply cannot believe that anyone would choose extinction in the name of preserving cultural identity or whatever other nonsense the *Treishya* are arguing. How useful is such an abstract concept if your entire civilization is dead?"

"Presider," Picard said, "it might be wise to at least consider postponing the conference until the situation here stabilizes."

Rising from her chair, sh'Thalis's expression darkened,

her lips tightening into an expression of determination. "Out of the question. There is simply too much at stake, and we cannot subject ourselves to the demands of a terrorist."

"I don't know if 'terrorist' is the best term to describe what the *Treishya* represent, Presider," Choudhury offered, her voice calm and neutral.

Nevertheless, sh'Thalis waved away the observation. "They can call themselves resistance fighters or freedom fighters or patriots, but threatening harm against innocents in the name of a political, social, or religious agenda is the very definition of terrorism, and it's something I cannot allow to sway me. Not now, and certainly not over something that could prove vital to the survival of the Andorian people."

"We could move the conference to the *Enterprise*."

Picard turned toward the source of the suggestion, Lieutenant Chen. Though she said nothing else, the captain noted the expression on the young woman's face, which conveyed, essentially, "Forgot about me, didn't you?"

"Go on, Lieutenant," Picard prompted. He had been ready to offer just such an alternative, and his young contact specialist had simply beaten him to the punch.

Realizing now that all eyes were upon her, Chen seemed to become very self-conscious for a moment before straightening her posture. "We'd have to reduce the number of spectators in actual attendance, of course, but the ship has ample facilities to host everyone on the list of invitees. One of the recreation decks or even one of the shuttlebays could be reconfigured to serve as a proper venue. Other guests and those wanting to observe the proceedings can do so via broadcast in other meeting rooms and common areas aboard the ship."

"Could such preparations be completed without having to delay the start of the conference?" Picard asked.

"It'd lack much of the pomp and circumstance that's been put into the Enclave chamber down here," Choudhury added, "but it would be more secure, sir."

Sh'Thalis shook her head. "I appreciate the concern for our safety, Captain, but just as canceling or delaying the conference is unacceptable, moving it off-world is out of the question. It must be held here, before the Andorian people and with Federation participation, to show everyone that we all are committed to solving the issues we face. This demonstration of solidarity is a vital first step toward illustrating the Federation's resolve to assist us with our ongoing reproductive crisis."

"While I certainly agree with you in principle, Presider," Picard said, "it's not simply the safety of the conference attendees that concerns me. There's also the matter of innocent civilians, who could become targets should the *Treishya* choose to act. An incident of that nature might very well trigger civil unrest across the planet. Given everything the Andorian people have suffered and continue to endure, is providing a possible trigger for such disorder truly worth what we might hope to accomplish at the conference?"

"Everything you describe might still happen," sh'Thalis replied, "with or without the conference. If we move it to your ship, onlookers could still be targets, as they would still be here, gathered to watch, support, or protest the conference as it's being broadcast." Rising from her chair, she fixed the *Enterprise* captain with an expression of utter conviction. "We cannot allow the *Treishya,* or anyone else, to dictate through fear how we are to lead our lives. The conference will go forward, and it will do so here, on Andor."

It was obvious to Picard that there would be no deterring sh'Thalis. He did not hear hubris or even inexperience on the part of a leader facing crisis. Rather, these were the words and emotions of someone committed to doing what she firmly believed to be for the good of the people to whom she had pledged her service. There was, he decided, much to admire about Iravothra sh'Thalis.

"Very well, then, Presider," he said, "but I hope you'll allow me to augment your security forces and Homeworld Security detachment as far as my ship and crew are able." He glanced to Choudhury, who nodded.

"Absolutely," said the security chief. "We'll do everything we can to make the Enclave chamber safe for participants and spectators. Commander th'Hadik has already submitted a revised security-deployment plan to deal with checkpoints, weapons and personnel scanners, defensive force fields, and so on. Captain ch'Zandi has also offered up several excellent suggestions, such as employing transporter inhibitors and equipment to thwart any efforts at disrupting communications." Looking to Picard, she added, "Something we discussed after your incident at the dig site, sir."

Picard nodded in approval before returning his attention to sh'Thalis. "Our presence and involvement in the conference is by your invitation, Presider. So, these are, of course, recommendations, but ones I hope you'll consider in the interest of safety." Despite the broad authority he currently enjoyed as Admiral Akaar's "roving troubleshooter" with respect to resolving planetary issues, the *Enterprise* captain had no desire to trample on the presider's authority or that of any duly elected official, on Andor or any other Federation world.

"I may be hopelessly optimistic and perhaps even naïve," sh'Thalis replied, smiling again, "but I'd like to think I'm not a fool. I welcome your continued assistance." Stepping around the desk, she took Picard's hand and cradled it in both of her own. "We will stand together, before the watchful and hopeful people of my planet, as we embrace the support and assistance of our friends and longtime allies."

Though he said nothing that might diminish the confidence the presider now felt, Picard could not help his own lingering feelings of uncertainty about the days to come.

26

Eklanir th'Gahryn noted his subordinate's dour visage as the younger Andorian entered his private chamber to deliver his evening meal, regarding the *chan* with no small amount of amusement.

"What troubles you, ch'Drena?" he asked as his aide, holding a tray that supported a large earthen bowl and a generous portion of what th'Gahryn recognized as *hari* bread, stopped before the round, multicolored rug in the chamber's far corner.

Loreav ch'Drena set the tray down on a small, short table positioned next to the rug. Straightening his posture, the *chan* said, "I apologize, Eklanir. It is just that I have not been sleeping well."

Rising from his chair and moving toward the rug, th'Gahryn regarded his subordinate with concern. "Are you ill?"

The expression on ch'Drena's face changed to one of embarrassment. "I simply miss my family, Eklanir. I've never been away from them for this long a period. Our newest child is still so young. I'm told she's walking now."

Th'Gahryn smiled as he sat on the rug, crossing his legs. He lifted the tray from the table and placed it atop his knees.

"I treasure such moments from my own children's youth," he said, "even though I missed my share of such milestones while away on duty. Your sacrifice is appreciated, Loreav, and it's important to remember that what we're doing here acts to protect all our children." He paused, regarding the thick stew contained in his bowl. "During times of stress or longing, I've always found tranquility in the outdoors. The forests, a park, wherever trees and grass are in abundance. Such places never fail to put my mind at ease."

"I was never one for the outdoors," ch'Drena replied.

Shaking his head in mock dismay as he dipped the bread into his stew, th'Gahryn said, "When I do fear for our future, it's because I hear things like that." During his own childhood, he had relished outdoor pursuits such as camping, hunting, and tracking, with his *thavan* and grand-*thavan* instilling in him an appreciation for respecting and living in harmony with the natural environment. By the time he reached adolescence, th'Gahryn enjoyed spending night after night in the wilderness, camping in the forests or up in the mountains. That reverence for nature continued upon his entry into military service and his enlistment as a foot soldier in Homeworld Security, where he often looked forward to his unit deploying to the field for an extended training exercise. He made a habit of volunteering for security patrols or any other activity that gave him a reason to venture out into the vast, untamed rough country that comprised a significant percentage of the military installation to which he was assigned. In addition to giving him an excuse to indulge in his love of the wild, it also kept him and his companions away from the watchful eyes of grumbling noncommissioned officers on the prowl for those unfortunate enough to be caught without something productive with which to occupy their time.

"You work very hard, Loreav," th'Gahryn said, "and for that I commend you, but there is more to living than simply being at your appointed place and carrying out your assigned duties. Life is meant to be cherished, to be celebrated. One of the ways I've learned to do that is by embracing this world of unmatched beauty that Uzaveh the Infinite has given us for reasons surpassing our understanding." He punctuated his statement with a bite of stew-drenched bread.

A pity you don't have the time to act upon such notions yourself.

Whether born of genuine admiration or a simple desire to avoid the appearance of disrespect, ch'Drena said, "Perhaps if I'd been fortunate enough to develop such an awareness for nature at an earlier age, my outlook might be different." Then, after a moment, he added, "On the other hand, one could argue that recent events might well provide me with an incentive to reexamine my attitude on such matters."

After taking another bite of his stew, th'Gahryn asked, "How so?" Sensing his subordinate's unease at how the conversation was evolving, he added, "It's all right, Loreav. You may speak freely."

"Well," ch'Drena said, casting his eyes toward the floor, "it's just that what you've been saying here has made me think about how much we've lost. I don't simply mean the loss of life, which is tragic, all the more so for the crisis our people already face. The Borg inflicted so much damage to our world, much of which likely will not heal within my lifetime. On the other hand, much also was spared. There are areas of Andor untouched by the Borg's hand, for which I'm thankful. Perhaps what we have here is a sign from Uzaveh, a reminder not to forget or otherwise take for granted that which has been given to us. Is that not essentially the message we as *Treishya* are attempting to impart to all who will listen?"

Nodding in approval, th'Gahryn replied, "It is indeed, Loreav." Throughout his professional military career, he had often sought advice and input from those much younger than himself, valuing the perspectives they held from being born and raised in a world markedly different from the one in which he was brought up. Problems often were seen in a manner completely dissimilar to what he might envision, sparking a host of creative resolutions and strengthening the bond of trust between not only senior and subordinate but also mentor and student. Indeed, it was only as he had grown older and achieved higher rank that th'Gahryn had come to view the latter relationship as being of greater importance.

It is but one benefit of not having died at a younger age.

The door to his chamber opened to reveal another Andorian, this one a *thaan* dressed in dark brown civilian attire, standing at the threshold. His expression was one of worry.

"Biatamar," th'Gahryn said by way of greeting, lifting the tray from his lap and returning it to the table.

"I apologize," said Biatamar th'Rusni, hesitating at the doorway. "I did not mean to intrude."

Waving the *thaan* into the room, th'Gahryn replied, "No, no. It's quite all right. What is it? If your face is any indication, you aren't bringing me pleasant news."

"I've just received a report from one of our contacts within the Parliament Andoria complex," th'Rusni said. "Presider sh'Thalis has directed that the conference proceed tomorrow as scheduled."

Nodding, th'Gahryn asked, "And this surprises you?"

After a moment, th'Rusni replied, "No, I suppose that it doesn't."

"Even with everything that's happened to this point,"

ch'Drena said, "after the messages you've broadcast and the actions we've taken, isn't the presider simply being stubborn or even foolhardy at this point?"

Th'Gahryn rose from the rug, smiling at his young aide. "Not at all. Presider sh'Thalis is acting as any strong leader should: not allowing her agenda to be dictated to her by those making threats. Were these other circumstances, her actions and decisions would be cause for admiration. Now, however, she simply is misguided. Woefully, tragically misguided."

Since the moment he had helped found the *Treishya* movement, that was precisely the view th'Gahryn had taken with respect to all the elected officials who chose to forsake their Andorian heritage and instead embrace the ideals held by other species as a matter of convenience. It was this perspective that had caused him to denounce even those officials who represented the Visionist party, the group supposedly devoted to ensuring that Andor's heritage and values were retained and respected. Despite commanding the support of a sizable percentage of the Andorian population, the Visionists, in th'Gahryn's opinion, had not done nearly enough to combat the ever-encroaching mindset held and celebrated by their political and ideological rivals, the Progressives.

It was true that Visionist leaders had stepped forward and taken direct action when they discovered that Progressivebacked scientists were developing genetic-manipulation schemes designed to alter Andorian physiology, polluting it with the unknown and potentially dangerous genetic code found in a still largely unknown species from across the galaxy. But that was years ago, and despite all their efforts the research continued and the scientists' creations were inflicted upon unsuspecting bondgroups—"test subjects," as they had been so callously labeled—and what had been the result? Even greater instances of aborted pregnancies or unexpected birth defects wrought upon the resulting off-spring. Not only had this reckless agenda not done any-thing to alleviate the very real crisis afflicting the Andorian people, it arguably had worsened it, and how had the Pro-gressives reacted? A call for even greater, more intrusive research, which carried with it the risk of further contami-nating an already weakened Andorian populace, possibly to the point of accelerating its headlong flight toward extinc-tion. Though Visionist leaders had protested this action, too, of course, they had done little else to see to it that their concerns, backed by a growing portion of the public, were heard by their political counterparts in the halls of parliament.

In the perceived absence of genuine action on the part of their elected leaders, private citizens had begun forming their own groups, instigating a new wave of social and political activism fueled by a desire to preserve not only the Andorian species, but also those intangible qualities that defined their race and set them apart from their interstellar neighbors. Most of these smaller guilds demonstrated their dissatisfac-tion with the government by staging protests or taking out advertisements for distribution via the media. They held ral-lies in attempts to grow their numbers, but even as their ranks swelled they appeared to have no plan for how best to utilize the resources now at their disposal.

Such was not the case with the *Treishya*.

"It's not just sh'Thalis," th'Rusni said, "but several mem-bers of parliament, as well, all of whom are supported by large portions of their respective constituencies. Even those mem-bers who oppose the Progressive agenda are encountering resistance from the voting districts in their home prefectures.

The issues we face have fractured the populace like nothing else in our history."

Th'Gahryn nodded. "Understandable, if not forgivable, given the circumstances. These are trying times, and it is natural to question one's own faith and principles when confronting adversity. Those whose convictions have faltered must be directed back to the beliefs that have defined us as a civilization, and it is our sacred duty to be their guide." Consisting of both civilians and former as well as active military members, the *Treishya* had during its brief existence moved with deliberate patience, remaining in the shadows and largely beneath the notice of government and law enforcement as it strove to fill its ranks. People from many walks of life pledged their commitment to the fledgling organization, citing the same concerns over the apparent decay of Andorian society that had driven th'Gahryn to form the group.

To the public at large, the *Treishya* was ephemeral, existing on the fringes of even the most vocal activist dissenters like the True Heirs of Andor. Though the *Treishya* had enjoyed only modest public notice during its infancy, th'Gahryn had watched as awareness and backing for the group's stated beliefs and mission increased. The spectacular failure of the Progressive-led science cabal to infect Andorian genetics with their "Yrythny solution" had raised concerns that further such injudicious actions were all but a threat to the security of the Andorian people. It was in this climate that groups like the *Treishya* had begun to thrive.

"The Progressive argument is persuasive," ch'Drena said. "After all, they do present what would appear to be salvation for our entire species. While I don't agree with them, I can see where others could come to do so."

"But at what cost?" th'Rusni asked. "Will those born in

the generations to come truly be Andorian, or something else? What heritage will your offspring embrace?"

Frowning, ch'Drena said, "It is not as though interspecies mating is unheard of. Other races are able to reproduce, though obviously with varying forms of medical assistance."

"Which is precisely the point!" th'Rusni countered. "If it were to be, would nature not have allowed for it to occur unaided? Also, there are no known examples of Andorians successfully producing offspring when including an out-worlder into their bondgroup. It cannot be done without artificial meddling, and isn't this the sort of meddling that drives much of what the Federation represents? They're never satisfied with just allowing people to exist; instead, they must insert themselves into matters about which they know noth-ing, or about which they demonstrate no appreciation or respect. Yes, the Federation and the Progressives, along with the puppets they control within our scientific community, may very well develop a solution that addresses the physical aspects of the issues plaguing our people. They do nothing for the larger matters at hand."

Clearing his throat, ch'Drena said, "I merely point out that there are those for whom such considerations are unimportant, and I wonder how we might go about address-ing them and perhaps rallying them to our cause."

"I don't believe such a thing is possible," th'Rusni said, shaking his head. "Not at this point. There is too much divi-sion, too many voices shouting for attention and no one lis-tening. We must take other, bolder actions if we are to make our message heard."

Remaining silent while his two companions engaged in their lively debate, th'Gahryn clasped his hands behind his back and began to pace alongside the floor-to-ceiling windows comprising his chamber's outer wall and affording an unfettered view of the night skyline of Lor'Vela. He very much enjoyed looking down upon the bustling city and the comparative tranquility that so characterized New Therin Park.

Perhaps a stroll through the park is in order after the day's business is concluded.

Th'Gahryn said, "While I agree with you, Biatamar, we must remember that there is a fine line separating the support given to us by some segments of the citizenry and the utter contempt with which others regard us. Many may concur with our message, but our methods of delivery will be the criteria by which we ultimately are judged. We must therefore tread with utmost care."

"By not taking more aggressive action," ch'Drena said, "do we not run the risk of alienating those who might be placing themselves in jeopardy simply for advocating our cause?"

Th'Gahryn shook his head. "Such people are a detriment to our cause, Loreav. There is a reason our actions to this point have been restrained. Anyone familiar with my career knows I'm not opposed to aggressive action when and if it's necessary, but I also prefer prudence and precision in an attack, rather than simply attempting to overpower an opponent. As with any battle strategy, planning and taking the time to understand your adversary is a crucial component of achieving victory." In truth, several of the earlier attempts at incursion into the parliament compound as well as against various Starfleet and other outworlder targets had been designed as probing actions, intended to expose vulnerabilities in the security protocols being employed at different locations. The assault on the power-generation facility was largely a ruse, designed to test the mettle of the Starfleet team and their supporters with respect to the assistance they had pledged to provide. As expected, the team from the Federation starship had evacuated rather than risk damage to Andorian persons or property.

Moving against the *Enterprise*'s commanding officer also had been something of a feint, to see if Presider sh'Thalis might decide that the risks to outworlders were too great to proceed with the conference, and cancel the event. If she had taken the extra step of evicting all outworlders from Andor, that would have been a delightful additional benefit. At worst, th'Gahryn thought the teams he had sent might capture Jean-Luc Picard, allowing him to be used as a bargaining tool against the presider. That the mission had failed on those counts did not mean th'Gahryn viewed it as a waste of time and resources. On the contrary, it had given him valuable new insight into the character of Iravothra sh'Thalis, and her determination to see through the current difficulties and do what she considered to be in the best interests of the Andorian people.

It's a pity that such conviction can be so completely misplaced.

As for the conference, that also would be an exercise in patience. With operatives already positioned within the parliament complex as well as utilizing various means to secure passes for entering the Enclave chamber, the *Treishya* would be ready to act if and when the opportunity presented itself.

"We've already made our position known," th'Rusni countered. "We've announced ourselves, and declared our intolerance for further intrusion by outworlders, and yet they remain, defying us. Law enforcement and the Starfleet ship no doubt are expending tremendous resources to find us. Our time may well be limited, so at what point do we demonstrate that their failure to respect our demands carries consequences?"

Turning back to the window so that he might take in the breathtaking vista before him, th'Gahryn sighed, disappointed in his aide's impatience. *Youth,* he mused.

"In due course, Biatamar," he answered after a moment. "In due course."

27

For the fifth time in as many minutes, Jasminder Choudhury reached up and ran a finger along the collar of her dress uniform. Was it her imagination, or had it shrunk since she had first donned it less than an hour ago?

I hate wearing this damned thing.

"Excuse me?" a voice said from behind her. "Miss? When you get a chance, I'd like to see the wine list."

Choudhury turned to see Lieutenant Rennan Konya standing in the doorway leading from the small antechamber, a command post for the *Enterprise* security team, wearing a standard-duty uniform and regarding her with a deadpan expression.

"Consider yourself assigned to waste reclamation once all of this is over," she said, narrowing her eyes and regarding her deputy security chief with a mock glower.

Stepping into the room and nodding to the three members of the security detachment assigned to duty in the command post, Konya shrugged. "For how long?"

"Until you stop annoying me," Choudhury replied, "or the universe collapses in on itself. Whichever comes first."

Konya chuckled. "Just so long as you don't make me wear

a getup like that." He paused, making a show of studying her. "Oh, but it looks good on you, though."

"I know," Choudhury said, tugging on the bottom of her jacket to straighten it. Captain Picard had ordered dress uniforms for himself as well as those members of the *Enterprise* senior staff who were scheduled to be in attendance at the conference, citing the formal nature of the event and their visibility to the attending dignitaries within the Enclave chamber. Everyone else from the ship's security cadre, including Konya, would be manning checkpoints and other stations around the complex, and the captain had directed that those personnel wear more practical attire.

Given a choice, Choudhury mused, *I'd rather be lying on a beach, wearing—*

"*Enterprise to Lieutenant Choudhury,*" said the voice of Commander Worf, erupting from the intercom.

She smiled. *Impeccable timing.* Moving to the workstation, she keyed the control to activate the communications frequency, and the image on her computer terminal changed from the UFP seal to the visage of the *Enterprise*'s first officer. "Choudhury here, Commander."

Regarding her with his usual intense glare, Worf said, "*With the conference about to start, do you require any additional personnel or equipment?*"

Choudhury shook her head. "No, sir. Between our teams and the troops ch'Zandi and th'Hadik brought along, we look to have everything covered."

"There're almost too many people running around down here, sir," Konya added.

Though she said nothing, Choudhury nodded in agreement. Several meetings with the leader of the local Homeworld Security brigade and the head of Presider sh'Thalis's security detail had been called in order to sort out assigned areas of responsibility during the conference and arrive at a scheme that would not see the three disparate units tripping over one another. Commander th'Hadik's primary concern was protecting the presider, though he had at his disposal sufficient personnel to augment the *Enterprise* team inside the subterranean complex where the conference was to take place. External security also fell under th'Hadik's purview, but he had transferred that responsibility to Commander ch'Zandi, who had deployed his brigade throughout the complex to supplement the Parliament Andoria complex's already formidable security. With the exception of protecting Presider sh'Thalis and several other high-ranking parliament members, everything inside of and connected to the Enclave chamber was Choudhury's to oversee. Accommodating all of the requests, suggestions, and even demands of her two Andorian counterparts had stretched Choudhury's patience almost to its limit.

What we really need to make this go off without a hitch is three or four more people wanting to be in charge.

On the screen, Worf said, *"If you feel that an excess number of personnel on the ground might hinder your efforts, I can speak to the captain about your concerns."*

"That won't be necessary," Choudhury replied. "I've already spoken to th'Hadik and ch'Zandi about it. We're creating a reserve component and staging them at the barracks used to house the parliament's security detachment. They can be deployed from there to just about anywhere in the complex at a moment's notice."

Konya added, "I've also set up transporter protocols for rapid response, just in case. Given what's happened during the past couple of days, we've also reconfigured access by the public. We've reduced the number of entrances from eight to four. It's making things a bit more crowded getting in, but by keeping attendees centralized, we're able to concentrate security details at fewer locations."

His features softening, Worf nodded. *"Excellent work."*

"All part of the service, sir," Choudhury said. During their own meeting earlier in the day, she and Konya had discussed with the first officer their joint belief that the *Treishya* would not pass up an opportunity to take some kind of action at the conference. Choudhury was somewhat confident that such an event was unlikely to occur on the first day, which was to consist mostly of introductory remarks by several speakers followed by a banquet and informal discussions to round out the afternoon and early evening. The meat of the conference would not take place until tomorrow, presented before a larger audience within the Enclave chamber as well as being transmitted across the global newsnets. To Choudhury, that was the ideal time to strike.

Of course, she reminded herself, *whoever's out there trying to outsmart you might be hoping you think that way.*

"We are standing by should further assistance be required," Worf said. Was it her imagination, or was there an added element of concern in the Klingon's voice? Even if that was not the case, she decided she still rather liked thinking it.

Choudhury raised her right hand to her temple, offering an informal salute. "You'll be the first to know, Commander. Choudhury out." Looking to Konya, she said, "Got everything you need?"

Raising the padd he now carried in his hand, her deputy replied, "I think so. Unless you need me for anything else, I'm heading back to the main entrance. Spectators are still filing in, and the extra screening procedures are taking a bit more time than we anticipated." He hesitated when applause erupted from the auditorium floor. "Showtime."

"Sounds like it," Choudhury said, glancing at the chronometer displayed on her computer terminal. "Let me know if anyone gives you any trouble about having to wait." It had been agreed that anyone not seated in the Enclave chamber when Presider sh'Thalis took the stage would have to wait until the first scheduled break after she and the first three speakers offered their introductory remarks.

"Acknowledged," Konya said over his shoulder as he left the room. Reaching for the communications panel set into her workstation, Choudhury tapped a control.

"Choudhury to all security stations. Be advised that Presider sh'Thalis is taking the stage. Protocol Alpha One is in effect for the duration of her remarks. All stations acknowledge."

She listened to the different checkpoints and other positions within and around the building check-in, watching on her screen as the Andorian presider moved toward the podium at the center of the raised dais.

Well, here goes nothing.

The applause had subsided, and from his vantage point, Shar was able to view the audience without shifting position in his seat or even moving his head. Based on facial expressions alone, those in attendance looked to represent a wide range of opinions regarding the matters for which everyone had gathered on this day. Shar knew that the number of actual delegates and scientists invited to attend and speak at the conference comprised but a fraction of the audience. Most of the seats in the chamber's tiered main viewing area had been reserved for other scientists and political figures from all across Andor. A large number of university students also were in attendance, with the remaining seats allocated to ordinary citizens who had requested access, taking advantage of the open forum Presider sh'Thalis had proposed as part of maintaining transparency to the public throughout the proceedings. The sight of the Enclave chamber filled to capacity, hosting so many people who—for whatever reason—had taken an interest in these proceedings was as inspiring to Shar as it was nerve-racking. Would he really be speaking to so many onlookers in the coming moments?

Now standing at the podium and waiting a moment for the audience to settle themselves after their warm greeting to her, Presider sh'Thalis raised her arms and gestured toward the assembled onlookers. "Welcome, citizens and friends of Andor," she said, her voice carried by the Enclave chamber's exceptional acoustics. "More than two centuries ago, our world joined a coalition of planets dedicated to mutual cooperation and support, in which all participants agreed to share their knowledge and resources for the benefit of us all. Since then, we have stood side by side and defended our homes against outside threats, and we have stepped forward to aid our fellow member worlds during times of individual planetary crisis. After the destruction brought by the Borg, people across the Federation came forward to assist those in need, including the countless volunteers who even now devote themselves to the rebuilding of our world. It's easy to forget or even dismiss such efforts, as the scars the Borg left are not easily visible here. Still those rebuilding efforts continue, and will do so for some time to come. However, that is not why we are here today."

Doing his best to present an outward appearance of calm, Shar nevertheless felt the twinges of anxiety playing at his stomach. Though he had considered and rehearsed the remarks he would be making in the next few moments, he had never felt comfortable speaking before any gathering of people. The notion of talking to the hundreds now seated before him had almost been enough to send him running in terror from the parliament complex, but he knew he could not refuse Presider sh'Thalis's request to address the conference.

If I can only do so without vomiting, it will be a grand day.

Despite himself, Shar could not help glancing to his right to where Captain Picard sat, unmoving as though cast from marble. His expression was composed, and he gave no indication that he was seated at the forefront of such a historic gathering. How was he able to remain so calm and appear as though he was perfectly at ease being the focus of such attention?

Sh'Thalis continued, "As you all know, we currently face the gravest crisis ever to affect our world, dwarfing even the devastation and tragic loss of life inflicted upon us by the Borg. Indeed, we face our very mortality as a species. Fate and biology have conspired against us to create the issues faced by bondgroups across our planet, who seek only to nurture the next generations who will assume caring for our civilization and all it represents."

She stepped away from the podium and moved to stand at the edge of the stage, her flowing white robes giving her a majestic air as she addressed her audience. "However, science and—dare I say it—faith may well provide us with solutions to the problems we face. I am aware that such courses of action are not without controversy; that they trouble a significant portion of our population, who worry about irreparable harm being wrought against the very essence that makes the Andorian people such a unique species in our galaxy." Her remarks elicited a chorus of murmurs and even some applause, which she acknowledged with a smile and a formal nod.

"I am not insensitive to such concerns," sh'Thalis continued, "but with the very future of our people at stake, it is my sworn duty to take whatever actions I deem appropriate and in our best interests. Much of the apprehension I've encountered seems born from uncertainty about the unknown, or perhaps a simple lack of understanding over what so many talented people are trying to accomplish on our behalf. There is also, quite frankly, no small amount of deliberate misinformation being spread, for the sole purpose of instilling fear among our people, playing on our fragile emotional state in the wake of all we have already endured. There are those who advocate an isolationist policy with respect to the crisis we face, choosing to ignore or even actively refuse the aid offered to us by our interstellar friends and neighbors. I find this unsettling, and nothing less than a monumental disservice to the Andorian people." When the applause came this time, it was louder and more enthusiastic, and accompanied by cheers.

Sh'Thalis turned to smile at Shar, holding his gaze for an extra moment before beginning to pace the length of the dais, making eye contact with people all across the audience. "I could spend the better part of the day standing here and speaking to you on this topic," she said, "but I am woefully unqualified to do so in anything resembling an intelligent fashion. For that, I have enlisted the participation and expertise of some of the Federation's leading scientific minds, including a few notable representatives of the Andorian people. One in particular is someone of whom I am quite proud; someone who has taken the talents with which he was blessed and channeled them toward a life of service. Not simply to the Federation Starfleet, but in this time of need he also has devoted his gifts and passion to his homeworld. Gentlebeings, allow me the honor of introducing you to Lieutenant Thirishar ch'Thane."

The mixture of applause and cheers was tempered by

more rumbling from different areas of the audience. Shar tried to ignore it as he rose from his seat and made his way across the dais to the podium.

Doesn't sound like everyone here is happy to see you.

Forcing away the errant thought, Shar nodded to the presider as she moved to meet him at the podium. She offered him a reassuring smile before stepping toward her seat at the back of the stage. Shar cleared his throat as he peered out at the audience, which now aimed their attention at him.

"Good afternoon. Whereas Presider sh'Thalis is happy to tell you that she is not qualified to discuss various aspects of the science behind what I and others have been asked to do on behalf of Andor, I am equally ill suited to talk to you about politics. I'm a scientist, dedicated to the pursuit of knowledge and its use for the betterment of the societies I represent."

He paused, gauging the audience reaction to his words, for which there was a mixture of approval and dissent. "Yes, that's right: societies. Andor is my home, and I've always felt a deep love and respect for it, as well as its people. I also wear the uniform of a Starfleet officer, and I have sworn an oath to uphold Starfleet's principles and defend its citizens even at the cost of my own life. I've been fortunate that my duties these past few years have allowed me to serve both of these allegiances, and it is that work which brings us here today.

"Much has been made of the research of my former mentor, Dr. sh'Veileth. She was vilified by some members of the media, as well as political and religious leaders. What was lost amid the controversy that sprang up around her work was that she was a dedicated servant of Andor, working tirelessly to address the issues that threaten us all. She pursued answers to those issues until the day she—like so many others—died at the hands of the Borg.

"Much also was made about the Yrythny ova, the genetic material I brought back from the Gamma Quadrant. There are those among us who believe that—despite the obvious benefits we stood to enjoy from using that material to address our physiological problems—we somehow were destroying the Andorian race. Such statements are perpetrated by those who hold their own agendas, rather than the welfare of our people, as their primary concern." The blunt statement elicited a range of reactions, from even greater applause to several shouts of disapproval. Facing the rear of the chamber, Shar was able to see several of the *Enterprise* security guards as well as members of the presider's protection detail scanning the crowd, searching for anyone who might be considering doing more than voicing their discontent. No one so much as rose from their seat, and Shar was thankful for the generally civil—if passionate—atmosphere permeating the room.

"As you are no doubt aware," he continued, "the Yrythny protocol developed by Dr. sh'Veileth did not prove useful. Indeed, many of the bondgroups who volunteered to be test subjects suffered miscarriages, and most of those offspring that survived pregnancy suffered a wide range of birth defects."

From the audience, an Andorian *thaan* chose that moment to stand, leveling an accusatory finger at Shar. "My bondgroup was one of those experiments!" he shouted, his voice carrying with utter clarity across the room. "Our child died less than halfway through the pregnancy!" The *thaan*'s outburst prompted renewed mutters from all around the audience, with several more spectators offering a wide range of hand gestures as they shouted at him.

"There will be order!"

The voice echoed through the chamber. Looking to his left, Shar saw Presider sh'Thalis standing at the podium, glaring at the audience with an expression that left no confusion as to who was in charge.

"This is not a street protest," the presider said. "These proceedings will be conducted with a proper decorum. If you are unable to abide such protocol, you will be escorted from the premises." She did not wait for acknowledgment, but instead simply looked to Shar and nodded for him to continue.

Turning his attention back to the audience, Shar studied the face of the *thaan* who had spoken with such conviction. He did not see anger in the Andorian's face; rather, he realized that behind the *thaan*'s eyes, pain and loss lurked, consuming him from within.

"I deeply regret the tragedy you've endured," Shar said, keeping his attention focused on the *thaan,* "just as I regret the loss of even one child, which might be prevented if we can learn to harness the knowledge in our grasp for the betterment of our people. To do otherwise is an act of fear and ignorance that is at best immoral and, at worst, criminal."

Now the reaction was even more polarized, with thunderous applause competing against even more animated displays of displeasure. When he had first composed his remarks, Shar was aware that some of what he might say likely would engender the effects he now was seeing. Though he had considered tempering his words, it was while reading over them just before coming onstage that he realized he did not care what sort of reactions he might provoke. With the fate of his civilization at stake, the time for watching one's words in order to avoid offending someone was long past. Now a line had to be drawn in the sand, separating for all time those who wanted to aid in the search for a solution, and those who wished to hinder it.

It should, Shar thought, make for an interesting few days.

28

From where he stood next to the oversized viewscreen mounted to the front wall of the president's office, Admiral Akaar watched the expression on Nanietta Bacco's face turn to confusion. Leaning forward in her chair, she clasped her hands together as she rested her forearms atop her desk, her attention focused on the screen and Akaar himself. Deep lines creased her face, and the skin beneath her eyes was puffy. Her hair, already gray, had turned completely white in the years since she had taken office. She nevertheless projected an air of dignity, confidence, and awareness that belied her age and the strain under which she had been operating for far too long.

But above and beyond all of that, she looked tired.

"The Gariman Sector?" she asked, frowning.

Akaar gestured to the screen's displayed image, which depicted a two-dimensional, computer-generated representation of a star chart. "We call it the Gariman Sector, mostly out of a desire to reduce or deflect the history surrounding that region." At the center of the map was a wedge of territory expanding outward from Federation space, flanked on one side by the Klingon Empire, and on the other by regions claimed by the Tholian Assembly. "But I'm fairly certain almost everyone in the galaxy knows we're referring to the Taurus Reach."

As Akaar expected, Bacco's features did not brighten with recognition, not at first. Then, as she studied the map, her brow furrowed as she recalled what she knew of the region. "That business with the Tholians a hundred years ago. Them, and the ancient race that once enslaved them. The Shedai?" Reaching for the coffee cup sitting in a saucer near her right hand, she asked, "Leonard, what's this all about?"

Stepping away from the screen and moving toward her desk, Akaar said, "The Taurus Reach was the focal point of a top-secret research, exploratory, and development effort unlike anything that's come before or since. The operation was conducted under some of the highest, most tightly controlled security measures ever utilized by Starfleet. An entire aboveboard exploration-and-colonization program was employed in that region for the *sole purpose* of providing cover for the clandestine missions being conducted there."

Bacco nodded. "I know the basics, I suppose. I'm old, Leonard, but not that old. It was long before my time." She smiled. "Just barely before yours, too, as I recall."

"Indeed," Akaar replied. "Many aspects of Operation Vanguard remain classified. Much of the official record has been altered so as to put forth the notion that our presence there was to search for signs of advanced weaponry or other technology that we thought shouldn't fall into the hands of our enemies. In reality, the entire mission was centered on a single discovery made in 2263: evidence of an astonishingly complex, artificially developed strand of DNA, millions of times more convoluted than anything encountered before or since. And I'm not talking simply about molecules intended to create life. This DNA contained within it the raw data needed to construct a *civilization*. Not just cities, Madam President, but *entire worlds,* and the life-forms to populate them."

"Yeah," Bacco said, still frowning as she cradled the coffee cup in both hands before her chest, "that wasn't in the reports I've read. You're talking about a blueprint or schematic of some kind? Created by the Shedai?"

Akaar replied, "That's right. They'd supposedly been dead for thousands of years, but that didn't stop them from giving us no small amount of trouble back in the 2260s." Shrugging, he added, "Of course, that was as much our fault as anyone else's, since we're the ones who woke them up and made them angry."

Now Bacco was nodding as she leaned back in her chair. "I remember some of this now. They weren't dead, just in hibernation for millennia?"

"Yes, Madam President," Akaar replied. "They once ruled the Gariman Sector, commanding technology on a scale that makes our most advanced weapons and starships look like clubs and stone knives by comparison. By all accounts, they were quite content to remain in hibernation until such time as conditions were ripe for them to emerge from seclusion, perhaps even to reassert whatever authority they felt they had over that area of space. Our entry into the region disturbed them, and they weren't too happy about that."

Waving away the rest of the dissertation, Bacco said, "I've read that much. Not one of Starfleet's or the Federation's finest hours, I'm afraid." Akaar knew her feelings on this, of course. They had spent a long night discussing the matter following a meeting with Tezrene, the Tholian ambassador, shortly after the formation of the Typhon Pact. During that meeting, the diplomat had reminded Bacco that "the crimes of the Taurus Reach have not been forgotten." After that conversation, the president had requested all available data on the events that had transpired there more than a century earlier.

What she and Akaar now knew was that the information they had reviewed a year ago was but the tip of the iceberg representing the cache of knowledge Starfleet harbored about the Taurus Reach, the Shedai, and the staggering technology they once had commanded. More disturbing than that, Akaar knew, was realizing that the knowledge they currently possessed was perhaps but merely a fraction of the ancient civilization's history and potential, which still lay beyond their grasp even after all this time.

Bacco indicated the viewscreen with a wave of her hand. "What does any of this have to do with why you're here?"

Clasping his hands behind his back, Akaar replied, "While the Shedai and our encounters with them are public knowledge to anyone who's read a history book, much of the information we've obtained about their technology and capabilities, particularly their so-called meta-genome, is shrouded in secrecy. Likewise, the official project files from the Starfleet effort to acquire and understand Shedai technology are still classified. Someone has—inadvertently, it seems—attempted to access information relating to the meta-genome." Wasting little time, Akaar explained the nature of the query submitted by the *Enterprise*'s chief medical officer, and the alerts it had triggered at the Starfleet Archives facility at Aldrin City.

"I don't see the immediate problem," Bacco said after a moment. "We've filtered the data being returned to the *Enterprise,* and redacted the information deemed beyond the scope of Dr. Crusher's request. She never needs to know what was flagged, right?" Akaar had no chance to reply before the president's features softened and she nodded. "Wait. I just realized what I'm missing. You're worried about how or why she made such an inquiry in the first place?"

"To a point, Madam President," Akaar replied. "I don't for a moment believe that Dr. Crusher is attempting any action deemed to be against our security or best interests. She's simply exploring and exhausting all avenues with respect to the research she's conducting with Professor zh'Thiin. I'm not even certain I'm worried about the professor, whose reputation is exemplary. However, given the nature of the request, particularly some of the parameters and formulae Dr. Crusher included to help narrow the search effort, I have to wonder how she came across some of the information she must have used to reach conclusions or at least make educated guesses about what to look for next."

"Dr. Crusher's a smart woman, Leonard," Bacco replied, "and one of Starfleet's leading medical minds. She's been conducting research like this for decades, and she did two tours as the head of Starfleet Medical."

Nodding, Akaar said, "A position for which she was eminently qualified. Again, Madam President, I'm not taking issue with Dr. Crusher's professionalism, integrity, or even her loyalty. What I'm saying is that she has in some way obtained access to data that, if only obliquely, has connections to information Starfleet and the Federation buried more than a century ago, because they believed it carried the potential to inflict more harm than good, particularly if it were to fall into the hands of our enemies."

"But it's been more than a hundred years, Leonard," Bacco countered. "There's no one left to remember any of this. If anything, unlocking those files, and doing it in a controlled manner, might give us access to information we might use to gain back some of the ground we lost to the Borg."

Akaar frowned. "That's a noble sentiment, Madam President, but we both know there is knowledge that's best left untapped because of the trouble—perhaps even evil—it represents. While our limited understanding of the Shedai technology has given us some improvements in the medical and other scientific fields, it also gave birth to Project Genesis. It's too late to put that particular genie back in its bottle, but that doesn't mean we open all the other bottles to see what else might come spilling out."

"I can't believe that," Bacco said, waving away Akaar's sentiment with a gesture. "That's the sort of thinking fascists and demagogues use to burn books or justify the suppression of contrary points of view. All knowledge is for good; only the use to which it's put can be for good or evil." Pausing, she chuckled. "Wow, did *that* sound Vulcan. I've been hanging around Sivak too long."

"Madam President," Akaar began.

Again, she waved him off. "I know. We're arguing semantics, and I see your point, anyway. We definitely have to tread softly here." Clearing her throat, she reached once again for her coffee, bringing the cup to her lips and taking a long sip. "So, what are your chief concerns?"

"That someone," Akaar replied, "either by accident or design, has accessed top-secret and potentially damaging information. These records were classified under multiple levels of security, including several layers of calculated distraction and disinformation. They were deliberately withheld from the materials provided to the various parties and organizations that requested genetic-engineering data in order to research the problem on Andor. The records are archived using compartmentalization within compartmentalization, with every component requiring separate authorization protocols submitted by you and me in order for *anyone* to review them, and even then such an approval only grants access to whatever subsection of data directly conforms to the request being submitted. The three archival containers flagged by Dr. Crusher's request represent twenty-eight such capsules, all filled with records pertaining to Operation Vanguard, and all protected with the same multiple security schemes."

"What's your point, Leonard?" Bacco asked.

Akaar replied, "That this information was buried for a *reason*, Madam President. If someone's trying to dig it up again I'd like to know why. My concerns are whether such attempts to access that data are confined to here, or are also taking place elsewhere."

Regarding him, Bacco pursed her lips. "By 'elsewhere,' you mean the Klingons, or the Tholians?"

"So far as we know, the Klingons possess no information of real, lasting value with respect to Shedai technology in general or the meta-genome in particular. However, the Tholians, with their genetic ties to the Shedai, are another matter. Given what Ambassador Tezrene told you while standing in this very office, they haven't forgotten what happened out in the Taurus Reach a hundred years ago, and they certainly haven't forgiven it."

Bacco nodded. "Add to that how I managed to screw up things with them during the Borg invasion, and you have to start wondering what they might be doing behind those silken cloaks of theirs." Looking up, she asked, "Leonard, you don't think they'd share Shedai information or technology with the rest of their friends in the Typhon Pact, do you?"

"Based on what we know of Tholian methods and their general xenophobia," Akaar replied, "that just doesn't seem likely, Madam President. Besides, everything we *do* know about what happened in the Taurus Reach indicates that even the Tholians don't possess detailed knowledge of Shedai technology. In fact, from the reports I've read so far, the Tholians lived in fear of everything the Shedai represented, owing to how their ancestors were treated. They were terrified at the very notion of us venturing into that area of space a hundred years ago, and it's why they never expanded into that region themselves. Hell, it's a century later and they *still* haven't branched out there."

"Yeah," Bacco countered, "but that wouldn't stop them from at least digging into whatever information they managed to collect, either from us or from other sources, and they've had a century to do that, just like we have. The question is whether they buried everything in a box somewhere like we did. Want to lay odds on that?"

Stepping around the desk, Akaar said, "We need to isolate any data that might have some connection to the research Professor zh'Thiin and Dr. Crusher are conducting, separating it from the files flagged in the search and returning the rest to Archives. For now, that's the safest place for that information." He had already informed the president of his intention for a full, thorough review of all records surrounding Operation Vanguard at his earliest possible opportunity, to be carried out in secret and with the assistance of one or two trusted members of his staff—once he granted them the proper security clearances, of course. "Next," he continued, "we start probing, trying to figure out how zh'Thiin and Crusher might have come across information that led them this way. I'm still not convinced we don't have a breach somewhere, but given the coincidental timing of the Tholians being mad at us and forming the Typhon Pact, I'm not ruling anything out at this point."

Bacco released an audible breath, shaking her head. "Not even noon, and already the day feels like it's eighteen hours

old." Turning from the window, she replaced the coffee cup in
its saucer. "You know, Leonard, there are times when I really
can't wait for the next person to come in here and boot me
out so I can go home."

"I take it from that, Madam President, that your security detail continues to thwart your efforts at constructing an
escape tunnel beneath the Palais?"

"Every night," Bacco replied, laughing. As she rose from
her chair, she offered Akaar a small smile. "By the way, Leonard, when it's just the two of us, you know you can call me
Nan, right?"

"I beg your pardon, ma'am?" Akaar said, maintaining a
neutral expression, as he always did whenever Bacco ventured
down this path. Alone in her private sanctuary save for Akaar,
with no aides or other staff members offering her information
or waiting on her to issue instructions, she seemed to welcome
the opportunity to relax and—for a few precious moments, at
least—shrug off the weight and responsibilities of her office.

Reaching up to rub her temples, Bacco released a tired
sigh before laughing again. "You're one of my most trusted
advisors and closest friends, Leonard. I feel more comfortable
talking to you than just about anyone else, and that includes
the people who've served with me for years. I like that you
and I come from such disparate backgrounds. You give me
a perspective I don't or can't have, and I like that you don't
mince words and will tell me what I need to hear, no matter
how badly I might not want to hear it. I think for all the value
you provide as my counsel and perhaps even my conscience
on occasion, you should call me Nan when we're alone."

"As you wish, Madam President," Akaar replied.

Unable to contain a chuckle, Bacco said, "Never mind."
She waved him toward the door. "Go away."

"Thank you for your time, Madam President," Akaar said, satisfied that he had done his part to help Bacco relieve some small amount of the stresses she carried along with her duties. Moving away from her desk, the admiral strode across the carpet toward the door.

"Leonard," he heard Bacco call out from behind him, and when he turned to face her, Akaar saw that the humor had faded from her features, her expression once again that of the dignified, committed Federation president.

"Yes, ma'am?" he prompted.

Gesturing toward the viewscreen, which still depicted the star chart highlighting the Gariman Sector—the Taurus Reach—she said, "Keep me informed."

Akaar nodded. "Understood, Madam President."

As he exited the presidential suite, the admiral's mind continued to process the just-ended conversation, as well as the information he had absorbed during the previous night's marathon reading of the unsealed records.

Something about all of this definitely did not feel right, and though Leonard James Akaar had no idea what might be wrong, he knew that when he finally discovered what troubled him, he most definitely would not like it.

No, he decided. *I do not think I will like it at all.*

29

"And that, my friends, is where baby Andorians come from."

Picard allowed himself a smile as Professor zh'Thiin's comment drew the expected chorus of good-natured chuckles from the audience. The atmosphere in the Enclave chamber had been relaxed throughout the professor's remarks, owing not only to her sense of humor but also the way she had presented what many might consider complex scientific principles in a straightforward, easily understood manner. Further, she had done so without talking down to her audience, responding to questions, comments, and criticisms with respect and enthusiasm. Even queries from those more interested in driving the discussion away from the science and toward the touchier social or political concerns were fielded with grace and aplomb.

"She's a very engaging speaker," Picard said, keeping his voice low as he spoke to Lieutenant ch'Thane, who was seated to his left at the curved table facing the audience. The low table had replaced the podium on the dais, affecting an ambiance somewhat less formal than that which had characterized the previous day's proceedings.

Ch'Thane nodded. "She's very passionate about her work."

That much was obvious to Picard. Zh'Thiin's devotion to helping Andor was matched only by her desire to engage in honest dialogue with the very people who would benefit from what she was trying to accomplish.

"All she wanted was an opportunity to speak," said President sh'Thalis from where she sat to Picard's right.

The captain nodded. "I'd say she's seized that opportunity." Zh'Thiin's approach was proving successful, if audience reaction was any indication. Even those who took exception to the professor's work had managed to do so in a civil manner. Most of the vitriol Picard had witnessed on the previous day had come from a small handful of spectators, who at first had been given every opportunity to comport themselves in a more appropriate manner before finally being escorted from the chamber by members of the parliament's security detail. Picard had instructed Lieutenant Choudhury and her people to let their Andorian counterparts assume responsibility for quelling such disturbances, not wishing to present even the merest hint of Federation or Starfleet influence on the proceedings. So far, that strategy appeared to be working, as those interactions he had witnessed between audience members and *Enterprise* personnel had been peaceful.

Picard caught sight of several raised hands, and zh'Thiin pointed to a female Andorian seated near the center of the room. Standing, she bowed her head in greeting, and the captain saw that she was an older woman, by his estimate long past childbearing age.

"Professor," the woman said, "you've been quite candid about your work and the possibilities it holds for us, and I appreciate that you've not tried to marginalize the processes involved; but there are those of us who worry about the possible, unforeseen long-term effects of introducing a new, artificial genetic sequence into Andorian DNA. Are you not risking some unintended complication that may cause even greater damage in the future?"

Zh'Thiin clasped her hands together as she regarded the woman. "That is an excellent question, and one that also poses several more questions. It would be dishonest of me to tell you that any attempt to manipulate genetic code is risk-free. There may well be unintended side effects to anything we attempt to do. That is the nature of biology, which as we all know does not remain static but instead adapts over time to be at harmony with its ever-changing environment. In fact, I believe that the problems we face are born from an apparent inability of Andorian physiology to evolve in accordance with a basic necessity for survival. Whether that is a natural phenomenon or perhaps the result of something artificial that has impacted us is an exploration for those with greater intellects than I possess.

"What I have attempted to do is to minimize what you might label the inherent risks of introducing non-Andorian genomes." Reaching into the folds of the multicolored robe she wore as part of the protocol for speaking in the Enclave chamber, she extracted a small device and pressed a control. A holographic projection appeared in the air before her, large enough to be seen throughout the chamber and displaying a computer-generated representation of what Picard recognized as a strand of Andorian DNA. "The new sequences I have developed are based on our own unique genetic code, though several components are composed of what I have come to call 'dynamic interlinks,' which are encoded into the chromosomes of a zygote taken after fertilization from the *chan*." Pressing another key on her handheld controller, zh'Thiin caused the projection to rotate, and a section of the DNA strand expanded outward, enlarging and taking on much more detail. .

"This intermediary process takes place in a laboratory setting," she continued, "during which the interlinking genetic code essentially examines its new environment and 'rewrites' itself in order to conform to whatever genetic gaps exist within the chromosomes. Once those changes take hold, the modified gamete is then introduced to the bondgroup's host *zhavey* so that the remainder of the pregnancy can proceed normally." Zh'Thiin paused, then offered another smile to her audience. "This is all a very sophisticated way of saying that the genetic code I have introduced is not that of an alien, but in fact an improved, adaptable form of our own, designed to accomplish in an artificial manner what I believe should have been a natural evolution of our physiology."

"There are those who would call that a usurping of Uzaveh's will!"

Shouted from somewhere near the back of the chamber, the comment had the immediate effect of causing everyone to turn in their seats, looking for the speaker. Picard's eyes narrowed as he saw a male Andorian standing up and shaking a fist in the air. He scowled at zh'Thiin, his eyes burning with such hatred that the *Enterprise* captain immediately looked to where two members of the parliamentary security cadre stood at the back wall, their attention focused on the outspoken spectator.

Zh'Thiin regarded the Andorian for a moment before asking, "Would Uzaveh go to such lengths to create something so unique as our species, only to see it wither and die? Why has Uzaveh given us the intellect and drive to seek knowledge, if the intention is not for us to employ what we learn as a means of surviving the tests nature sets out for us?

Is Uzaveh's will not that we take the gifts bestowed upon us and use them to better ourselves not only as individuals but also as a society?"

The Andorian remained where he stood, shouting invective at zh'Thiin. "Perhaps this is a test, and we have failed! We lack the will to trust that Uzaveh will see us through these trials, and instead we choose to meddle with what we have been given. We are being punished for our arrogance!"

Picard glanced toward the chamber's upper tier and saw Lieutenant Choudhury standing near the ramp, tapping her combadge and pointing toward the main floor. At the back of the room, the two Andorian security officers moved from their positions and began heading toward the dissenter. Everyone around him moved aside in order to allow the security officers access, but the angry spectator stood his ground. Around the chamber, several animated conversations were breaking out, with audience members turning to one another, their expressions dark and their words heated. Both Andorian and *Enterprise* security personnel were on full alert now, watching the evolving situation and waiting for instructions.

"Choudhury to Captain Picard!"

Startled by the anxiety in his security chief's voice, the captain tapped his combadge. "Picard here. What is it, Lieutenant?"

"Sir, we've got a situation developing outside. Our security perimeter has been breached, and we have protesters on the grounds. I've put all forces on alert."

As if to accentuate Choudhury's point, a trio of security officers from sh'Thalis's protection detail emerged from behind the curtain at the left side of the stage, brandishing sidearms as they closed on the presider. Within seconds sh'Thalis was out of her chair and surrounded by her bodyguards.

"Presider," said one of the Andorians who obviously was in charge of the detail. "Please come with us."

Picard felt a hand on his arm and turned to see Lieutenant Peter Davila and Ensign Ereshtarri sh'Anbi standing behind him, both wearing their Starfleet dress uniforms. A glance to their waists told the captain that—for the moment, at least—their phasers remained in their holsters.

"Sir," Davila said, "I've been instructed to take you, the professor, and Lieutenant ch'Thane to a secure area."

At least three dozen *Enterprise* security personnel and Homeworld Security soldiers had now entered the chamber, most of them dispersing among the crowd while others took up station at each of the exits. "I don't think that will be necessary, Lieutenant," he said, shaking his head.

Davila frowned. "Sir, with all due respect, Commander Worf gave me explicit instructions to remove you from any perceived danger, and he also told me you'd say something like that." His expression remaining deadpan, he added, "He also said that if I allowed you to overrule him, he'd kill me."

Despite the growing tension permeating the room, Picard managed a wry grin. "And we wouldn't want that to happen, now, would we? Very well, Lieutenant. Make it so."

Rennan Konya hated technology. At least, he did at this particular moment.

"Get that damned thing back up!" he shouted over his shoulder at Lieutenant Robert Mars, who bent over the portable computer workstation, his fingers tapping a frantic sequence of keys as he shook his head in frustration.

"It's not responding!" Mars called out. "My screen shows the entire force-field grid is off-line! It's reading like a power failure, but I'm checking the relays and everything else is functioning normally."

Frowning, Konya asked, "No power interruptions? What about communications and the rest of the security grid?"

A moment passed as Mars fed the necessary queries to the computer interface. "Everything else is up, including transporter and weapons inhibitors. It's just the force fields."

What the hell? The question rang in Konya's ears even as the answer presented itself with startling clarity. "Somebody may have targeted them deliberately. There might be a network infiltration. Notify Commander La Forge," he said, returning his attention to the unsecured entrance to the Parliament Andoria main building, and the two *Enterprise* security officers who now served as the only barrier preventing entry. Konya suddenly felt vulnerable out here in the building's wide, high-ceilinged main corridor, which stretched to either side of him and curved behind him, encircling the Enclave chamber at the heart of the structure. Eyeing the set of six computer monitors set into the portable security workstation, he took note of the status reports being generated by checkpoints throughout the building. So far, the situation inside appeared to be under control.

Well, let's just see what we can do about that.

Konya turned at the sound of running feet and saw a detachment of Andorian security officers jogging down the hall toward one of the chamber entrances. He had seen the reports of things beginning to get out of hand within the meeting hall, as well as Choudhury's status update directing additional personnel there. Conspicuously absent on any of the computer screens was anything relating to what had happened to the intricate force-field protection grid Commander La Forge and his team of engineers had established.

"Th'Hadik to Lieutenant Konya," said the voice of the parliament's security detail commander. *"We have intruders on the grounds, heading toward your position."*

"Did everybody just take the day off around here, or what?" Konya snapped, letting a bit of his own irritation vent with the words. To Mars, he said, "Get us some help." Drawing a breath to calm himself, he tapped his combadge. "Konya here. Acknowledged, Commander." He was about to ask if any of the intruders might be armed when he heard the unmistakable report of disruptor fire, but not from outside. Turning toward the sound of the weapon, he saw a member of the Andorian security detail dropping to the corridor's polished floor.

"How the hell are they inside already?" Konya shouted, drawing his phaser from the holster at his waist. Tapping his combadge again, he called out, "Konya to Choudhury! We've got intruders inside the building!" He indicated for Mars to stay on station as he moved down the corridor, extending his weapon arm and letting his phaser lead the way.

There was a pause before the *Enterprise* security chief replied, *"All stations have reported no breaches."*

"Then somebody's asleep on the job," Konya hissed as he rounded the bend in the corridor, coming to a halt at the scene before him. The prone form of an Andorian security guard lay on the floor near the wall. A quick inspection revealed that the guard's disruptor pistol was still in its holster.

"Lieutenant Choudhury," he said into his combadge. "We've got an armed intruder in quadrant four, heading toward three."

"The inhibitor systems are still active," the security chief replied. *"The only ones with live weapons should be our people and the Andorian security teams."*

Resuming his jog up the corridor, Konya replied, "I'll be sure to ask him about it when I catch up to him." He came to another bend in the passageway in time to see an Andorian running away from him. The runner was wearing dark clothing, and it took Konya an extra second to realize it was the uniform of one of the Homeworld Security details.

Son of a . . .

"You!" he shouted, and the Andorian stopped running. He turned to face Konya, his left hand coming up and wielding a disruptor pistol, which he fired without hesitation.

"Konya! Answer me, damn it!"

Choudhury heard the report of weapons fire coming through her combadge as she jogged down the passageway toward a ramp at the end of the hall. There followed what to her ears sounded like Rennan Konya grunting in shock and pain. Then she heard nothing.

Tapping her communicator, she said, "Choudhury to command post. Scramble react teams to all stations."

"Acknowledged," replied the voice of Lieutenant Kirsten Cruzen, a member of her command post staff. *"It's getting crazy outside, Lieutenant. Some of the checkpoints are reporting that people are climbing over each other to get through the gates."*

"What the hell set them off?"

Cruzen replied, *"We're still trying to figure that out."*

Reaching the spiral ramp, which had been reserved for use by the security details and was therefore off-limits to conference attendees and civilian spectators, Choudhury sprinted to the ground level. Her first sight upon emerging from the Enclave chamber's main concourse was that of dozens of Andorians running across the courtyard lawn beyond the large bay windows forming the ground level's outer wall.

She also saw figures wearing the uniforms of *Enterprise* personnel as well as Homeworld Security. Voices carried through the thick transparasteel—shouts she could not understand, along with commands to halt or to cease some activity or another.

Louder voices came to her from elsewhere in the corridor, and Choudhury turned to see a pair of *Enterprise* security officers taking into custody a trio of Andorians dressed in civilian garb. The three intruders were facing the wall, their hands behind their heads as the security guards applied wrist restraints. In this part of the complex, at least, some semblance of order seemed to be returning.

Tapping her combadge, she said, "Choudhury to Davila. Are Captain Picard and the others secure?"

"Affirmative, Lieutenant," Davila replied. *"We're at the emergency rally point on level two."*

Level two? Why the hell had the captain not been transported back to the *Enterprise,* as outlined in the conference security protocol? As soon as she asked herself the question, she rebuked herself for posing it in the first place. Regulations, security protocols, or even the wrath of Commander Worf would not force Picard to retreat to the safety of the ship while members of his crew were in danger. As infuriating as that might be from the perspective of someone charged with ensuring the captain's safety, Choudhury could not help the admiration she felt toward the man. In all likelihood, Picard had consented to being taken to the rally point solely for the purpose of obtaining a weapon for himself.

"Understood," she said, resigning herself to the inevitable. "Wait there for further instructions. Choudhury to command post, I need sitreps from all stations."

"La Forge here," replied the voice of the *Enterprise*'s chief

engineer. *"We're recycling the entire force-field grid. It should be online within sixty seconds."*

Happy to hear that news, Choudhury said, "Any idea what caused the outage, Commander?"

"One thing at a time, Lieutenant. La Forge out."

"We don't have time for one thing at a damned time," she said as the connection went dead. Touching her combadge again, she said, "Choudhury to command post, where are my sitreps?"

"I'm sorting through them now," Cruzen replied. *"We're starting to get condition-green reports from stations around the building. Some stations are reporting civilian casualties, Lieutenant."*

Through gritted teeth, Choudhury hissed one of the more vile yet audibly satisfying Klingon oaths she had goaded Worf into teaching her. Second only to the safety of all attendees, avoiding casualties had been a priority for the concert even with the specter of protests and possible attack by the more aggressive activist groups hanging over her head. "Acknowledged," she replied, shaking her head in anger and dismay.

No sooner did that link sever than another was established, this time by Commander th'Hadik. *"Lieutenant Choudhury, the situation in the exterior compound is being brought under control,"* reported the Homeworld Security commander. *"We have teams at all exterior entrances, and those citizens who managed to enter the grounds are being detained."*

Nodding in satisfaction, Choudhury replied, "Excellent news, Commander. We're still mopping up inside, but I think we've just about got a handle on it."

"Lieutenant!"

Choudhury flinched at the loud voice echoing in the passageway at the same instant something moved in her peripheral vision, and she turned in time to see a lone Andorian coming around a bend in the corridor, a satchel slung over his left shoulder. Her eyes caught the disruptor in his left hand at the same instant the Andorian saw her. He moved with surprising speed, raising his weapon to aim at her. Choudhury was faster, her arm snapping up as her thumb pressed the phaser's firing stud. Brilliant orange energy leaped from the weapon, crossing the empty space and striking the Andorian in the chest. The intruder staggered back a step before stumbling over his own feet and falling against the nearby wall, where he slid unconscious to the floor.

Running footsteps came up from behind her, and she turned to see one of the security officers, Lieutenant Austin Braddock, approaching with his phaser aimed at the fallen Andorian.

"Are you all right?" he asked, his gaze never leaving the stunned intruder.

Choudhury shrugged. "I've been better," she said as she stepped forward and confiscated the Andorian's weapon. "What about you? Everything secure?"

"Affirmative," Braddock replied. "I also got word that Lieutenant Konya's okay. He was just stunned."

Relieved to hear that, Choudhury scowled as she regarded the Andorian's disruptor. "This is standard Homeworld Security issue. How the hell did he get his hands on one?" The weapons-inhibitor systems installed by Commander La Forge and his engineering team had been programmed so that only Starfleet phasers and Andorian sidearms issued to authorized security personnel were functional within the parliament complex. The only way someone else should be in possession of an operational weapon was if he or she had taken it from one of the security guards.

There's a happy thought.

She nodded toward the three Andorians that Braddock's partner, Ensign Jeffrey Moffett, still watched over with his phaser rifle. "What about them?"

"They came in from the street," Braddock said, "taking advantage of the commotion outside to run around like idiots."

Reaching for the satchel still slung over the unconscious Andorian's shoulder, Choudhury opened the bag and examined its contents. Inside was a portable computer interface. It was still active, and Choudhury turned it so that she could examine its display. When she saw the screen's contents her eyes widened in surprise.

"I'll be damned."

Braddock frowned. "What is it?"

She held out the computer for him to see. "It's a schematic of the force-field grid. Somehow, this clown got into our network." *Might this Andorian be the one responsible for the network's failure?*

"You're saying he hacked us?" Braddock asked, his eyes widening in surprise. "Someone can do that so easily?"

"They're not supposed to be able to," Choudhury replied, "but it's not impossible, especially if you know what you're doing."

Or, you had help.

The unwelcome thought did nothing to improve Choudhury's mood.

"Well," she said, releasing an exasperated sigh, "I sure hope things get more exciting around here real soon. I'm starting to get bored."

30

Seated behind his desk and taking in the flurry of information streaming across multiple newsnet broadcasts, Eklanir th'Gahryn found himself plagued by mixed emotions. Should he feel satisfied at what had been accomplished, or disappointed at the lengths he had to go to to ensure that his message—and that of the *Treishya*—was heard?

"They've announced three deaths and dozens of injuries," said Biatamar th'Rusni from where he stood next to a large computer display set into the wall of th'Gahryn's private chamber. "Several of those are critical, and early reports are that at least two of the injured may not survive the night."

Shaking his head, th'Gahryn leaned forward in his chair and reached for the almost-forgotten cup of tea sitting next to a report th'Rusni had brought to him. "That is unfortunate, though if the end result is the parliament and the Federation heeding our demands, then the sacrifice made by those individuals will not have been wasted." Sipping his tea, he reflected on what had transpired, wondering what could have been done to prevent the loss of innocent life. From the moment he and his advisors had begun planning *Treishya* actions against the conference, th'Gahryn's single, unwavering order had been to avoid civilian casualties, knowing that any such injuries or deaths that could be attributed to the group would serve only to undermine its message and purpose. Despite that, th'Gahryn knew that such a goal, though noble, was unrealistic. That did not diminish his desire to see to it that such regrettable incidents were minimized, if not altogether avoided.

People die in war, he reminded himself, *and it is a war that you're waging.*

"The conference protests are beginning to elicit reactions across the world," th'Rusni said. "More gatherings are taking place in other cities, both supporting and objecting to the continued Federation assistance. The genetic-enhancement issue is the primary focus for many of these assemblages, but the incidents at the conference are fueling calls for the presider to deport all Starfleet personnel and even all outworlders."

Th'Gahryn also had seen those reports, several of which had been provided by a small number of news organizations that had long been accused of slanting their news with a notable bias toward staunch Visionist party views. Of course, other outlets were offering contrary perspectives more in line with values and positions held by those claiming allegiance with the Progressives. The truth, th'Gahryn knew, was often found somewhere between the cacophony being produced by extremist factions from both parties, and was just as likely to be ignored in an atmosphere of media sensationalism.

"Law-enforcement agencies in several of the larger cities are reporting personnel shortages," th'Rusni continued, "with their forces being overtaxed as they're called upon to keep such protests from escalating."

At this, th'Gahryn nodded in satisfaction. "Excellent. See, Biatamar? It's as I told you. We enjoy a growing level of approval from the populace. Now that we've taken our message to the public, those who share our vision are rallying to our cause." Even better than the reactions of the civilian populace was the fact that they were being elicited without the need to expose actual members of the *Treishya*. A handful of agents, used judiciously, had been more than sufficient to engender such support, and momentum soon would take over, with more and more citizens voicing their opposition to the government's actions. That, th'Gahryn knew, would be the right time for the *Treishya* to make an even larger, bolder statement, which the parliament, the Andorian people, and perhaps even the Federation itself would not be able to ignore.

In time, he reminded himself. *In time.*

"Have there been any reports from the presider's office?" he asked.

Th'Rusni replied, "One of our contacts inside parliament reports that she's meeting with her security commander as well as the Starfleet captain to discuss canceling the conference."

"I sincerely doubt it will be that easy," th'Gahryn replied. "Sh'Thalis may be inexperienced, but she's certainly not a coward. She has remained steadfast in her beliefs to this point, and the events of the day, while certainly tragic on a personal level, are likely insufficient to force such a change of heart." Rising from his desk, he released a tired sigh. "No, Biatamar, there is still much work to do."

Moving away from the computer display, th'Rusni said, "I'm also receiving reports that Homeworld Security has taken at least two of our people into custody, including our agent who infiltrated Starfleet's computer network."

"That was expected," th'Gahryn replied. "Based on what we know of the security detail's deployment plan, anyone inside the complex was likely to be captured."

"I don't understand," th'Rusni said. "It will take them only a short time to discover what he did, after which they'll reconfigure their protocols to prevent a recurrence of that breach."

Th'Gahryn nodded, offering a small smile. "Yes, exactly." Seeing the perplexed look on his advisor's face, he added, "Remember what I told you about patience, Biatamar, and the need to study and learn from your adversary before engaging them in direct confrontation. We have sufficient support within the government and even the military to pursue our agenda, but we are still outnumbered by those who would stand against us. Therefore, we must be deliberate in our actions so as to avoid revealing our true presence among our enemy. Let Starfleet and Homeworld Security and even the presider's personal protection staff scramble to address or prevent external threats to their security. Their efforts will ultimately prove futile, as the true danger already lurks among them."

Picard watched Presider sh'Thalis pace the length of her office, noting and understanding the frustration and anguish that was evident on her face. It was easy to empathize with the emotional turmoil she had to be enduring, given that he felt much the same way himself.

"When did she die?" sh'Thalis asked, referring to the latest civilian casualty—the fourth, from the small riot at the conference—which the newsnet broadcasts were now confirming.

Standing in front of sh'Thalis's desk, her assistant, Loqnara ch'Birane, replied, "Just a few moments ago, Presider. According to the report I received, she was trampled when a group of protesters charged one of the compound's open perimeter gates. What's not being reported is that she was a *zhen,* and in the final stages of her pregnancy. I've already contacted the hospital, and it seems the pregnancy was a normal one, proceeding without complications. However, surgeons were unable to save the unborn child."

A wave of sadness washed over Picard as he considered the tragic loss. Despite the obstacles before them, this bondgroup had managed to cultivate a child, only to have it and its bondmother torn from them in a senseless act of violence, and for what purpose? None that Picard could fathom. For a moment, he was unable to keep his thoughts from turning to young René, safe with his mother aboard the *Enterprise.* What would his life be if circumstances or fate were—suddenly and without mercy—to take them from him? It was a cold, empty existence Picard did not want to contemplate.

"Such a waste," sh'Thalis said, shaking her head as she continued to pace. Picard had come to realize that this was the way in which the presider released pent-up emotion, rather than directing her anger toward an undeserving subordinate or an inanimate object. "Do those fools not realize what they're doing when they allow something like this to occur? With everything that's happened to us, and with the problems we're still facing, is turning on one another really a viable solution for anyone who's *not* insane?"

Allowing her a moment to gather her composure, Picard exchanged glances with Geordi La Forge and Commander th'Hadik, both of whom stood silent. Given what both men had come to say, the captain figured that any control sh'Thalis might have over her emotional state would be severely tested in the coming minutes.

"Presider," Picard said, "with all that's happened, I think perhaps it may be prudent to reconsider canceling the conference."

Sh'Thalis stopped her pacing, directing a withering stare at Picard. "Is that what you think we should do?" The anger behind her words was palpable.

"There is the safety of the attendees to consider," he replied. "Though we were able to control the situation inside the Enclave chamber, we have exposed several vulnerabilities in our security. If the *Treishya* or some other group attempts another such scenario, we cannot guarantee that there won't be additional loss of innocent lives."

Frowning, sh'Thalis gestured toward La Forge. "Commander, I thought you reported that you had discovered the culprit responsible for breaching your computer network and overriding your security protocols."

La Forge looked first to Picard, who nodded for him to proceed, before replying, "One of the intruders was carrying a portable computer, which, from what we can tell, was used to access our secure optical data network, using credentials he forged. Where he got the information necessary to craft such access and then employ it from an outside interface is something we haven't figured out yet."

"But you've been able to close that breach, yes?" sh'Thalis asked. "That point of access is no longer viable, is it?"

The chief engineer nodded. "Correct, Presider. The person who did this was an expert in computer systems, and he managed to defeat our network security. Further, he did it in such a way that we had no hint someone else was in our system. Still, the fact that he did it from an outside point of entry worked in our favor. Bouncing our system and resetting its encryption scheme was enough to cut him out, at least for the few minutes that passed before he was taken into custody."

"Mr. La Forge," Picard said, "What are the chances such a breach could be repeated?"

Pausing as though to consider the question, La Forge replied, "If someone's that good, I suppose they could get past any protection schemes we put up. Resetting our system was a temporary fix, but I've got computer techs on the *Enterprise* working up something more permanent right now. They're adding new layers of encryption and authentication, and the only way someone should be able to get inside our system from now on is if they're a member of our crew." He shrugged, adding, "And then only if they're one of the less than thirty people with the proper authorization codes and the expertise to use them. If someone tries another infiltration from an outside terminal, the new schemes should trap them and help us trace their location."

"That is but one part of the equation," said Commander th'Hadik, speaking for the first time since arriving in the presider's office. "We are vulnerable from a personnel standpoint, as well."

Sh'Thalis regarded him with unabashed confusion. "Please elaborate, Commander."

The burly Andorian stepped forward, his glossy black leather uniform stretched taut over his imposing, muscled physique. "We inventoried and accounted for all weapons issued to our security details. However, the disruptor carried by the intruder came from the reserve arsenal we have on the complex grounds."

"Which explains how he had a functioning weapon even with our inhibitor systems in place," La Forge said.

Th'Hadik nodded. "Our working theory is that someone here provided the weapon to him. We checked the arsenal's access log, but there is no record of an unscheduled entry."

"Computer records can be forged," Picard said.

"Indeed," the Andorian replied. "And on that point, we

also conducted identity verifications on everyone we took
into custody, to include retinal scans. One of those arrested
has a profile in the parliament's security system. His clearance
grants him access throughout the compound, but upon further investigation the computer record appears to have been
fabricated."

"How is that possible?" sh'Thalis asked, her mouth all but
falling open in shock.

Shaking his head, th'Hadik replied, "In theory, it should
not be possible. Our computer networks carry multipoint
encryption and authentication protocols, which can only be
issued by authorized personnel. All requests to create access
for anyone are channeled through a central office charged
with overseeing data-network security. We attempted to
ascertain the identity of the security officer who created the
access credentials used by the intruder, and we discovered
that the access ID attached to the record in question was itself
a forgery." He paused, clearing his throat. "The author of *that*
record is listed as being *you,* Presider."

The revelation caught everyone in the room by surprise.
"What?" sh'Thalis asked, making no attempt to hide her
shock. "That makes absolutely no sense. I don't even use a
computer. I leave all of that to Loqnara." She gestured toward
ch'Birane, who now looked every bit as anxious as the presider
herself.

Th'Hadik nodded. "That's correct, and he does not possess the requisite authorization or expertise to create such an
access entity. No, it appears that someone else on staff at the
compound is responsible."

"You're suggesting the *Treishya,* or another group, has
contacts or sympathizers within the presider's administration?" Picard asked.

"I am not *suggesting* it, Captain," the Andorian countered. "I'm stating it as a point of incontrovertible fact. It's the only reasonable explanation that fits all of the information known to us. To do what this person accomplished requires a specialized level of technical acumen as well as knowledge of how our system is deployed, including security protocols. We've suspected the possibility of *Treishya* supporters or sympathizers within our government for some time, but law-enforcement agencies have had no success ascertaining the identities of anyone who might have such an affiliation."

La Forge said, "The level of expertise you're talking about can't be held by a large number of people, even if you count the entire data-systems and network-security staff."

"That is our contention, as well," th'Hadik replied, nodding. "We have intensified our efforts to compile a list of likely suspects, but it is a time-consuming affair."

"Presider," Picard said, "with this new information, I strongly urge you to cancel the conference, or at least move it to a safer venue, such as the *Enterprise*."

Sh'Thalis shook her head. "We've been over this, Captain. I cannot capitulate to these extremists. To do so only legitimizes their position, and weakens my authority. How can I command respect as the leader of my people if I do the *Treishya*'s bidding? What will be their next demand, and what if I then refuse? I cannot believe that my failing to comply won't have consequences."

"At least wait awhile before resuming the schedule," La Forge said. "Give my people time to retrofit the computer security and harden our defenses."

Th'Hadik added, "Such a delay would also allow us further time to seek out anyone in the administration who may be aiding the *Treishya*."

After a moment, sh'Thalis nodded. "Very well. That is a sensible course."

Still standing behind her near the desk, Loqnara ch'Birane said, "Presider, you have adversaries in parliament who will take advantage of this decision and use it to portray you as indecisive and perhaps even cowardly, waiting for Starfleet to come to your aid rather than boldly standing up to those who would seek to undermine your noble efforts."

"When they assume responsibility for the safety of innocent bystanders," sh'Thalis replied, "then their observations and portrayals will mean a great deal more to me than they do today." To Picard and La Forge, she said, "Any assistance you can provide, as always, is greatly appreciated." Turning to th'Hadik, she added, "If we have traitors in our midst, Commander, I want them found."

The Andorian nodded. "Understood, Presider."

Picard was about to offer th'Hadik any personnel or other support from the *Enterprise* that the commander might desire in order to assist in the search efforts, when he was interrupted by the sound of his combadge beeping and the voice of Commander Worf.

"Enterprise *to Captain Picard.*"

Tapping his communicator, the captain replied, "Picard here. What is it, Number One?"

The Klingon's response came in a series of terse, clipped words, belying his anxiety even as he endeavored to retain his professional bearing. "*Sir, long-range sensors have detected the approach of a vessel into the system and on a course for Andor. It's broadcasting a hail on all frequencies. Communications confirms that the hail is intended for the* Enterprise."

His brow furrowing as he digested this latest news, Picard

asked, "Have you identified the ship? Does it appear to pose a threat?"

"*The vessel appears to be unarmed, sir,*" the first officer replied, "*but sensors have identified it as being Tholian in origin.*"

"Tholian?" Picard repeated. "Are you certain?"

Worf replied, "*Affirmative. If it maintains its present course, it should enter standard orbit of Andor in less than two hours.*"

With rare exceptions, which were detailed in Picard's intelligence briefings, the Tholians had become all but invisible since forming their controversial, highly publicized allegiance with the other key stakeholders of the Typhon Pact. In the year that had passed since the forming of the unlikely consortium, the governments representing the Pact had kept mostly to themselves, though intelligence reports theorized that their stated intentions to work together for the betterment of their respective peoples was little more than a hopeful fantasy. The organization's true goals remained as shrouded in mystery as its members.

So, why here? Why now?

Picard suspected he would find the answers to such questions anything but pleasant.

31

"The Tholian vessel has dropped out of warp, Commander, and is now on course to assume standard orbit."

"Sensors," Worf said, glancing to the tactical station. "Conduct a full sweep. Confirm that they're unarmed."

At the tactical station, Ensign Abigail Balidemaj did not look up from her console as she replied, "Aye, sir." Her fingers moved with impressive speed over the workstation's rows of illuminated controls, and several of the display monitors arrayed before her jumped in response to her queries. "Sensors are detecting no signs of any weapons systems, Commander. According to the recognition database, the ship appears to be a diplomatic courier vessel. They do have deflector shields, but they are currently inoperative."

"Diplomatic?" asked T'ryssa Chen, who at Worf's direction had taken the seat to the right of the captain's chair and normally reserved for the first officer. "They sent someone to talk? I don't recall the Tholians ever being particularly chatty. They make the Klingons sound like Bolians."

Glaring at the outspoken lieutenant from the corner of his eye, Worf nevertheless grunted in agreement. His own infrequent encounters with the notoriously standoffish race lent credence to Chen's observations. The original hail from the ship, directed at the *Enterprise,* had been nothing more than an automated message notifying the starship of its peaceful intentions and requesting to enter orbit above Andor. After relaying this information to Captain Picard, who in turn had consulted with Presider sh'Thalis, Worf had dispatched a response to the Tholian vessel conveying the presider's permission for the ship to proceed with its approach. The message had not been answered, nor had any further hails or requests for dialogue been received, despite repeated attempts by Balidemaj to establish communications.

Typical Tholian obstinence, the first officer conceded.

"Put the ship on-screen," Worf ordered, and a moment later the image on the main viewer of Andor from high orbit changed to a display of the Tholian vessel against a backdrop of black space. Unlike warp-capable ships constructed by other races, this vessel showed no distinct nacelles or other similar design concepts. Everything required for the ship's propulsion system was carried within the smooth lines of its angular, arrowhead design.

"They've opened a hailing frequency," Balidemaj called out from her station. "Standard linguacode greeting and a request for an open channel."

"Establish communications," Worf ordered.

The tactical officer turned in her seat, her expression one of confusion. "The message isn't being sent to us, sir. It's being directed at Andor, though we can certainly pick it up."

Perplexed, Worf scowled as he attempted to discern what the Tholian vessel might be planning. "Open a channel." A moment later, the image on the viewscreen shifted once again, this time to the silhouette of a Tholian, the reddish hue of its crystalline body dominating a broad-spectrum background. The image at first appeared to be wavering, and it took Worf an extra moment to remember that this actually was an indicator of the extreme heat aboard the alien vessel, in keeping with Tholian environmental requirements.

"People of Andor," it said, the intercom system's universal translator rendering the Tholian's speech into a high-pitched, almost feminine voice, *"I am Ambassador Nreskene, special diplomatic envoy of the Tholian Assembly. On behalf of my people, I bring you greetings, and my assurance that our presence here is peaceful."*

"Do Tholians lie?" Chen asked.

Considering the question, Worf shook his head. "Actually, they don't. At least, they're not known for employing deception." Of course, it was entirely possible that the Tholians, through their close association with certain other Typhon Pact member states, had acquired some new skills and habits.

"I come to you today with information of great importance to all your citizens," Nreskene continued. *"It is my intention to be heard by everyone, not simply your government or military leaders, so that you may understand the sincerity with which we are reaching out to you. While our reputation of being intolerant with respect to other species is well deserved, it is our intention to establish a new era of communications with our interstellar neighbors. We realize that many will view this with great suspicion, which is why I am here today."*

Shifting in his seat, Worf said, "Ensign Balidemaj, is this signal being received at the parliament complex?"

The young woman nodded. "Yes, sir. As the ambassador stated, it's being relayed through all newsnet broadcasts across Andor."

On the viewer, Nreskene said, *"For some time, we have known about the difficulties facing the Andorian people. How-*

ever, it is only recently—within the past few years, according to Federation standard measurements—that we have become aware of information which we believe may be of use to Andor in finding a possible solution for your dilemma. To that end, we have contacted one of the leading representatives of your scientific community, Professor Marthrossi zh'Thiin, who has already devoted significant time and effort toward researching the Andorian reproductive crisis. Indeed, having been kept apprised of the professor's progress using the information we furnished to her, we are delighted to see that the work she has performed to this point holds such great promise."

"What is he talking about?" Chen asked. Worf turned to her, realizing that the puzzled look with which she regarded him likely matched his own.

"It appears," he said, "that Professor zh'Thiin, either knowingly or unknowingly, has benefited from collusion with Tholian sources." Though no open state of warfare currently existed between the Federation and the Tholian Assembly, the latter party's coalition with the Typhon Pact and its other member states, all of whom had some history of aggression with the Federation, was a matter of no small concern.

"As for the information we provided," Nreskene said, *"it will interest many to know that it has actually been in our possession for quite some time, though it was suppressed by our leadership caste more than a century ago, not long after the discovery of an astonishing form of artificially engineered genetic code. It was found on a world near our territorial boundaries by a Starfleet research vessel, and was later determined to have been created by an advanced yet extinct race of beings calling themselves the Shedai."*

Worf frowned upon hearing the name. It was familiar, though he could not recall where he had seen or heard it.

Turning to the science station, he said, "Lieutenant Elfiki, search the computer banks for any mention of this Shedai race, along with any coordinating references to Starfleet research missions."

"Aye, sir," replied the science officer, already turning to the task at her workstation.

"They've been dead for millennia," Chen said, "but the Tholians share an ancestral link with them." As Worf cast a questioning glare in her direction, she added, "I read about them while doing research on various Starfleet first-contact missions."

Nreskene said, *"The Shedai once ruled a vast empire, which included subjugating our ancestors. That period of our history is largely unrecorded, but we do know that their empire fell. It was believed that they had all perished, but a few remnants of their civilization survived, and were found along with this artificial genetic code. Though this discovery was made so long ago, we have only just begun to explore its potential ourselves, owing to the shroud of security in which it was concealed. It did not take us long to realize the unique eugenic properties the genetic code possessed, and several of our scientists even postulated that such potential might well assist in the curing or even prevention of biological anomalies such as that affecting the Andorian people."*

The Tholian paused, and to Worf it seemed as though the ambassador might want his audience to ponder that last point for a moment. He reviewed what Nreskene had said, sensing there was something deliberate about the way in which the information was being imparted. Having engaged in diplomatic debate on more occasions than he could count, the Klingon had learned to discern when someone was laying an oratorical trap. It was exactly the sensation he was now experiencing as he listened to the Tholian's words.

Wait . . .

Even before Nreskene resumed speaking, Worf realized that the ambassador had already provided the clues to detect that trap, which he now was about to spring.

"Despite the enthusiasm within our own scientific community," the Tholian said, *"what also was intriguing was the apparent fact that this same information has been in the hands of Federation and Starfleet officials since its discovery. While the Federation has made available to Andorian scientists a great deal of data and materials in the areas of genetic research, they appear to have taken deliberate steps to avoid disclosing this information. Considering the potential it represents, as evidenced by Professor zh'Thiin's work and progress, one must wonder what could have motivated anyone to keep such knowledge hidden."*

"Talk about cutting our legs right out from under us," Chen said, her voice barely a whisper.

Worf could only nod in agreement. Whatever this Tholian was playing at, whether truthful or complete fabrication, his revelations likely would be having an immediate, tangible effect down on Andor, sending the government officials, media outlets, and ordinary citizens scrambling for understanding. An all-new flurry of explosive emotional responses would surely follow, compounding that which already was coursing through the Andorian populace.

Nreskene said, *"More than a century ago, the discovery of the formidable power once wielded by the Shedai was the cause of much strife between the Federation, the Klingon Empire, and even my people. Escalating tensions all but led to open warfare between the three parties. With that in mind, it seems obvious why the information was concealed and an earnest attempt made to obscure if not deny what happened. However, that was long ago, and the interstellar political situation has since drastically*

*changed. With all the Federation currently faces with respect
to rebuilding in the aftermath of the Borg invasion, one would
think they would want to assist those in need, and most especially
one of their oldest, most trusted member states. After two centuries of steadfast alliance, should the Federation not be doing
everything in its power to help Andor, especially if they hold in
their grasp a potential answer to your problems? As one member
of a race that was also once subjugated for the benefit of another
civilization, I find such actions to be most disgusting."*

"Subjugated?" said Lieutenant Elfiki. "Did he just imply
that the Federation *enslaved* Andor? This guy is definitely a
politician."

Worf glanced at Chen, who was regarding him with an
expression of troubled skepticism. "They're really taking us
out for a ride, aren't they?"

*"Perhaps they are unwilling to extend every effort on behalf
of a trusted ally,"* Nreskene continued. *"Only their leaders can
confirm or deny that. However, those I represent have decided
that a new approach is in order: one of candor, not only among
ourselves but also to those with whom we must share this quadrant of the galaxy. Therefore, as our first official act of goodwill,
we publicly acknowledge our role in Professor zh'Thiin's research,
and pledge to provide her with our continued support, in the
hope of bringing about a true solution to the problems Andor
faces. We await your answer with utmost enthusiasm."*

With that, the Tholian's image disappeared, replaced on
the viewscreen by that of the ambassador's ship. Around the
bridge, crew members had turned from their stations staring at one another with varying degrees of confusion and
disbelief.

"Lieutenant Elfiki," Worf said, still trying to process
everything he had just heard, "package a copy of that mes-

sage and stand by for transmission to Starfleet Command."
He would not send it just yet; he would wait until Captain
Picard weighed in on the matter, but it was likely that the
captain would soon be having an animated conversation with
someone back on Earth. Regardless of whether the Tholian
was being truthful with the revelations and insinuations he
had made, the effects on the Andorian populace were sure to
be nothing less than explosive.

T'Ryssa Chen, it seemed, had reached the same conclusion, and when she looked to Worf, it was with her right eyebrow arched.

"I could be wrong, but you might want to think about
setting the ship's phasers to stun the whole planet."

Her suggestion, Worf decided, was not completely without merit.

32

"Madam President," Sivak said as the doors to Nanietta Bacco's office parted to admit the Vulcan, "the Tholian ambassador is here."

Occupying one of the chairs in front of Bacco's desk, Admiral Akaar turned to regard the president's assistant. "Did she travel here via the Delta Quadrant?"

"I do not have her itinerary here with me, Admiral," Sivak replied, his right eyebrow arching, "but I can certainly obtain that information if you desire."

Bacco pulled herself to her feet. "That won't be necessary," she said, offering their banter a dismissive wave. "Send them in, Sivak." She then directed a mock glare at Akaar. "You. Behave."

Moving from his chair to stand to one side of the desk so as not to be standing next to or in front of Bacco when her guest arrived, the admiral replied. "I have always endeavored to conduct myself with utmost tact, Madam President." That he managed to say that without cracking a smile was almost enough to make Bacco laugh, which would have provided a nice lift to her current mood. Her ire at having been forced to await an answer to her request for this meeting, coupled with the added delay as the diplomat's estimated time of arrival seemed to shift with the direction of the breeze blowing across the River Seine, was beginning to wear on her patience. It seemed as though every meeting she had with Tezrene, former Tholian ambassador to the Federation and now one of the diplomatic representatives of the Typhon Pact currently residing on Earth, was less productive and more contentious than its predecessor.

"Well, let's put on our happy faces and make nice for our guest," Bacco said just before her office doors slid apart to once again admit Sivak. This time, her assistant was followed by four members of her presidential protection detail, who in turn accompanied a lone Tholian. As always, the ambassador wore her environmental suit, comprised of golden silk and containing the harsh, toxic atmosphere native to her homeworld and deadly to most humanoid life-forms.

"President Bacco," Sivak said, stopping in front of her desk and speaking with the official tone he reserved for making such introductions, "I present Tezrene, Tholian ambassador to the Federation and official representative of the Typhon Pact."

"Thank you, Sivak," Bacco said, and the Vulcan took his cue to exit the office. Bacco waited until the doors closed behind him before directing a stern gaze toward Tezrene. "Well, Ambassador, thank you for taking the time to meet me, though I have to say that for a people who place such a high value on punctuality, you sure do like to keep others waiting." Standing as he was just behind and to the ambassador's left, Akaar was not within the Tholian's line of sight when Bacco saw his eyes widen and he regarded her with a mixture of surprise and amusement. Every feature of his wizened visage seemed to ask, "Did you not just tell me to behave myself?"

Rank hath its privileges, Leonard.

To her credit, Tezrene at least attempted to appear repentant. *"I apologize for the delay in answering your request for a meeting, Madam President,"* she said, her native language interpreted through her environmental suit's embedded vocoder device and offering a translation that seemed to give the ambassador a flat, computer-like voice. *"I was unavoidably detained by urgent matters requiring my immediate attention."*

Bacco said, "Yes, you have been busy, haven't you?" Stepping away from her desk, she moved to stand directly before the Tholian, though not so close that her protective detail could not step in to block Tezrene's path should the Tholian be so bold—or stupid—as to attempt a direct physical threat against her. "That was quite the proverbial bombshell your Ambassador Nreskene dropped on Andor."

"We prefer to think of it as correcting a glaring omission of fact, Madam President," Tezrene replied. *"Given the unprecedented success Professor zh'Thiin seems to have found with her research, and the obvious benefit it would appear to represent for the Andorian people, my government thought it prudent to disclose the truth behind the wondrous discoveries the professor has made."*

Her eyes narrowing in suspicion, Bacco said, "So, you're claiming credit for zh'Thiin's work?"

The ambassador emitted a series of clicks and snaps that were not translated by her suit's vocoder, before answering, *"Not at all. Indeed, we celebrate the progress Professor zh'Thiin has made with the limited information we provided to her."*

"So," Akaar said, moving forward so that he was now in the Tholian's field of view, "if I understand you correctly, Ambassador, you did not give Professor zh'Thiin a complete record of the information you possess regarding the Taurus meta-genome?"

"That is correct, Admiral," Tezrene answered. *"I am authorized to tell you that while our grasp of the full potential to be found within the Shedai data repository is by no means complete, we have been making great strides to further our understanding of all it represents."*

Frowning, Akaar said, "Forgive me, Ambassador, but that seems a bit far-fetched. It has been more than a hundred years since the meta-genome's discovery in the Taurus Reach. Considering everything that happened in the years following that find and the genetic links between your people and the Shedai, one would think Tholians ideally suited for decrypting that information."

"You would be correct, Admiral," Tezrene said. *"That much was demonstrated more than a century ago. However, for a time, we believed that shunning the Shedai and everything associated with them was the best course of action for our people. As time has passed and new perspectives are gained, we have begun revisiting those earlier decisions."*

Bacco was certain that she did not at all like what the ambassador seemed to be implying. After all this time, were the Tholians truly digging back into the secrets of the Shedai, and the immeasurable power they once commanded? So great was their influence, at least according to what Bacco had learned, that the Tholians had feared traversing the Taurus Reach, that section of space over which the Shedai once had ruled, for millennia after the ancient race was believed to have died out.

Well, it sounds like they've gotten over that, she mused, her thoughts briefly turning to the conversation she had shared with Akaar just a few nights earlier. Despite the admiral's estimation of the Tholians' motivations, might they actually be considering sharing with the other members of the

Typhon Pact any of the Shedai's secrets that had lain dormant all this time?

"You seem to be making rapid progress," Akaar said.

Tezrene replied, *"It was only after the rescinding of such mandates and following prolonged research that our scientists were able to comprehend those facets of the meta-genome which allowed my government to offer assistance to Professor zh'Thiin."*

"It's a very magnanimous gesture on the part of the Tholian Assembly," Bacco countered. "Tell me, Ambassador: why not simply approach us directly? This sounds like the sort of collaborative venture that seems to have eluded us all these years." As Tezrene formulated her reply, Bacco was sure that if the Tholian could shrug, she would have done exactly that.

"My government saw no gain to be acquired by taking such action, Madam President."

Despite the fact that Tezrene appeared to have deliberately phrased her response in such a fashion as to provoke a reaction, Bacco still felt the momentary urge to suggest to the ambassador other possible courses of action, several of which involved inappropriate acts which might be undertaken individually or perhaps with the assistance of various relatives. She forced herself to count to ten before saying another word, all the while regarding the Tholian with what she hoped appeared to be polite indifference. Even as she studied Tezrene's shielded face, which of course offered no visual clues as to what that ambassador might be thinking, Bacco doubted that her own charade was having any tangible effect.

Damn, but I bet Tholians make hellacious poker players.

"And just how long have you been supplying Professor zh'Thiin with this information?" she finally asked.

"More than a year, as you would measure it," Tezrene replied.

Of course, Bacco thought. It would not have been long after the Tholian Assembly's decision to join the Typhon Pact, but their research into the Taurus meta-genome obviously predated even that bold political maneuver. Whether they had planned all along to use whatever knowledge they gleaned from the long-dead Shedai in a bid to make life difficult for the Federation was anybody's guess, and Bacco knew she would never receive a straight answer to such a blunt question.

She asked it, anyway.

"So, all of this—the theatrics, the lurking in the shadows, coming out on an interstellar stage to show how much you can stick it to the Federation—is just a bid to screw with us?"

Tezrene paused, and Bacco figured the ambassador's vocoder was translating some of the colloquial idioms she had thrown into the middle of their verbal joust. Then, the Tholian replied, *"It appears that your arrogance continues unabated, Madam President. As we have tried to communicate to you in the past, it should seem obvious that our goals are to benefit our people. Any secondary effects the attaining of those objectives might have upon the Federation, and you personally, are secondary in nature, though they of course do not pass unappreciated. Perhaps I was simply being too subtle during our past discussions, so allow me to be clear: How you choose to react to any action we take is of little consequence, either to my government or the Typhon Pact. Nothing we have done is in violation of any interstellar law or treaties currently binding on our two peoples. Therefore, any concerns you might raise are simply not relevant."*

Then, as though suddenly made aware of something she might have forgotten, Tezrene shifted her stance on the set of six limbs supporting her squat, crystalline body. *"I do apolo-*

gize, Madam President, but as I expect we have nothing further to discuss and I am due at another appointment, I must therefore take my leave of you."

"So what happens now?" Bacco asked, willing the words to sound measured and controlled and offering no hint of her mounting frustration.

Lifting her two foremost limbs, Tezrene brought them together before her. If she had possessed hands like a humanoid's, Bacco would have expected the ambassador to interlace her fingers. *"I am but an observer to these proceedings. My government does not see fit to inform me with respect to certain facets of its agenda. I expect that I will discover their plans just as you do. Good day, Madam President."*

Despite her instinct to call Tezrene on the abrupt nature of her leaving, Bacco waited until her protection detail escorted their charge to the exit, and even until the doors opened before she called out, "Ambassador." She watched as the Tholian halted her departure, turned to face her once more.

"Yes, Madam President?"

"Just one more thing before you go," Bacco said. "It's possible that I *also* was too *subtle* earlier, so let me explain this for future reference: I don't like to be kept waiting. I don't tolerate it from the people I *like,* so you can imagine how little regard I have for anyone else. So, while you're on my planet and enjoying the hospitality of the people who live and work here, when I call for you, I expect you to be here before the echo dies. You want to get in a political pissing match with me, you can do it from your own damned planet. Am *I* making myself perfectly clear, Ambassador?" She counted the seconds Tezrene spent in silence, regarding her with the implacable façade afforded her by her environmental suit. The count was twelve when the Tholian finally responded.

"*Duly noted, Madam President. Good day.*"

Akaar, to his credit, waited until Tezrene and her escort had left the office and the doors had slid closed behind him before deigning to say anything.

"And to think, all this time I believed I was the diplomatic one."

"Shut up," Bacco said, reaching up to rub her forehead. A sudden pressure, slight yet still noticeable, was beginning to build behind her eyeballs. With luck, she decided, her brain would explode, and all of this would be someone else's problem.

I don't have that kind of luck.

"Madam President," Akaar said, his tone impassive, "what would you like to do now?"

"All sorts of things, Leonard," Bacco said, "most of which would end up having me tried for one charge or another. In the meantime, it looks like I'll be spending some time with the Council, because nothing solves problems better than a gaggle of politicians talking it all to death."

33

"*All requests for interviews with the presider or any member of her administration continue to go unanswered. We are also awaiting official comment from the Federation ambassador as well as the Starfleet liaison. The scene outside the parliamentary compound as well as the Federation embassy is one of intense activity, with hundreds of citizens converging on each location and demanding answers in the wake of the unexpected yet controversial message from the Tholians.*"

"'Unexpected yet controversial,'" Beverly Crusher echoed. "That's an understatement and a half."

Watching the report on the viewscreen in Presider sh'Thalis's office, Picard simply nodded. The newsnet broadcasts had been offering some variation of the report without respite since Ambassador Nreskene's message to Andor, three days ago. Presider sh'Thalis had spent much of the ensuing time in closed-door meetings not only with Professor zh'Thiin but also with the other members of parliament, no doubt receiving updated status reports about the escalating instances of civil unrest as well as contingency plans for dealing with the constantly evolving situation. Though the presider had not said as much aloud, Picard was left with the distinct impression that his presence, or that of anyone else who was not an Andorian, was not welcome in the parliamentary chamber.

"Did you watch the earlier report?" Beverly asked after a moment. "It seems Presider sh'Thalis has at least one person on her staff with a big mouth."

Picard nodded. "Yes. I believe 'unnamed sources' is the correct term." According to those sources, Presider sh'Thalis had been in almost constant discussions with parliament about the Tholian ambassador's startling revelations and their potential impact on Andorian society, to say nothing of the possible damage to Andor's relationship with the Federation.

Looking away from the viewscreen, Beverly asked, "Is it true the presider's getting pressured to expel Federation diplomatic staffs?"

"Not just them," Picard replied, "but all Starfleet and Federation personnel. There have even been a few calls to order all non-Andorians from the planet at once." Concerned for the safety of anyone affected by such demands, the captain already had ordered Worf to contact all Federation and Starfleet offices with instructions for anyone who wished to be evacuated to the *Enterprise*. More difficult would be informing non-Andorian civilians about that offer, but at last report, Worf and Choudhury were already working on a means to accomplish that task.

Beverly regarded him with a quizzical expression. "Do you think she'll give in to those demands?"

"She's resisted them to this point," Picard said. Indeed, sh'Thalis had expressed to Picard her regret at having to entertain the suggestions at all. Despite whatever understandable desire she might have to vent anger and betrayal at Picard as the face of the Federation and Starfleet in closest proximity, she had elected not to focus on placing blame or pointing fingers and had instead concentrated on determining the next correct course of action. However, Picard knew that she faced a vocal opposition in the parliament. Several of the representatives had made public their shock and displeasure stemming from the Tholian's message. The newsnet broadcasts were using clips from those interviews to maximum advantage, flooding the airwaves with ceaseless discussion and theorizing on the subject while waiting for the presider to make any kind of official announcement.

Turning from the viewscreen, Picard moved to stand before the massive curved window at the front of the office. Looking across the compound, he was able to see a large crowd assembled in the street outside the complex's main gate. Even through the thick transparasteel, he still could hear the faint shouts, horns, and other noisemakers coming from the crowd. There were far too many people to count, but Picard estimated that the gathering numbered at least two hundred. As had happened during earlier such gatherings, some of the participants held up placards with words and phrases rendered in Andorii as well as Federation Standard. Unlike past demonstrations, there were far more signs printed with anti-Federation slogans than those voicing support.

"It's interesting how quickly opinions and stances can change," Beverly said after a moment. "When we first arrived here, the point of contention was whether to allow genetic manipulation at all. Now, the argument seems to be focusing on why the Federation didn't help their friends, the Andorians, to do precisely what so many people didn't want done in the first place."

Drawing a deep breath in a vain attempt to relax, Picard replied, "Ambassador Nreskene did a masterful job framing the discussion in that manner. I have to say, his approach was almost Romulan. It would seem the Tholians are benefiting from their association with the Empire." He clasped his hands behind his back, continuing to study the scene beyond the perimeter gate.

"For a year we hear almost nothing from the Tholians," he said, "and now this. At least we know they've been busy." Relations between the Federation and the Tholian Assembly had all but disintegrated in the aftermath of the Borg invasion. The Tholians, angered over President Bacco's strong-arm tactics during her attempt to pull together a combined force to stand against the Borg, became one of the founding member states of the Typhon Pact. While the Pact's other major stakeholders—the Romulan Empire, the Breen, Gorn, Kinshaya and Tzenkethi—had all been involved in activities that had garnered the Federation's notice during the past year, the Tholians had largely remained quiet. Had they been biding their time?

"They're obviously playing some kind of angle," Beverly said, beginning to pace the office, "but what? Are they trying to get the Federation to bicker among itself? Why?"

Picard shrugged. "By causing internal strife, they might draw our attention away from something they consider to be of greater importance." Whatever that might be, he could not guess. Territorial expansion? While the Tholians had always been keen to extend their borders whenever the opportunity presented itself, their habit had been to do so away from Federation space. Boundary disputes were rare, owing as much to Federation diplomatic policies aimed at giving the Tholians a wide berth as to the mysterious race's hesitation to expand into areas where a dispute with the Federation might arise. At least, that was the status quo until a year ago. Since then, the Tholian's motives were known only to the Tholians.

And they're certainly not talking. At least, not to us.

All attempts by the *Enterprise* and Andor's own orbital space control to contact the Tholian courier vessel in the wake of the ambassador's message had been met with silence, even after the ship had settled into a geosynchronous orbit above the capital city of Lor'Vela. It had mimicked the *Enterprise*'s orbital path for the better part of a day before abruptly and without announcement departing the system, continuing the tradition of inscrutability that so characterized the Tholian Assembly.

The door to the presider's office opened and Picard and Beverly turned to see Professor zh'Thiin enter. She looked tired, the captain thought, her hair not quite so neat, her clothes a touch rumpled. Her antennae drooped. It was obvious that the past few days had also taken their toll on her.

"Captain Picard. Dr. Crusher," she said, stopping just inside the room as the doors closed behind her. "I'd hoped to find you here."

Offering a formal nod, Picard said, "What may we do for you, Professor?"

"It's what I can do for you, Captain," zh'Thiin replied. "I wish to apologize. I know that sounds so inadequate, but I hope you'll believe me when I tell you it's offered with all sincerity." She paused, casting her gaze toward the floor. "I never imagined something like this would happen. I simply wanted to help my people."

Gesturing for zh'Thiin to join them in the sitting area near the front window of the presider's office, Picard asked, "Professor, how did you come into possession of the research materials you were given?"

"I never had contact with any Tholian," zh'Thiin said, shaking her head as she took one of the proffered seats and folded her hands in her lap. "I was contacted more than a year ago by a Gallamite named Eronaq Sintay. At least, that's the name he used. He told me that a client he represented had taken an interest in the situation here on Andor, and that they held information they believed might be of use to those of us in the scientific community researching genetic therapies."

"And you had no idea this Sintay's client was Tholian?" Beverly asked.

Zh'Thiin shook her head. "No. Sintay said that his client wished to remain anonymous, and that maintaining that secrecy was a condition of our 'partnership.' He told me he'd been instructed to provide me with a sample of the information that I could study, and that if I wasn't interested in continuing the relationship, that would be the end of it. However, once I saw what they had given me, there was simply no way I could ignore whatever else they might have."

"The meta-genome," Picard said, his words low and soft.

"I suppose that's right," the professor replied, "but I had no way of knowing that."

Picard was able to sympathize. Though he was aware of Operation Vanguard and other forays into the Taurus Reach more than a century ago, much of that effort remained classified to this day. Included among those closely guarded secrets was information on the meta-genome itself. From what Picard had read, even the limited level of understanding into the complex strand of artificial DNA that had been achieved by Federation scientists had been sufficient to later guide the development of what would come to be known as Project Genesis. That awesome process, in which matter could be rearranged at the molecular level in order to transform lifeless planets and moons into thriving habitable worlds, had caused its fair share of trouble on more than one occasion in the century since its development. As impressive and even awe-inspiring as Genesis had been, Picard realized with a shudder that it represented the merest fraction of the power once commanded by the Shedai, the blueprints for which had been encoded into the meta-genome. All that was required was for someone to find a key to open the lock protecting that knowledge from those who might use it for reprehensible purposes.

"We know the Tholians have been in possession of this information since the time of the original Vanguard missions," Picard said, "and that for reasons known only to them, they did nothing to further their understanding of its potential for decades after the operation concluded. Why now?"

Beverly countered, "We don't know for sure that they did nothing. It could just be that they lacked the technology to help them understand what they had."

"While that might once have been possible," Picard said. "I don't believe that's the case now. I think there are at least some Tholians who know precisely what that meta-genome represents, even if they lack the technical expertise to do anything with that knowledge. Of course, that begs the question as to why we didn't make more progress with our own understanding of the meta-genome even after all this time." Pausing, he shrugged. "I suppose some of that could be attributed to the information being kept hidden for so many years."

"That doesn't explain the Tholians," Beverly said. "Correct me if I'm wrong, but aren't they supposed to hate everybody?"

Looking to his wife, Picard offered a small, humorless smile before turning to zh'Thiin. "Perhaps they didn't even need to know its precise potential. After all, why waste time with that sort of knowledge gathering when another party is already working on something in a similar—though far more primitive—vein."

"Enter you, Professor," Beverly added. "The Tholians essentially got you to do the difficult work."

Wringing her hands in her lap, zh'Thiin asked, "But why help us at all? Are they not part of an alliance that stands at odds with the Federation?"

"To be honest," Picard replied, "we're not entirely sure. While some members of the Typhon Pact have made quite clear their animosity toward the Federation, a few parties have taken a more composed, deliberate approach." As for the Tholians, for now they seemed content simply to have the Andorians angry with the Federation.

That much was working, at any rate.

"This is unbelievable," Crusher said after a moment. "Considering everything the Federation and Starfleet Command have given to the professor and other scientists working on the reproductive problem, why hold this back? It's not as though they couldn't redact unnecessary yet still-classified information before sending it here."

It was a question Picard had asked himself more than once during the past three days, particularly of Admiral Akaar himself. As the Starfleet Commander had explained it, "simple preservation" fueled that original decision. To reveal such knowledge now, while the Federation continued its struggles to rebuild as possible enemies lurked about, was too dangerous. The second reason Akaar had provided was the one Picard found the most saddening, especially now that one had the virtue of observing the decision in hindsight. With so much of the wondrous artificial DNA's true potential still shrouded in mystery, someone had thought that the odds of Andor benefiting from the classified information did not outweigh the risks incurred should that knowledge fall into the wrong hands. Given the success zh'Thiin had been able to achieve with even the limited information she had been provided, such paranoia hardly seemed justified.

"What will happen now?" zh'Thiin asked, and Picard heard the despair in her voice. "Don't misunderstand me, Captain; I don't blame you for the actions of your government, but what might my people's situation be if the Federation had offered information about the meta-genome a century ago, or even a decade? Where would we stand as a civilization?"

For that, Picard had no answer. The simple fact of the matter was that the effects of the Tholian ambassador's message were continuing to fuel an underlying current of resentment and betrayal among the populace. In the days since Nreskene's broadcast, many people were coming to view the Federation's actions as willful withholding of assistance despite its potential usefulness to Andor.

In truth, Picard could not blame them.

And where do we go from here?

34

Turning his face upward, Eklanir th'Gahryn closed his eyes and relished the soothing rays of the late-afternoon sun. If not for the pressing matters at hand, he would remain here until the last of the daylight faded, only to stay and watch the city around him come alive in a celebration of nightfall.

There should be laws against being indoors on a day like today.

Whenever circumstances and opportunity permitted, th'Gahryn retreated to the sanctuary he had created on the roof of the building that housed his private residence as well as the informal base of operations for the *Treishya* cell in Lor'Vela. The building, constructed atop a plateau on the outskirts of the city, was taller than those around it and as such received unobstructed sunlight for most of the day. Th'Gahryn had used that to his advantage, installing a solar-energy collector array as well as cultivating a lawn and garden to include an *elka* tree to provide a modest amount of shade. The garden also sported a gazebo along with a pair of benches and a stone table with metal chairs. From here, th'Gahryn enjoyed a spectacular view of the city, and he was high enough that the cacophony of Lor'Vela street life was little more than a faint buzz. This was where he often came to read, eat a quiet meal, or simply sit and watch the teeming hive of activity that was the new Andorian capital. Would that he could be allowed to partake of those treasured pastimes on a wondrous day like this.

"Eklanir."

So much for that notion, th'Gahryn mused, turning toward the voice and seeing Biatamar th'Rusni standing near the lift vestibule at the center of the roof. His advisor held a data reader in his hands, and his features were clouded with concern.

"What is it, Biatamar?" th'Gahryn called out, stepping away from the gazebo and making his way across the roof toward the lift.

Th'Rusni held up his reader. "Parliament remains in closed sessions. Our contact inside informs me that those representatives who support us are making little progress convincing Presider sh'Thalis to expel Federation and Starfleet personnel."

Smiling at the report as he approached the lift, th'Gahryn shook his head. "She is uncompromising in her beliefs, and for that I will extend her my sincere admiration. It cannot be easy, attempting to govern during a time of such turmoil."

Fate, it seemed, had blessed him with a wonderful gift, in the form of the Tholian ambassador and the incredible message he had delivered three days earlier. The newsnet broadcasts had done nothing since that moment but regurgitate the Tholian's startling revelations, in many cases inadvertently or deliberately misconstruing several points in order to slant the story so as to better fit within an outlet's particular political bias. The results had fueled the fires of discontent seizing hold among the populace. Calls for the eviction of not only Federation and Starfleet representatives but all non-

Andorians were on the rise. Denouncements from members of parliament representing the Visionist party were dominating the broadcasts, competing and in many cases winning out against contrary public statements distributed by their Progressive counterparts. Th'Gahryn did not see how Presider sh'Thalis, pilloried in the public eye, the media, and even within her own administration, could withstand that sort of mounting coercion for any appreciable length of time.

Stepping past th'Rusni, he made his way toward the lift. The doors parted at his approach and he stepped into the car, pressing the control for the lift to return him to his office. "I am confident when I say we have more than a few acquaintances within parliament who will agree that the time for the presider's commendable yet misguided nobility is at an end. Do we have endorsement for our plan?"

"No one has spoken for the record, of course," th'Rusni replied, "but I gather from the updates I'm receiving that certain parties would not object if we were to take matters into our own hands in decisive fashion."

Th'Gahryn considered his advisor's words, listening in silence to the hum of the lift as it descended into the bowels of the building. The next step in demonstrating the *Treishya*'s resolve, whether the result was success or failure, very much hinged upon the sanction of several members of parliament, who through various means had espoused views and positions very much in keeping with the activist movement th'Gahryn had forged almost with his own hands. Once he and his people set into motion their next act of protest, there would be no retreating from the attention their actions would engender. In one bold strike, the *Treishya* would advance from being just a group of concerned, dissatisfied citizens slightly more vocal than their rival factions to the focus of global attention by every law-enforcement and intelligence agency on the planet. The foremost question requiring an answer was whether those organizations would be governed by friends or enemies in the government. Would the *Treishya* be hailed as heroes, or shunned as terrorists? If all went according to plan, the actions undertaken today by th'Gahryn and his people would reward him with several allies enjoying new positions of power.

The lift eased to a stop and th'Gahryn barely waited for the doors to open before he exited the car and entered his expansive private chamber. Moving with a deliberate stride, he crossed the room and stood before the workstation built into the wall before his desk. The arrangement was an elaborate amalgam of communications and computer equipment, much of it fabricated to th'Gahryn's personal and exacting specifications. In particular, the comm system had been fashioned with several purposes in mind, not the least of which was being able to transmit and receive messages and hold secure dialogue with other *Treishya* cell leaders without worry of being traced.

"How much time do our people require before they are ready to implement the plan?" th'Gahryn asked. As he did so, he glanced at the chronometer display on one of the workstation monitors. It would be dark soon, which would be ideal for covert action.

Th'Rusni replied, "Five hours."

Nodding in approval, th'Gahryn said, "Alert them to begin their preparations immediately. We shall commence operations in six hours." By then, he knew, it would be well into late evening. Though the parliament's security contingent would doubtless be on the alert, by that point fatigue and monotony would have begun to take hold. A bored sentry was an inattentive sentry, not that stealth would be a requirement for the plan th'Gahryn had devised. On the contrary, he intended the *Treishya*'s forthcoming actions to provide a bold statement.

As th'Rusni turned and headed for the door to carry out his instructions, th'Gahryn recalled the multi-part encryption key he had created for accessing the system and which he shared with no one. Keying a set of instructions to the workstation's manual interface rewarded him with one of the computer monitors flaring to life. The blank screen was replaced with text informing him that the frequency was being established, which th'Gahryn knew would take at least a moment or two as the party he was trying to contact would need that time to establish secure communications on their end. After an appropriate interval, the text was supplanted by a video image of another Andorian, this one dressed in semiformal robes of the sort common to mid-level government employees.

"Threlas," he said by way of greeting. "I hope you're well."

On the monitor, Threlas ch'Lhren nodded. *"Indeed I am, my friend. I hope the same can be said of you."* An information technology specialist working within the labyrinthine government bureaucracy, ch'Lhren was one of th'Gahryn's closest friends as well as one of the *Treishya*'s first members, recruited by th'Gahryn himself. *"What can I do for you, Eklanir?"*

"The time for action has come," th'Gahryn replied, "and we have need for your particular talents. I trust you're ready?"

Ch'Lhren nodded, though th'Gahryn noted that he did so only after pausing, his eyes leaving the video pickup as though verifying that no one was in proximity to eavesdrop on the conversation. *"I can be ready, yes. Everything is in place and only awaits the proper instructions."*

Satisfied, th'Gahryn paused, giving one final consideration to what he was about to do. Once begun, there would be no turning back.

So be it.

"Very well, then, my friend," th'Gahryn said, already feeling the weight of his decision beginning to press down upon him. "Let us proceed."

The turbolift doors parted and Worf stepped onto the bridge, taking in the scene of subdued yet focused activity before him. It was well into beta shift—a few short hours before the start of gamma shift, actually, and he noted the familiar faces of several of the officers who, like him, had already been on duty during the previous rotation. With Lieutenants Choudhury and Konya off the ship, Ensign Balidemaj had taken on their alpha-shift bridge responsibilities and, as she had earlier in the day, was currently manning the tactical station.

"Commander," said Lieutenant Commander Havers, rising from the captain's chair after noticing Worf's arrival. "What brings you to the bridge?"

Worf held up his hand to indicate that the beta-shift watch officer should keep his seat. "I was just on my way to my quarters." He paused, then added, "To be honest, I've always been restless whenever the captain is off the ship." Such feelings of anxiety had plagued him from his earliest days as an ensign, and only deepened upon his transfer to the previous *Enterprise* under Captain Picard's command. From the ship's very first encounter with danger, Worf had always balked at the notion of the captain placing himself in harm's way while he and other subordinates remained safe. As he advanced both in rank and responsibility, eventually succeeding his late friend and colleague Natasha Yar as the ship's security chief, his commitment to the safety of the entire crew, Picard in particular, grew ever stronger. Now that he served as the *Enterprise*'s first officer, protecting the captain was one of his primary responsibilities.

And yet here he was, safe aboard the ship while Picard tended to matters down on the planet's surface. The very thought burned in his stomach like the fires of the Kri'stak Volcano.

"I'm sure Lieutenant Choudhury has the situation well in hand," Havers said. "Between our people and the Andorians, there's a small army down there."

Unsatisfied with that observation, Worf began to pace a slow circuit around the bridge's perimeter. "Do not discount the possibility of anyone among the Homeworld Security brigade or even Presider sh'Thalis's own protection detail taking exception to the continued presence of Starfleet personnel or just non-Andorians in general on Andor," he said, his attention divided between Havers and the various workstations he walked past. "There may even be members of the *Treishya* or one of the other anti-Federation groups among their ranks." No one fitting that description had yet been found, but avoiding discovery was the hallmark of any well-trained covert operative. That was just one more reason for Worf to feel anxious about the current situation, and he would continue to feel that sensation until Captain Picard was back aboard ship and the *Enterprise* was on its way to its next assignment.

"I shall be in my quarters should you require me," he said as he completed the circuit, returning his attention to Havers.

The watch officer nodded. "Understood, sir. I . . . "

He paused as lights all suddenly flickered and several of

the workstations around the bridge wavered or blinked, as though somehow losing their power connections. Then Worf heard a noticeable stuttering in the ubiquitous hum of the ship's engines reverberating through the bulkheads.

"What is that?" he asked, his gaze drifting over the confused, even concerned expressions of the bridge crew.

From where she sat at the ops station, Ensign Jill Rosado did not look up from her console as she said, "I'm registering power fluctuations across the ship."

At tactical, Balidemaj said, "Sir, we received an incoming burst transmission just before the power interruption. Somebody was attempting to contact us from the surface."

Worf looked to Havers, who tapped his combadge. "Bridge to engineering. What's going on with the ship's power?"

There was a pause before the voice of Lieutenant Commander Taurik replied, *"Engineering. Taurik speaking, Commander. We are experiencing a ship-wide interruption in power-routing systems. The cause is as yet unknown, but we are performing diagnostics."*

A moment later, everything on the bridge went dark, and Worf heard the sounds of computer consoles and other control stations powering down. He felt a fleeting disorientation as his eyes adjusted to the sudden absence of light, but within seconds secondary illumination was activating across the bridge. Looking from station to station, he saw that consoles were already returning to life. Confusion clouded the faces of everyone around him.

"Bridge," Taurik said. *"We have lost all main power. Backup systems are online."*

"What is the cause, Mr. Taurik?" Worf asked, feeling his annoyance beginning to rise.

The Vulcan engineer replied, *"I do not yet know, Commander. We are continuing our investigation."*

At ops, Rosado said, "Sir, I'm locked out of all primary systems, including weapons and defenses. They've all been taken off-line, or else security protocols have been enabled and are preventing me from gaining access."

Frowning at the report, Worf asked, "How is that possible?"

Rosado shook her head. "I don't know. It shouldn't be possible, at least not without command authorization."

Worf stepped down into the command well and moved to stand behind Rosado. "Computer," he called out, "remove security-lockouts on primary systems and resume normal operations."

"Unable to comply," replied the computer.

Now struggling with the urge to vent his rapidly intensifying irritation, Worf said, "Computer, override all previous security lockout instructions and restore normal functions. Authorization Worf three seven gamma echo."

"Unable to comply," the computer repeated.

Frustration now was being replaced with simple anger. Clenching his fists at his sides, Worf snapped, "Engineering! The main computer is not responding to command authorization directives."

"We are experiencing similar difficulties here, as well, Commander," Taurik replied. *"I have already alerted computer operations to the problem."*

"What the hell is going on?" asked Havers, still standing in front of the captain's chair. "What about that communication just before all this started? Could that have been some kind of attack?"

"Our systems are designed to withstand such infiltrations," Worf replied.

From the tactical station, Balidemaj said, "Commander, we're receiving an incoming message. It appears to be coming from the surface, but I'm unable to pinpoint a source."

That only added to Worf's mounting confusion. "You can't locate the signal's point of origin?"

The tactical officer shook her head. "No, sir. It's being routed through the global satellite network. Whoever's hailing us, it looks like they don't want to be found, and they definitely seem to know what they're doing."

"On-screen, Lieutenant," Worf said, "but continue your efforts to track the signal's source."

The image on the main viewer of Andor from orbit shifted to display an Andorian that Worf did not recognize. He looked to be of middle age—at least, so far as the first officer could tell with respect to Andorian physiology. His stark-white hair was cut close to his skull, and his visage was marked by deep lines in his forehead, along his cheekbones, and around his mouth.

"This is Commander Worf, first officer of the *U.S.S. Enterprise.*" Stepping around the ops station, he approached the viewer and glared at the image displayed upon it. "What is the purpose of your communication?"

The Andorian smiled, though it was the sort of expression that to Worf implied insincerity and even arrogance. *"My purpose, Commander Worf, is to tell you to take your ship away from my planet, and not to return."*

At once galled and yet impressed by the Andorian's bluntness, Worf said, "And who are you to be making such demands?"

"I am the one currently holding your ship hostage," the Andorian replied. *"My name is Eklanir th'Gahryn, leader of the* Treishya. *We have given you ample opportunity to leave in*

peace, and you have ignored our requests. Therefore, I have been compelled to undertake more aggressive action."

Forcing himself to remain still, Worf clasped his hands behind his back. "From what I have observed, you are a coward, content to lurk in the shadows and hide your face while you send others to do your bidding."

Th'Gahryn smiled again. *"I thought you might say something like that. Knowing how much a Klingon respects an enemy who will face him, I thought revealing my true identity would convince you that I'm sincere about what I'm saying, even if you disagree with my position."* He paused, shrugging. *"Not that I require your affirmation. You will remove your starship from planetary orbit and depart Andorian space. Failure to do so is ill advised."*

Worf exchanged disbelieving looks with Havers before returning his attention to the screen. "Even if I were to agree, my captain and several members of my crew are still on the planet's surface. I will not leave without them."

"They will be dealt with, Commander," th'Gahryn said. *"As we speak, I have dispatched teams to collect them, after which they will be handled accordingly."*

There was no mistaking such an obvious threat. Struggling to keep his mounting rage in check, Worf glowered at his adversary. "Any hostile action you take against any member of this crew, or any Starfleet officer, is a criminal offense." For a brief moment, he almost wished the *Enterprise* was a Klingon ship, manned by a Klingon crew. At least then, the options for dealing with such an overbearing, dishonorable opponent would be far more fulfilling.

"Commander," th'Gahryn said, *"I've just threatened a Federation starship and its crew. In comparison, any action I might take against your captain would be rather restrained.*

Your concern should be those under your immediate command. Leave now, or I will destroy your vessel." He looked away for a moment as though consulting someone or something off-screen.

From just behind him, Worf heard Rosado say, "Commander, primary antimatter-containment systems have just gone off-line!"

Incredulous, Worf turned and glared at the ops officer. "What?"

Rosado offered a frantic nod. "Backup systems are deactivating, too."

Stepping forward so that he could have a better look at the ensign's console, Havers said, "If we lose those . . ." The words trailed off.

On the viewscreen, th'Gahryn completed Havers's report. *"If your redundant safety features are removed, your ship will self-destruct."*

"Worf to engineering," the first officer growled. "Status report!"

Despite Taurik's Vulcan heritage, Worf still heard the first signs of strain in the assistant engineer's voice as he replied, *"Commander, the main computer has just issued instructions for a complete shutdown of all antimatter-containment systems with the exception of one fail-safe protocol. We are unable to countermand or override the process."*

Returning his attention to the viewer, Worf glowered at th'Gahryn. "What have you done to my ship?" How was any of this even *possible*?

"I control its main computer," th'Gahryn said. *"Now, I believe we were discussing your imminent departure."*

Havers said, "We could evacuate."

"That would prove problematic, I think," th'Gahryn replied.

Rosado said, "He's right, sir. Transporters are off-line and all shuttlebays have been locked out and depressurized."

"What about the escape pods?" Havers asked.

"Control systems have been locked down and encrypted," the ops officer replied. "It could take a week to descramble the codes, but manual control should still be available."

Despite his responsibility to see to the crew's safety, Worf did not view the escape pods as a palatable option. Abandoning the ship was itself a dishonorable act, but compounding that action by setting off in small, defenseless craft that may well have been affected by whatever scheme th'Gahryn had already perpetrated against the *Enterprise* did not seem at all prudent.

Shaking her head, Rosado sighed in mounting exasperation. "How the hell did he manage all of this?"

"Commander," called out Balidemaj from the tactical station. "I've still got sensors, and I'm picking up two vessels on an intercept course from the other side of the planet." She paused, apparently gathering more information, before adding, "They appear to be civilian freighters, sir, but sensors are picking up military-grade weapons and shields."

"*The benefits of having supporters and sympathizers within Homeworld Security,*" th'Gahryn countered. "*They are to be your escort from our system, Commander. I suggest taking no hostile action against them. In your vessel's diminished capacity, it wouldn't fare well in any serious confrontation.*" Leaning closer so that his weathered visage all but filled the screen, the Andorian's expression turned hard. "*If you do not leave orbit and set a course away from Andor immediately, I will destroy your ship with my entire world watching. Decide, Commander. Now.*"

Seething at his apparent helplessness, Worf clenched his

jaw so as to avoid howling at his adversary. "Commander Havers, take us out of orbit. Set a course for Starbase 7. Contact Captain Picard and alert him as to our current status."

"That won't be necessary, Commander," th'Gahryn said. *"Rest assured, we shall communicate your message to him in short order. Thank you for your cooperation."* The insufferable *petaQ* even had the audacity to smile just before the transmission ended.

Worf ignored the questioning stares of the bridge crew, turning from the viewscreen. Commander Havers regarded him, his own features clouded by uncertainty.

"What do we do now, sir?" he asked.

As much as it infuriated him to have to admit as much, Worf knew there was nothing to do except comply with th'Gahryn's demands and worry about the captain and the rest of the crew still on the surface.

35

Picard stood in the main foyer outside the meeting chamber of the Parliament Andoria, regarding himself in the reflection of one of the windows overlooking the courtyard surrounding the building. His dress uniform was immaculate, though he noted the puffiness around his eyes. It had been a long day, he reminded himself. Though local time here in the capital city was early evening, Picard's internal clock was still in tune with shipboard time aboard the *Enterprise*, which at last check was coming up on 2330 hours. Gamma shift, which presided over the starship during its equivalent of the "wee hours," would soon be starting, greeting the onset of a brand-new day.

Here on Andor, the old day was still proceeding at high warp.

As had been the case for the past three days, Presider sh'Thalis and the rest of the parliament had been locked in closed-door discussions, emerging at infrequent intervals for brief respites before returning to the chamber and resuming their dialogue. Sh'Thalis and a few other representatives had expressed their worry to Picard over much of the rhetoric being put forth by some of the ruling body's more vocal Visionist members, though disagreement on the current issue did not fall along party lines. Several Progressive advocates also had voiced their concern and displeasure over the Tholian ambassador's contentious broadcast to the Andorian people, and such negative feelings were only being exacerbated by the Federation Council's seeming reluctance to comment on the matter.

It was the last point that most concerned Picard. For what reason could President Bacco and the council be wavering? At least some of the secrets of the Taurus Reach that had been buried for all these decades were now revealed. The only thing that could be done now was to acknowledge the decisions made for better or worse more than a century ago, reiterate the Federation's dedication to aiding the Andorians by any means available, and find a way to move forward in united fashion.

Apparently, he mused with no small amount of cynicism, *some things are easier said than done.*

"You look tired," Beverly said, standing behind him and raising a hand to brush at his shoulder.

"Well, that's exactly how I feel," Picard replied. Satisfied with his appearance, he turned from the window and offered his wife a warm smile. "How's René?" He had not seen his son since very early in the morning before he beamed down from the ship in order to await word of any progress from the parliament.

Beverly returned his smile. "He misses his father." Reaching out, she placed a hand on his arm. "You know, I would've thought that all of us being aboard the same ship might mean you'd get to see him every night before his bedtime."

Feeling a pang of regret, Picard took his wife's hand in his own. It was a tender gesture, one he supposed was at odds with the sort of proper, composed bearing expected of a senior Starfleet officer. He forgave himself the momentary lapse of protocol, though habit did make him glance to where Lieutenant Rennan Konya and Ensign Ereshtarri sh'Anbi stood at a respectful distance, their attention on the passageway leading from the foyer and ensuring the captain and Dr. Crusher's privacy.

"Presider sh'Thalis has asked me to speak to the parliament," Picard said, "but I had no idea I'd be waiting this long." The presider had come to him in the fervent hope that he might be willing to address the assembled representatives and attempt to somehow defuse the sharp tensions currently being directed at the Federation and Starfleet. After three days of being shut out of all such discussions, he was choosing to take this as a sign that the situation was taking a positive turn. Of course, the presider had extended the invitation much earlier in the day, and since then he had been waiting without any further information or updates.

"I know," Beverly said. "Duty calls. That sounded more accusatory than I intended."

Picard smiled again, squeezing her hand. "There's no reason you have to stay. You should go back to the ship, if for nothing else than to kiss him good night for me."

"I already did that," Beverly replied. "He's asleep, and Dr. Tropp is the perfect babysitter. Besides, I didn't want to miss your big speech to the parliament."

Releasing a small sigh, Picard said, "In that case, I should probably prepare some remarks. Wouldn't want to disappoint my audience, now, would I?" In truth, he had only a vague notion of what he might say once he stood before the assembled politicians. Though he had received reluctant permission from President Bacco and Admiral Akaar to address the parliament, they had given him no direction as to what to convey on the Federation's behalf. Instead, they were trusting in his judgment and experience to help ease the swelling turmoil now gripping the Andorian government and populace. Everything Picard had considered as part of a formal opening statement had sounded too trite to his own ears. There definitely needed to be some form of acknowledgment and concession in the wake of what had been revealed by Ambassador Nreskene.

"Choudhury to Captain Picard," said the voice of the *Enterprise*'s security chief, emanating from his combadge and interrupting his thoughts.

"Picard here. What is it, Lieutenant?"

Her voice carrying a slight yet still noticeable tinge of anxiety, Choudhury asked, *"Sir, have you been in contact with the* Enterprise?"

Exchanging frowns with Beverly, Picard replied, "I haven't. Is there a problem?"

"That is *the problem, Captain,"* Choudhury said. *"I've tried several times to reach them, but there's no answer. I've also had a few of my people try on their own, and no luck."* After a moment, and in a lower voice, she added, *"If I didn't know any better, sir, I'd think communications were being jammed."*

Not liking the possibilities that notion engendered, the captain said, "Stand by, Lieutenant," before tapping his combadge to initiate a new frequency. "Picard to *Enterprise.* Come in, *Enterprise.*" When there was no answer, he repeated the call and received the same lack of response. Switching back to Choudhury, he said, "Lieutenant, put all of our people on alert, and wait for further instructions." By now Konya and sh'Anbi had adjusted their stances so that they could divide their attention between the corridor and Picard. Both regarded him with expectant looks, awaiting his orders.

"What are you thinking?" Beverly asked, studying him with no small amount of concern.

Picard shook his head. "I don't know yet, but something here is definitely wrong."

"Captain," Choudhury said, *"there's something else. Our security grid's pick—"* Her voice disappeared in a brief burst of static before the channel went dead.

"Lieutenant?" Picard called out, before attempting to reestablish contact. When that failed, he looked to his security detail. "Ensign sh'Anbi, go to the security command post and get me an update from Lieutenant Choudhury."

The young Andorian security officer nodded. "Aye, sir," she said, turning to leave the foyer, when a piercing alarm began filling the corridor. Pulsing indicator lights stationed at regular intervals along the curved, high-ceilinged passageway began to flash, casting frenzied shadows on the walls.

"That's an intruder alarm, sir," Konya said, his hand moving to rest on the phaser in its holster near his left hip.

Sh'Anbi activated her tricorder. The warbling tone of its internal sensors echoed in the foyer. "The security grid is down, sir. Force fields are inactive, but the transporter and unauthorized-weapons inhibitors are still operating. I'm picking up activity at all of the security checkpoints. Dozens of bio readings."

"The *Treishya*?" Beverly asked.

Was this it? Had the activists decided that the time for bold action finally had come? As if in response to his unvoiced thoughts, the lights in the foyer and corridor promptly extinguished, to be replaced seconds later by smaller, dimmer substitute emergency illumination. The shadows around them now became longer and more foreboding.

"We can't stay here, sir," Konya said, having drawn his phaser.

Picard nodded, his hand reaching as though of its own accord to take Beverly by the arm. "To the command post, Lieutenant."

Everything, it seemed, had gone crazy.

In the feeble glow of emergency lighting within the security detail's command post, Geordi La Forge scowled at the array of status displays and computer monitors before him. The workstation had been dedicated to overseeing the force-field grid and other protective measures requested by Worf and Choudhury for the duration of the conference. All of them were telling him the same thing: He was locked out of the system he had devised.

"What the hell?" La Forge said, tapping out strings of queries and other interrogative commands on the workstation's manual interface. None of the status readings changed in response to his instructions. In fact, it was not evident that the system was even acknowledging his attempts.

"I can't get in, either," said Ensign Maureen Granados from an adjacent workstation. "It's like my credentials have been deleted from the system."

La Forge nodded. "Same here. Did we lose anything with the shift to backup power?" The sudden loss of main power had caused a momentary degradation of system performance for the handful of seconds it had taken for the secondary systems to engage, but so far as La Forge could tell, everything was back online.

"It's up and running," Granados replied. "We just can't do anything with it."

Turning away from his console, La Forge saw that

Choudhury and the three other security officers on duty had donned tactical gear over their uniforms, and each had retrieved phaser rifles from the weapons locker in the corner of the room. Though Choudhury had silenced the raucous and annoying alarm siren, the tension in the room was still conspicuous. "Lieutenant," La Forge said, "I can't explain what's going on."

"Can you get me communications?" asked the security chief, not looking up as she examined the phaser rifle cradled in the crook of her left arm.

"Working on it," he said. "Whoever's behind this knew what they were doing."

That seemed to give Choudhury pause. "You think it's the same people who were interfering with us before." It was a statement, not a question.

"I think so, yeah," La Forge replied. "The transporter inhibitors are still active. We could try to destroy them outright, but their force fields are still working." Somebody had definitely thought through their plan of attack, if indeed that's what this was. "We'll have to move clear of them if we want to beam back to the *Enterprise*."

Completing the inspection of her weapon, Choudhury shifted her gaze to La Forge. "Already ahead of you on that count, Commander," she said, "but we've got another problem." She held up the phaser rifle. "Our weapons have been neutralized."

"What?" La Forge asked. Incredulous, he turned back to his workstation and brought up the status displays for the weapons oversight protocols. "I'll be damned. If this is right, all particle weapons on the grounds have been deactivated, which should be impossible. That command can only be issued from here, and only by you or me."

"Well," Choudhury said, handing the rifle back to one of her subordinates, who returned it to the weapons locker, "if neither of us did it, then we *definitely* have a problem."

La Forge released a frustrated sigh. "This doesn't make any sense," he said, studying the station's readouts in the vain hope that some new clue might present itself. Following the incident with the intruder and his unauthorized accessing of the security grid, the chief engineer and Granados had reconfigured the entire system, adding new layers of authentication and encryption to ensure such an infiltration could not be repeated. So far as he could tell, that had not occurred; this was something new.

"Lieutenant," said another of her people, Ensign Ron Hanagan, from his station. A tricorder was in his right hand, and he held up the device for them to see. "I'm picking up an influx of bio readings on the complex grounds. We've got intruders all over the place."

For the first time, La Forge saw signs of genuine annoyance clouding Choudhury's face, even more so than when she had been cut off during her conversation with Captain Picard moments earlier. "We're blind and deaf up here," she said, moving toward Hanagan. She reached for the hand phaser on her belt, then, realizing it was as useless as the weapon she had just discarded, shook her head in apparent disgust before looking back to La Forge. "I need communications, Commander. I don't care how you get it, or if it means you and your people stand at the windows and shout at each other, but I want to talk to my security teams. *Now.*" There was no malice behind the security chief's words, but rather simple determination and singular focus. She was uninterested in causes or details. All that mattered right now were results, by any means necessary.

"We're on it," La Forge said. Then, seeing that Choudhury and Hanagan were heading for the door, he asked, "Where are you going?"

Choudhury gestured downward. "To the main level checkpoint. It's the quickest way over to the parliament building."

"Captain Picard?" La Forge prompted.

Nodding, Choudhury said, "Konya knows to bring him here, but I want to make sure he has backup if he runs into trouble." She then pointed to him. "With all due respect, Commander, let me worry about the captain. I need you to get us back in control of our systems, or else blow up the whole damned thing. I don't care, but if we can't use it, I don't want whoever's doing this to have it, either. Got it?"

"Got it," he said, but by then Choudhury and Hanagan were gone, leaving him and Granados alone with two junior security officers, neither of whom looked old enough even to have been born when La Forge had first reported for duty aboard the *Enterprise*-D.

Don't be an ageist. The joke came unbidden, serving to relieve his tension only the smallest bit. But, it was a start.

"Okay, Granados," he said, returning his attention to the hash that made up the status readouts on his monitors. Though it still all seemed like gibberish, he forced himself to look at it as though it were fresh, searching for some hint, some clue that might be useful. "Let's see what we can do about this mess."

36

"Commander Worf."

Standing near the front of the bridge, his arms folded across his broad chest as he regarded the image on the main viewer of the two Andorian ships following close behind the *Enterprise,* Worf turned at the sound of Ensign Balidemaj's voice. As he beheld the young tactical officer, he saw the look of uncertainty in her eyes, but there also was something else. Hope? Triumph? The first officer could not be sure.

"Have you found something, Ensign?" he asked.

Balidemaj nodded. "I think so, sir." Waiting until he crossed the bridge to her station, she pointed to one of the computer monitors set at eye level into the wall of her console. "I've been going over the sensor and communications logs from the moment we encountered the power fluctuations. Remember that burst transmission we got just before everything started going haywire? It makes sense that it had something to do with all of this, but what I couldn't figure out was how." She shrugged. "Then I started breaking it down, piece by piece. That wasn't a broad-spectrum hail like we normally get, or even like the one th'Gahryn sent before we established communications with him. It was focused, sir, for a particular receiver."

His eyes narrowing in suspicion as he contemplated what this revelation might mean, Worf asked, "Can you pinpoint the location of that receiver?" Such a discovery implied the presence of an intruder aboard the ship, or even possibly a collaborator among the crew. Despite himself, he thought immediately of the seventeen Andorian members of the *Enterprise* complement. Could one of them be working in concert with Eklanir th'Gahryn and the *Treishya*? As much as he did not want to consider the notion, common sense told him he could not dismiss the possibility.

"That's what I've been trying to do, sir," Balidemaj replied, indicating another monitor with a wave of her left hand. "The signal's no longer active, so I only have the previous logs to go on. Still, I've been tightening the search radius, and so far I've narrowed it to the secondary hull."

Deflector control, engineering, cargo storage, and the aft shuttlebay were areas of the ship with sufficient space to offer isolation for someone to work in relative privacy. Even with the limited area, searching the ship for a single person who might not want to be found posed a significant challenge.

"I think I've got it, sir," Balidemaj said, pointing again to one of her status monitors. "When the burst signal was sent, there also was a reply, but on a frequency so low that it's below our system's normal operational range. Very weak, which explains the short duration. It wasn't meant for anything more than one or two short dispatches."

"Were you able to decipher the message?" Worf asked.

The tactical officer shrugged. "There wasn't much there. All I found was a simple command: 'Proceed.' Nothing else."

Worf considered that. "Perhaps nothing else was needed. It's in engineering, isn't it?"

Turning in her seat, Balidemaj frowned. "Yes, sir. How did you know?"

"There are only a few places aboard the ship that lend themselves to the kind of widespread systems infiltration and interruption we are experiencing," Worf replied. "Assuming our systems are otherwise secure from outside penetration, that means something or someone has to have allowed such unauthorized access in the first place."

Her attention once more on her instruments, Balidemaj shook her head. "I'm not picking up any unexplained communications or other readings coming from engineering."

"Notify Commander Taurik of what you've found," Worf said. "His team will take it from there." Then, before turning away from the station, he added, "Excellent work, Ensign."

Balidemaj nodded. "Thank you, sir."

Stepping down into the command well, Worf moved to take his seat in the captain's chair. He studied the images of the modified Andorian freighters on the screen, already feeling his anticipation rising at the thought of finding and quashing the source of whatever influence Eklanir th'Gahryn used to hold the *Enterprise* hostage.

Once that was accomplished, the danger to the ship was averted, and the safety of Captain Picard and the other members of the crew secured, Worf would be only too happy to turn his attentions to th'Gahryn himself. The Andorian's arrogance and impudence could not be allowed to go unchallenged.

That, Worf decided, would be a worthy pursuit indeed.

Running at a full sprint, Lieutenant Peter Davila crossed the final dozen meters of the portico leading to the side entrance of the parliament building and threw himself through the partially closed door.

"Lock it!" he shouted as he sailed past the two *Enterprise* security officers manning the door, hitting the floor an instant later. He tucked his body and rolled with the impact, coming up on one knee with practiced ease, his uniform and the extra padding of his tactical gear absorbing most of the impact. In front of him, Lieutenant Kirsten Cruzen slammed the controls to lock the door from the inside just as the first of the charging horde of Andorians reached the portico. Davila watched through the transparasteel portals set into the double doors as the protesters beat at them with their fists, their faces contorted into all manner of furious expressions. Ignoring them, Cruzen reached for the doors' manual-override locking controls. The locks settled into position with a satisfying click, and Davila knew that even if whoever had compromised their security grid had also gotten into the parliament complex's own systems, they could not open any of the doors secured in this manner.

So let's all hope everybody else managed to get their doors locked.

"They look more than a bit miffed," said Ensign Michael Baker from where he stood on the side of the doors opposite Cruzen.

"Maybe it was something I said," Davila replied, reaching up to wipe sweat from his brow as he fought to get his breathing under control. He had been outside, patrolling the compound's exterior when the intrusion alarms sounded. There was time only for a brief report from Lieutenant Choudhury before he lost communications with her, and since then he had experienced no luck reestablishing contact.

And that was when everything went straight into the toilet.

According to the protocols Choudhury had established in

the event of a breach like the one they currently were experiencing, the *Enterprise* security details were to abandon their positions along the perimeter and fall back to the main compound, taking shelter inside the various buildings and underground facilities while avoiding direct confrontation with any civilians. Though concerned for the safety of his people, Captain Picard had been firm in his conviction that no Starfleet officer be responsible for the injury or death of an Andorian citizen, except when acting in self-defense and as a means of last resort. To Davila, it seemed like an overly passive strategy, but after considering it further, he came to realize why the captain had made such a decision. The political turmoil surrounding Andor's reproductive crisis and the controversial involvement of the Federation in trying to remedy it would also come to bear here. As ridiculous as it might sound to any rational person, the death of even a single Andorian at the hands of a Starfleet officer—unfortunate in its own right— would only be taken and twisted out of all meaningful context by those opposed to Federation "meddling" in Andorian affairs, and seen as a deliberate assault on the sanctity and sovereignty of the Andorian people.

So, here we are.

"How in the hell did someone get into our grid *again?*" he asked. Whatever had happened, it was not the result of a random system attack, of this Davila was certain. "According to Choudhury, she wasn't able to contact the *Enterprise,* either. Somebody's going to an awful lot of trouble to mess with us like this." He shook his head, studying the growing mass of Andorians gathering outside the doors. There were at least three dozen of them standing there, pounding on the portals. More could be seen beyond them, running in different directions across the courtyard, illuminated by the compound's exterior floodlights. Assuming all of the entrances had been secured in accordance with the fallback protocol, none of the dissenters would get in, of that Davila was sure. Nothing short of an armor-penetrating missile was coming through those doors.

Of course, with our luck . . .

"This doesn't make any sense," Cruzen said, shaking her head. "They disable our force fields and cut off our communications, and for what? So the locals can run around out there and tear up the grass or maybe break a few windows?"

Davila shrugged. "Wouldn't be the craziest thing." He had read reports and accounts of activist groups on other planets, including Earth in the late twentieth and early to mid-twenty-first centuries, who indeed had expended considerable effort working to convey their message or agenda, often going to elaborate extremes in order to make a demonstration such as the one he and his companions now were witnessing. "If they believe the message is important enough, then they won't think anything within reason is off-limits."

"Even destroying property?" Baker asked, nodding toward the doors. "That's not a protest. It's a mob. What if they hurt or kill somebody out there, including some of their own people?"

"Then we've got a big problem, don't we?" Davila paused, considering what he had just said. "Maybe that's what someone wants. Throw open the doors, let all the protesters who've been clamoring to get in here have free run of the place, and we'll be tied up figuring out what to do. Meanwhile, maybe somebody else is waiting for us to have our backs turned before they do whatever it is they're really planning." He pointed to Baker before gesturing down the hall. "If Lieutenant Braddock left the line and fell back to his rally point, he should be at Checkpoint Bravo. Get over there and see if he's heard anything."

Baker nodded. "Aye, sir."

Something like fingers snapping caught Davila's attention and he jerked in the direction of the noise, but not before Baker staggered, one hand reaching for his neck. Davila saw something there, but by then the ensign had sagged against a nearby wall and begun to slide toward the floor. Reaching for his phaser, Davila turned at the sound of someone approaching from behind him. His weapon cleared its holster at the same time he heard Cruzen call out in surprise before she too collapsed. Davila pivoted in search of the new threat, his hand coming up and leveling the phaser at the chest of the Andorian standing near an open doorway. The intruder was holding something in his right hand and pointing it at Davila, who flinched at the sight of the weapon but still managed to keep his phaser trained on its target as his thumb pressed the firing stud.

The weapon did not fire.

There was time only for one quizzical glance at the phaser before Davila felt a sharp sting in his left arm. Then his vision swirled out of focus and he was overwhelmed by the sensation of falling before everything dissolved to black.

"Fall back! Move move *move!*"

Lieutenant Austin Braddock yelled to be heard over the chorus of shouts and the clamoring of bodies beyond the perimeter wall's metal gate as he stepped away from the small shelter that served as a guard house. Placing his hand on the shoulder of Ensign Theresa Dean, he forced the younger officer away from her post at the gate checkpoint and aimed her toward the parliament administration building fifty meters behind them.

"Get to Checkpoint Bravo!" he shouted. "Now!"

On the other side of the guardhouse, Ensign Nordon fell to the grass, knocked over by an Andorian who had cleared the gate and charged him like an enraged bull. The young Benzite rolled onto his side, curling into a fetal ball and covering his head with his arms to protect himself as a second Andorian came at him, lashing out with a foot that connected with the back of Nordon's thigh.

"Hey!" Braddock shouted, drawing his phaser and aiming it at the protester. The Andorian looked up, saw the weapon, and turned to run away, leaving Nordon on the ground. Crossing to where the security officer still lay huddled, Braddock knelt beside him and tapped him on the arm. "Nordon, are you okay?" He divided his attention between his fallen comrade and the dozen or so Andorians who had scaled the gate, though the protesters seemed content to leave the *Enterprise* people alone as they ran off across the courtyard.

The Benzite rolled onto his back, wincing as he reached to where the Andorian had kicked him. "Yes, Lieutenant."

"Good," Braddock said, offering Nordon's arm a reassuring squeeze. "Then let's get the hell out of here."

A shadow fell across the grass to his right and Braddock turned his head in time to see an Andorian bearing down on him, his face a mask of hatred. The lieutenant raised his phaser, but he had no time to fire before Dean crossed into his field of vision and tackled the Andorian, driving them both to the grass. The Andorian attempted to punch Dean, but the ensign was smaller and faster, using her speed to land several quick jabs with both hands to the sides of her opponent's head. He fell back to the grass and Dean pushed him away before regaining her feet.

"What the hell was that?" Braddock asked, his eyes watch-

ing for new threats, but there were none. However many protesters had breached the gate here, they were all gone now,
presumably heading for other areas of the compound.

Catching her breath, Dean said, "My phaser wouldn't
fire."

Braddock examined his own weapon. The power level
was fine, but when he took aim at a patch of grass and pressed
the firing stud, the phaser did not fire. "Son of a bitch." He
cast a look toward the parliament buildings. "Somebody's
modified the weapons inhibitors to block us." Without a
functioning weapon, Braddock now felt more than a little
exposed outside.

Helping Nordon to his feet, Braddock reached for his
combadge. "Braddock to Choudhury," he called out, not
really expecting a response, given that he had lost contact
with the command post mere moments after the force field
protecting the gate had deactivated. Tapping his badge again,
he said, "Braddock to *Enterprise*," and received the same notable lack of response. "Well, things are just getting better by
the minute, aren't they?"

"Do you think Lieutenant Choudhury was able to contact the ship and report our situation before communications
were lost?" Nordon asked, still favoring his leg.

Braddock shook his head. "I'm not counting on it. Until
we hear otherwise, we need to proceed as if we're on our own.
If the *Enterprise* can help us, they will, but for now, we make
do." Eyeing something hanging from a belt around the fallen
Andorian's waist, he crossed over the unconscious intruder
and retrieved the item. It was a long, slender cylinder, and
he tested its weight in his palm before using his thumb to
press the single control embedded into its casing. In response,
the cylinder extended outward from both ends, achieving a

length of just under one meter. Braddock could not help the smile that curled the corners of his mouth.

"What's that?" Dean asked.

"Stun baton," Braddock said. "Police-issue. You're lucky he didn't use this thing. You'd be out cold until morning." He had carried something similar during his brief tenure with the security detachment at Starfleet Academy, where his responsibilities consisted mostly of patrolling civilian establishments near the Academy grounds and rounding up cadets who had imbibed intoxicating beverages in quantities that could be considered unhealthy. Such unglamorous duty was but one of the reasons he had requested transfer to a starship assignment.

Kneeling beside the Andorian, Braddock patted the intruder's clothing before reaching into one pocket and extracting a thin, hexagonal-shaped card. "This says he's a sentinel with the Lor'Vela Constabulary." He shook his head. "Figures."

"If a police officer can condone and even participate in such action," Nordon said, his eyes widening, "who's to say there isn't some more tangible form of support from local institutions for what's going on here?"

Braddock sighed. "That's what I like about you, Nordon. You're always an optimist. Come on, let's go." With communications unavailable, the teams would likely have to use runners back and forth between the different checkpoints and other defensive positions, and that worked only if the runners knew where to go. In the case of Braddock and his team, that meant getting to Checkpoint Bravo. Lieutenant Choudhury would be expecting her people to follow the contingency plan she had put into place for such eventualities, which in this case was the same as when facing a breach of the compound's defenses: rally at positions inside various structures closest to the perimeter, take stock of the current situation, and wait for further instructions.

Piece of cake, right?

"Where the hell is everybody?" Dean asked as Braddock led the way across the courtyard's open expanse.

"Good question," the lieutenant replied. He could hear shouts in the distance, but other than the occasional lone figure running between buildings; it was almost as though he and his team had been forgotten as the protesters ran off to partake of more interesting activities. That notion did nothing to alleviate Braddock's anxiety. The stun baton in his hand was comforting, but he still felt all but naked without a phaser. There was every reason to believe that the person who had incapacitated the Starfleet sidearms within the compound had probably not done so for other types of particle weapons, such as the disruptors used by Homeworld Security soldiers. Of course, that presupposed every Andorian on the grounds was automatically an enemy not to be trusted. Braddock did not believe that, but it was certainly plausible that more than a few soldiers might be in league with the protesters, to say nothing of whoever might be directing this little bit of chaos.

If it were me, I'd shut down everything, he mused. *Why take that chance?* Of course, that begged the question of what someone who might need a weapon would use in the event such measures were enacted. The stun baton he carried was one example, but what about weapons of greater lethality?

Now there's a pleasant thought.

37

Beverly spotted the first intruder.

"Jean-Luc," she hissed, barely audible even though Picard was less than a meter in front of her. He saw what she meant in the same instant she issued her warning, and instinct made him reach back and push her toward the nearby wall just as he saw the dark silhouette of an Andorian move into view. He stepped from behind a large support column, raising his arm and pointing something in their direction.

"Incoming!" Lieutenant Konya shouted, also reacting to the new threat by dropping to a crouch and scrambling for the feeble concealment offered by a large ornamental statue. A distinctive metallic snap echoed in the wide corridor, but the captain neither saw a flash of energy nor heard any burst of sound coming from where the Andorian lurked in the shadows. What kind of weapon was he employing?

"Stay down!" Konya barked over his shoulder as he adjusted his position behind the statue in order to take aim at the Andorian. He raised his phaser, and Picard heard the click as the lieutenant's thumb pressed the weapon's firing stud, but the phaser did not fire. Another sharp crack sounded in the passageway, and this time Picard heard something striking the wall over the lieutenant's head.

"Konya!" he called out, watching as the security officer dropped back under cover. He looked over his shoulder, holding up his phaser. "It's dead."

"Mine, too," sh'Anbi said, from where she had positioned herself behind another column.

Indicating for Beverly to move back the way she had come, Picard considered his officer's ineffectual weapons. Their adversary was employing something that fired projectiles at its target, and was his hearing playing tricks on him, or were the projectiles themselves traveling at a far lower velocity than would be considered harmful, at least to most humanoids?

"Whoever brought down the force fields must have also deactivated the phasers," he said, trying to keep watch along the corridor in both directions. He tried to spot the Andorian, but their assailant was once again cloaked in the near darkness. Konya was backing toward them, using whatever furniture, plants, and other decorative items scattered about the expansive corridor might offer some degree of cover. Somewhere ahead of the lieutenant, Picard heard footsteps, at least two sets. Their opponent had a friend.

He likely had more.

"We can't stay here," Picard said, keeping his voice barely above a whisper. Looking to Konya, he asked. "Where's the nearest exit?"

The security officer gestured with his head back the way they had come. "About fifty meters up the passage, sir, but that'll put us out in the open."

Picard nodded. "I think the weapons they're using are of limited range. We're better off outside, where we can get some distance."

"There are probably more of them outside," Konya said,

glancing over his shoulder and trying to keep track of their attacker's movements. "Then again, at least out there, we might see them coming."

"Agreed." Rising to his feet, Picard was preparing to move around Beverly and take the lead toward the exit when he heard footsteps behind him. A shadow broke away from those cast upon the walls in front of them, and the captain saw the faint illumination of the backup lighting reflecting off a head of stark-white hair. His muscles tensed in anticipation as he saw the Andorian's arm come up, his weapon aiming at them.

An earsplitting howl reverberated off the walls, and Picard saw a dark blur crossing the corridor toward the Andorian, who recoiled as he took notice of the abrupt movement. By then sh'Anbi was on him, driving him into the wall with the full weight of her own body. The Andorian was knocked off balance, grunting in surprise as he tried to recover from the sudden attack, but sh'Anbi gave him no quarter. She lashed out at his head with the edge of her left hand, and Picard heard bone against cartilage as the ensign's hand struck the Andorian's nose and he cried out in pain. The strike was followed by another, this time a knee to her opponent's solar plexus, and the Andorian groaned in protest as air was forced from his lungs. He bent forward, his free hand reaching for his midsection, and sh'Anbi brought her fist down on the back of his neck. The Andorian fell forward, crashing down atop a decorative low-rise table, with the sound of the impact echoing in the corridor.

"Behind you!" Konya yelled, already moving as another figure emerged from cover. Picard pushed Beverly back out of the way just as he heard another metallic crack, and this time he felt something whip past his left ear. That was the only shot the Andorian managed to get off before Konya reached him, the lieutenant swinging at the Andorian's arm and sending his weapon up and out of the way. Konya stepped closer, gripping the shooter's arm and pivoting to his left, yanking his opponent forward and over his hip. The Andorian was pulled off balance and crashed with a heavy thud to the floor. Twisting his attacker's arm, Konya wrenched the weapon from his hand before driving a knee into the side of the Andorian's head. There was a grunt of pain before his opponent went slack, and Konya released his arm, where it fell limply across the prone Andorian's body.

Stepping forward, Picard regarded his two security officers. "Are you both all right?"

From where she knelt next to the Andorian she had dispatched, sh'Anbi said, "Yes, sir." Beverly stepped toward the fallen Andorian, and the ensign added, "He's only unconscious, Doctor."

"Mine is, too," Konya said, rising to his feet, "though he'll probably have a headache for a few days." He held up the weapon he had taken from his assailant. "Other than a knife, this is the only weapon he was carrying, sir."

Moving closer, sh'Anbi offered Picard the weapon she had taken from her own opponent. "It looks like a tranquilizer, sir." She held up a small cylinder, perhaps two centimeters in length. "I've seen these used by animal handlers, such as veterinarians and trained specialists at zoos. The weapon has a magazine that carries ten of these, and he was carrying two additional magazines. The projectile's exterior casing is composed of an organic material that breaks down once introduced into the bloodstream."

"A tranquilizer?" Beverly frowned. "Could be poisonous?"

Sh'Anbi shrugged. "Not normally, though it's certainly possible, Doctor."

"Seems like an awful lot of trouble just to kill us," Konya

said. "Even after disabling phasers and disruptors, they could've used any of a number of lethal weapons. I think they want to take us alive, sir."

Examining the projectile sh'Anbi had given him, Picard shook his head. "They're going to have to work a bit harder for that."

Konya smiled. "Due respect, sir, but I like the way you think."

"Captain Picard!"

Despite himself, Picard flinched at the sound of his name being shouted in the corridor, and he turned to see a trio of Andorians moving up the passage toward him. He tensed at the sight, relaxing only slightly upon realizing that all three wore the polished black leather uniforms of Homeworld Security, and that the apparent leader was the local brigade commander, Captain Eyatra ch'Zandi.

"Are you all right, Captain?" ch'Zandi asked as they drew closer. His eyes fell on the unconscious Andorians lying on the floor behind Picard, and he regarded the captain with concern. "Is anyone in your party injured?"

Picard shook his head. "No. Captain, what can you tell us?" As he spoke, one of ch'Zandi's subordinates moved to inspect the fallen Andorian intruders.

"It appears that the *Treishya* have launched an assault on the parliament grounds," ch'Zandi replied. "At least sixty, by our count, possibly more. They only seem interested in non-Andorian personnel, particularly you and your people, Captain. We need to get you to a secure location."

"I need to verify the status of my people," Picard countered, "and contact my ship. Our communications have been cut off."

Nodding, ch'Zandi said, "Ours, as well. We're operating

under the assumption that the *Treishya* has assistance from someone on the grounds."

"Probably the same people who disabled our security grid," Beverly said.

"We can worry about that later, Captain," ch'Zandi said. "I have orders to take you to Presider sh'Thalis's secure bunker on the complex's lower level."

Taking Beverly by the arm, Picard said, "Very well, Captain." Light reflected off the sidearm on ch'Zandi's right hip as the Andorian turned to lead the way down the corridor, and Picard glanced at the holstered weapon. It took an extra second for him to realize that its handgrip was the same as the tranquilizer pistols the intruders had carried.

No.

Something clapped in the near-darkness and Picard heard a whimper of surprise from behind him. He turned to see one of the Andorian soldiers stumbling before he crashed into the nearby wall. To his left, he saw sh'Anbi, the weapon she had taken in her right hand as she crouched low, taking aim at the other soldier accompanying ch'Zandi.

"Jean-Luc!"

Picard heard Beverly's shout of alarm at the same instant he sensed motion next to him. He ducked just before a blue fist sailed past his head, and ch'Zandi's hand struck the wall. The Andorian grunted more from frustration than pain, drawing back his hand and reaching for the pistol on his hip. The weapon had not yet cleared the holster when Picard ran into him, forcing the Andorian backward until he slammed into the wall behind him. Reaching for the weapon, Picard rammed the heel of his other hand into ch'Zandi's jaw, snapping back the Andorian's head. Somewhere behind him he heard the now-familiar reports of at least two of the tranquilizer guns firing, but he ignored them as his hand wrapped around ch'Zandi's own weapon and pulled it clear of its holster. Ch'Zandi released a howl of rage, his eyes burning with fury as he yanked his arm free and lunged toward Picard, raising a fist to strike. Then he jerked to an abrupt halt and Picard saw the dark stain on the Andorian's neck where the tranquilizer had struck him.

Not waiting for the sedative to take effect, Picard lashed out with the pistol in his hand, striking ch'Zandi across the face. The Andorian drew back, wincing, and Picard pressed forward, knocking him backward until he tumbled off-balance to the floor.

Picard whirled at the sound of an anguished cry to see sh'Anbi kneeling next to Konya, who was lying on the floor and all but consumed by a series of spasms. His skin had gone pale and his eyes were wide with terror. "What happened?" Picard asked as Beverly moved to kneel beside the stricken lieutenant. Even in the dim light, the captain could see that sweat had broken out on Konya's forehead despite the moderate temperature inside the vast meeting hall.

"He was hit," Beverly said, reaching to where the small projectile had entered Konya's left arm. She placed the first two fingers of her right hand against the side of the lieutenant's throat. "Pulse is racing, and he's got a fever. She reached for the tricorder secured to Konya's waist and opened it, running it over the lieutenant's body. "He's having an allergic reaction to the sedative."

"How bad is it?" Picard asked.

"It's slow moving, but if we don't treat him . . ." She looked up at Picard. "He probably has about ten minutes. I need a medkit, or sickbay."

Despite his concern for the well-being of one of his officers, Picard forced training and experience to guide him. "Ensign sh'Anbi, where's the nearest security checkpoint for our people?" He had to repeat the question before the young Andorian focused her attention on him.

"Section B7, sir," she said, pointing past him. "About a hundred meters in that direction."

Nodding, he pointed to Beverly and Konya. "Stay with them."

"I can go, sir," sh'Anbi countered.

"Stay here," Picard said. "That's an order. Watch out for other intruders, or any of our people. I'll be right back."

"Traitor."

The single word, barely audible, stopped Picard just as he was turning to leave. Looking down, he saw the prone form of Captain ch'Zandi, who was glowering at sh'Anbi with unfettered hatred.

"What did you say?" sh'Anbi asked, her expression one of horrified disbelief.

Ch'Zandi's eyelids fluttered and his speech was slurred, obvious effects of the tranquilizer he was fighting. "You forsake your race for those who would watch our world die. You're . . . you're worse than they are." The last few words trailed away as the Andorian slumped to the floor, succumbing to the sedative injected into his body.

"Ignore him, Ensign," Picard snapped, his voice hard. "He's the traitor. He has betrayed you, along with everyone who would stand with him and actively impede those who work to save your people. Don't ever forget that."

"Jean-Luc," Beverly said, "I need that medical kit."

Picard nodded. "I'm on my way."

Shar dared not breathe, holding his hands away from his body as he stared down the muzzle of what to him appeared to be a rather large weapon.

"What do you want?" he asked the gun's wielder, a tall, muscled *thaan* wearing simple reddish-brown clothing of a type commonly available at merchants throughout the city. As for the Andorian himself, he appeared to be of mid-age, with deep lines around his eyes and mouth, and thinning white hair atop his head. Behind him, standing outside Professor zh'Thiin's office, was a second Andorian, also brandishing a weapon like his companion, though he was dividing his attention between the scene before him and the door.

"You, off our planet," the Andorian said, offering Shar an insolent sneer.

Scowling at that, Shar replied, "Your planet? I'm a citizen of this world, as well, in case the obvious escaped you." He indicated his own visage with a wave of one hand.

The *thaan* reacted to the sudden movement by tightening his grip on his weapon. "Don't do that again," he hissed through gritted teeth, the tone behind his words leaving no doubt as to their meaning. "You shed any claim to your birthright the moment you put on that uniform. You submitted yourself to willing slavery for the very people who would destroy everything we value; everything with which we identify ourselves as Andorian." Glancing at Professor zh'Thiin, who stood next to Shar, her hands also raised, he added, "You're no better than he is, polluting our children with that filth. What's the point of saving us if we're going to be nothing more than crossbred clones you engineer in a lab?"

"That's not what I'm doing," zh'Thiin snapped, her tone forceful. The Andorian's response was to turn the weapon toward her, a silent warning that future such outbursts might be costly.

Satisfied that the professor understood his threat, the Andorian returned his attention to Shar. "Well? Where are your reasons? What justifications do you offer in your own defense?"

Shar had heard his rhetoric, or some variation of it, on numerous occasions, and as before, he rolled his eyes in contempt. "I have plenty of reasons, but trying to explain them to you would be a waste of time. You don't possess the minimum number of functioning brain cells necessary to understand the more complex words I might use. Stop regurgitating what your Visionist mouthpieces feed you over the newsnets and then, perhaps, we might have an actual, constructive dialogue." In actuality, his response was far harsher than he normally would offer when confronted by people of this Andorian's ilk, but there was a reason for that, as well.

The response from the *thaan* was exactly as Shar hoped. Baring his teeth, he stepped closer, aiming the weapon's muzzle at a point between Shar's eyes. "You have no idea what you're talking about. We have no use for politicians of *any* ideology who put their own interests above those who elect them to office. This is about doing what's necessary to preserve the purity of our people."

"You'd rather die than explore every option science might provide to help us through this crisis?" Shar said, adding an edge to his voice. "Is that what you truly believe?"

"If we're meant to survive, then Uzaveh will show us the way," the Andorian said. "Otherwise, I accept the fate ordained for me."

Shar shrugged. "Then what are you waiting for?" He gestured toward the gun with a nod. "Put it in your mouth and pull the trigger."

Now genuinely angry, the Andorian stepped closer, the weapon's muzzle mere centimeters from Shar's face, so close that his eyes began to blur from trying to keep it in focus.

Close enough, Shar decided, lashing out with his foot and driving it into the Andorian's groin. The *thaan* howled in pain, but by then Shar had ripped the gun from his hand. Outside the office, the *thaan*'s companion, startled by the sudden explosion of movement, turned toward him, but zh'Thiin was faster, her hand slamming down on the control pad set into her desk. The door to her office slid shut.

Shar, not yet finished with his opponent, brought the butt of his purloined pistol down on the back of the Andorian's skull and the *thaan* dropped, barely able to extend one arm in an attempt to keep himself from crashing face-first into the floor.

"The door's locked," zh'Thiin said, her expression anxious as she regarded him, "but I don't know how long it will keep them out."

Ignoring the pounding on the other side of the door, Shar gave his captured gun a quick examination. It was not a disruptor or other particle-beam weapon. "What is this?" he said, ejecting the pistol's magazine and examining what appeared to be projectiles loaded into it.

"Those are sedatives," zh'Thiin said, pointing to the Andorii text inscribed along one side of the topmost dart. "Nonlethal, if that label can be believed."

"We're not supposed to kill you," said the *thaan*, from where he lay on the floor trying to reorient himself. "Only capture you."

Shar frowned. "For whom? Are you with the *Treishya* or the True Heirs?" The *thaan* nodded, but did not respond further. "And why? I thought they wanted us off the planet."

"Maybe they wish to make some sort of example of us," zh'Thiin offered. "As for how and to what end, I'd rather not speculate."

Shar nudged the *thaan* with his foot. "Is this true?" He shook his head in disgust when the Andorian did not respond. The pounding on the other side of the door was louder now, and more insistent. Then the door itself shuddered as though struck by something heavy. "We should get out of here." Looking about the room, he nodded toward the window. "Can we go that way?"

Nodding, zh'Thiin said, "Yes."

"Get it open," Shar said just as he heard another heavy thud against the door and a dent appeared in its surface. They did not have much time.

Reinserting the magazine into the weapon, he checked to see that a tranquilizer was loaded before turning his attention back to the *thaan*. "Did it ever occur to you that Uzaveh may have already shown us the way to save ourselves, rather than sit around and wait for salvation to be handed to us? Have you considered that perhaps the professor has found that way for us?" When the *thaan* did not answer, Shar regarded him with a mixture of pity and derision. "It's so easy to be misled when you let someone else do your thinking for you."

Without another word, he aimed the tranquilizer gun at the *thaan* and fired a single shot into his leg. The snap of the weapon as it spat forth the low-velocity projectile rang out in the office's cramped confines, and the effect of the sedative was immediate, with the Andorian collapsing unconscious to the floor.

"We need to go, Shar," zh'Thiin said, her voice anxious.

Regarding the insensate *thaan*, Shar sighed in resignation. "They're such fools," he said, more to himself than to the professor.

The next impact against the door pushed it out of its frame, creating a gap wide enough to see into the room beyond. A shadow appeared in that aperture and Shar greeted it with another of the tranquilizers. The figure fell away and Shar stepped to one side, out of any line of fire and listening for other movement on the opposite side of the door. Hearing nothing after a moment, he was satisfied that there were no additional intruders lurking in the outer office. Despite that confidence, Shar turned and directed the Professor to the window.

"Where are we going?" zh'Thiin asked as he helped her over the transom and onto the narrow ledge running the length of the building, one floor above the ground.

"The Starfleet command post at the Enclave chamber," Shar said, levering himself up and through the window. "We'll find help there."

Using the surrounding foliage for cover and trying to navigate a path beyond the compound's exterior floodlights, Shar led the professor away from the building, his senses on the alert for danger as they disappeared into the cool, foreboding darkness.

38

"Found it."

Reaching for the underside of the engineering workstation, T'Ryssa Chen moved her hand until her fingers brushed across the smooth-edged object that most definitely was not any standard component for a Starfleet control console. She held it up as Taurik and other members of the *Enterprise* engineering staff approached her.

"What is it?" asked Ensign Hogan, one of the junior engineers.

Chen held the device in front of her tricorder. "Scans say it's a miniaturized transceiver array, but I'm not picking up any activity."

"Excellent work, Lieutenant," Taurik said. "How did you find it?"

Holding up the transceiver, which was contained within a black octagonal shell two centimeters in thickness and ten centimeters in diameter, she said, "Its battery's composed of zantraetium, a mineral indigenous to Andor, but not used in Federation starships."

"So, an Andorian put it there?" Hogan asked.

Taurik said, "It would be unwise to jump to conclusions, Ensign, but based on circumstantial evidence alone, it would seem to be a rational hypothesis." Nodding toward the device, he asked, "Lieutenant Chen, have you found any information of value on the device?"

Shaking her head, Chen replied, "Its data-storage module is wiped clean. If th'Gahryn or one of his friends was in contact with it while he was communicating with us, then he may have instructed it to erase itself so as not to leave anything we might use to track him."

"But if it's clean," said another engineer, Lieutenant Whitsitt, "and we still can't get back control of the computer, that means it must have inserted something into the system: some kind of software addition or modification."

Nodding, Taurik said, "It would have to be an extensive modification, but something on that scale should be detectable." To Hogan, he said, "Ensign, notify information systems and have them begin a Level One diagnostic."

"That could take hours," Chen countered. "The operating system alone is hundreds of kiloquads worth of programming code. Whatever they stuck in could be anywhere, and it makes sense that it's something low-level or out of the way."

Taurik said, "Such an investigation is necessary if we are to locate whatever software has been added or compromised by the infiltrator's actions."

Sighing in growing irritation, Chen said, "Commander, whoever did this has an in-depth knowledge of computer systems. They probably knew we'd go this route if and when we figured out there's a problem in the first place. For all we know, they *want* us to waste time poring through the software looking for whatever they've done."

"Given that time is of the essence, Lieutenant," Taurik said, his right eyebrow arching, "I am open to suggestions."

How does he do it? The question burned at Chen's consciousness, and it irritated her more that she knew the answer. She possessed all of the same discipline and training Taurik employed in order to keep his emotions in check and his focus on his duties. Perhaps there was some value in emulating his example? *Okay, but I'm sure as hell not telling him that.*

"What about a full system reboot?" Whitsitt asked. "Bring it all down, and then up again."

"Or restore the system from the backups," Hogan suggested.

Chen shook her head. "Either one of those will take too long, and what do you want to bet whoever set us up has something in the system that's watching for a move like that?"

"The lieutenant is correct," Taurik said. "It is a logical course of action, and one to be expected by someone possessing the expertise needed to commandeer our systems in the first place. There may be a protocol to send a signal back to Andor in the event an attempt at system restoration is detected."

Shrugging, Chen said, "Hell, why not just go all the way and send a command to drop that last safeguard on the antimatter containment system?"

"An unpleasant, yet viable scenario," Taurik said. "Therefore, prudence demands we explore other alternatives."

"We need another operating system." The words came unbidden, all but spilling forth from her mouth, and Chen's eyes widened when she realized she was the one who had spoken them. The assembled engineers provided a host of reactions, from confusion to incredulity to curiosity, in the case of Taurik.

"Lieutenant?" prompted the Vulcan, after several seconds passed without her saying anything else.

Chen said nothing at first, her mind racing in an attempt to force the half-formed thought to coalesce. She opened her mouth, struggling to articulate what she saw in her mind, but the images were coming too fast for her to translate. "We need another operating system," she repeated, "something those bastards haven't anticipated. We need something that can interface with the main computer, immune to whatever was done to it and capable of overriding its instructions, while still being able to tell it how to route and store data." She waved her hands in front of her face. "It doesn't have to do it for very long, and it doesn't even need to take over everything. It just needs to handle a few primary systems and give Commander Worf control of the ship."

Nodding, Taurik said, "An impressive summation of our predicament, Lieutenant, but do you have a suggestion?"

Maybe.

Without answering, Chen turned and started running for the exit. "Taurik, I need your help!"

"Lieutenant!" Taurik called out, but then Chen heard the Vulcan running to catch up with her as she plunged into the corridor leading from engineering, sprinting up the passageway toward the nearest turbolift. "Where are we going?"

Glancing over her shoulder, she replied, "To get our other operating system."

Beverly applied the cold, wet towel to Konya's forehead. Thankfully, the lieutenant had slipped into unconsciousness, instead of continuing to squirm and convulse in obvious discomfort due to the attack on his nervous system.

"His blood pressure's dropping," she said, eyeing her tricorder while continuing her ministrations. She had been able to diagnose Konya and come up with a treatment that could be rendered even with a standard-issue Starfleet field medical kit, but that solution would do neither her nor Konya any good if such a kit were not procured in short order. How long had Jean-Luc been gone?

"Is there anything I can do, Doctor?" asked Ensign sh'Anbi.

Shaking her head, Beverly replied, "No, Ensign, but thank you."

Between the two of them, they had managed to move Konya into one of the smaller meeting rooms off the grand, curved passageway, and sh'Anbi had taken the additional step of disabling the room's emergency lighting so as to provide further concealment in the event someone came looking for them. The air in the room was warm, and Beverly had already unzipped the top of her uniform jumpsuit and opened the closure on her tunic in an attempt to cool herself. Sh'Anbi had taken up station near the door, holding it open just enough to be able to see into the passageway while hiding in the darkness and keeping watch for Captain Picard's return. They had seen no one since the captain's departure, which by itself was enough to unsettle Beverly.

"Listen," sh'Anbi said, holding out a hand and indicating for Beverly to stop her movements. "Do you hear that?"

Deactivating her tricorder, Beverly closed her eyes and listened, hearing nothing at first. Then, after a few moments, the faint sound sh'Anbi must have detected with her superior hearing finally became audible to her comparatively inadequate human ears. It was a low-pitched rhythmic click, repeating once or twice a second, and growing louder. As it increased in volume, Beverly realized the clicks were coming faster, and now she was certain she heard footsteps in the corridor, as well.

Then she flinched as a beam of light played across the floor out in the passageway.

They're tracking us.

Moving so that the meeting room's octagonal conference table was between her and the door, Beverly motioned toward sh'Anbi, but the young Andorian was already moving with deliberate slowness away from the door as though trying to meld with the surrounding darkness. Beverly's own muscles tensed as the brightness of the beam increased and the clicking sounds grew ever louder. Raising the tranquilizer pistol Konya had earlier confiscated, she felt her hand tighten around the weapon's grip as she laid its barrel atop the table and waited. Her gaze shifted between the tiny gap from the open door to her patient, who was still lying on the floor in the far corner of the room.

Seconds—a handful at most, Beverly guessed—seemed to stretch into infinity. She focused on a point to the left of the door, knowing the tricks the human eyes could play when trying to look directly at an object in darkness. She caught the faint shadow falling across the slice of weak light along the door's edge. Her finger pressed against the tranquilizer pistol's trigger, and it took physical effort not to fire as she watched that gap of light widen. A bead of sweat dropped down from her hairline and began tracing a path down her temple, but she ignored it, refusing to risk even the slightest movement.

Something dark and narrow poked through the opening at about chest level, and it took Beverly a moment to realize it was the barrel of another weapon. Her jaw clenched as the object moved farther into the room, the door opening wider to admit the new arrival. Beverly waited until light from the corridor washed over Konya's unconscious form and

the Andorian was framed in the doorway before she pulled
the trigger. The sound of the pistol firing was jarring in the
silence of the small meeting room. Beverly knew she had hit
her target when the Andorian's body jerked as the tranquilizer struck him. He staggered back, his free hand reaching for
his chest before he stumbled out of view.

There was more motion outside and sh'Anbi fired her own
confiscated gun, which was followed by someone else crying
out in surprise. Footsteps scrambled and then a flashlight
beam flared in Beverly's vision. She had time to make out
another silhouette in the doorway before she ducked beneath
the edge of the conference table, firing one last time without
truly aiming. Something skipped across the surface of the
table and smacked the wall behind her, but Beverly ignored
it, shifting her position and moving to her right in a desperate
bid to stay out of the shooter's line of sight. On the other side
of the room, sh'Anbi was moving, too, lunging forward and
shouting at the top of her lungs. Beverly rose from her couch
in time to see the young security officer strike the intruder
across the face with the muzzle of her pistol, catching the other
Andorian off guard. The beam of his flashlight danced across
the ceiling as sh'Anbi followed her initial attack, striking the
side of her opponent's head with her left fist. Instead of firing her weapon, she was using it as a club, hammering at the
Andorian's head as they both lurched from the room.

"Sh'Anbi!" Beverly called out, dashing forward, gun held
out in front of her and searching for other targets. In the hallway, the Andorian had fallen to the floor and sh'Anbi was
rolling away from him, regaining her feet. Lying in disjointed
heaps on the floor outside the meeting room were two more
Andorians, both sedated and unconscious.

"Are you all right?" Beverly asked, eyeing sh'Anbi.

The ensign nodded, holding up her tranquilizer gun. "Empty."

More running footsteps sounded in the hallway and Beverly turned toward them, bringing her weapon's sights around to level on the chest of Jean-Luc Picard. Behind him were two more *Enterprise* crew members, Lieutenant Choudhury and Ensign Hanagan. The captain looked flushed and was breathing hard, and he carried a small satchel slung over his left shoulder. He slowed his pace as he caught sight of Beverly and sh'Anbi, and Beverly sensed him relax just a bit as his eyes met hers.

Not wasting time on greetings, Jean-Luc pulled the satchel from his shoulder and handed it to her. Recognizing the medical kit, Beverly grabbed it and ran back to the conference room to kneel beside Konya, who still was lying undisturbed even after the brief skirmish.

"Can you treat him?" Jean-Luc asked, stepping into the room behind her and wielding a Starfleet-issue flashlight.

Beverly ignored him, opening the medical kit and extracting a container holding various medications as well as a pair of hyposprays. Running her fingers across the selection of vials, she quickly settled on one marked NEUROPINEPHRINE as well as a dose of tricordrazine, which she loaded into the hyposprays. She opted against subtlety, applying the hyposprays to either side of Konya's neck and pressing their injector studs. Retrieving the medical tricorder from the kit, she activated the device and waved its hand scanner over the security officer's body, feeling relief wash over her as she noted the change in his readings.

"I think we got to him in time," she said, nodding in satisfaction as the indicators settled within ranges normal for a healthy human.

"Excellent," Jean-Luc said, patting her shoulder.

Even with just the single word, Beverly could tell he was tired from his exertion. Looking up from her patient, she studied him. "Are you all right?"

Jean-Luc nodded, reaching up and using his uniform sleeve to pat perspiration from his forehead. "Just wishing I was that cadet who could still run marathons." Smiling at his own remark, he turned to Choudhury. "Have you been able to contact your people, Lieutenant?"

The security chief replied, "No, sir. Whoever's behind this, they did a good job cutting us off. I haven't been able to reach the *Enterprise* yet, either."

"How many intruders do you think are on the grounds?" Jean-Luc asked.

"There's no way to be sure, sir," Choudhury said, "but I think we're looking at two distinct groups: the protesters just seem interested in causing mischief and maybe some property damage, but that's the kind of diversion I'd set up if I wanted to get onto the grounds and tie up security forces."

"Can there be that many?" Beverly asked, having returned to treating Konya. "If they had large numbers, I think we would've seen more of them by now."

Jean-Luc said, "They may be separating into smaller groups in order to go after multiple targets. Has the parliament chamber been secured?"

"Yes, sir," Choudhury replied. "I got a report from Commander th'Hadik himself. Presider sh'Thalis and the rest of the representatives have been locked in their meeting chamber and are currently under guard."

"I wouldn't trust th'Hadik," sh'Anbi said. "Remember Captain ch'Zandi?"

"She's correct," Jean-Luc added. "We have to be careful.

Some of the Andorians are loyal to the *Treishya,* or whoever's responsible for this."

"That's right. They are."

Beverly turned from Konya toward the new voice, looking past Jean-Luc, Choudhury, and sh'Anbi to see five Andorians standing in the corridor outside the meeting room, each of them aiming a weapon. Behind them, another Andorian stood holding the blade of a long, curved knife to the neck of Ensign Hanagan.

At the Andorian's command, Jean-Luc and the others dropped their weapons. Beverly considered the tranquilizer gun next to her left leg, but didn't want to risk Hanagan's safety.

Nodding in approval, the Andorian smiled as he gestured toward Jean-Luc with the muzzle of his weapon. "Come out of there."

"Why? What are you going to do with us?" Jean-Luc asked, keeping his hands away from his body.

The Andorian scowled. "If you don't come out of there, I'll have to shoot you, then carry you. If I have to do that, I promise it won't be a gentle experience." He paused, and Beverly felt a chill course down her spine as he eyed her, then sh'Anbi and Choudhury. "For any of you."

Rising to her feet, she locked her gaze with Jean-Luc's and saw in his eyes an earnest attempt to reassure her that everything would be all right. Despite the strength she drew from him, there was no ignoring the veil of unease settling over her as she and the others were led from the room.

39

L a Forge had exhausted all options, it seemed, except one.
"We could blow up the building."

Sitting at her adjacent console, her face illuminated by its
small, recessed lighting panels, Maureen Granados eyed him
with understanding, no doubt feeling the same frustration that
currently gripped him. "I'd like to think of that as a last resort."

"That's where we are," La Forge said, shaking his head
and reaching up to rub his temples. Everything they had tried
in order to regain control of the security grid—every trick
in the book and more than a few not to be found in any
book—had failed. Whoever had infiltrated the system he and
Granados had set up had done so with remarkable, even awe-
inspiring adroitness. It seemed as though the perpetrator had
anticipated every contingency, including attempts to power
down the equipment or reroute from one console to another.
The field-deployable workstations such as those currently
operating in the command post were designed to work autonomously as well as in concert with other such stations, each
acting as a hub within the tactical network. They were easily
reprogrammable even by someone with little to no computer
expertise, and were adaptable to changing conditions on the
ground that might necessitate rapid network reconfiguration,

such as loss of personnel and equipment during battle, without degradation of systems oversight.

And that flexibility, La Forge knew, was what currently was working against him. That, and an admitted unfamiliarity with tactical systems such as these. While he obviously was familiar with the technology in broad, general terms and was therefore aware of its capabilities, he had never spent a great deal of time working with such hardware intended for deployable applications.

And to hell with me for not knowing.

"Commander La Forge!" called Ensign Steven Perkins from where he had taken up station near the door. "Someone's coming again!"

La Forge felt a fresh knot of worry forming in his gut. They already had been visited by a trio of Andorians looking to gain access to the command post, but Perkins and his companion, Ensign T'lira, had managed to overpower them. T'lira's Vulcan self-defense training in particular had come in handy as she dispatched two of the opponents in seconds before either Andorian could fire a single shot. She and Perkins had secured the unconscious Andorians in an unused room down the hall, and now the security officers were armed with the odd tranquilizer guns their would-be attackers had been carrying. The weapons were a fortunate acquisition, after La Forge had discovered that their phasers were also inoperable thanks to the commandeered security grid.

Another problem that needs fixing, and damned quick.

That was a problem for another time, he reminded himself as he and Granados extinguished their respective console work lights and he reached for the tranquilizer gun Perkins had given him. Moving toward the door, he asked in a low voice, "What've you got?"

Perkins gestured toward T'lira. "Don't ask me. She's the one who can hear them."

The Vulcan nodded. "Two people, moving slowly in this direction from the ramp." After a moment, she stepped back from the wall next to the door. "They are approaching our position."

To everyone's surprise, there was a knock on the door, followed by a muffled voice. "Open up. It's me. Regnis."

Waiting for T'lira's nod of confirmation, Perkins tapped the control pad next to his arm and the door slid aside to reveal Lieutenant Bryan Regnis and another *Enterprise* security officer, Ensign Shayla Cole.

"Sorry," Regnis said, his expression flat. "I thought this was the men's room."

Despite the tension, La Forge was unable to help the short chuckle that escaped his lips. He shook his head in mild irritation as he waved for Regnis and Cole to come inside before Perkins relocked the door. "What's going on?" La Forge asked.

"The way people are running around out there," Regnis replied, "you'd think the Pioneers had finally won a title." Looking around the room, he asked, "No luck getting us back online, I take it?"

La Forge shook his head. "Not yet."

"Whoever hijacked our system is still in there," Granados added. "It's like they're waiting for us to try something and they know what it will be. Then they either reroute or else just lock us out."

Regnis pursed his lips, looking away as though lost in thought. "You've tried resetting the system?"

"Sure," La Forge said, "but you know how these consoles work. One resets, the others reconfigure to deal with it."

His gaze returning to regard the chief engineer, Regnis arched an eyebrow in almost Vulcan-like fashion. "But the master control setup is still here, right?"

"That's right," Granados replied.

Regnis smiled. "Then we still might have a play." Moving to the workstation La Forge had set up as the master operations console for the deployable network, he reached for the station's interface panel and opened it, raising it up to expose the console's innards. Among the optical cabling and other electronic components was a row of twelve isolinear optical chips. Pointing to the chips, Regnis asked, "These oversee the core software, right?"

"Yes," La Forge answered, frowning as he watched the lieutenant at work.

Nodding, Regnis reached into the console and removed the first, second, eleventh, and twelfth chips from their respective slots. "Then what we want to do is give the protected firmware a hard reset, so that it reverts back to the default configuration it was given when it was first put together."

"You mean the original settings, as in new from the depot?" La Forge asked. "You can't do that, not without an A7 computer specialist's software-configuration kit." Indeed, the chief engineer had already considered that option, but discarded it upon learning that such a kit had not been included in the equipment brought down from the *Enterprise.*

Regnis chuckled as he worked, exchanging the first and second chips with their respective eleventh and twelfth counterparts. As the last chip snapped into place, the entire console went dark, but only for a few seconds before a series of beeps and clicks accompanied the workstation's reawakening. In response to this action, other consoles around the room blinked and emitted their own sets of alert tones and indicators, with monitors refreshing their displays. On La Forge's console, the primary computer display now offered a new message in simple text: SYSTEM RESET COMPLETE. ENTER CUSTOMIZATION PARAMETERS.

"I'll be damned," he said.

"I think I love you," Granados added.

"Get in line," Regnis replied, still smiling. To La Forge, he said, "With all due respect, Commander, these are field units, designed for tactical environments where we don't always have the luxury of the right tool for the right job. A lot of these systems have work-arounds that might not be by the book, but they work."

T'lira replied, "Most ingenious, Lieutenant."

La Forge nodded. "I'll say. Where the hell did you learn that?"

"A friend of mine figured it out, a long time ago. It came in handy on AR-558, when the Dominion kept trying to hack the communications relay there."

His eyes widening, La Forge recalled the name, belonging to a small, desolate planet in what at the time had been the Cardassian-occupied Chin'toka system, and the bloody battle fought there during one of the most intense periods of the Dominion War. "You were on AR-558?"

Regnis said, "I was sent in as one of the replacements. You know, after."

"Yeah," La Forge said, "but after was no picnic, either." As harrowing as the original siege of that Starfleet installation had been at the hands of Jem'Hadar ground troops, it was but a prelude to what had come later, when the Dominion had finally taken the planet and the Starfleet communications relay it housed, along with the entire Chin'toka system.

Once again, the young security officer looked away, as

though remembering something he had not thought about for some time. "No, it wasn't."

At the console, Granados said, "Okay, we're back up. I've got oversight of pretty much everything. It'll take a few minutes to bring up the grid and reestablish comm, but after that it should be simple to reinstate all systems."

Feeling new energy and determination coursing through him at this unexpected and most welcome turn of events, La Forge said, "Do it."

Chen gritted her teeth, biting back growing irritation.

"I can't just do it," she said, looking away from the computer interface terminal and glaring at Taurik. "If I rush this, we might trip some kind of alarm, or some other signal, and that might make somebody decide to blow up the ship. That would be a bad thing, right?"

Standing next to her in the service corridor leading to the *Cousteau*—the captain's yacht, which was currently stored in its customary home on the underside of the *Enterprise*'s primary hull—Taurik's expression was unreadable. "Sarcasm is a most unbecoming trait, Lieutenant."

"It works for me," Chen snapped. Returning her attention to her console, she studied the technical schematic it now displayed. Though the yacht itself had been sealed off as just another aspect of the commandeering that had affected most of the *Enterprise*'s computer systems, Chen had still found a way to access its computer by means of the smaller vessel's self-contained diagnostic-and-maintenance computer system. After first navigating past the software protocols linking the *Cousteau* to the *Enterprise*'s main computer, Chen was able to integrate her portable interface directly with the yacht's primary data core. A few checks of her own confirmed her theory that she had managed to effect her infiltration without triggering any alerts or other booby traps that might be lying in wait.

"All right," she said, "according to this, once I establish the link between the yacht's main computer and the ship's protected backup core, I should be able to connect to our shuttlecraft fleet and slave their computers to the *Cousteau*'s. Once that network's up, it should only take a few seconds to switch out the *Enterprise*'s operating system for ours."

Taurik said, "The *Cousteau* acts in lieu of the *Enterprise* main computer, directing software applications from the backup memory core, rather than trying to install those components to the primary systems." He nodded as he pondered her scheme. "An unorthodox yet shrewd strategy. However did you think of it?"

"I did something like it when I broke into the records system at my school and changed my grades," Chen said. Sensing Taurik's surprise at her admission, she looked away from her terminal and smiled. "I wasn't always the stolid, forthright Starfleet officer you know and love, Commander."

His right eyebrow rising, the Vulcan offered no other reaction. "Indeed."

An indicator tone sounded from the console, and she nodded in approval at the monitor's status displays. "Okay, we're set." She reached for the interface, but stopped when the terminal emitted another signal. "Uh-oh."

"I beg your pardon?" Taurik asked.

Reaching for the control pad, Chen began scrolling through screens and pages of data, studying the flurry of constantly streaming status updates. She caught the signs of new activity in the system, events being recorded and procedures being enacted, which she had hoped not to see. "We've got a big problem. I must have tripped something. I'm seeing new instructions being sent to the engineering subprocesses. Something's querying the status of the antimatter-containment systems." She could feel her heart racing as the potential consequences of what was happening before her within the vast computer network hammered home. "Taurik, I think they know we're here." Then, she tapped a new string of commands into the terminal. "We have to do this, right now."

Taurik extended his hand, resting it atop hers. "Should we not contact the bridge and inform them as to what we are doing?"

"No time," Chen snapped, shaking her head. "Besides, why spoil the surprise?" Without waiting for the Vulcan's response, she entered a final, furious string of instructions to the terminal, new protocols she was making up as she went, creating them in the heat of desperation and near-panic. There was no time to test what she was writing. It would either work, or not.

"Lieutenant," Taurik said, his voice rising an octave as he pointed to the display monitor. "There's been an update to the antimatter-containment protocols."

Chen ignored him, her fingers pressing down on the control pad's smooth surface as she executed her new commands. She drew a deep breath, held it, and shut her eyes. If the ship was going to explode around her, she decided she would rather not see it coming.

Nothing happened.

At first.

The lights were the first signs that something was amiss, extinguishing an instant before Chen heard a fluctuation in the omnipresent hum of the *Enterprise*'s warp engines. Despite safety features in place to prevent injuries to the crew in the event of a power failure, her stomach still registered the wavering of artificial gravity and even the inertial damping systems as emergency backups took over in response to loss of connectivity with the main computer. On her terminal's monitor, she watched as dozens of status indicators danced, racing to keep up and register thousands of changes taking place across the ship as one software platform was replaced by another at the speed of light. The display was receiving information not only from the *Cousteau* itself but also from each auxiliary craft in the *Enterprise*'s shuttle fleet as they carried out Chen's instructions, establishing access between one another and surrendering their autonomous control systems to the captain's yacht. When the screen went dark, Chen released the breath she was holding, and smiled as the display coalesced into a new image, that of an introductory LCARS screen and a banner that read: COUSTEAU. U.S.S. ENTERPRISE, NCC-1701-E. MAIN ENABLED.

When the ship did not explode around her, Chen looked to Taurik. "I think that's it." Before the Vulcan could respond, she tapped a series of commands on the terminal's control pad, verifying the status of various systems, her heart pounding harder with every beat as she saw the results of her work scrolling before her eyes. "We're back!" she said, slapping the edge of the console in her excitement. According to her readouts, the *Enterprise*'s primary computer core had been entirely bypassed, with her patchwork amalgam of computer processes from the shuttle fleet standing in for the starship's comparably larger and more complex systems. "Links to the protected backups are functioning, and the system is executing protocols there rather than from the main platform. All antimatter-containment protocols are back online. Communications is coming back. Defensive systems are still running up, and we should have weapons in about a minute."

"Commander Worf will certainly be gratified to hear that," Taurik said, his expression neutral and his tone impassive, but it was still more than enough to elicit from Chen an unrestrained belly laugh. Without thinking, she reached for him and drew him to her, wrapping her arms around him and squeezing for all she was worth. To her delight, she felt Taurik's hands on her back, and she smiled as she buried her face in his neck.

Then, she was struck by an amusing thought.

Wow. What I wouldn't give to be on the bridge right now.

Alert sirens sounded across the bridge, and the entire chamber was bathed in dull red lighting. On the main viewer, a tactical schematic appeared, superimposing itself over the images of the Andorian freighters, which were breaking from their formation and veering off on different vectors.

"They're locking weapons," reported Ensign Balidemaj from the tactical station.

At the center of the bridge, Worf leaned forward in the command chair, muscles tensing as he studied the tactical readout. "Status report."

"Shield generators are recycling," replied Rosado at the ops console. "They completely reset, pretty much like everything else, sir. We're not going to have them for another minute or so. Weapons are coming online, too."

How long had it been since the ops officer had reported the sudden reset of the *Enterprise*'s main computer system? Less than a minute, by Worf's measure. He had no idea what had happened, or why, or by whose hands, and he did not care. All that mattered was that his ship had been returned to him, and it was now time to bring this ridiculous situation under his control.

"Bring us about," he ordered. "Stand by all weapons."

Rosado glanced over her shoulder at him. "Sir, weapons aren't online yet."

"They will be by the time we're ready for them," Worf said, imagining the three-dimensional picture of the *Enterprise* and the two freighters, moving about one another. "Mind your station, Ensign."

From her station, Balidemaj said, "Commander, we're being hailed by one of the ships."

"I imagine we are," Worf replied. "Ignore them." There would be plenty of time for talk once the events of the next few minutes played out.

Balidemaj shouted, "They're firing!"

The effects were felt an instant later as the *Enterprise,* without benefit of its deflector shields, absorbed the full force of the Andorian freighter's disruptor strike. The reverberations channeled up through the ship and through the deck plates beneath Worf's feet, and he even felt them in the arms of the captain's chair.

"Damage report!" Worf ordered.

Rosado replied, "Minor hull buckling on deck eleven, near deflector control. No breaches detected, but force fields have been activated, anyway." The ship shuddered again as the second ship opened fire, and Rosado reported more minor damage, this time further aft near the main shuttlebay. Even with her skilled evasive maneuvers, Worf still winced every time he felt the disruptors slamming into the hull. How much longer before some actual damage was inflicted?

"Commander," Balidemaj said, "weapons are now online."

Despite himself, Worf actually smiled at that report. "Target both freighters' engines and prepare to fire on my command."

"They know we're hot, sir," Rosado said, and even with her back to him Worf could see that the ops officer was smiling.

"Pursuit course on the lead ship and overtake, Ensign," Worf ordered. "Fire phasers." The lights around the bridge dimmed as power was routed to the weapons systems, and on the main viewer the first officer saw twin beams of fiery orange energy lance across space to strike the freighter near its aft section. Wasting no time, Balidemaj followed with a second strike, and this time Worf noted the surge of energy as the phasers found their mark.

Rosado nodded with satisfaction. "Their primary propulsion system is off-line, sir. Life support is holding steady."

"Excellent," Worf said, his eyes focused on the main viewer as the image shifted back to that of the other freighter. "Where is the other ship?"

Balidemaj replied, "They're trying to sneak in behind us, sir."

"Evasive," Worf ordered. "Target its propulsion systems and fire when ready." Seconds passed until the phasers fired again, and this time Balidemaj's aim was true on the first attempt.

"Nice shooting," Rosado said.

Balidemaj looked to Worf. "They're not going anywhere, sir, but their life-support systems are operational." She looked down at her console in response to a new alert tone. "The lead ship is hailing us again."

Rising from his chair, the Klingon moved between the ops and conn stations until he stood mere meters in front of the main viewer. He folded his arms across his chest and regarded the image of the now-wounded freighter.

"Very well. Let's see what they might wish to discuss now. Open the channel, Ensign."

When the image of the freighter's now harried-looking captain appeared on the screen, Worf forced himself not to sneer in triumph.

40

The fist drove at his face, and Austin Braddock jerked his head to his left and dropped his shoulder, avoiding most of the strike. He still felt a graze as the Andorian's hand whipped past his right ear, and he lunged to his left, trying to get around his opponent to gain some maneuvering room.

Damn, this guy's fast.

Releasing an angry grunt, the Andorian shifted his feet and turned to face Braddock, who now was dancing on the balls of his feet and watching his attacker for any opening he might exploit. The lieutenant held his arms loose and low in front of him, flexing his fingers and leaving his face exposed, essentially daring the Andorian to take another swing at him. Out of the corner of his eye, he saw Ensign Theresa Dean struggling with her own opponent, lashing out at him to keep him at bay. Somewhere behind him, Braddock knew Ensign Nordon lay unconscious, a victim of the tranquilizer gun carried by his own assailant.

That weapon was not part of the current equation, at least not after Braddock had managed to wrest it from the Andorian. He had tried to use it himself, but the Andorian was just too quick, lunging at him and forcing Braddock to go on the defensive in order to avoid being tackled and dropped to the ground. Likewise, the Andorian, who obviously had some form of unarmed combat training, had managed to separate Braddock from the police-issue stun baton he had taken from the protester near the gate checkpoint. It bothered Braddock that the Andorian had tossed away the weapon rather than trying to use it. So far as Braddock could tell, his opponent was actually enjoying their little impromptu melee.

Just my luck.

The Andorian was grinning at him now, his stark-white teeth looking as though they might be more at home on some predatory animal. Was he cocky, or just that confident in his own abilities? Braddock was in no real mood to find out, one way or another.

"Okay, sport," he said, gesturing to the Andorian to come forward, if he so chose. "Let's get this over with."

"All security teams, this is Lieutenant Regnis."

The voice exploded from his combadge, startling Braddock. He could not help looking down at the communicator affixed to his uniform, knowing the Andorian would take advantage of that error even before he sensed his attacker springing forward.

"All hands," Regnis's voice said, *"the security grid is back online. Repeat, the grid is back online."*

"Now he tells me," Braddock said, moving back and to his right to avoid the Andorian's attack. His opponent's strike was half-hearted—a feint. The arrogant bastard was actually playing with him. *Well,* he decided, *here's something new for you to—*

A beam of orange energy struck the Andorian in the chest, stopping him in his tracks. His body shuddered from the phaser blast and his eyes rolled back in his head before he went limp and collapsed to the ground. Blinking in disbelief, Braddock turned to see Ensign Dean advancing, phaser out and aimed ahead of her. Behind her, he saw the inert form of her own opponent, lying facedown in the grass.

"Are you deaf, Braddock?" Dean asked, moving to verify that the Andorian indeed was out of commission. "Regnis said the grid was back up. That means phasers, too."

Clearing his throat, Braddock made a show of straightening his uniform. "I heard him. I was just . . . you know . . . taking care of this guy my way."

"Uh-huh," Dean said, shaking her head. Then, she and Braddock cocked their heads at the same time, listening to the sounds of energy-weapons fire elsewhere in the compound. "Sounds like everybody else is getting the word." She pointed over his shoulder. "Look. Force fields are back up."

Braddock looked in the indicated direction and saw the energy barrier now once more covering the entrance at the compound's perimeter wall. "We're not in the clear just yet. More people might not be able to get onto the grounds, but who knows how many are still here, and now they're trapped *inside*." Other than this skirmish, they had managed to avoid contact with other protesters or whoever was responsible for the compound breach. Thanks to the communications blackout, information was scarce with regard to whoever or whatever the security forces were facing. With comm apparently restored, hopefully the situation would become more clear in short order.

Moving to where Nordon was still unconscious on the ground, Braddock asked, "Is he okay?"

"Sleeping like a baby," Dean said. "I have no idea how long those sedatives last."

Bending down to maneuver Nordon into a sitting position, Braddock levered the Benzite to his feet and then crouched low enough to first hoist the unconscious ensign over one shoulder, then drape one arm over his other shoulder. "There are medkits at Checkpoint Bravo. Maybe there's something in them that'll snap him out of this." Adjusting Nordon's weight to a more comfortable position, he gestured to the phaser in Dean's hand. "Okay, you're on point. Let's keep moving."

Though not as opulent as the Enclave chamber, the large meeting hall in which Picard and his party now found themselves was still very well appointed, far more impressive than even the main assembly hall at Starfleet Academy on Earth. The only things detracting from the chamber's atmosphere were the forlorn faces of dozens of *Enterprise* crew members as well as other non-Andorian civilians, and the twenty Andorians standing watch over them. Studying the Andorians with a critical eye, Picard noted even in the room's reduced lighting that they carried weapons that most certainly were not tranquilizer guns, but likely far more dangerous or even lethal. Whatever all of this was about, he surmised, it would begin here.

"Get away from the door," said his Andorian captor, who had identified himself as Biatamar th'Rusni, an apparent advisor to whoever was behind the attack on the compound. He gestured with his pistol for Picard to move deeper into the hall. He carried a satchel slung from his left shoulder, in which he had deposited the combadges taken from Picard and his people.

"Why are we here? What is it you want with us?" the captain asked, for the fifth time.

As with his earlier attempts, this one also was met with

disdain. "Your primary concern," th'Rusni said, "should be that you arrived here at all, and that you remain in reasonably good health for the time being." He stood next to Beverly, his large left hand gripping her right arm. He had taken her aside from the moment Picard and his group were captured, obviously figuring the captain would be easier to deal with so long as his wife was part of whatever coercion tactics th'Rusni chose to employ. Picard bristled at the notion, but, for the moment at least, the Andorian was correct. Indeed, th'Rusni saw the captain looking at him and, to emphasize the control he enjoyed, pulled Beverly closer.

Focus, Jean-Luc.

Even as he struggled with apprehension over Beverly and the rest of his crew, the part of his mind still trying to formulate a way out of the current predicament noted that whatever had been done to seize control of the security grid and the weapons-inhibitor systems, an exception had been made for the model of pulse rifles these Andorians carried.

"If you were going to kill us," Picard said, "you'd have done it already. You obviously want us alive, so what's the reason?"

Th'Rusni replied, "A minor point of clarification, Captain: we want you alive *for the moment*. The *Treishya* will soon demonstrate what happens to outsiders who pollute our world, subvert our leaders, and enslave our people for their own ends."

"Enslave your people?" Picard asked. "Andor is a founding member of the Federation, an ally for more than two centuries, joining of their own free will."

"'Free will'?" th'Rusni repeated. "I believe you mean that our leaders were maneuvered into an alliance after first being subjected to enemies for which we were not prepared, all while asking us to devote people and resources to help fight battles you humans brought upon yourselves. And now this filth you conspire to inflict upon us, by introducing alien genes into our population? Even that is motivated by your desire to subjugate us. Here you have a possible cure for the affliction my people suffer while preserving our genetic integrity, but instead you pursue an easier solution that allows you to control our numbers and keep us in line."

"That's not true at all," Beverly said, spitting the words even as she tried without success to break th'Rusni's grip on her arm. The Andorian responded by yanking on her arm hard enough to elicit a pained grimace.

Picard felt his jaw slacken as he listened to th'Rusni's words. "You've already found a way to twist even those facts to fit your agenda," he said, regarding the Andorian with pity.

"Do you realize what you're saying?" sh'Anbi said, moving to stand next to Picard. "It's insanity to think anyone would do something like that."

"Ensign," said Lieutenant Choudhury from behind sh'Anbi, her tone one of caution. She was helping Lieutenant Konya, who was conscious and able to move but still disoriented.

"What's insane," th'Rusni said, "is that the Federation and Starfleet would place the protection of their precious secrets above helping a supposed ally." He glared at Picard. "You would either offer us substandard treatment with only a slim chance of success and the very real possibility of actually worsening our problem, or stand by and watch us die as a race in order to keep buried whatever wondrous mystery you unearthed and chose not to share. Are those the actions of an ally, Captain?"

Picard said nothing. What would be the point? Th'Rusni

had made up his mind, at least for the time being, operating as he was with whatever partial or deliberately distorted information he had been given. There would be no reasoning with him. Not here, and certainly not now.

His attention was drawn to the meeting hall's subdued secondary lighting, which had begun to flicker. Everyone in the chamber was looking around, eyeing one another in confusion. Then the room was awash in much brighter illumination as the main lights flared to life, and Picard was forced to blink several times to clear his vision.

"What's happening?" he heard th'Rusni ask. When he turned, he saw confusion on the Andorian's face.

One of his companions replied, "They weren't supposed to restore the lights until we made our report."

Th'Rusni nodded. "Something's wrong."

"All security teams, this is Lieutenant Regnis," said a voice, carried over the meeting hall's intercom system. *"All hands, the security grid is back online. Repeat, the grid is back online."*

A chorus of murmurs rolled over the assembled hostages, and Picard took heart in the looks of uncertainty beginning to cloud the faces of th'Rusni and his companions.

"Excuse me."

Picard turned at the sound of Lieutenant Choudhury's voice and saw the security chief walking toward one of the Andorian guards, who promptly shifted his position and aimed his rifle at her.

"Stay back," the Andorian warned. When Choudhury continued her advance, the Andorian pressed the weapon's firing stud, but there was no discharge of energy.

"That's what I thought," Choudhury said, before lunging at the guard. She grabbed the rifle's barrel and yanked it toward her, pulling the surprised Andorian forward until she was within arm's reach. Her right arm lashed out, the edge of her hand striking the bridge of the Andorian's nose. He cried out in pain but Choudhury ignored him, swinging her left fist into the guard's stomach before grabbing his right arm and pivoting to her left, pulling the Andorian across her hip and over onto the floor.

Around the room, the other guards were now realizing they were outnumbered and all but weaponless. A few of the Andorians attempted to brandish knives or other implements but that proved futile as two or three *Enterprise* crew members converged on each of them.

Picard turned toward th'Rusni in time to see Beverly yanking herself free from the Andorian's grip. She staggered away from the Andorian even as he began following after her, but he took only a few steps before the familiar report of a phaser echoed in the room. His body spasmed as an orange beam struck him in the back, and he sagged to the floor. Then there was a rush of movement near the door and Picard saw more *Enterprise* security officers clamoring into the meeting hall, each carrying a Starfleet-issue phaser rifle. Within seconds they targeted th'Rusni's companions, dispatching them with surgical precision. It happened with such speed that Picard was certain he had to be imagining the sight unfolding before him.

Movement to his right caught his attention and he turned in time to see another Andorian barreling toward him. His attacker was mere meters away when something hot and orange screamed past Picard's head, striking the Andorian in his chest and sending him tumbling to the floor. Picard turned to see Ensign sh'Anbi standing beside the still shaken-up Rennan Konya, wielding what the captain recognized as a compact Type 1 phaser in her hand. Noting Picard eyeing the undersized weapon, she shrugged and indicated Konya with a nod.

"The lieutenant had it hidden in his boot, sir."

Despite himself, Picard could not help smiling at the elegant simplicity of Konya's unorthodox tactics. He nodded in approval. "Well done, the both of you."

"Captain," a voice said from behind Picard as he moved to Beverly, who had fallen to the floor and was pulling herself to her feet. Verifying that she was uninjured, he turned to regard the young brunette woman wearing lieutenant's pips on the collar of her uniform tunic.

"Lieutenant," he said, frowning. "I'm sorry, but I seem to have forgotten your name."

The woman nodded. "Walker, sir. Lieutenant Katherine Walker. I'm usually on gamma shift, but Commander Worf sent me and my team with his compliments."

Smiling as he glanced over his shoulder to see Walker's security team taking the now-quite-unconscious Andorian dissidents into custody, he said, "Excellent work, Lieutenant. What's our current status?"

"Commander La Forge was able to reset the security grid, sir," Walker replied. "After that, I'm told it was a piece of cake to restore the force fields and reconfigure the weapons-lockout systems. He basically programmed it to recognize Starfleet phasers and deactivate everything else."

Choudhury said, "I'm sure Homeworld Security will be happy to hear about that."

"You let me worry about that, Lieutenant," Picard said. "What about the *Enterprise*?"

Walker said, "We had our share of problems there, too, sir, but the engineers figured it out just like Commander La Forge did down here."

"Do they know what happened?" Beverly asked, rubbing her right arm as she stepped forward to join the conversation.

"The ship's main computer was hijacked, by an expert. I don't have all the details, Captain, and I'm likely too dumb to understand most of what I was told, anyway; but the way I understand it, whoever wormed their way into our systems knew what they were doing. We're talking about a level of expertise you normally only find with people serving aboard starships."

Picard turned at the sound of Choudhury gasping, watching as her eyes widened before her expression took on an abrupt shift, from shock to . . . anger?

"Or," the security chief said, "someone who *used* to serve on starships."

The office was empty.

"Damn it," Choudhury snapped, lowering her phaser as she cleared the last room in the lavishly decorated work space that dominated this floor of the towering building located in the heart of Lor'Vela's business district. Moving back into the office's main area, she saw Commander th'Hadik standing behind the expansive desk, which was the room's most prominent furnishing. Behind him, the lights of the city as seen through the bay window's darkened glass reminded her of the view from her cabin aboard the *Enterprise,* and the stars that were the last thing she saw before falling asleep and that greeted her with each new day. The sudden odd thought reminded Choudhury just how tired and worn-out the last hours had made her.

Yeah, my bed would feel pretty good right now.

"He could not have left here that long ago," said th'Hadik, indicating a cup sitting near one corner of the desk. "This beverage is still warm."

Choudhury said, "What about access logs for the building? Is there anything like that we can check?"

"I will ask the city police to investigate that possibility," th'Hadik said, "but given the resources th'Gahryn supposedly commands, masking his movements would be a simple task."

Sighing in disgust, Choudhury turned from the desk and glared at the Andorian currently standing between Lieutenants Regnis and Braddock. "Where would he go?"

Threlas ch'Lhren regarded her with an implacable expression. "Any number of places, Lieutenant."

"What, are you his travel agent?" Choudhury asked. "Being able to move around without attracting attention requires help, including the kind of help you're obviously capable of providing."

Ch'Lhren shook his head. "I am nothing more than a loyal subordinate, and a humble follower of the *Treishya*. I do what is necessary to further our cause."

Feeling her teeth grinding together as she clenched her jaw, Choudhury said, "Tell it to the magistrate." For a fleeting moment, she imagined what she might do to the Andorian if left alone in a locked room with him for but five minutes.

Upon hearing Worf's report about the nature of the infiltrations that had affected the *Enterprise*'s main computer, including the strange device of Andorian origin discovered in the engineering section, Choudhury had known instantly and without doubt who was responsible. Threlas ch'Lhren possessed the precise expertise that would have been required to so thoroughly assume control over a Starfleet computer system, particularly one so advanced as to be found installed aboard a *Sovereign*-class starship. After nearly a decade of service, the *Enterprise*-E and her sister vessels remained at Starfleet's technological forefront, employing the most advanced information-processing systems to be found. Understanding and being able to exploit such sophisticated computer hardware and software would almost certainly require a very specialized skill set.

Such as that belonging to someone who once held a Starfleet A6 computer-expert classification.

Despite whatever her gut had told her, such a theory, based as it was at best on circumstantial evidence, needed proof. Fortunately, ch'Lhren himself provided that corroboration when Choudhury and Commander th'Hadik found him at his office on a lower level of one of the parliamentary administration buildings, packing a travel case and looking very much like someone who wanted to leave in a hurry. Choudhury had deferred to th'Hadik so far as questioning ch'Lhren, and it was the commander who had found in the Andorian's packed belongings a duplicate to the odd transceiver device discovered by engineers aboard the *Enterprise*. Even if ch'Lhren was not directly responsible, he was at least somehow involved.

Choudhury was absolutely certain it was the former.

"You did it during the tour, didn't you?" she said, glowering at ch'Lhren as she levied the accusation. "All that crap you spewed about Starfleet failing Andor. You knew I was from Deneva and that talking about the war would rile me. You were counting on me getting flustered so I'd walk away, and give you the opening you needed to plant that thing. Tell me I'm wrong." Even as she spoke the words, the images of the scorched husk, which was all that remained of her homeworld, danced once more in her mind's eye. Again, she saw her family, lost and perhaps now nothing more than yet more nameless, faceless victims of the Borg.

Ch'Lhren shrugged. "You are not wrong."

It required every iota of self-control Choudhury possessed not to draw her phaser and shoot the Andorian where he stood. Her right hand twitched, yearning to reach for the weapon. She willed it to stay at her side.

Stepping around the desk, th'Hadik held up the transceiver for ch'Lhren to see. "You have much to answer for. Conspiring to destroy a Starfleet vessel? There won't be a hole on this planet deep enough for where Presider sh'Thalis will want to throw you."

"He wasn't going to do it," Choudhury said, regarding ch'Lhren with disdain. "It was all a bluff. If they'd wanted to kill people, they could've started with the captain. Instead, they weren't even carrying real weapons. It was all a show they wanted to put on."

Ch'Lhren cocked his head as he returned her critical gaze. "I have no idea what Eklanir was thinking, but I do not doubt he would have ordered your ship's destruction if he felt it was warranted, just as he would have killed your captain and anyone else if it served his purpose."

"To what end?" th'Hadik asked, shaking his head in disbelief. "You would make an enemy of the Federation, now, when they've extended the hand of friendship to us yet again?"

"Is that what they've done?" ch'Lhren asked, though his tone and the way he looked away from the commander suggested he was not truly seeking an answer.

"Do you really think we're your enemy?" Choudhury asked, aghast. How could someone harbor such sentiments? Did Andor's long, shared history with the Federation mean nothing to people such as this?

Pausing as though to ponder that question, ch'Lhren

pursed his lips. "Whatever else you may be, I am certain you're not my friend."

"Nor am I," th'Hadik said, "and neither is Eklanir th'Gahryn, as he isn't here to come to your aid. That's unfortunate for you, as you'll be the one standing trial for treason, conspiracy, and whatever other charges Presider sh'Thalis and the parliament see fit to bring against you."

For the first time, ch'Lhren smiled. "I suspect Presider sh'Thalis will be dealing with other issues in short order, which will certainly deflect her attention from someone such as myself."

"What's that supposed to mean?" Choudhury asked. "What are you talking about? Another threat? Another attack?" She stepped forward, stopping herself before she could take things too far. "What's left? We found you, and we'll find th'Gahryn. It's over. Soon, the entire planet will know what you tried to do, and what you were willing to do. They'll see you for the renegade gang of lawless thugs and terrorists that's all the *Treishya* really is. That's what you're celebrating and defending?" What had they missed? What was this bastard hiding?

Ch'Lhren's only reply was to stand in silence, smiling.

41

A chime sounded, echoing across the parliament chamber, and the gentle murmurings permeating the ornate hall faded.

"*Please be seated,*" said a disembodied voice through the intercom system. "*These proceedings will now come to order.*"

Standing at the rear of the Enclave chamber, Picard watched as the members of the Parliament Andoria moved to their designated places in the expansive meeting hall. Civilians and other members of the government who had been invited to observe the proceedings took seats around the chamber's upper tiers. In accordance with the customs and traditions pertaining to formal gatherings of the esteemed governmental body, each of the parliament members wore formal, brightly colored robes. Picard knew that this hall, a substitute for the original Enclave chamber once located in Laibok and another casualty of the attack that had destroyed that city, lacked much of the grandeur of that revered meeting place. The assembled parliament members seemed not at all foiled by the missing splendor of their former meeting place, carrying on as best they could in their new surroundings. The gathering was still one of solemnity, with the members sitting in a circle on the main floor of the chamber's lowest level. At the center of the assemblage, dressed in an alluring red robe that covered her from neck to feet, was Presider sh'Thalis.

She looks tired, Picard thought, studying the presider as she watched the group before her. Sh'Thalis had spoken to no one since entering the chamber, skipping all pretense of geniality and instead moving directly to her station. Picard had watched as her security escorts, chief among them Commander th'Hadik, rebuffed the attempts of various representatives to approach her. For her part, the presider had busied herself with some manner of report or other work on the data reader she had brought with her, though Picard suspected her interest in whatever she might be reading was minimal, if it existed at all.

"Jean-Luc."

Picard felt a hand on his arm and turned to see Beverly smiling at him. Without a word, he followed her to where Professor zh'Thiin and Thirishar ch'Thane stood near one of the chamber's exits. The captain had not seen ch'Thane since the end of the *Treishya* raid on the parliament complex two nights earlier. While Picard and Beverly donned their Starfleet dress uniforms, ch'Thane and zh'Thiin wore formal black robes.

"Good afternoon, sir," ch'Thane said as the captain and the chief medical officer approached.

Nodding, Picard replied in a soft tone, "Mr. ch'Thane," before offering a greeting to zh'Thiin. Both Andorians looked none the worse for wear after their experience, which according to ch'Thane had primarily consisted of moving from one stand of shrubs to another, making their way from the building that housed the professor's office to the Enclave chamber and the command post manned by members of Lieutenant Choudhury's security detail. Their greatest challenge, according to zh'Thiin, had been avoiding the bushes with thorns and the occasional nest of bothersome insects.

"I was startled to see that you had tendered your resignation from Starfleet," Picard said, eyeing the young Andorian.

Ch'Thane nodded. "I considered the matter at length before making my decision, Captain. I thought it was best so far as my continued working with Professor zh'Thiin. With everything that's happened and the way public sentiment has shifted in its opinions of Starfleet and the Federation, I did not want to be an additional burden on the professor, not when we're so close to being able to demonstrate to the world that her ideas will work."

Not exactly her work, Picard mused, though he kept the thought to himself. However Professor zh'Thiin had come into possession of the knowledge that ultimately had helped guide her research, and whatever judgment she may have lacked, her motives had been pure.

"I understand," Picard said, "and I respect your choice. Even though Starfleet has lost a talented and valuable officer, I cannot disagree with the desire to help your people. I wish you the best of luck, Thirishar."

Offering a slight, formal bow of respect, ch'Thane said, "Thank you, sir." Then, he turned to regard the parliament members. "Do you know what's going to happen?"

"I honestly have no idea," Picard replied. The *Treishya*'s assault on the compound and its attack on the *Enterprise* had fueled no shortage of activity within the parliament as well as regional governments at every level around the planet. In only the first few hours after the incident, reports of civil unrest were on the rise, with citizens massing in support as well as protest of the continuing Federation and Starfleet presence on Andor. Large, vocal groups had gathered outside the grounds of the Federation embassy as well as the headquarters of the Starfleet liaison in Lor'Vela. The on-site commander had already been in contact with the *Enterprise*, working with Lieutenant Choudhury to prepare in the event an evacuation of the embassy or the Starfleet installation became necessary.

A hush fell over the chamber and Picard watched as Ledanyi ch'Foruta, the parliament's deputy presider, rose to his feet. He took a moment to study the audience assembled before him, offering an occasional nod to a colleague. Picard's gaze shifted to President sh'Thalis, and he saw that she was looking back at him. The captain felt an abrupt chill as he beheld the sadness in her eyes.

"Greetings, representatives and honored guests," ch'Foruta said, his voice carrying throughout the cavernous Enclave chamber. "I also welcome those of you watching us from points across our planet, as these proceedings are being broadcast live via all newsnet outlets. We are gathered here today to discuss matters of grave concern not only to the people of Andor, but also to those we would call friends and who, like the citizens of this world, desire only peace and security when they come to us in the spirit of inclusion and mutual cooperation." His opening statement had an immediate effect on the representatives, many of whom turned to one another, speaking in tones far too low for Picard to hear from his perch.

"The incidents of discord that have plagued us in recent days trouble me, my friends," the deputy presider continued, "just as I know they trouble you. There are many who view the incident that took place on these grounds to be an act of dissatisfied citizens yearning for their government to recognize them and to hear their pleas. While that may be true of some of those who feel disenfranchised or simply forgotten altogether, what took place here two nights ago was nothing less than a criminal act; an act of aggression, intended to sow the seeds of fear not only into our society, but also into those sworn to lead it. It was, quite simply, terrorism. And we allowed it to happen right before our very eyes."

Now Picard saw several more animated responses from the audience, including both the nodding and shaking of heads, mild applause, and even a few fists shaken in the air. All of this, despite whatever rules of etiquette likely existed in this place.

"I know that there are many among us in this room who agree with at least some of the ideals the *Treishya* claims to espouse," ch'Foruta said, "just as I know that these same supporters have denounced that group's violent tactics. Many of you represent segments of the population who also support the views of such groups, who wish to be heard, but we must entertain divergent viewpoints in civilized fashion. An agenda or ideal cannot be forced upon a citizenry through fear and threats. If we allow that, then we risk descending into chaos.

"However, what we also cannot afford, what can simply not be allowed, is failure to act. We have been entrusted with a sacred responsibility, and it is our duty to take those actions we feel are necessary to preserve order, and to ensure the safety of those to whom we have pledged our service. Our actions must be swift, they must be bold, and they must be decisive. We must demonstrate that we, and not groups like the *Treishya,* are in control." This generated raucous applause from the assembled representatives, their reaction cascading around the chamber. Picard, Beverly, and ch'Thane sat motionless, but the captain was certain he heard zh'Thiin emit a snort of derision.

"He supports the *Treishya*," she said, shaking her head in obvious disdain. "This is all theater; chest thumping to stir up the masses."

Ch'Foruta waited for the applause to dwindle before saying, "There is also the matter of the controversial research into altering Andorian physiology in order to resolve our pro-creation crisis. Whatever your view on this sensitive topic, arguing from a position of ignorance is not constructive. Gifted individuals like Marthrossi zh'Thiin have devoted great time and effort to solving this problem, and we must be open-minded in the spirit of helping our people through these dark times. And while it's worth noting that their work was assisted in large part by a former enemy, this is offset by the knowledge that this one-time adversary may well have delivered to us our salvation." There was renewed applause, but ch'Foruta held up a hand, ushering everyone once more to silence. "The larger issue is the very lack of assistance from our friends, who have by their own admission been in possession of the same knowledge given to us by the Tholians."

This is it, Picard thought. *This is why we're here.*

"Our friends," ch'Foruta said, pointing to where Picard and Beverly stood, "have held this knowledge in secret for more than a century." Nearly everyone in the chamber looked to Picard, and it took all of the captain's self-control not to react to the hundreds of eyes now focused upon him. In his peripheral vision, he saw Beverly remaining equally still, and there was no mistaking the escalating tension that had just filled the room.

"They kept it cloaked in shadow," ch'Foruta said, "all while watching as our civilization dwindled. Were they simply ignorant, or was this a deliberate choice? We do not know. We may never know, not that it matters. The damage has been done."

Picard watched as the deputy now directed an accusatory finger at sh'Thalis. "And even as we come to terms with the deception, the indecisiveness, or the simple cowardice exhibited by our supposed partners in peace, there are those among us who continue to court the Federation's good graces. Why? Our world has suffered calamitous destruction on a scale never before seen in its history. Many of our largest cities have been wiped from the face of our planet, because the Federation squandered every opportunity to prepare for an enemy of which they've been aware for decades. When the time came to defend against that threat, they were not ready, and now dozens of worlds and billions of people have been lost. Our planet might well have been counted among those casualties if not for the wildest stroke of good fortune."

Not giving the audience time to react, ch'Foruta's voice rose until it echoed off the chamber walls. "Honored representatives, we cannot lead while hoping for fate to smile upon us, just as we cannot govern in the face of the chaos these grievous failures have inflicted upon our people. Presider sh'Thalis would have us believe that we cannot proceed until we discuss the matter—amongst ourselves and with our Federation partners. Meanwhile, our streets are filled with those looking to us for guidance, and we must show it to them now, without hesitation or evasion, or we will be showing them nothing more than the dishonesty and betrayal they already have suffered at the hands of our alleged friends. None of that is possible, so long as our leaders fail to act, or take action believed by our people to be detrimental to their best interests."

Leaning closer to Beverly, Picard asked in a low voice, "Where is all this going?" The question burned in his mind even as he looked once more to Presider sh'Thalis. While she sat ramrod straight in her chair, a look of defeat clouded her features, and Picard realized at that moment what ch'Foruta was about to do.

No.

"For the sake of returning stability to this government," the deputy presider said, "so that we can proceed with leading in a responsible manner for the safety and security of all our people, I now move for a vote from the floor, to determine President sh'Thalis's fitness to retain her office."

42

Nanietta Bacco did not so much recline into her chair as collapse into it. She felt drained. No, that was not at all right. She felt *numb*. It was as though every iota of energy had been siphoned from her body, leaving behind a spent shell.

And this shell needs to pull itself together, and get back to work.

Leaning back in her chair, she closed her eyes, drawing what she wished could be a deep, calming breath. The events of the past few hours still weighed on her, and Bacco knew that the sensation washing over her was but the beginning of what she would feel in the hours, days, and weeks to come. All she wanted at this moment was to run from this place as fast as her legs would carry her, and find some private beach on which to lose herself. Better yet, she wanted a dark hole, in which she could hide until the present madness faded, assuming it ever did.

"Madam President."

Bacco opened her eyes with a start, blinking in rapid succession and turning in her chair to see Admiral Akaar standing just inside the entrance to her office. Behind the tall, imposing Capellan, Sivak regarded her with the Vulcan equivalent of embarrassment. Obviously, Akaar had barged past her personal assistant's desk, determined to see her without the pomp and circumstance—to say nothing of simple courtesy—involved in a proper announcement or introduction.

"If you're not here to tell me I've been imagining the past couple of days," she said, eyeing Akaar, "then get out."

The admiral shook his head. "I'm afraid not, Madam President."

Bacco said, "Fine. You can stay. In fact, why not take my job? I'm apparently not very good at it, anyway."

Akaar stepped farther into the office, allowing the doors to close behind him, and regarded her with an almost paternal air. "Madam President," he began, but stopped when she held up her hand.

"No, Leonard, I mean it. What the hell happened? How did we let things get this far? After everything the Federation has endured, it's come down to this? Petty squabbling among ourselves?" The news of Presider sh'Thalis's removal from office by the Parliament Andoria had begun rocketing through Federation News Service broadcasts within moments of the official announcement. During the ensuing four days, the FNS and other news media outlets had been forced to fill air time and space in their various publications with speculation as to the current political situation on Andor, owing to a planetwide blackout for news and communications ordered by the parliament for all data traffic going off world. No one, it seemed, knew anything, and speculation was running rampant.

As shocking as this development was, Bacco had suspected something like it might happen from the moment the parliament locked themselves in their meeting chamber for days of intense debate. Bacco had been kept apprised of the situation by the presider's aides as well as sh'Thalis herself, as the parliament members argued over how best to proceed in the wake of the Tholian ambassador's contentious message to the Andorian people. According to the updates the president had received, the parliament was sharply divided on the issue. Less than half of the representatives supported sh'Thalis as she sought to move away from the desire to cast blame on the Federation and instead focus on what she considered to be the topics of primary importance. Pursuing Andor's ongoing reconstruction efforts and resolving the reproductive crisis were her agenda, neither of which—sh'Thalis believed—could be accomplished without continuing Federation support and assistance.

The majority saw things differently.

"Unbelievable," Bacco said, reaching up to massage the bridge of her nose. "It's been four days since they ousted her. We should have been able to do something. *I* should've done more."

"I doubt there was anything you could've done, Madam President," Akaar said. "Presider sh'Thalis and her allies in the parliament were simply outnumbered by their enemies. We knew when she was elected by such a narrow margin that she would never have an easy time of it."

Bacco nodded. "I remember the heat she took when she announced her support of the research Professor zh'Thiin's predecessor was doing. And that was *before* the Borg came." In the aftermath of the attack on Andor, sh'Thalis, at the time recently elected to the office of presider, had endured much criticism for her staunch support of Starfleet and the Federation. She had held her ground even as her political opponents and their operatives painted her as a puppet of the Federation Council, beholden to her "masters" despite Starfleet supposedly having abandoned Andor to whatever fate the Borg might bring. Sh'Thalis had weathered most of that condemnation well enough, at least in public, but Bacco knew from private communications that the presider was feeling the pressure of being portrayed in such a negative light. Bacco's despair was only worsened by the knowledge that sh'Thalis—though thrust into her office by tragic circumstance—had exhibited an honest, legitimate desire to make life better for the Andorian people.

Now, she was gone. Recalled from office and dismissed in disgrace, and why? Because of the fear and uncertainty some politicians allowed to rule their own lives and govern their decisions.

What a damned waste.

The sound of her doors opening once again was enough to rouse Bacco from her momentary reverie, and she looked up from her desk to see her assistant standing near the entrance to her office. "What is it, Sivak?"

"Madam President," her assistant replied, "the Andorian ambassador has arrived and is requesting an audience."

Well, Bacco mused as she exchanged questioning glances with Akaar, *this is interesting.*

Blowing out her breath between pursed lips, she rose from her chair and gave herself a cursory inspection to ensure her clothes were presentable. Her ensemble sported a few wrinkles here and there.

Much like the body wearing it.

"Send him in, please," she said, steeling herself for what she suspected would be a very short, very intense few minutes.

The doors opened again a moment later to admit Sivak, and behind him followed a slightly built Andorian of moderate height, just a few centimeters taller than Bacco herself. He wore a flowing black robe featuring an intricate web of dazzling embroidery in various shades of blue and white, which complemented his bright cerulean skin and the stark, pallid tint of long hair that fell below his shoulders.

"President Bacco," Sivak said, stopping in front of the desk and speaking with the official tone he reserved for making such introductions, "may I present Gilmesheid ch'Pavarzi, Andorian ambassador to the Federation."

Offering a formal bow, ch'Pavarzi said, "Madam President." Then, he repeated the greeting to Akaar. "Admiral."

"This is an unexpected surprise, Ambassador," Bacco replied, hoping her words sounded congenial. "I know things have to be hectic for you right now. What can I do for you?" She gestured toward one of the chairs in front of her desk, and was slightly startled when ch'Pavarzi declined the offer, opting instead to remain standing.

"What I have to say will not take long, Madam President," he said. "I was instructed by my government to deliver this information to you in person, and to do so as quickly as possible. The parliament-ordered blackout decree will soon be rescinded, but the new presider believed you were deserving of advance notice regarding this matter." He paused, as though choosing his next words with utmost care. "Before I proceed, I would like to state for the record that while I have been honored to serve as an ambassador to the Federation, I was most distressed to learn of the information kept from my people, which apparently holds vital clues as to how we might solve our procreation dilemma. This is not the sort of behavior one expects from supposed friends and allies."

"You know it's not as simple as that," Bacco snapped, then immediately checked herself. Feeling her cheeks flush from embarrassment at the momentary lapse, she forced herself to wait a full five seconds before continuing, "My apologies, Ambassador. What I'm trying to say is that the matter is far too complicated to be condensed into a talking point for a speech or a news broadcast."

The Andorian said, "From my people's perspective, Madam President, the matter seems rather straightforward. The Federation, for more than a century and while being fully aware of the problems faced by my planet, has kept secret information which, ultimately, is proving to be of great benefit to us in our time of greatest need."

Feeling her frustration mounting, Bacco struggled to maintain her composure. "Ambassador, you must first understand that Admiral Akaar and I only became aware of the significance of this information shortly before it was made known to the people of Andor. *That's* how far down this mess was buried. At the time the information about the meta-genome was classified, what little was known about it told our best scientists that it represented awesome power, the likes of which might well prove dangerous to the safety of the entire Federation were it to fall into the wrong hands. We had barely scratched the surface of its potential, and that's still largely true to this day."

"And yet," ch'Pavarzi countered, "your limited grasp of what meta-genome represents allowed your scientists to devise your so-called Genesis Device, as well as further your knowledge in the area of medicine, including aspects of genetic engineering that you have, admittedly, applied for the betterment of people throughout the Federation. So, it seems controlled application of that very dangerous knowledge you claim not to understand is possible, when you are motivated by your own self-interests."

Bacco could feel the discussion spiraling out of control, and saw no way to keep it from slipping completely from her grasp. "Decisions made decades ago, Ambassador. Now that we know the meta-genome offers hope for Andor, there's no reason not to explore it to the fullest extent possible. Professor zh'Thiin will enjoy far more support and assistance working with us than on her own."

Ch'Pavarzi shook his head. "The time for that has passed, Madam President. I have been sent here to inform you that my government has approved a global referendum, which was conducted during the past four days. All votes have been counted, and the parliament in turn has cast their own vote. Andor will shortly be announcing its secession from the Federation."

"What?" Bacco all but shouted the question despite her best intentions. Her eyes felt as though they might bug right out of their sockets as she digested what ch'Pavarzi had just said. "You can't be serious."

The ambassador appeared to be having difficulty reigning in a smug expression of superiority. "I'm afraid I am, Madam President. Our government has already extended overtures to the Tholian Assembly, with the hopes of opening a continuing dialogue. As such, we will no longer require Federation aid or assistance. All of this will be made clear when the new presider broadcasts our secession declaration via the Federation News Service. Effective with that announcement, all Federation and Starfleet personnel will be expelled from the planet. I trust you will see to it that this is accomplished with all available efficiency."

"This is outrageous," Bacco said, scarcely daring to believe her ears. Was this really, truly happening?

"Any non-Andorian civilians will be allowed to stay, if

they so desire," ch'Pavarzi said, "though by doing so they rec-ognize that Federation law will no longer apply on Andor."

Stepping toward the desk, Akaar said, "That sounds like rhetoric, Ambassador. The laws of any sovereign member always supersede Federation law. You're making an issue of something that is pointedly *not* an issue, and never has been since the signing of the Federation Charter."

Ch'Pavarzi replied, "We prefer to think of it more as clarifying our government's position, Admiral."

"Your government would throw away everything for which we've worked for more than two hundred years?" Bacco asked. "Over a secret that's been buried for a century; an error that we can address right here, this very minute?"

"My government is acting in accordance with the will of our people, Madam President," ch'Pavarzi said. "While the vote was by no means an overwhelming majority, the separa-tion between those for and against this action was still signifi-cant, and their message is clear: the Federation can no longer be trusted so far as our welfare is concerned."

"That's categorically not true, Ambassador," Akaar said.

Turning his attention to the admiral, ch'Pavarzi said, "All evidence to the contrary, of course."

"And what of those who voted against secession? What happens to them?"

"Nothing 'happens' to them, Madam President," the ambassador said. "They remain Andorian citizens, with all the inherent rights and privileges therein. Anyone wish-ing to leave Andor, even to live on a Federation-controlled world, is free to do so. I have been sent here to reassure you that while Andor will no longer be subject to the Federa-tion's laws, we have no wish to cut off all ties." He paused again, then added, "We have simply decided that the role we play in such a relationship will be more to our benefit than yours."

"Ambassador," Bacco said, stepping around her desk, "Andor is a founding member of the Federation. We've stood together as allies for more than two centuries. Do you realize the precedent this will set?"

Ch'Pavarzi nodded. "Indeed we do. Our action will send an unambiguous message to all the worlds of the Federation, reminding them that they are not obliged to subordinate themselves to a governmental body that would place secrets of dubious value over the welfare of those in need. They will know that there are alternatives to such blind devotion." With a cursory nod to Akaar, he bowed once more. "Thank you for your time, Madam President. Good day."

Forcing herself not to call out after him, Bacco watched as the ambassador turned and walked out of the office. She waited until her doors closed before releasing the breath she only now realized she had been holding.

"Damn it," she whispered. "Somewhere, that bitch Tezrene is laughing her ass off."

Akaar turned to face her, his wizened face a mask of concern. "Madam President?"

Bacco began to pace her office. "We have to do something," she said. Reaching up to rub her temples, she felt the ache mounting behind her eyes. "We can't just let this happen. Diplomatic overtures, a resolution to assist Andor by any and all means possible, *something.*"

As she crossed her office, casting her gaze down at the carpet, she recalled the unpleasant meeting she had had here, more than a year ago, with the Tholian ambassador. Tezrene had warned her that the Federation would soon know what it felt like to be surrounded by a rival power, the Typhon Pact.

What Tezrene, and Bacco herself, had not anticipated was that this upstart alliance would be so brazen as to attempt recruiting new membership from those they called adversary.

In other words, Bacco mused, *and as Father might've said, they've got balls.*

Lost in thought, she did not realize Sivak had entered the office until she nearly ran into him. Startled, she looked up to see her aide standing before her, and this time there was no mistaking the worry he harbored as he regarded her.

"Madam President," the Vulcan said, "what do you wish me to do?"

Drawing herself up, Bacco forced away the fatigue, the defeat, the uncertainty that had permeated her every waking moment these past few days. There was little to be gained from wallowing in denial about what had happened, to say nothing of the events soon to unfold. Now, she decided, was the time to act, for the good of the people who had elected her to this office and to whom she had pledged her unfailing commitment to keep them safe and secure.

"We need to call the Council into session," she said to Sivak, and as she spoke she saw Leonard James Akaar nodding in approval. "We've still got a lot of work to do."

And it starts today.

43

With the lights out and her feet resting on the edge of the low-rise coffee table positioned in front of the sofa in her quarters, Choudhury sat in her favorite recliner, facing the sloping windows and watching the stars streaking past at warp. The mesmerizing sight, which almost never failed to calm her, was having no such effect this evening. Likewise, the drink in her hand also was proving to be of no assistance in that regard. The dismal mood in which she had chosen to wallow was showing no signs of abating.

I should probably shake this off, she decided. *I'm thinking the captain probably doesn't want a drunk, depressed chief of security standing behind him on the bridge.*

The door chime sounded, and Choudhury continued to sit in silence until whoever stood outside her quarters pressed it twice more, before she finally called out, "Come in." She heard the door's pneumatic hiss as it slid open, and she could see a dark figure reflected in the window before her. There was no mistaking the tall, muscular silhouette standing at her threshold.

"Since when do you knock?"

Worf hesitated before replying, "I did not . . ."

"It's an expression, Worf," Choudhury said, not turning

from the window. "What I mean is, since when do you need an invitation to come in?" She watched him step far enough into the room that the door closed behind him, returning her quarters once more to near-darkness.

"I was . . . distracted," he said. She heard him stepping around her, coming around her left side and moving between the coffee table and the sofa. "I've been in a debriefing with Captain Picard. He has asked me to reiterate to you the exemplary performance demonstrated by you and your team. Your preparation and training likely prevented an already unfortunate situation from becoming even more tragic."

Choudhury did not feel deserving of such praise, and had harbored similar sentiments when Captain Picard personally thanked her following the resolution of the crisis on Andor. Despite the best efforts of her and her team—to say nothing of Commander th'Hadik and his people as well as loyal members of the Homeworld Security brigade—there had been casualties. At least eight Andorian civilians had been killed during the near-riot, which almost had engulfed the parliament complex. Dozens more had sustained injuries of one sort or another. Only one *Enterprise* security officer, Ensign Jacob McPherson, had died during the incident, but for Choudhury that was still one too many. Several more of her people also had various broken bones and other wounds, all of which were being treated by Dr. Crusher and her sickbay staff.

"How's the captain?" Choudhury asked, trying to change the subject. Despite her motive, her question was one of genuine concern. The past days had been a strain on everyone, but she knew the toll they must have taken on the captain had to be greater than the burden shouldered by anyone else.

Worf replied, "He is tired, of course, and distressed over what has happened."

"I'll bet." Choudhury sighed, shaking her head. "I never thought I'd see the day that a planet willingly left the Federation. It just sounds so ludicrous." There was no denying that the past year had brought its fair share of challenges to the Federation. Threats of secession by a handful of planets—among those Alpha Centauri, itself a founding member—had been put forth. Alliances and the time-honored tradition of mutual collaboration had triumphed in the face of those obstacles, shedding the light of hope on one of the darkest chapters in Federation history, but such was not the case on this occasion. The effects of Andor's decision would send shockwaves throughout the quadrant, Choudhury guessed, having tangible effects not only on other member worlds but also the Federation's political rivals. Chief among those, of course, would be the Typhon Pact. How they might benefit from what had happened today remained to be seen. Would Andor seek membership in that unlikely coalition?

Wouldn't that be something, Choudhury mused, with no small amount of cynicism.

"I suspect the captain blames himself," Worf said, "even though I cannot see where he would be at fault."

"That's what captains do, Worf," Choudhury said, smiling. "They take the blame even when it isn't deserved. They take it so that those they command won't have to. It's how they inspire loyalty and respect."

"Captain Picard does not *need* to inspire loyalty *or* respect," Worf countered. "I would give my life without hesitation in order to save his." His conviction was palpable, even more so than at any time since Choudhury had known him. It had taken her little time to realize just how seriously Worf considered his Klingon heritage and the concepts of honor that permeated every facet of his life. It was fascinating to see how he had struck a balance between the ethos imbued in a warrior society and the standards of duty and integrity expected of a Starfleet officer. Somehow, and despite more than a few occasions where those two seemingly divergent perspectives had been at odds with each other, Worf had attained a sense of equilibrium that helped to guide him throughout his career. It was but one of the many things Choudhury found so intriguing about him.

And it's quite the turn-on, too.

"You really do admire him, don't you?" she asked, after a moment.

Worf nodded. "There is no one I hold in higher esteem."

"Coming from you," Choudhury said, "that's saying something. I'm pretty sure the captain knows that, which is probably just one of the reasons he wanted you as his first officer. He needed someone he could trust without question, and who better than a Klingon warrior who pledges the kind of allegiance you offer him? He's a better captain because you're by his side, Worf." Her words seemed to have an effect, as Worf now appeared to be standing just a bit straighter.

"It's interesting you should say it that way," he said, moving so that he could sit on the sofa. "During our meeting, the captain asked me to consider pursuing a command of my own."

Making no effort to hide her surprise, Choudhury pulled her feet from the coffee table and sat up in her chair. "Really?"

Worf nodded. "He said that it was important to consider my options, but that with all Starfleet has lost, there is a need for good captains. I found it an odd discussion, considering how long it took for him to assemble a senior staff that works well together. I'd think he would want to keep us together, at least for a while."

"He might be getting pressure from higher up," Choudhury suggested. "I've heard rumors Starfleet Command's been trying to promote him to admiral for over a year. Maybe he's eyeing you to replace him here."

Casting his gaze down to the coffee table, Worf replied, "I am not a suitable candidate for command. I have several reprimands in my personnel file that would disqualify me from such consideration."

"I've seen those," Choudhury countered, "and you know what? All of that was a lifetime ago. Since then, you've earned a record that a lot of captains would kill themselves to call their own. Besides, if having Jean-Luc Picard ask for you by name to serve as his first officer on the Federation flagship isn't a referral, I don't know what is. Hell, they'd probably make *you* an admiral if he told them to do it."

Worf waved away the suggestion. "This is all irrelevant. Captain Picard will never accept promotion. He's already refused several offers. No, his place is here, on the *Enterprise.*"

Smiling, Choudhury reached across the table, extending her hand and waiting until Worf took it in his own. "And will your place always be by his side?"

After several moments spent in silence, Worf said, "I honestly do not know. Though it would be a great honor to succeed him, if given a choice, I might well remain here for as long as the captain wanted me as his first officer." He shook his head. "I will have to give this a great deal of thought."

Choudhury rose from her chair, keeping her grip on his hand and pulling him to his feet. Wrapping her arms around him, she pressed her cheek into his broad chest. "Yes, you should do that."

He could do it tomorrow, she decided.

Chen ran her hands over the pages of the real book, savoring its texture. Her fingertips registered the rough page edges, and if she closed her eyes she imagined she could feel the words themselves, rising from the paper to greet her. She had enjoyed reading as a child, and while that interest had followed her into adulthood, she possessed very few physical books. Though the book she now held was an obvious reproduction of a book originally published a century ago, that did not at all diminish her present enjoyment.

"Lieutenant?"

Only upon hearing the voice did Chen realize she had closed her eyes, and she opened them to see Geordi La Forge standing across the table from her, eyeing her with an expression of curiosity and even mild amusement. Offering a small, sheepish smile, she glanced around the crew lounge to see if anyone else might be looking at her, but it appeared that her admittedly odd behavior had attracted no notice. Of course, she realized that was no mean feat, given the somber mood affecting pretty much everyone aboard ship. That vibe had permeated even the unfailing atmosphere of good humor that normally characterized the Happy Bottom Riding Club.

"Commander," she said, starting to stand.

La Forge gestured for her to keep her seat before indicating the chair opposite her. "May I join you?"

"Of course," Chen said, nodding as she cleared her throat. "What brings you here, sir?"

Taking his seat, La Forge replied, "I was told you'd be here."

"You were looking for me?" she asked.

The chief engineer smiled. "Absolutely. Commander Taurik told me what a tremendous help you were, but I hadn't had a chance to thank you in person before now. What you did was really something. It was inspired. I love that kind of unconventional thinking, especially in an engineer."

Unsure of what to say, Chen did not want to spoil the moment with something inappropriate, so she offered a simple nod. "Thank you, sir."

"I don't suppose you'd want to be assigned to me full-time?" La Forge asked.

Now Chen laughed. "Well, I don't know about that. I certainly don't mind helping out, especially during the long stints where there's really no need for a contact specialist. I know Captain Picard would rather I keep up with the cross-training, and to be honest I'm enjoying it. Engineering, flight ops. It keeps things fresh." Then, more comfortable with the conversation, she added, "Unless you're wanting to train me to take over your job?"

"One step at a time, Lieutenant." La Forge chuckled, then his features softened and he looked down at the table, running his fingers across its smooth surface. "It's nice to laugh, especially after everything that's happened." He gazed out at the rest of the crew lounge. "The news about Andor's really gotten everybody down."

You think? Chen only just managed to avoid hurling the sarcastic question across the table. Instead, she said, "I have a feeling we'll all be thinking about this for a while." The impact of Andor's decision had already been felt among the crew, with half of the ship's seventeen Andorian crew members resigning their commissions and transporting to the planet's surface prior to the *Enterprise*'s departure. Those who had remained were receiving the support of their friends and shipmates, but no one was pretending that such a startling development would not have a dramatic impact on the political landscape the Federation now faced.

"Did you know any of the Andorian officers who resigned?" she asked.

La Forge shook his head. "Not that well, no. What about you?"

"No," Chen replied. "I feel bad about that, now."

"Well, it's going to take a long time to sort things out," the chief engineer said. "I'm already hearing rumors about background checks for any Andorian who opts to stay in Starfleet. Somebody somewhere probably thinks of them as a security risk now." He released an exasperated sigh. "I hope they don't push things that far. It's not like everyone on the planet was even for this idea, let alone everyone in the Andorian government. You'd think we'd know by now that there's nothing to be gained by ostracizing people just because they're of a certain species or were born on a particular planet."

Chen shrugged. "Let's hope someone in charge is smart enough not to repeat those same mistakes. I'm betting that's President Bacco."

"Me, too." Leaning forward in his chair, La Forge drew a deep breath as though attempting to change mental gears. He gestured toward the book still lying on the table before her. "What are you reading?"

Smiling as her attention returned to the book, Chen said, "I actually haven't started reading it yet. I found it in my quarters when I came off shift this evening. Apparently, it's a gift, from Captain Picard."

"Really?" La Forge asked. "What's the occasion?"

Once again uncomfortable, Chen replied, "I did a favor for Dr. Crusher. She asked me to repair that flute he keeps. You know, as a memento."

"Oh yeah," the engineer said, nodding. "I know."

"Right," Chen said. "So, I fixed it, and I guess she gave it to him, and he gave me this, as a way to say 'Thank you.' I have to admit, I feel weird about it."

La Forge laughed again. "I suppose that's understandable. He is the captain, after all, and he's also pretty reserved."

"That's one way to put it," Chen countered. "Anyway, the book's an interesting choice. It's a novel, published a hundred years or so ago, about the first contact between humans and Vulcans."

Frowning, La Forge said, "I know that book. Captain Riker gave that to him as a birthday present several years ago. It was after . . . well . . . let's just say whatever happens in that book isn't the way things really went."

"I've read the reports, Commander," Chen said, unable to suppress a small giggle. "What I thought was most interesting is that he wrote an inscription." Opening the book, she turned it to the first page and rotated it so that La Forge could see what he undoubtedly recognized as Captain Picard's unique, exacting penmanship.

Reading aloud, La Forge said, "To T'Ryssa Chen. Things aren't always as they seem, and sometimes they surprise you. Thank you. JLP." Impressed, he leaned back in his chair. "For what it's worth, I've known the captain for almost twenty years, and while he's not the most outgoing person, he's definitely become less aloof than when I first met him." He pointed to the book. "That said, he must be very impressed with you to make a gesture like that."

"You don't think it's just fatherhood mellowing him?" Chen asked, garnering another chuckle from La Forge.

"I don't think I'll be testing that theory any time soon," he said, looking up as someone else approached their table.

"And now, if you'll excuse me," he offered as he rose from his chair, "my dinner date's arrived."

Chen turned in her seat to see Dr. Tamala Harstad walking toward them. She smiled as she greeted La Forge, whose face seemed to brighten as he regarded her.

Guess the rumors are true.

"It's a pleasure to meet you, Lieutenant," Harstad offered after La Forge made the introductions.

"And you, Doctor." To La Forge, she said, "Enjoy your evening, Commander." She forced herself to keep a straight face even as she added a small lilt to the end of her sentence, which had the intended effect of causing the chief engineer to struggle at suppressing a small grin despite himself.

Clearing his throat, he said, "Thanks again, Lieutenant. Like I said, that was some fine work. I won't forget it."

The couple made their way to another, unoccupied table on the other side of the room, leaving Chen sitting alone at her table. She sighed, contemplating whether to eat her dinner here, or simply order something from the replicator in her quarters. Her right hand played across the surface of the book, and she once again was drawn to the exquisite tooling of its imitation leather cover.

At least I'll have something to read tonight.

"Lieutenant?"

Startled by the new voice, Chen jerked herself upright in her chair and was surprised—pleasantly so, she realized— to see Taurik standing to her left, hands clasped behind his back. "Commander," she said. "I apologize. I was just . . . never mind. What can I do for you?"

Taurik's right eyebrow arched, and he indicated the empty chair on the table's far side with a nod. "I was curious as to whether you cared to have dinner with me?"

44

Sitting in the small office in his quarters, Picard regarded the weary visage of Iravothra sh'Thalis depicted on his desktop computer screen. She seemed to have aged a decade in the few short days that had passed since he had last seen her.

"I apologize for not having an opportunity to see you before you left, Captain," she said, offering a small smile. *"As you know, I've been rather busy these past few days."*

Buoyed by her attempt at humor, Picard replied, "That's quite all right." He stopped himself before referring to her by her former title. "I understand completely. I hope you won't take what I have to say as simple courtesy, but I was supremely disappointed in the parliament's decision to remove you from office. From where I sit, you carried out your duties to the people of Andor with integrity and compassion. I'm only sorry that did not appear to be sufficient for some parties."

Sh'Thalis warmed upon hearing that. *"Very kind words, Captain, particularly coming from someone of your stature. While politics had never been an aspiration of mine growing up, I came to love my work. I really did want to help people; to make their lives better. Hopefully, I'll be able to do that again."* She paused, looking away from the comm unit's video pickup as though contemplating a brighter future just within her grasp. *"And since we're on the subject of helping people, I also did not get to properly thank you and your crew for everything you did while you were here. From the conference to assisting in our reconstruction efforts, your support was invaluable. I only wish we had been able to show our appreciation in some meaningful way."*

"That's not necessary," Picard said. "As my first officer has been known to say from time to time, the honor is to serve. I only wish that we could have done more."

Pausing again, sh'Thalis released a small sigh. *"I predict that the parliament will come to regret the action they took in haste, fueled as it was by emotion. I don't understand how they think this will bring stability to our world. The decision has sparked all manner of dissension, given that a sizable portion of the population opposed secession. There's even talk of trying to orchestrate a new referendum in order to revisit the original vote and see if a call for rejoining the Federation can't be approved. And of course, none of this changes the agenda of groups like the* Treishya. *They will continue to oppose the work of Professor zh'Thiin and those like her, despite the potential it harbors for the survival of our race."*

Picard had read the latest reports coming from the now-"liberated" world of Andor as provided by the Federation News Service, which had been granted provisional permission by the parliament to remain on the planet and report current events. The news organization was, by some accounts, already coming under fire from hard-line Visionists and outspoken representatives of the *Treishya,* the True Heirs of Andor, and other activist groups. Eklanir th'Gahryn, the mysterious yet oddly charismatic leader of the *Treishya,* had come out of hiding and resumed his infrequent broadcasts to the Andorian people, calling for the ousting of the Federation "propaganda machine."

As for Professor zh'Thiin, from what Picard had been able to learn, the Andorian Science Institute had not forced her to cease her work. With the first bondgroups expecting the birth of healthy children aided by the genetic research she had devised, there was little practical argument against what she had accomplished. Assuming those children developed no unforeseen side effects as a result of zh'Thiin's protocol, it was a veritable certainty that public opinion would soon begin to swing toward supporting her work.

"I hope such a referendum comes to pass," Picard said. "Andor's role in Federation history is an honored one, and we are lesser without you." He tried not to dwell on that comment, having read Admiral Akaar's report regarding President Bacco's final meeting with the Andorian ambassador and how that conversation had ended.

Andor, joining the Typhon Pact? Picard simply could not believe it, and the Andorian government was neither confirming nor denying such speculation. Would the next weeks and months see the Pact boasting of a momentous expansion of their fledgling coalition? The ramifications of such a radical shift in the interstellar political landscape were staggering. Admiral Akaar had already sent a message to Picard, wanting his insights into the Andorian situation with respect to how it might affect the Typhon Pact. It was a question that would be receiving no small amount of critical attention in the days and weeks to come, and that discussion was one to which Picard was not looking forward.

"Rest assured there are many here who feel as you do," sh'Thalis said. *"I only hope that their voices are heard, sooner rather than later."* When she smiled again this time, it seemed to Picard as though some of the fatigue bearing down on her had faded. *"I know you're a busy man, so I won't keep you any*

longer. Once again, thank you for everything. Thiptho lapth, *Jean-Luc."*

"Until we meet again, Iravothra," Picard said. When the transmission ended, he sat in silence for a moment, contemplating the people of Andor. Trying times still lay ahead for them, made only the more difficult, he thought, by the loss of someone as dedicated and forward-thinking as Iravothra sh'Thalis.

A damned pity.

Something rubbed against his leg, pulling him from his reverie, and he looked down to see René staring up at him with wide, expectant eyes.

"Up," the boy said, his small hands gripping Picard's trouser legs as he tried to pull himself into his father's lap.

"Come here," Picard said, lifting the boy and turning him so that he faced the desk, and in doing so his gaze fell upon the familiar ornate box sitting to the left of the computer terminal. Reaching for it, he opened the box and smiled as he beheld the flute. "Hello, old friend," he whispered as his fingers caressed the instrument. Though he had come to terms with perhaps never again being able to play the cherished keepsake, simply looking at it was enough to sadden him at the thought of losing not only that treasured pursuit but also the tenuous connection to everything the flute represented. He had never voiced that sorrow to Beverly, but she obviously had sensed his despair despite his best efforts to keep it concealed, and it had spurred her to action. The result of that devotion—with the able and wondrous assistance of Lieutenant T'Ryssa Chen—was a gift beyond measure, in ways that to this day Picard could articulate solely through the music he and the flute created. That it was here, restored and waiting for him, filled him with a joy he had missed for far too long.

"There you are."

Picard looked up to see Beverly standing at the doorway to the small office. Seeing her, René held out his arms and offered a near-toothless grin of greeting.

"Escaped your clutches again, did he?" Picard asked.

"He knows it's time for his bath," Beverly replied, "and he's stalling." She stepped over and lifted René from his father's lap. "Everything okay?"

"I was just talking to Presider sh'Thalis," Picard said. "Excuse me, *former* Presider sh'Thalis."

Nodding in understanding, Beverly asked, "How is she?"

"Tired," Picard said. "Unhappy. Worried for the future."

Beverly shifted René so as to support the boy on her right hip. "She should join the club. You don't have to be a planetary leader to worry about things like that."

Sensing that there might be more to his wife's words than she might be letting on, Picard asked, "Something on your mind?"

"I suppose so, yes," Beverly said, turning from him to regard René for a moment. "When we were down on Andor, during the . . . incident?"

"Yes?" Picard asked.

As though wary about how he might react, Beverly glanced to the ceiling before replying, "To be honest, once that was over, I thought about you and René, and how I'm starting to feel that I don't want to have to wonder whether I might never see either of you again because of one dangerous mission or another. I don't want to wonder what might happen to you when duty calls."

Suddenly uncomfortable with the turn the conversation was taking, Picard said, "This is the life we chose, Beverly. Indeed, one could argue that this life chose us."

"I know, believe me," she said, "but I've been through it all before, and I'm finally starting to realize that maybe I don't want to do it again."

Though his first instinct was to ask what Beverly might be suggesting, Picard realized that what he wanted to say was what actually came out of his mouth. "Sometimes, I think I feel the same way."

This, of course, took his wife by surprise. "What?"

Drawing a deep breath, Picard said, "I'm not saying I'm ready to retire or anything, but there have been times during the past year when I've considered what it would be like to do . . . something else. I don't know that I'd feel the same way if René weren't here, but I do know that with him as part of the equation, things *are* different. I'm not just talking about any potential danger from a hazardous assignment, for either of us, though that's certainly a point to consider. Sooner or later, his needs will require us to make a decision. I guess what I'm trying to figure out is whether I want to wait for the decision to come on its own terms, or do something about it now." There was Akaar's seemingly open-ended offer to promote him to admiral, and what if the rumors of a possible ambassadorship were true? And what of still another option, the one that saw him and Beverly returning to Earth or some other quiet planet and finding a nice, small house near a lake or river? Not for the first time, Picard considered the appeal of raising his son far away from the world of starships along with the interstellar crises, political strife, and everything else the universe might throw at him.

How long would that last? Really?

As usual when he pondered such questions, Picard had no ready answers. Instead, he reached across his desk to retrieve the small metal box from where it rested next to his desktop computer interface. Lifting the box's lid, he beheld the treasured flute, finally restored thanks to the generous talents of T'Ryssa Chen.

Hello, old friend.

"Well," Beverly said, still holding René as she stepped into the office and took a seat in the chair on the other side of his desk, "we certainly don't have to make any decisions tonight." She nodded toward his computer terminal. "Don't you have that message from Admiral Akaar you're supposed to answer?"

Casting a glance toward the monitor, Picard considered Akaar's communiqué for a moment, before deciding that whatever response he might offer probably would be the same if he offered it now, or an hour from now. "It can wait," he said.

Beverly leaned back in her chair, situating René so that he could see his father, "Well, if that's the case, then how about some music? Think you can still play that thing?"

"I believe it's well past time we found out," Picard said, lifting the flute from the box and cradling it in his hands, his fingers finding the proper positions almost of their own accord. He closed his eyes, feeling the music well up within him. It had been there all along, imprisoned and demanding escape. When he began to play, it was as though no time had been lost, with the music carrying away the burdens of command, the consequences of duty, the aggravations of politics, and the uncertainty of what the future might bring.

Now, there was only the music, and Beverly, and young René. For a time, at least, Picard was at peace.

Afterword

Readers interested in learning more about Operation Vanguard, the Shedai, the Taurus Reach, the mysterious Taurus meta-genome, and how the Tholians are involved with all of that are encouraged to seek out the *Star Trek: Vanguard* novel series from Pocket Books. Set in the twenty-third century, the series features a cast of new characters with storylines that run parallel to the events of the original *Star Trek* television series. As of this writing, the ongoing series consists of the following books:

Harbinger, by David Mack
Summon the Thunder, by Dayton Ward and Kevin Dilmore
Reap the Whirlwind, by David Mack
Open Secrets, by Dayton Ward (story by Dayton Ward and Kevin Dilmore)
Precipice, by David Mack
and
Vanguard: Declassified, with stories by Kevin Dilmore, David Mack, Marco Palmieri, and Dayton Ward (June, 2011)

There is also a "prequel story" to the *Vanguard* saga, *Distant Early Warning* from the *Star Trek: Corps of Engineers* series, by Dayton Ward and Kevin Dilmore, available as an e-Book. The story is also collected in the trade paperback omnibus *Star Trek: Corps of Engineers — What's Past.*

Acknowledgments

Thanks of the first order are due to Jaime Costas, who stepped into the breach with bayonet fixed, ready to do battle against the forces of chaos and perhaps even those of evil while settling into her new role as my editor.

Thanks also to Emilia Pisani, who's hunkered down within the eye of the editorial storm affecting Pocket Books this past year, keeping everything on schedule while doing her level best to soothe the fragile egos of various writers requiring feeding and attention, this one included. Always ready with answers, contracts, checks, and even those cool blue pencils we use to mark up our manuscripts, Emilia's been a rock. Somebody buy that woman a drink!

Tips of the hat are offered to Christopher L. Bennett (*Greater Than the Sum*), Keith R.A. DeCandido (*Articles of the Federation*, *A Singular Destiny*), David R. George III (*Rough Beasts of Empire*), Bill Leisner (*Losing the Peace*), David Mack (the *Destiny* trilogy, *Star Trek: Vanguard*, as well as the *Typhon Pact* novel *Zero Sum Game*), and Michael Martin (*Seize the Fire*) for establishing characters, concepts, and situations that provide "points of continuity departure" for various events in this novel.

As has become almost second nature now, I'd like to thank the volunteers who maintain the Memory Alpha (http://www.memory-alpha.org) and Memory Beta (http://memory-beta.wikia.com) *Star Trek* Wikis. Both sites provided points of reference during my research throughout the writing of this book.

A high-five and a hearty "Thank ya!" to Paul D. Storrie, author of "The Old Ways," which appeared in the Andorian issue of IDW's *Star Trek: Alien Spotlight* series. Paul's tale provided some helpful continuity fodder and other points of inspiration. Likewise, much appreciation is extended to S. John Ross, Steven S. Long, Adam Dickstein, and Christian Moore, authors of *Among the Clans,* a sourcebook for the late, lamented *Star Trek Role-playing Game* created by the equally late, lamented Last Unicorn Games. This book also provided more than a few nuggets of inspiration.

And very special thanks are reserved for Heather Jarman, author of *Andor: Paradigm,* which appeared in *Worlds of Star Trek: Deep Space Nine – Volume One.* It's her portrayal of Andor, and Lieutenant Thirishar ch'Thane in particular, that guided me during the Andorian-centric portions of this story. I hope I was able to pay the proper respect to her creations.

On that note, I offer thanks to Ian McLean, longtime *Star Trek* fan and Andorian aficionado, for taking the time to give the manuscript a rather hurried beta read at my request. Any errors or omissions of detail with respect to Andorian culture are entirely my fault, despite Ian's best efforts to steer me toward the light.

I would be remiss if I didn't recognize John William Corrington and Joyce Hooper Corrington, writers of the screenplay to *Battle for the Planet of the Apes* (1973). The line spoken by President Bacco in Chapter 28 ("All knowledge is for good; only the use to which it's put can be for good or evil") is an homage to one of my favorite scenes from that film, with this line of dialogue spoken by the orangutan philosopher Virgil. It's one of those quotes that have stuck with me over the years, and I've always wanted to find a way to incorporate a salute to it in one of my own stories.

Thanks to my best bud, frequent writing partner, and hetero life mate, Kevin Dilmore, who kept me sane throughout this process by offering me the occasional distraction, often in the form of chicken wings or, on more constructive occasions, magazine articles and other stuff that needed writing. I'm already looking forward to our next team-up, which should be (HA!) one for the books.

Even my daughters, Addison and Erin, rate a thank you this time around. Why? Because they help keep me grounded and remind me every day what's really important. Oftentimes, it involves trips to the park or McDonald's, sometimes without their mommy's knowledge.

And finally, I offer my heartfelt thanks and undying devotion to my wife, Michi, for . . . well . . . for everything.

About the Author

DAYTON WARD. Author. Trekkie. Writing his goofy little stories and searching for a way to tap into the hidden nerdity that all humans have. Then, an accidental overdose of Mountain Dew altered his body chemistry. Now, when Dayton Ward grows excited or just downright geeky, a startling metamorphosis occurs.

Driven by outlandish ideas and a pronounced lack of sleep, he is pursued by fans and editors as well as funny men in bright uniforms wielding tasers, straitjackets, and medication. In addition to the numerous credits he shares with friend and co-writer Kevin Dilmore, Dayton is the author of the *Star Trek* novels *In the Name of Honor* and *Open Secrets,* the science fiction novels *The Last World War, Counterstrike: The Last World War, Book II,* and *The Genesis Protocol,* as well as short stories which have appeared in the first three *Star Trek: Strange New Worlds* anthologies, the Yard Dog Press anthologies *Houston, We've Got Bubbas* and *A Bubba in Time Saves None, Kansas City Voices Magazine,* and the *Star Trek: New Frontier* anthology *No Limits.* For Flying Pen Press, he was the editor of the science fiction anthology *Full-Throttle Space Tales #3: Space Grunts.*

Dayton is believed to be working on his next novel, and he must let the world think that he is working on it, until he can find a way to earn back the advance check he blew on strippers and booze. Though he currently lives in Kansas City with his wife and daughters, Dayton is a Florida native and maintains a torrid long-distance romance with his beloved Tampa Bay Buccaneers. Visit him on the web at http://www.daytonward.com.